DOUBLE FALSEHOOD

A SHAKESPEAREAN THRILLER

VAUGHN ENTWISTLE

MASQUE PUBLISHING LLC

Double Falsehood: A Shakespearean Thriller

Ebook edition: ISBN 978-1-8381568-0-0

Print edition: ISBN 978-1-8381568-8-6

Published by Masque Publishing LLC

First Edition: August, 2020

GET A FREE SHORT EBOOK!

Get a free copy of my short ebook, *The Necropolis Railway*, by signing up for my occasional newsletter at my author website: www.vaughnentwistle.com

CHAPTER 1: I AM MURDERED

The bullet missed my heart but punctured my lung, which explains why my breathing is wheezier than usual. I'm leaving a blood trail my murderer is surely following through the White Hart Inn. Worse yet, I'm bleeding all over the most priceless manuscript in all the world: a long-lost play by William Shakespeare, a sheaf of brittle paper so authentic the pages quiver with the Bard's own jittery handwriting—scratch-outs, ink blots, drips and all . . .

. . . including that crippled signature:

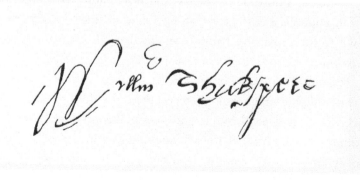

I hear the distant creak of my office door easing open and shamble my wobbly legs faster. In my bloody bumblings through the Inn, I am writing the final act of my life the police forensic boys will have no trouble reading. As I reach the taproom I'm dizzy and going saggy at the knees. I stop to lean against the wall to catch my wind and notice the Scotch I poured waiting for me atop the bar. I snatch it up and take the briefest sip only to cough explosively, spattering droplets of blood and single malt across the white lath and plaster wall. How long can a podgy, middle-aged bastard like me last with such a chest wound? Will I faint before I reach the secret passage? I tripped the silent alarm so I know the police are on their way, but as usual the Rozzers will likely arrive too late to affect the outcome of this little drama.

A crash as something topples to the floor in my office. From the sound I know exactly what it is: the strong box with the day's take. My murderer has pry-barred it open looking for the manuscript. He'll be lucky to find a pitiful fifty quid in bills and coins. Still, it lets me know my assailant is close.

Too flaming close.

I push away from the wall, smearing a bloody handprint, and totter toward the kitchens.

The narrow hallway that leads from the bar to the kitchens is pitch-friggin'-black—the bulb blew a week ago and I never got around to changing it. I've been effing and jeffing every time I flipped the switch and nothing happened, but now I am grateful, because the gloom conceals me. I grope along the wall until I reach the stairs down to the cellar and stumble rubber-legged down the break-neck steps and crash into the cellar door.

The murderer would have to be deaf not to have heard that.

I fumble the rough iron latch and the cellar door groans open onto darkness. I stagger through and bump the door shut behind me, leaning with my back against it, sucking in a breath of chill, subterranean air all yeasty from the beer barrels. For a moment it's reviving, but then weakness surges through me in a hot flash. My knees quiver and threaten to buckle.

CHAPTER 1: I AM MURDERED | 3

Outside, footsteps scuffle along the passageway—the quiet steps of someone trying to be stealthy, a hunter pursuing his quarry. The footsteps grow distant, but then stop and double back. I strain to listen, but catch only faint, indecipherable scraping noises. Is that someone creeping down the cellar steps?

I stiffen as a footfall crunches on the other side of the door. How could my murderer track my blood trail in the dark hallway? I rummage in the pocket of my cardigan and draw out the pistol. The gun is still warm and exudes the sharp, bitter smell of cordite. I have five shots left.

Suddenly, the door barges open behind me, pitching me forward. I don't even have time to get my hands up before my nose ploughs into the stone flags and air chuffs out of me in a pained grunt. I keep hold of the manuscript, but the gun flies from my hand and skitters away into the shadows. The cellar door flings wide, spilling just enough light to sketch a human silhouette I do not recognise.

I am surprised. My guess was wrong.

My murderer is not who I expected.

CHAPTER 2: A BLOODY MURDER

The blast of a hunting horn snared the rider's gaze from the sun-dappled road and drew his eyes into the tenebrous depths of the forest. A second horn blast. He slowed from a canter to a trot and edged the steed into the shadows beneath the towering oaks. At first sight, he could have been taken for a gentleman riding the Great West Road[1] on business, but the handsome chestnut bay and the sumptuous clothes he wore were of a quality that only the purse of a nobleman could afford: a puce velvet cap plumed with purple feathers, a gold brocaded cape thrown about his shoulders, tooled leather gloves, knee-high riding boots, and a gold-hilted rapier dangling from his belt.

The hunting horn meant poachers. No doubt a brace of tres-passing knaves driving a hart[2] toward a confederate who lay coiled in wait, arrow knocked to the bowstring, straining for the kill.

But he was wrong. The horn blasts were not the work of poachers. They were meant not to drive, but to lure. The hunt was a pursuit not of the wild hart, but a man's heart. Not poachers, but villains plotting murder.

His murder.

Another horn blast.

Close by.

The prick of a sharp spur goaded the horse to splash through a shallow brook. But on the far side, the snarl of greenery proved too dense to ride farther. The rider dropped from the saddle, lashed the reigns to a withered sapling, and squeezed through a clump of prickling holly bushes. With one stride he plunged from bright summer sunshine into arboreal gloom.

In ancient times these giant oaks, crowned with mistletoe, had been sacred to the druids, and in these groves they sacrificed to their heathen gods. Today, the blood-hungry wraiths still hovering would slake their thirsts once again.

Ahead, a shaft of sunlight pierced the forest canopy and painted a circle of light upon the recumbent trunk of a fallen tree, illuminating an object set atop it. The lustrous curve of a hunting horn drew him toward it. His fingers stroked its polished smoothness, but then his eyes turned up at a sound like the mewling of a wounded cat. What he saw ripped the breath from his lungs: a young woman dressed in nothing but a white burial shroud, a torn rag blindfolding her eyes, her wrists bound by a rope looped around a tree. Blood ran from the corners of the woman's mouth and shock-red drops spattered the shroud. Even beneath the blindfold and blood it was a face he knew well and his heart lurched up.

"Dear God!" he called out, stumbling toward her. "My beloved!"

Hearing his voice, the woman turned her head his way and let out an inhuman wail.

But then a weird, foreshortened form stepped from behind the tree she was tied to: a goblin. Or rather, a man disguised for evil. His clothes were hidden beneath a buckram[3] cloak and hood. His face concealed behind a hideous green mask. The dwarfish figure came on, drawing a rapier. A second figure emerged from behind another tree, sword drawn. This one was of normal height and likewise wore a buckram robe and hood, but hid its features behind a Greek Tragedian's mask, the frowning mouth and eyes drooped in mournful despair.

The nobleman flung off his cloak and drew steel as a third figure emerged from hiding; this one wore a Satyr's mask, the goat like face set in an obscene leer with waggling tongue. As the masked figures advanced, the nobleman backed away. But unseen behind him, a fourth figure uncoiled from the shadow of a gnarled oak. This one also wore a rough cloak and hood, but the face was hidden behind a fiery Devil's mask. The Devil clutched a dagger, and now swept up fast and silent and buried the blade to its hilt in the small of the nobleman's back. He roared with pain and whirled, slashing wildly with his rapier, forcing his devilish attacker to retreat. Gasping, he reached around with his free hand, seized the dagger by its leather grip, and drew it out with an anguished howl.

"It will take more than a single dagger thrust to kill me!" he bellowed, but then shuddered, legs quivering, threatening to buckle. "What wickedness is this? My limbs grow cold!"

From a distance, the bound woman heard his words and moaned piteously.

The nobleman stared wide-eyed at the bloody dagger in his hand. A clear liquid dripped from the blade's hollow tip, releasing white smoke with a hiss when it fell to the mossy ground.

The Devil, newly emboldened, took a step closer.

"A poison dagger!"[4] The man groaned and sank to his knees. He threw a despairing look at the woman. "Oh, my beloved," he cried out. "I am dead! I am murdered!"

The four masked figures converged upon the kneeling man to gloat at his death-throes.

The nobleman glared up at the red-masked demon, his eyes aflame with hatred. "Masked though you be, I know who you are!" he cried, his body wracked by dreadful convulsions. "I see your devil's heart. Such evil cannot hide from the world forever. You chose your vizard[5] well, for you are truly Satan's progeny! Damned to burn in hell!"

The Devil had hung back slightly, but now rushed forward with an angry snarl, snatched up the fallen dagger from the forest floor and fell upon the kneeling man, stabbing him frenziedly, drawing piercing screams with every plunge of the blade.

Hearing his cries, the bound woman wailed, tugging at the rope that bound her to the tree and then threw back her head and unleashed a despairing shriek.

As the blade plunged in for the umpteenth time, the Goblin grabbed the Devil's arm and wrenched the dagger free. "Enough!"

The Devil tore loose of his grasp, stood up, and stalked away silently into the forest. The Satyr dithered, clearly unsure whether to stay or leave, but then stumbled away, hurrying to catch up.

"Wait! What shall we do now?" the Tragedian shouted at the Devil's back. "Hold, I say! What shall we do?" But the Devil and pursuing Satyr had vanished into the forest gloom.

As the Tragedian went to follow, the Goblin jerked him back by his sleeve. "Peace! Keep your wits! Take up his cloak from the ground and help me bear his bloody corpse away."

Gasping and grunting, the two masked figures dragged the nobleman's body through the tangling brush to the edge of the brook. Here, the Goblin removed the dead man's hat, rings, gloves, and boots and piled them in the Tragedian's arms. "Put these on. If you are seen riding the West Road folk will think you are he and it will confound all reports."

The Goblin knelt over the corpse and flourished the dagger. "I must cut off his nose and ears and hack the face so that none may recognise his visage.[6] Then we'll roll his trunk down the bank into yonder brook."

The Tragedian had to look away as the Goblin set to butchering the dead man's face, quailing at the rasp of knife on bone. When he had finished his gory work, the Goblin gave the corpse a mighty kick that rolled it into the shallow trickle where it flopped face down, staining the water with an aura of red.

When the Tragedian had donned all of the dead man's clothes save for the feathered cap the Goblin asked: "Have you a blade?"[7]

The mournful face shook slightly: *No.*

The Goblin held out the poison dagger. "Take this. You know what must be done."

The Tragic Mask turned its sorrowful gaze to look upon the

bloodied dagger, but would not touch it. "Why murder her? She cannot confess our guilt. You have cut out her tongue."

"Aye, but she can groan our guilt. Make a dumb show of it."

"Nay, do not ask. I cannot slay her."

"You must. You will. Take this bodkin.[8] Make an end of it."

"NO!"

"You know what awaits us should this enterprise fail?"

"Aye . . . the scaffold."

The man behind the Goblin mask choked out a mirthless laugh. "If we fail then death, when it comes, will be a blessed balm, for first we will walk the long, tedious road to the scaffold hand in hand with Richard Topcliffe."[9]

"But she is innocent of all stain. I'll not have her blood on my hands!"

"There is no one innocent in all England while a heretic bastard sits upon the throne."

"By Jesu, I would not murder her unshriven of her sins."

"Do it. Prove yourself! Or do you lack even a woman's heart?" The Goblin pushed the dagger into his hands. "Tie her to the horse and lead her away from here. Find a place much overgrown. There cut her throat and hide the body in the nettles. Then ride the horse a goodly distance east along the Great Road. Remove the saddle and reins and set the horse loose. Dig a hole and bury the raiments.[10] When you return, keep to the woods so that none may see your face. I shall await you beneath the bridge at Wexdale."

And with that, the hideous Goblin strode away in a flurry of buckram, tramping the same woodland path the Devil had taken.

The woman, although blindfolded, stiffened at the swish of approaching feet. She fell to her knees, clutched both hands in prayer, and began to babble. Even though her words had no tongue to form them, it was clear she was reciting the Lord's Prayer. A great sob of pity ripped from the murderer's throat. "Desist, I beg you, for your prayers steal my bravery and my dread deed be left undone!" The woman trembled as he took a step closer. Her garbled prayers became louder, more earnest. He drew the poison dagger, his own hands shaking. "Hasten your prayers, sweet lady. I cannot slay you while you pray. And fear not. Your soul shall fly straight to heaven."

He wiped a gloved thumb in the blood trickling from the corners of her mouth and daubed a bloody cross on her forehead, muttering a benediction. "Enough!" he said in a cracking voice. "Prepare your soul!"

She raised her hands to heaven, praying faster.

He brought the dagger up, and hesitated, gathering himself. The woods darkened as the sun plunged into clouds. Somewhere a crow cawed. The blade quivered in the air, inches from her bare throat. Finally, he lunged forward, yelling out in despair, but instead slipped the dagger beneath the rope binding her wrists together and drew the blade upward, cutting her free.

"I cannot murder you. There is blood enough on my hands. And more to come."

He froze at the sound of approaching voices: a man singing, shouted curses, laughter—travellers on the Great West Road.

The woman knelt in the damp leaf mould, awaiting death. Instead, she heard the crash of running footsteps and then the drum of hoof beats as a horse galloped away. It was some while before she reached up and tugged the blindfold loose.

Alone in the forest.

CHAPTER 3: THE PLAYERS' QUARREL

"Will Shakespeare, you are a prating coxcomb!"[1] Thomas Pope bawled and flung a chestnut that bounced off the crown of Shakespeare's head. The Stratford player combed a careless hand through his thin brown hair, but never looked up, thinking it to be yet another bite from the horse-flies that had been banqueting on the blood of the Lord Chamberlain's Men[2] for the last mile. Instead, he continued to mumble to himself as he walked along, eyes cast down to the hard-packed dirt road, gesticulating with arms and hands as he played out the scene he was writing in his head.

"See," Pope crowed. "There is no sense in that Warwickshire head and hence no feeling."

"Nay," Richard Burbage argued. "That man's head teems with princes and kings. With foredoomed lovers and valiant heroes—an entire world compassed within one mind."

"Aye," said Will Kempe, who was juggling four apples as he jigged along. "But if that be true, then John Sincler must have even more folk tramping about, for see how they wear thin his hair like the grass on an over-trodden verge."

The rest of the players cackled except for Sincler who dashed forward, snatched a nut from Pope's open hand and hurled it at Kempe in retaliation for the insult.

It was the summer of 1570 and the Lord Chamberlain's Men trudged the Great West Road that ran from London to Bath following a rickety horse cart laden with chests of costumes and props, and stacked with planks and sawhorses that could be lashed together in an inn-yard to form a temporary stage. The players were on tour. It was not uncommon for acting troupes such as theirs to quit the playhouses during the summer months when the warm weather crept in on the feet of a squealing horde of plague rats. But this year the capitol city slipped through the Grim Reaper's bony grip and the death carts had not trundled through the streets groaning beneath heaps of buboed[3] corpses.

In a rare season, the cackling Angel of Death swooped over London in his tattered grey shroud without alighting, although tongues wagged with rumours of plague in the outlying towns. But by a stroke of irony worthy of a master dramatist, a play was the very reason the theatres had been closed. Rival playwrights of Shakespeare's, Ben Jonson and Thomas Nashe, had penned *The Isle of Dogs*, a scandalous and seditious play that mocked the Privy Council[4] and lampooned the queen herself. After a single performance the Master of the Revels[5] had seized and burned all copies, arrested Jonson (Nashe fled to France), and nailed shut the doors of every theatre in London.

"A pox on this road," William Sly complained. "I am hotter than a boiled pig. My feet burn and my bones ache."

"A pox on Ben Jonson ..." Henry Condell said.

"... and Thom Nashe." George Bryan added.

"... Aye, and a pox on Thomas Nashe!"

"Verily," Burbage agreed. "With their *Isle of Dogs* they birthed a beast which has eaten up every playhouse in London. These rogues are the reason we wear out the day in walking."

Jostling around in the back of the cart was John Heminges, who served as actor, stage manager, and money-handler for the troupe. He sat perched on a cushion atop a small iron-banded chest that was always kept locked. The chest held the day's take. The key to the chest hung from a cord around Heminges' neck. "What would you have me do?" he said in answer to their complaints. "The Master of the Revels has closed the theatres. We have no choice but to tour."

"Aye, tis part of a strolling player's life," Burbage chided.

"This player's tired of strolling," William Sly said, sitting down amid the ruts of the dusty road and folding his arms.

The Lord Chamberlain's Men stumbled to a halt and Burbage shouted to Young Sam to stop the cart.

"We pause for rest?" Shakespeare asked, as always the straggler, sauntering up to rejoin the others. He was arguably the most handsome of all the players, with an open, intelligent face, a fastidiously trimmed beard and moustache of a lighter shade of brown than the wavy hair of his head, and a fine straight nose that rose to meet a pair of eyebrows perpetually arched in curiosity. "Tis well," Shakespeare said. "I have lines to write down lest I forget."

"No, sweet Will," Burbage said. "We do not pause for rest but for unrest—mutiny."

"Mutiny?" The Stratford player's eyebrows arched even higher as he looked about at his fellow players with puzzlement.

William Sly curled a surly lip. "I am done with this tour, Master Shakespeare."

Several other players joined in the chorus: "Aye, me too!" And with that, Henry Condell, George Bryan, and John Sincler plumped down on the road and refused to take another step.

Will Kempe dropped an apple, and another, and then the rest thumped to the ground at his feet. The theatre's most famous clown yanked off his cap with its jingling bells and threw a gravely unfunny look at his fellow players. "Tis an ill omen for the Lord Chamberlain's Men."

"What is your complaint?" Shakespeare asked of all.

"The heat, the miles," William Sly answered. He lifted a foot to show the many holes in the sole of his shoe. "Look you. I walk upon nothing."

"Shoes can be patched," John Heminges said sagely. "Holes stitched."

"A dozen holes stitched together is still a hole."

Young Samuell Gilbourne, a boy actor who played most of the women's roles, being the youngest and farthest from arthritic, had been given the spine-jolting job of driving the unsprung cart, which juddered, clattered and bounced over every rut, pothole, and upturned stone. His attention was still fixed on the road ahead. He had been warned to keep watch, as highwaymen and footpads[6] lurked everywhere on the Great West Road, eager to unburden travellers of their goods and money—and if needs be, their lives. He was the only one to notice the rising dust that meant someone fast approached from the opposite direction.

"The beggars in London are fatter than we," George Bryan said. "If Henry Condell grows more narrow he will appear as naught but a barrel stave, and then who shall play Falstaff?"

Sam Gilbourne stood up in the cart and peered at the rapidly approaching figure. "A horseman rides this way," he piped in a child's voice yet to break. At twelve, "Young Sam" was a tall, slender, fine-boned excuse for a boy; but in makeup, a wig and a dress he made a fetching Juliet and acted many of the leading women's roles. But none of the other players heard his warning, as their argument grew more contentious.

"How much did we take last night at that farmer's house?" Sly demanded.

John Heminges harrumphed, and then grudgingly muttered, "Thruppence."

"That's less than this dulled jade[7] eats in a day," Thomas Pope said and pinged a chestnut off the horse's arse, causing it to whinny and lurch to one side, nearly toppling Heminges from the back of the wagon.

"Perhaps we should eat the horse and pull the cart ourselves," George Bryan laughed.

"A meagre meal that would make," Pope crowed, "tis naught but bone and gristle."

Heminges saw mutiny boiling into full-scale insurrection. "Come friends," he wheedled. "Are we not all players? We play tragedy one day, but the next comes comedy. The Lord Chamberlain's Men have faced adversity before and remained a whole body."

"My body will no longer be whole at this rate."

By now, the dust plume had resolved itself as a rider, head down, cape flying, galloping his horse at full tilt toward them.

"A horseman," Young Sam shouted, "riding fast this way!"

"Tis different for you fellows," William Sly said. "You are all sharers;[8] the rest of us are but paid players."

"*When* we are paid." Richard Cowley spoke up. "Here we play for country pennies when before we played for city crowns."

"I could earn more in London," Bryan said. "I have an honest trade."

"Aye, you are the honest doorman of a swiving house," Shakespeare quipped, prompting bawdy cackles.

"Fellows!" Heminges interrupted. "We are but a day from Marlborough where there are many great houses we may play. Marlborough has always smiled upon the Lord Chamberlain's Men."

"Alarum!" Young Sam shouted, his voice stretched to a shrill squeak. "Look to!"

The rider swept down upon them in a thunder of hoof beats. He weaved around the cart and plunged straight through the body of the Lord Chamberlain's Men. Players flung themselves out of the way. Shouts. Yells. Apples thumped to the ground as Will Kempe dodged aside. Shakespeare did not see the horseman coming until too late. The rider brushed hard against him, spinning him around and hurling him to the ground. Horse and rider galloped on as the surprised players flung curses at his retreating back.

"Whoreson!"

"Villain!"

"Did you see the fellow?"

"A nobleman by his dress: a fine plumed hat and cape."

"Rogue, more than nobleman!

"An arrogant fop!" Richard Burbage snarled and spat on the

ground. "Riding hard from Bath to London. No doubt anxious to warm the bed of some pox-rotten whore."

William Shakespeare had taken the hardest fall and now he clambered to his feet, rubbing his sore shoulder only to find something smeared on his sleeve. He wiped his hand across his doublet and showed it to Burbage. "Mud," he said.

"Aye," Burbage agreed. "Tis made of water and dirt and can be found at the bottom of any pond. What of it?"

"It has not rained for two months. And yet his cape was beslubbered[9] with mud and the horse's hooves flung clods as it galloped by. This fellow has not ridden the West Road more than a few miles."

But before Shakespeare could pursue the thought, the Lord Chamberlain's Men fell back to arguing. Nearly being ridden down by the horseman was the final insult for many. Although John Heminges tried to dissuade them, in the end five of the company: George Bryan, William Sly, Henry Condell, John Sincler, and Augustine Phillips asked to be paid their share of the take and bidding their fellows good bye, turned and walked away, heading back toward London.

Vexingly, after being the main instigator of the rebellion, Thomas Pope had changed his mind and decided to stay on.

"How shall we manage?" John Heminges asked, watching his fellow players grow small in the distance.

"We must each take double roles." Burbage said.

"What?" William Kempe asked. "Act for two and do all removing and mending?"

"Aye, as need be." Burbage stared them down, one by one. "We are players. Tis the business of show." He turned to Shakespeare. "Will, you must amend some of your plays. Shorten each player's speeches. Remove a scene here and there."

William Shakespeare uttered the worst curse word he could think of and stalked away, kicking at the brown grass at the edge of the hard-baked road.

"The Lord Chamberlain's Men warring and divided," Will Kempe worried. "Tis an ill omen." Bells jingled in his cap as he shook his grizzled head ruefully and sighed. "Tis an ill omen."

CHAPTER 4: THE QUEEN'S PURSUIVANTS

The black mare cantered along the narrow road, hooves spooling dust. The horse's haunches were salted with dried sweat, its breathing ragged and laboured, but the rider atop its back neither noticed nor cared. The horseman was head to toe dressed in the black of a Puritan: black boots, black breeches, a black doublet, a wide-brimmed black hat jammed on his head, from beneath which lank strands of black hair blew in the wind. The sweat-stained collar of the plain white shirt was the only relief to a blackness that seemed to have migrated even to his eyes, which were such a dark shade of brown as to appear obsidian.

The road ahead divided. Without hesitation he guided the horse onto the left fork. A half-mile later, a great manor house loomed through the trees: a magpie building of black and white half-timber and stucco in the fashion of the age. The narrow lane that wound to the house uncoiled ahead and he swung the horse onto it.

Lush green lawns framed the manor's frontage where several of the Queen's soldiers in Cabasset[1] helmets and breastplates, shouldering muskets and pikes, stood guard on either side of the front door. As the lone horseman rode up, one of the soldiers quit his post and rushed over to meet him.

"Pursuivant Scrope."

"Sergeant at Arms," the rider nodded. The horse beneath him was panting and radiating heat. A pungent whiff of hot flesh clung to man and horse. Rivulets of sweat ran from beneath Scrope's hat and trickled down the hollows of his gaunt cheeks.

"A long, dusty ride from London, sir. Will you take meat and drink?"

"The Queen's business comes first," the horseman said, leather creaking as he swung from the saddle and dropped from his mount.

Up close, Oswyn Scrope had a long hooked nose mottled with blackheads. While mostly clean-shaven, his upper lip and chin were fuzzed with the slightest wisp of beard and moustache—tolerated only because the many pockmarks, warts and moles that sprouted on his forehead, brows, cheeks and chin defied the close scraping of a razor. He drew an iron rod from beneath his saddle and banged it against the side of his boot as he strode toward the front door of the manor house. The Sergeant at Arms called for one of his men to take the horse's reigns and hurried after.

"How many days, Sergeant Crugg?" Scrope asked as the soldier fell into step.

"Four, sir."

Gravel crunched as the Pursuivant[2] spun and hurled a withering glance at his Sergeant at Arms. "Four days and you have discovered naught?"

Sergeant Fen Crugg dropped his gaze, stirring the gravel with the toe of his boot. "Perhaps the intelligence was lacking, sir."

"Clearly, the only thing lacking is the thoroughness of your search."

Scrope's dark eyes narrowed to a squint as he scanned the roofline of the manor, counting chimneys. "Where is Pursuivant Munday?"

"In the library, sir."

There was a loud whinny from behind as the black mare, over-heated and driven beyond exhaustion, collapsed to the ground, where it thrashed, eyes rolling, mouth foaming.

"Give the beast water," Scrope commanded. "If in an hour it still cannot stand, kill it and cook it. It will provide meat for our supper." With that he strode away, and plunged into the shadows of the open doorway.

Inside, a great many soldiers busied themselves dismantling the manor, prying loose wainscoting, thrusting long metal skewers into cracks and chinks in the masonry, measuring the walls and hallways using wooden rods.

As Scrope marched the length of the hallway, the eyes of the portraits lining the walls watched his progress. He glanced up at them, scowling at what he saw: fine ladies and fine gentlemen dressed in the high-fashion gewgaws and trifles he found wicked and impious in their self-glorifying vanity. At last he strode into a large library where a young man of thirty-some years sat at a table piled high with books, poring over a slim tome.

"Master Munday."

The young man started. He dropped the book and leapt up from his seat.

"Pursuivant Scrope."

Scrope strode over to the large table and picked up a book at random, eyeing it with disdain.

"Nothing heretical thus far," Anthony Munday said. "Although these books bear the stain of controversy." He indicated a stack of no more than six or seven volumes with a sweep of his hand.

Angered, Scrope flung the book aside. "Four days and this is all you have discovered?"

"Perhaps we were mistaken. Perhaps—"

Oswyn Scrope silenced the younger man with a mawkish look that warned: *proceed no further.* "Where is the recusant?"

"As you instructed, the lady of the house, her children, and all servants are locked in her chambers,"

"What of the man of the house, Sir Edgar Broughton?"

"In the churchyard at Marlborough. The plague swept through here some three months past. She is a recent widow, much to be pitied."

Scrope shook his head to differ. "Those who refuse the Queen's religion and cling to papacy deserve not our pity. Any mercy they receive will be given by God alone, on the day they are judged." The rookish eyes swept the room, prying into every corner and crevice, and then lingered upon the great open hearth. "How many fireplaces? Surely you have made note of that?"

Munday stood open-mouthed, transfixed by the dark gaze, then shook himself free of it and scrabbled about the tabletop, tossing aside books until he snatched up a sheet of paper.

"Yes master, I have it here." His eyes flew across lines of his own scribbled handwriting as he read the line aloud. "Eight fireplaces. Four downstairs and four upstairs."

Scrope's gaze retreated inward as he groped his memory. "Eight fireplaces," he repeated. His gaze returned and fastened upon Munday's face. "And yet I counted nine chimneys. A strange disparity, think you not?"

Anthony Monday's mouth opened as he strained to find words and produced only a choked-off grunt.

Scrope clomped to the huge fireplace and stroked a hand along the immaculate white stone of the fireplace mouth, tugging and pushing, testing for loose stones.

"The fire is laid with faggots, ready to be lit."

"Yes, Master Scrope, as they are throughout the house."

"And yet we swelter in warm summer?"

"Aye, but it is the fashion. For appearances."

Scrope made a disapproving noise in the back of his throat and crouched down to examine the inside of the fireplace, peering up the chimney and wiping his fingers along the chimney back. He brought his hand away and held it up for Munday to see. Even his hands were warty.

The younger man goggled at Scrope's fingers and shrugged his shoulders, at a loss.

"Observe, Master Munday. No soot. Neither the throat of the chimney nor the hearth are in the least blackened." He stood up. "A great fireplace in a great room. And yet it has never been lit." The dark eyes bored into Munday's. "Why, pray tell?" But instead of waiting for an answer, Scrope turned his head and shouted to his men in the hall-way. "Bring fire! Someone go to the kitchen and fetch fire!"

Moments later, a soldier rushed into the room bearing a burning tapir. Scrope took it and knelt at the fireplace, kindling the stacked faggots, which crackled and popped as the dry wood lit. After watching the flames grow for a few moments, he decided it wasn't enough. "The books," he said to Munday. "Fetch them."

"Master?"

"We need more fire. Fetch the books here."

"But sir, they are not heretical. These are books of great learning: Greek poetry, mathematics, medicine."

"The Bible is the sole book of any import. The extra chimney is a sham, a tube to draw down air to a priest hole.[3] We must have a greater fire to smoke out a Jesuit."

Munday fetched an armful of books and piled them at his master's feet. The Pursuivant snatched one at random, tore out a handful of pages and tossed them in the fire. Munday looked at the book in his hands. It was beautiful leather bound volume of Ovid. Slowly, and with pained reluctance, he tore lose a clutch of pages and fed Ovid's immortal words to the flames.

The two Pursuivants threw volume after volume into the fireplace —Euclid's *Elements*, a rare copy of DaVinci's Notebooks, an illumi-nated Canterbury Tales of great antiquity—until smoke and burning pages fluttered up the chimney flue and the blaze of the fire scorched their faces, forcing them to back away.

From somewhere came the sound of coughing. The two men exchanged a look. The coughing turned to hacking and then to choking. Strangely, the sound appeared to come from the centre of the fire. Then something burst up from the flames, scattering burning faggots that tumbled from the fireplace and rolled across the floor. A trapdoor, built into the floor of the hearth flung open, and a human figure appeared, engulfed in smoke. As the two Pursuivants watched, the figure crawled from the blazing fire and collapsed on the floor, clothes and hair singed and smouldering. Still wheezing, the charred figure looked up into the merciless eyes of

Oswyn Scrope who smiled and said in a gentle voice, "Father John Pryce, I presume?"

~

Oswyn Scrope's boots thundered up the bare wooden stairs and Anthony Munday struggled to keep up, followed close behind by the Sergeant at Arms and two of his men. Scrope reached the second floor landing and threw a questioning look at the younger man. "Where is milady's room?"

Munday nodded the direction. Scrope stomped along the hallway to the final door. Munday fumbled to key the lock open, then Scrope thrust him aside and crashed through the doorway.

The air inside the bedroom was hot and steamy and funked with the stink of many bodies crowded into a small space and the chamber pot in the corner overflowing onto the floorboards. A dozen people huddled together, mostly servants. In the middle of them, Lady Ester Broughton, the mistress of the house, kneeled upon the floorboards, both hands clutching a wooden crucifix that dangled from a cord around her neck. Her children, two girls and a boy, a babe of two years, clung to her petticoats. All eyes looked up in fear as Pursuivants and soldiers crowded into the room. The children began to cry. Lady Broughton tore her gaze away from the men and continued praying.

"Lady Ester Broughton," Scrope's voice boomed. "I arrest you for treason."

The Lady snarled back, defiantly, "I have committed no treason, sir!"

"Your guilt is proven, Madam. We have found one priest, already! Plucked from the flames like the Devil himself. Where are the others? Reveal to us their hiding places."

"There are no more priests!"

"YOU LIE!"

Terrified, the boy flung his arms about his mother's neck and began to sob.

"Even if there were more priests, wild horses could not drag the truth from me."

A smile floated to the surface of Scrope's gargoyle face and soured there. "And so they shall." With that, he drew back his boot and kicked the child from his mother's arms. The lady screamed as her babe flew across the room and tumbled to the floor, his sobbing pitched to a hysterical wailing. A kerfuffle of shouts, screams, and imprecations burst out, but affected Scrope not in the slightest. He lunged forward, grabbed the Lady by her hair, yanked her to her feet and hauled her from the room. Ignoring her pained wailing, he dragged her down the staircase, along the hallway and out the front door, where he savagely hurled her to the ground, tearing loose a great hank of auburn hair. Lady Ester knelt on the gravel drive, weeping with shock and terror, but fell silent when she saw that Oswyn Scrope truly did mean to drag loose the truth using wild horses.

On the front lawn, Father John Pryce hung suspended between five horses, a rope tied to each limb and one looped around his neck.

"I ask you again, madam. Where are the others? We know you have provided shelter to two Romish priests who landed at Dover a month since. I have knowledge of the devices fashioned to hide priests, hidden places and secret holes carved into the foundations of a house. If need be I will tear this manor apart stone by brick. I will find all the hiding holes in time. Or perhaps I will nail the doors shut with you and your children inside and burn it to the ground."

"There were two others," the Lady quickly confessed. "Gone. Three weeks hence. They stayed but one night and left."

"Bound for where?"

"I know not. They did not give their names nor did I ask. That is our agreement."

"Cunning, like all popish tricks, but destined to fail nevertheless."

The dark eyes lingered on the Lady's face. Scrope could tell when interrogants were lying. It was a skill that made him most useful to his master Richard Topcliffe, the Queen's own torturer and the most dreaded name in England. For Topcliffe knew that, while torture loosened all tongues, even the innocent could be inveigled to confess anything on the rack. However, Scrope's inscrutable mind could sieve truth from falsehood.

The Pursuivant considered her words for a moment and said. "Very well. I believe you."

He abandoned the Lady where she knelt and stalked across the lawn to where Father Pryce hung suspended in space. "I trust you are comfortable, Jesuit. I imagined you would wish to stretch your limbs after such close confinement for four days." He chuckled, "Most ingenious, a chamber wrought beneath the hearth of a fireplace. The work of the evil dwarf, Thomas Hyde, I'll wager."

"God hate you," the priest muttered between clenched teeth.

"Save your oaths. You shall kneel before God's throne soon enough. Here is what I know. Your name is Father John Pryce. You came by Dover a week hence to join with two other Romish priests. Our spies have already provided us with their names. Here is what I do not know and what you will reveal to me. Why so many Jesuits come to this Bourne? You are plotting something. What?"

Pain had narrowed the priest's eyes to slits, but he opened them long enough to glare up at his tormentor and snarl, "Your hideous visage is punishment from God!"

The Pursuivant's face blackened at the insult. He looked up and nodded at his Sergeant at Arms. "Lead on the horses, Master Crugg." Father Pryce groaned as the horses shuffled a half step forward and the ropes stretched and creaked. "I ask you again. Is there a Romish plot afoot in England? Speak Pryce, or prepare to pay the price!"

Instead of answering, the Priest began to recite a prayer in Latin in between gasps for breath. Scrope threw another quick nod at the Sergeant. The horses stirred. The ropes creaked louder and then two sharp pops announced that the Father's arms had been pulled from his shoulder sockets, dislocating them. His screams rose to a nerve-shattering shriek then faded as he fainted. Scrope called for water. A soldier ran forward with a leather bucket and doused the Priest who jolted awake, moaning and dripping.

"Consider that a second Christening," Scrope mocked. "I know there is a Popish plot. Name me the house the priests are bound for."

"Oh, Lord!" Father Pryce shouted aloud. "Prepare to receive my soul!"

The father's words dissolved into screams as Scrope gave the nod and this time the horses tied to his legs were goaded forward, threatening to split him in two at the crotch.

Anthony Munday, who stood close by the flank of the black mare, fumbled a needle he had palmed in his hand.

"Enough! Enough!" Father Pryce screamed. "Stop, for Christ's pity and I will tell you all!"

Scrope raised a warty finger to signal an end to the torture. The horses were eased back, loosening the strain. "Where?" he demanded. "Where are the Jesuits headed?"

The words lurched out between gasps for breath: "They … are … to … meet … at … "

Anthony Munday dug the needle into the black mare's flank. The horse whinnied and reared up, vaulting forward. The rope around Father John Pryce's neck snapped taught, stretched … and ripped the head from his body. The decapitated head catapulted loose of the rope and bounced across the ground until it rolled against the hip of the kneeling Lady Ester, who fell over in a faint.

Anthony Munday looked up to find the black eyes of Oswyn Scrope boring into his. "The words trembled upon his lips, ready to fall into my hands." Scrope's words were choked with retribution.

"It was a horse-fly," Munday said quickly. "I saw it land upon the beast and bite before I could prevent it."

For a moment it looked as though the Pursuivant would combust with rage, but then he shook his head knowingly. "No, Master Munday," he said, fixing the younger man with his dread gaze. "It was the Devil in the form of a horse-fly. Come to silence his servant before he could speak God's truth."

The two men crunched across the gravel to where the decapitated head of Father John Pryce lay, lips still twitching, stunned-wide eyes staring into the unconscious face of Lady Ester.

"Three Jesuit priests have journeyed to Wiltshire," Scrope said. "Three that we know of. Mayhap there are more."

"They travel from house to house of recusants[4], performing popish mass."

"No," the Pursuivant shook his head. "Never have we had so many Jesuits in one place. I fear there is some fell purpose to this flocking of jackdaws. But I shall not rest until all mount the steps to the scaffold."

The large wooden crucifix that hung around Lady Ester's neck lay in the gravel at her side and the ruddy flow still oozing from the torn stump of John Pryce's neck crept across the ground . . . until it drowned the cross in blood.

CHAPTER 5: EXEUNT, PURSUED BY A GHOST

They had walked for hours, through loosely sprawled clutches of shabby dwellings too small to be considered a hamlet let alone a village, past rolling downs in tillage where a ploughman whipped the haunches of oxen who lowed and bellowed in harness, straining to pull a plough stuck fast in its furrow, unable to break through ground baked hard as iron by weeks of drought and sun. By the middle of the day, they had penetrated the edge of a great forest and were thankful of some shade as the sun directly overhead broiled their scalps even through their caps. Between the dense press of trees, Shakespeare spotted the glitter of moving water.

"A brook," he said. "We need to water the drab and shade us from the sun. And I have pages to write."

Footsore and sweaty, the remaining players shouted their happy agreement and the Lord Chamberlain's Men quit the road and ambled into the shadows beneath the towering oaks.

Shakespeare took quill, inkpot and a sheaf of papers from one of the iron-banded chests in the back of the cart and strolled off into the green, walking some distance from the others until he found a low, flat-topped rock that would serve as a table. He spread his papers out, then anxiously sharpened a new nib on his goose quill, dipped it into his inkpot and began to empty his pent-up mind onto the blank sheets. He wrote for a good half-hour, the words flowing from him. From his spot, he could hear the other players laughing and talking as they tucked into a small lunch of the remaining victuals fetched from the farmhouse they stayed in overnight, and passed around a wine skin.

A rod-like shape flitted across the page and perched on the end of his quill as if it had alighted upon a reed in a swamp: a tiny dragonfly with wings of glittering mica, its body a slender glass tube lit by a luminous blue gas. He pursed his lips and blew gently upon it, smiling as it flew off to hover over the brook, darting here and there as it snatched small insects from the air. Movement in one of the higher branches of an oak caught his eye. A horned owl perched on a branch, seeming to dissolve into the trunk until it revolved its head the other way and stared down at him. Shakespeare set down his quill and let out a languid sigh, for a moment transported to the days of his youth when, released from grammar school, he would run wild through the forest of Arden.

On the far side of the brook, a bush shivered. Shakespeare's hand flew to the dagger at his belt, fearing a lurking robber, but then a huge stag drifted free of the shadows and stepped silent to the muttering brook where it bowed its extravagant crown of antlers to lap the cool water. The sight touched Shakespeare more profoundly than he could have imagined and his vision starred. A clumsy footfall snapped the stag's head up, water still dripping from its mouth, ears twitching this way and that. Then it reared up and sprang away.

"Will, there you are!" Richard Burbage stumped over and held out a wine skin.

"Your bumbling steps just frighted away a great hart."

"No doubt these great woods are as thick with deer as fleas on a badger's arse," Burbage replied, settling himself on the mossy ground next to Shakespeare.

Remembering his thirst, Shakespeare took the wine skin and squirted a fine jet of vino down his throat, pausing only to wipe the beard of his chin and then his eyes with the back of one hand.

"Why do your eyes water so, Will?"

"Sight of the beast put me in mind of my sweet boy, Hamnet."

"Ah, you grieve for him still?" Burbage was Shakespeare's closest friend, from whom he could hide no secrets.

"Tis past a year since he died. The last time I was in Stratford … the last time I saw my darling boy, I took him hunting the hart in the Forest of Arden."

"You and your poaching, Will. You are a young roister-doister no longer. Next time you will not escape with a whipping, you will be hanged for it!"

Shakespeare ignored the barb and continued, "I showed Hamnet how to mark a trail and how to stalk. We hid us behind a bush and as we sat talking, a great hart—a full-grown doe—stepped into a shaft of light and burned there, no more than ten paces distant."

"Did you slay it?"

Shakespeare shook his head wonderingly. "I raised my bow, sited, and drew back the string. But the hart looked at me straight with its soft eyes. My hands trembled at its beauty and I could not loose my arrow. And so it sprang away, back into the forest." He raised the wine skin and quaffed more. "Thus ended my boy's first hunting lesson as we skulked home with no venison for the table. I had to stop at John Fletcher's farm to buy a goose for supper. I never heard the end of it from my *good lady*." The way Shakespeare said the words *good lady* made it clear he thought she was neither. "God's wounds, that woman has a voice like a Lincolnshire bagpipe. I could still hear her drone half the way back to London."

They fell quiet for a time. Drowsied by the wine, Burbage lay back on the mossy ground and closed his eyes. Shakespeare took up his quill and scratched out a new line. A chinking of coins announced the arrival of John Heminges, who trudged over carrying the small chest that held the take. He thumped the chest down on the ground next to Burbage and sat upon it. "What are you penning now, sweet Will?"

"A new play."

"Excellent! Have you a name for it?"

"Tis a mystery as yet. But I will discover it anon."

"What is your subject?" Burbage asked, sitting up, suddenly wide-awake. It was clear he was already speculating what new role would be his, and what great lines he would thunder from the boards to blow back the hair of the groundlings and set the rafters of the Theatre buzzing.

"Double dealing," Shakespeare said. "Double speaking. Double falsehood."

"I like it," Burbage grinned.

"Murder."

"I like it better."

"More murders. The stage will groan with bodies."

"I could not like it more!" He rubbed his hands together like a man set to tuck into a feast.

"Treason. The murder of a prince."

"I like it not!" said Burbage as his grin suddenly collapsed

Shakespeare arched his eyebrows at his fellow player.

The big man cleared his throat with a rumble like collapsing masonry.

"Will, plays about treason invoke the wrath of the Privy Council.[1] Richard Topcliffe, the Queen's own torturer spoke directly with Jonson, who I heard tell answered every question put to him with naught but 'Aye and Nay.' Tramping the Great West road wears thin our soles, but Topcliffe's road to the Tower will wear our souls into ghosts. Even now, Jonson lies in chains in Marshalsea prison[2] and Nashe has fled for France. Having roared, the lion of state has gone back to sleep. Let us not tweak its whiskers further."

"Why not a pastoral romance?" Heminges suggested. "And comedies are very popular—depending upon the situation."

"Tis a bloody play," Shakespeare said, continuing to write without looking up.

Burbage's face tightened with excitement. "The groundlings love blood. Nothing packs them in like your *Titus Andronicus*."[3]

"This story will have bloody action. It will gush forth fountains."

"Sounds costly," Heminges frowned.

Burbage frowned back. "What, a little pig's blood in a bladder?"

"Aye that and we must daily wash our garments. Therein lies the greater expense."

Burbage nodded agreement. "Aye, Thom's argument has a point. Perhaps just a little blood, and screams and groans cost nothing."

"I'll leave it anon," Shakespeare said, ignoring their chatter as he scribbled lines.

But Heminges was worried and would not let the matter drop.

"Why not write us a masque,[4] Will? The play houses are closed but no law forbids us to perform a masque, for there can be no sedition or treason in a masque."

Shakespeare stopped his scribbling and gave Heminges a crusty look. "No? Look for it and you can find treason or sedition in anything, even a masque. But then, I am no writer of masques. Perhaps we could have a masque within a play. I could share the writing of that with another."

Meanwhile, young Samuell Gilbourne stood solitary by the edge of the road, baking in the noon sun. The other players called for him to join them in the cool shadows beneath the trees, but he was a town boy and clearly afraid of the shadow-tangled gloom beneath the trees.

"There may be ghosts in yon forest," he said in a trembling falsetto. "The woods are dark and I am fearful."

"Peace," Shakespeare called out. "There are no ghosts in the woods, boy. Ghosts cling to dark places: houses and castle dungeons where murderous deeds were done and where they left their lives behind."

Burbage grunted, remembering something. "But Will, you told me once of things you had seen in the Forest of Arden. You fell asleep out hunting and woke to see wondrous sprites and fairies dancing in the trees. You said it was where you got the idea for A Midsummer Night's Dream."

"Fell asleep hunting?" John Heminges mocked. "I hear they brew a wondrous strong cider in Warwickshire. It makes many a man fall asleep and sets his head adance with fairies."

"God's wounds!" Shakespeare exploded, slapping down his goose quill on the stone. "Did you two pursue me here to babble?"

Heminges and Burbage muttered apologies and promised to keep quiet and let Shakespeare write in peace, but no sooner had he uttered the promise when Burbage turned his head and bellowed out: "Young Sam, quash your childish fears. Unhitch that drab and lead it down to drink."

Shakespeare threw a murderous look at his friend, but went back to his writing.

With obvious reluctance, Young Sam unhitched the horse and led it down to the shallow brook. As the horse guzzled, Sam's eyes darted about, probing the shadows as if he expected boggarts[5] to leap out at any moment.

Shakespeare had just finished penning a troublesome couplet when Sam's girlish shriek shattered the peace, springing every man to his feet. Young Sam abandoned the horse drinking at the brook and ran back to the road, where he danced about, screaming in terror.

"Hell's teeth!" Burbage shouted. "Cease your caterwauling, boy!"

"What is it, Sam?" Will Kempe rushed over and laid a comforting hand on the boy's shoulder. Wild-eyed, Samuell Gilbourne pointed a trembling finger at the brook. "The water ... it bleeds!"

Shakespeare left his writing and joined Burbage as the two men strode down to the brook to see for themselves. The old horse slurped away, unperturbed by Young Sam's screams. When the two players reached the spot, they were shocked to find that the boy had not been imagining it. A faint crimson current flowed along the middle of the brook, swirled about the horse's lapping muzzle, and then eddied away downstream.

John Heminges arrived and gasped when he saw what the other two men were staring at. The three shared a look, and then each drew the dagger from his belt. They followed the meandering brook upstream until they came upon a horrible sight: a dead man lay sprawled on his back in the shallow water, his face hacked into a raw, bleeding mass. The figure of a woman kneeled over him, keening piteously, her long blonde hair snarled with twigs and leaves. The woman had her back to them as they crept up, but their splashing footfalls gave them away and she turned to look.

The men gasped aloud. Not a woman, but a ghost. The ghastly pale face was besmirched with blood, and fresh blood trickled from the corners of its mouth. The ghost wore a white funeral shroud as if it had just sat up and climbed from its coffin. Seeing them, the lurid apparition rose up and stumbled toward them reaching out with bloody hands. It opened its mouth and let out an inhuman moan and as it did so fresh blood dribbled out.

One of the players screamed, or more likely they all did.

Suddenly, all three were running away, feet skidding on the slippery pebbles of the brook, each vying not to be the last. As they burst from the bushes, howling and yelling, Will Kempe looked up in open-mouthed surprise.

"A ghost! A ghost!" They cried. "We are haunted!"

"Master Kempe!" Burbage shouted. "Run! Take the horse! We must away from this cursed place!"

John Heminges dallied only long enough to snatch up the money chest, and when he looked back, the gory woman appeared, lurching after them and wailing most horribly. Heminges cried out with fear and almost dropped the heavy chest, which banged against his thighs as he ran to join the others.

The appearance of the ghastly woman struck terror into the rest of the players. Amid shouts and cries, and without bothering to hitch up the horse, the Lord Chamberlain's Men laid hands upon the cart and pushed it up the road as fast as their legs would allow, most too frightened to cast a backward glance.

The woman stumbled onto the road after them, but they were already too far away to be caught. Wailing and moaning, bloody hands tearing at her hair, she sank to her knees, bowing until her forehead touched the ground as she sobbed out her desolation.

CHAPTER 6: GHOSTS AND
BURNED PIES

"We must never speak of what we have seen."

"I tremble to think on it."

The strolling players were once again strolling the Great West Road, albeit at a faster pace than before. Thomas Pope clutched the bridle of the nag in harness and seemed to drag along both horse and cart as The Lord Chamberlain's men sought to put more miles between them and the haunted spot they had rested in.

"You three discovered the grisly scene," Thomas Pope said. "What did you see?"

"A dead man much bloodied," Burbage answered. "As we watched, the ghost tore the heart from his chest and gnawed upon it so that blood drizzled from its lips."

"I did not see that," Will Shakespeare said. "I would have spoke to it had not Thom Heminges screamed."

"You screamed first!" Heminges countered. "And louder than Dick Burbage and I together ... like a milk maid with a mouse up her skirts."

"I screamed only because you screamed."

"It had wings like a bat," Will Kempe said. "Great leathern wings."

"How would you know?" Shakespeare asked. "You ran away even as we three sprang from the forest."

"Aye, but before I ran, I did see the creature. It flew after us on leathern wings ... and breathed fire."

"We must never speak of this again," Heminges repeated.

"Aye, not for our own sake," Burbage said. "For the sake of Young Sam. Look you all, we frighten the boy further with such talk."

Since the ghost incident, Samuell Gilbourne hid himself in the back of the cart and refused to come out. He remained there, squeezed in between two chests, a sack pulled over his head from beneath which his frantic eyes peered.

"Aye," Heminges agreed, "But not just for Young Sam's sake. If we speak of having found a dead man, the local constable will hold us for the inquiry. And we must make haste for Marlborough."

"Agreed," Shakespeare said, starting to doubt what he had seen, but still shaken. "We shall speak of it no more. Not until we are back in London. There we may converse on such philosophies of death and ghosts over a tankard of ale in the comfort of *The Witch's Tit.*"

The rest agreed with a murmured "Aye."

The players paced off another thirty yards in uncomfortable silence.

"Its face was ghastly white and beslubbered with blood," muttered Will Kempe, unable to let the matter drop.

"SILENCE!" Burbage shouted, throwing his arms wide in a kingly gesture. The players stumbled to a halt and looked to their lead player, expecting him to continue the argument of the ghost. But instead he raised his head and made a show of sniffing the air.

"What?" Shakespeare asked.

"Pies," Burbage spoke dreamily, the mossy caverns of his nostrils flaring as he snouted the breeze that zephyred in their faces.

The rest sniffed the wind, but could smell only road dust and summer pollen.

"Meat pies," Burbage continued. "Roasted pork in a golden pastry crust ... a peat fire ... and brew kegs. I smell ale brewing." He sniffed deeper, filling his lungs. "And a cider press."

"He's always right," Pope said. "He has the best nose of the company—"

"And the biggest ..." Will Kempe added.

Richard Burbage grabbed his crotch and winked at his fellow players. "And you know what they say about men with big noses?"

"Aye," Shakespeare said. "Big noses drip a good deal in the cold winter."

"I scent an inn, gentleman!" Burbage roared. "No more than a mile away."

"What colour is the tapster's apron?" Shakespeare asked. "Can you nose that out, too?"

"Tis a good omen!" Will Kempe said.

The players laughed and smiled at one another, the horror of the ghost quickly forgotten at the prospect of hot pies and cool ale. They struck off with a renewed spring in their step but after only a dozen yards Burbage threw out his arms again, halting them as he snuffled the air and made a sour face.

"What now?" Shakespeare asked.

"Burned!" Burbage said, his voice cracking with dismay. "The pies have been left in the oven too long. The crusts are black!"

"Tis an ill omen," Will Kempe muttered, shaking his head. "Tis an ill omen."

CHAPTER 7: STOLEN BY A FOXE

The ancient beggar crept along the Great West Road, bent double beneath the burden of an enormous sack—evidently all he owned slung upon his broken back—feeling the way ahead with the tapping of a gnarled stick. His ragged dress: a serf's hooded tunic of scratchy wool, worn through and patched in many places, testified to his crushing poverty. The beggar's hood raised slightly at the drum of approaching hoof beats.

A rider in much haste galloped toward him: a gentleman from the cut of his clothes, a fine, plumed hat and cape billowing out behind.

"Alms," the old beggar cried aloud, holding out his hand in supplication. "Alms for a poor old man, in Jesu's name."

But the horseman cantered by without so much as a glance. The beggar turned to watch him go and stood upright, slipping back the hood to reveal the handsome face of a young man not quite into his thirtieth year. He sported waxed moustaches twirled in a fashion favoured by gallants and a beard trimmed into two forks, like upside down horns on his chin. An ostentatiously large pearl earring dangled from one ear.

The rider continued on for several hundred yards, and then veered his horse off the road into the trees.

The young fellow, who gave his name as Rafe Foxe (amongst many others), looked both ways up the Great Road to see if any more travellers could be seen. The way was empty. He tossed his sack into the bushes—it was actually filled with nothing more than hay and rags and weighed almost nothing—then hiked up his tunic and ran toward the place he had seen the rider leave the road.

When he got there he found a handsome chestnut bay tied to a tree. The horse's rider had dismounted and was standing knee deep in the middle of the nearby stream. He had stripped to the waist and was now busy washing his hands in the stream and splashing water over his face and neck, all the while shouting aloud in Latin. Foxe could not speak Latin, but recognised it as the language of the Catholic Church, a service now forbidden by order of the crown.

Seeing that the rider was preoccupied with his prayers and fevered ablutions, Rafe Foxe turned his attention to the horse. It carried two saddlebags that bulged with the promise of riches. Even more miraculously, like a gift from heaven, were the clothes piled on the ground close by: a pair of fine riding boots, a gorgeous cape with gold brocade, a purple plumed hat, a rapier with a jewelled handle. Laid atop the neat pile was the most handsome pair of leather riding gauntlets Foxe had ever seen.

The young man put his hands together in mock prayer and raised his eyes to heaven. "Ask and you shall receive. I thank you, oh Lord, for these alms."

Moments later, the chestnut bay whinnied as Rafe Foxe, dressed in the accoutrements of a nobleman, spurred the horse from the trees and galloped back the way the rider had just come, back toward Marlborough.

CHAPTER 8: THE WHITE HART INN

W ill Kempe danced a jig as he walked, the bells in his cap
jingling. Six apples whirled in the air between his quick,
clever hands. The rest of the Lord Chamberlain's Men were almost
jigging themselves, for they hurried toward a goal that drew them
ever faster to it.

In the far distance stood a roadside Inn—a large handsome
building of black timbers and whitewashed stucco. This close, it did
not need a nose as keen as Burbage's to see and smell the smoke from
its kitchen fires.

But long before they reached the inn, their paths crossed with
another group of travellers: six men and women who trudged toward
them, each one carrying a bundle of possessions on their backs.

"God by you," Shakespeare called out as the two groups converged.

The women were weeping, and all were distraught and walked
with their eyes cast down.

"What ails you, good lady?" he asked of a white-haired woman old
enough to be his mother. "Why weepest you?"

"We are undone, sir. All of us."

"How so?" Burbage asked. "Have you been robbed?"

"Robbed of our living. We were once the servants of Wexcombe

House, a great estate, dismissed now by the lady."

"A whole retinue, cast off at once?"

"Aye, sir," the white-haired lady said. "Maid servants and cooks, gardeners and gamekeepers, scullery maids and ostlers—all sent packing without regard for age, rank, or years of loyal service."

"For what cause?" Shakespeare asked.

"Because we are of the old faith, and therefore not to be trusted," the woman said, her words iced with bitterness.

Anger flared in the eyes the young man who walked behind her, by resemblance most likely her son, "There was a time when no one cared about religion in these parts, but now the state comes between man and God." He turned his head and spat upon the road. "I wish the Protestant bastard Elizabeth were dead!"

The players visibly blanched at treason shouted aloud for all to hear.

"Speak not!" John Heminges growled in warning to his fellow players. "Say nothing."

Shakespeare stepped to where Will Kempe jigged on the spot, snatched an apple in mid-juggle and pressed it into the old woman's hands. "We are poor players also much distressed, but take this, sweet lady, and our prayers."

"My name is Winifred," the old lady said, a smile returning to a face creased with years of worry and hard work. "May God bless you for your kindness, sir."

The players watched in sad silence as the masterless servants plodded away.

"Tis wicked," Burbage said, "to be cast off so cruelly."

Heminges cleared his throat. "Not our concern, gentlemen. Remember, ours is the business of show. We must to Marlborough. There lies our salvation."

The players strolled on, and soon were close enough to see the inn sign swinging on its iron rod.

"The White Hart," Thomas Pope read aloud.

"Will Shakespeare saw a great hart just before the ghost attacked us," Will Kempe blubbered. "Tis an ill omen."

"Peace, Kempe, you fool," Burbage said. "Every third inn in England is named 'the White Hart.'"

They reached a crossroad a short distance from the inn. As was common in many parishes, a pillory had been erected at the side of the road. A horse and cart were drawn up and two men stood close by.

"The Constable and his man!" Heminges said. "Remember, say nothing."

The two men were in the process of removing a ragged fellow from the pillory who was wrestled to the back of the cart and lashed to it with a rope. The prisoner had a wild mane of dishevelled hair and a shaggy beard stiff with filth. His shirtless body was black with grime and oozing sores. He called out to the passing players. "Turn back! Death awaits! You enter a poisoned land where men speak in false tongues and the whore of Babylon strikes at the heart of England with a dagger of fire. Turn back! Turn back!"

"Peace!" the Constable shouted. He nodded to his man who cracked the whip first on the haunches of the horse and then on the prisoner's back. The players watched in silence as the cart rumbled past, the wild man howling like a beast, the Constable trudging behind. The players muttered greetings and doffed their caps to the queen's man, but the gimlet-eyed officer replied only with a suspicious glare.

"A poor tom o'bedlam whipped from the parish!" Shakespeare muttered in a low voice.

"Another bad omen!" Thomas Pope said. He crossed himself and spat on the ground.

The players hurried away from the crossroads toward a cluster of buildings: a tiny, tumbledown church in ruins, two farmhouses and the inn.

The White Hart was a large and handsome building of three stories, the biggest inn they had seen in all their travels. It boasted an inn yard with stables and now a flock of honking geese chased each other around the yard with necks stretched out. Behind the stable yard, pigs wallowed in a sty, and sheep bleated in a pen. At the side of the building, a young maid drew water from a well. A great flock of hens and cocks spilled across the road in a feathery wave of reds and golds and tawny russets, rooting beneath stones and pecking at the ground. Several nibbled at the dangling ties of the players' stockings as they waded through the clucking mass.

"I am hungered enough I could eat one of these fat capons[1] with the feathers still on," Burbage said, rubbing his stomach.

Two figures stood by the front door where a cart was unloading barrels. A wiry, hatchet-faced fellow in a tapster's leather apron spun the barrels away from the back of the cart and walked them in through the open door, while the innkeeper, a short, podgy, round-faced man in a white apron urged and scolded his progress. The innkeeper fell silent when he saw the players approaching. Plastering on a fawning smile, he stepped forward to greet them.

"I bid you welcome, travellers. If you seek meat, drink, and rest, the White Hart is the best inn on the Great Road." The innkeeper's piggy eyes crawled over the Lord Chamberlain's Men, taking their measure and then rummaged among the chests in the horse cart. "Tell me, are you merchants travelling to Bristol market?"

Hoping to impress such country bumpkins, Richard Burbage stepped forward, thrust out his barrel chest, and gestured theatrically as he spoke, filling the air with the rich basso profundo of his voice: "We are The Lord Chamberlain's Men, London players of great renown, bound for the richest houses in Marlborough where we may delight the nobility with plays of passion, bombast and fury. We would honour you humble inn by tarrying here a night. Years from now, travellers will point to the White Hart and say: 'Here, Richard Burbage, the greatest player of Elizabeth's reign, rested his head.'"

Burbage's speech failed to inspire the awe he had intended. The Innkeeper's smile sagged into a frown. "Players, eh?" He made the face of a man scraping shit from the sole of his shoe. "In that case, money for the rooms up front, if it please you. I've had players in my Inn before. They are wont to leave in the night and forget to pay."

"Be reassured, good sir," John Heminges said, stepping forward with the money chest cradled in his arms. "I have the chinks[2] for you, locked in here." Coins clashed as he shook the chest. (In truth there was but a double handful of coins mixed with a scattering of stones and bent nails tossed in to make noise of a higher currency.)

The sham worked. The promise of money chased a smile back onto the innkeeper's face. Reassured, he laughed and rubbed his hands together. "But I can see you are a company of honourable fellows so the reckoning may wait until the morn. How many rooms shall you require?"

Will Shakespeare gripped Heminges's arm and muttered a threat in his ear. "Not three a-bed, Thom. I'll not sleep three-a-bed again. Burbage snores like a rutting boar and the vapours from Will Kempe's feet could strike a man blind."

John Heminges's eyes spoke that he would have argued the point had the two not been in public, but he forced a smile and pried his arm loose.

"We are five men and a boy, who does not mind to sleep on the hard floor—it gives good posture in a young back.

"Excellent!" the Innkeeper gushed. "First, you must meet my family. I am John Thomas."

"Oh, well named!" Burbage muttered. He and Shakespeare choked back rude laughter.

The innkeeper slapped a hand on the brutish fellow's shoulder. "This is my coz, Walt Gedding. There is no more honest a tapster in England."

At John Thomas's words, each player put a guarding hand on his money purse. Walt Gedding threw them a surly nod. He had a red scarf tied around his head. With his knife-scarred face and stringy blond hair brushing his shoulders, he looked more like a pirate than a tapster.

"Now you must meet the mistress of the household and my young babe." The Innkeeper turned and shouted into the house. "Come wife, come daughter, we have guests." He turned back to the players and grinned like the Devil welcoming sinners to hell. "Believe me, there is none like my wife in the kitchen."

"We believe you, sir," Shakespeare said innocently. "Her skill in baking led us here from afar by our noses."

They heard a loud, girlish giggle as a voluptuously plump woman scurried from the door—the innkeeper's wife—who he introduced as Maud. Evidently, Maud had been caught in the act of plotting more culinary arson, for her face, neck, and bare arms were dusted white with flour. The lady had wide hips, a well cushioned behind, and enormous, juddering bosoms, which threatened to spill over the top of her dress. Her immense breasts—with a cleavage as deep and dark as a mountain gorge—were sprinkled with flour, at which she batted with her pudgy hands as if dusting prized family heirlooms.

Shakespeare leaned close to Burbage and whispered into an ear sprouting tufts of red hair: "There's a pair of loaves needs kneading."

"My dough is already rising."

A moment later and something young and coltish flitted from the door. "This chaste young maid is my daughter, Constance," the innkeeper said, draping a father's jealous arm around her neck.

"Cu-cu-Connie?" Burbage stammered, straining to keep a filthy laugh gated behind his teeth.

"A name I would fit myself into," Shakespeare whispered.

The young girl, perhaps sixteen, was fair of face, and though pleasingly buxom, was less bovinely proportioned than the she-cow that birthed her. Constance curtsied shyly, batting her eyelashes at the men.

Richard Burbage ogled mother and daughter with a lascivious grin. "I would those two would make me a Burbage sandwich, and I the meat in the middle."

"Greedy fellow," Shakespeare whispered. "You may devour the mutton, I will savour the lamb."

Three rooms was finally decided upon which meant Young Sam got half a bed to sleep in and John Heminges shared his room with the luggage.

After the players had unpacked and argued the toss over who got what side of the bed, they drifted down to the Inn's great room. As they crowded around a table, they noticed other guests. A sad-looking fellow with white hair and a scrawny white beard sat at the next table, morosely pouring ale down his gullet. He was already staggering drunk and the pile of coins stacked ready by his elbow suggested he meant to stay that way for some time.

Then Thomas Pope noticed a well-dressed gallant with a forked beard, sitting alone at a small table in the snug. "Wait," he said. "I know yon fellow by the feathered cap and the fine cape. That's the rogue that nearly rode us down this morning!"

The Lord Chamberlain's Men looked at one another and then, without another word, rose as one and clomped over to where Rafe Foxe sat, chair rocked back against the wall, shiny boots propped up on the table. Although confronted by five able-bodied men, each with a dagger in his belt, Foxe did not seem the least bit afraid and nodded to them over his tankard of ale with a pleasant smile.

"I know you!" Thomas Pope said.

Foxe shook his head carelessly and said, "I think we have ne'er met."

"I think we *have*, sirrah," Pope spat. "This morning, on the Great West Road. You nearly trampled us!"

Rafe Fox shook his head. "You are mistaken, good fellow. This morning I travelled west, toward this very inn."

"Why then it must have been another rogue wearing your clothes," Burbage put in. "Same boots. Same cape. Same feathered cap."

"Same riding gloves," Shakespeare added, eyeing the handsome gauntlets and noting the stylised letter *W* in the leather working of the cuff. "I know something of gloves, and these are passing fine—the gloves of a nobleman. You wear fine boots, fine gloves and a fine hat, yet they do not match the condition of the rest of your apparel. Could they be stolen?"

Stool legs smacked the floorboards as Rafe Foxe's boot heels came off the table. The hands of the Lord Chamberlain's Men all flew to their daggers, but Rafe Foxe merely smiled ingratiatingly. "Come to think, I do recall we very nearly clashed on the road this morning. Gentlemen, I humbly beg your pardon. I was in a mad haste to visit the bed of a doxy I keep in a village close by."

Burbage threw a knowing look at Shakespeare and muttered, "I told you."

"But here," Rafe Foxe said. "Let me make amends." He thumped a bulging coin purse on the table. "I'll treat you all to a dinner of pie and ale."

The spending of money is always the fastest way to make friends. The Lord Chamberlain's Men let out a cheer and the argument was instantly forgotten as Rafe Foxe was invited to find a place at their table. Moments later, Maud and Constance bustled from the kitchen, each bearing a tray of trenchers steaming with hot pies: pork pie, game pie, and something called fish pie (although the pastry casing seemed to contain nothing but fish heads).

No one was surprised to find that the pies were burned black on the bottom.

After the pie fillings were picked from their blackened crusts, Will Kempe sprang to his feet and danced a jig, and then followed it with antic faces and pratfalls until Rafe Foxe and the Lord Chamberlain's Men barked with laughter.

Drawn by the sounds of mirth, the mistress of the house deserted the kitchen to lean against the doorframe as she watched. She held a large bowl beneath her wondrous bosom and stirred something with the consistency of pudding batter with a wooden spoon. Burbage looked up at her and their eyes locked. She winked at him, then dipped a chubby finger in the batter, pushed it between her plump lips and sucked the finger clean. Burbage's leg spasmed and kicked the underside of the table so hard it bounced trenchers and toppled tankards.

"Careful, Dick!" Thomas Pope shouted angrily.

"Sorry," Burbage said. "I feel a stiffness coming on." With that, the Great Thespian muttered an excuse about draining the serpent and left the table.

Throughout it all, the dour man seated opposite sluiced ale down his gullet as if he were swallowing poison and stared blankly at the table in front of him.

The greasy Tapster scowled back into the room lugging a large tray and banged down fresh tankards of ale. "Tapster," Shakespeare said, grabbing Walt Gedding by the arm. "What ails yon gloomy fellow?"

Before consenting to answer, the tapster glared at the hand gripping his elbow until Shakespeare removed it. "He is Ned Smedley," the tapster said; his voice was a spade shovelling gravel. "Until late a servant at Wexcombe House. He and his fellows are all dismissed."

"Aye, we met them on the road. Why did he not tarry with them?"

"He is old and will find no service with a new master, so Ned has pledged to stay and drink himself to death."

"Better than jumping in the river," Shakespeare reasoned. "I would rather drown myself in sack[3] than in water."

A nine man's Morris[4] had been carved into the tabletop. Will Kempe and Thomas Pope began a game, using groats[5] as counters and wagering against each other.

Rafe Foxe watched them play a game as he sipped his ale. He finally smiled and spoke up, "If it's games you fellows like, I bought these a week since at Bristol market." He pulled a cup and dice from his doublet and set them down on the table. "Being but a simple country wight, I have little knowledge of dicing, but perhaps you clever London fellows could teach me how to play?"

Will Kempe and Thom Pope shared a knowing grin across the table: the trout had not only put himself upon the hook, he had kindly supplied the rod and line. The three moved to another table that was free of trenchers. John Heminges flung a worried look at Shakespeare and rose from his seat.

"I had best go with them," Heminges said. "To keep watch and lend a cooler head. Both men are rash and foolish gamblers."

As the day still had plenty of light and his room had a small table and a large window, Shakespeare excused himself and went upstairs to work on his play. He wrote steadily for an hour until he had filled five pages, then stood to stretch and drifted to the window, rubbing at the knotted muscles burning in his neck. Throwing wide the shutters he leaned far out the window, his hands resting on the sill. His room was on the roadside, and now he looked down on the chickens scurrying about. He noticed smoke rising above the dense stand of trees opposite and frowned—at first fearing that some careless charcoal burner had set the woods on fire. But a minute's study showed that the smoke was constant and he realized that it must come from the chimneys of a great house just beyond the trees.

The clopping of hooves pulled his gaze back to the road. Two horses approached at a slow walk. A gentleman in fine clothes with a haughty face sat astride the first one. He rode past looking neither left nor right. Following twenty paces back was a woman on a brown mare. She rode sidesaddle, and by her fine clothes was evidently the Lady of the haughty gentleman. As they drew close, Shakespeare could see that she was a beauty—her fiery red locks pinned up by jewelled brooches and capped by a feathered bonnet. The woman seemed to sense his stare, for she looked up and their eyes embraced in a lingering gaze. Shakespeare made a flourish with his hand and bowed deeply to the lady, who smiled demurely and acknowledged him with a slight nod of her plumed bonnet. As her horse clopped past his window, something white fell from the lady's hand and fluttered to the road.

Shakespeare fled the room, thundered down the narrow stairs and ran outside to snatch up it up.

A handkerchief.

It was of fine French linen with the letter V embroidered into a corner. He pressed the handkerchief to his face and inhaled. Perfumed! Shakespeare dithered for a moment. His first impulse was to run after the lady and act the gallant by reuniting her with her dropped handkerchief, but by now the lady and her dour husband were distant smudges on the twilit road.

And then he tumbled to it. She had not dropped the handkerchief by accident: it was an invitation. The notion set his heart pounding and he felt the same giddy excitement that tingled through him when poaching deer on another man's land.

William Shakespeare knew he was about to do something he would find himself in trouble for. Still, he could not help himself. But what he could not know was just how much trouble, for the scented handkerchief would soon draw him into a web of treason and murder.

CHAPTER 9: FOUR DAYS EARLIER— HOW THIS WHOLE BLOODY MESS BEGAN

As usual, I have to exit the bus Kamikaze-style.

The Number 46 from Marlborough to Chisbury doesn't actually stop outside the White Hart Inn—once again logic and sanity fails to jibe with bus company timetables and routes. So my only way of avoiding a quarter-mile walk is to wait for the bus to slow at the roundabout and commando off the open platform.

I rise from my seat and sidle toward the back of the bus past grim-faced pensioners gripping bulging Sainsbury's shopping bags. I make it to the open, breezy platform at the rear of the bus where I stand clutching the shiny silver handrail. When I press the big red button, the bell "dings" and the bus shudders Jurassically as it slows. As it leans into the roundabout, the Number 46 has lost most of its speed and so I leap. My feet slap the blurring pavement and I run it out. For a podgy little man in his forties, I pull it off quite deftly, but it's an undignified exit from public transport for a man of my age—and a local business-owner to boot. Unburdened of me, the bus accelerates, swaying dangerously around the curve of the roundabout, and growls up the bypass road, trailing a wisp of black diesel soot.

I plod toward the black and white half-timbered Tudor building in the distance. There's a gnarled oak growing in the narrow parking lot and an inn sign swinging above the front door—The White Hart Inn. My name is Harvey Braithwaite and, God help me, the White Hart is my domicile, my business, and my personal albatross—or at least until the bank takes it away.

The 1971 Jensen Interceptor FF[1] parked in my designated spot is in mint condition, but hasn't turned a wheel since the day I took possession of the Inn, a year ago. (My driving ban expires in just a few days.) The Jensen is—or rather was—a deep shade of royal blue. Judging by the white splatters across the bonnet and windscreen, the colour evidently has a laxative effect on the owl that perches in the oak tree and keeps me up half the night with its hooting. Sadly, I count only one other car in the parking lot—and this is the lunchtime rush. I sigh and push through the front doors.

As I step inside, the familiar smell of beer, cigarettes and ennui washes over me. You never get completely get rid of that smell—cigarettes that, is—even though the inn has been non-smoking for years. I brush past a naked coat rack and step into the taproom. Sidney, my bar tender, lurks in his usual spot behind the bar. Built like a cigar store Indian and about as animated, Sidney came with the fittings when I purchased the business. He's still here, nearly twelve months later, and like the damp mould stain beneath the stairs I can't seem to get rid of either. Sidney is a study in inertia—ponderous and slow. He's recalcitrant to serve and offers me an inexhaustible supply of insubordination no matter how little I pay him. I mainly tolerate him because I suspect he's too dozy to steal from me . . . much.

"Guvnor," he grunts as I step behind the bar. As always he has one hand cradling the bowl of a pipe jammed in the corner of his mouth.

"What've I told you about that pipe?" I ask, irritatedly. "The pub's non-smoking! Go outside if you want to light up that chimney stack."

He pulls the pipe from his wet lips. "Not lit," he grunts. The chewed stem glistens with saliva as he tilts it to show me the bowl. "No tobacco."

In fairness, he did give up smoking four months ago, and now he uses the pipe purely as a pacifier, sucking the last remaining molecules of nicotine from the wood fibre.

I plant both hands on the bar—a sea captain steadying himself at the wheel—and look around at my doughty vessel. Some people may think it's quaint to live in a crumbling ruin. I could disabuse them of that notion in short order. The inn is made of horse shit, straw and bloody big boulders and was built around the year 1500—before people had brains. The plumbing is early Victorian. The wiring is late Victorian—I think Edison and Faraday knocked it up between them while on a dirty weekend here. If you even think of plugging in the toaster while the microwave is on it you'll blow every fuse and blackout half the county.

The nautical reference is apt, since the warped floors pitch and roll like a troubled sea. Everything is sagging and settling and tilted. People who love old-fashioned crap lap it up—I did too, which is why I paid too much for the business. But now I find its age a pain in the arse. Try hanging a picture straight when the whole friggin' building has a ten-degree list to starboard. When I bought the place I thought: Oldie Worldie quaint. Main road location. Just outside Marlborough. Tourist magnet.

How bloody wrong can you be?

About the time I took possession of the keys the local council finished the new bypass, which siphoned off the traffic and all my customers with it. Yes, now that you ask, I was out of my mind when I bought it—or closer to bonkers than usual. In my defence, it was only a month after my divorce became final. My ex-wife now owns my old pub, along with half my life savings.

What can I say? Life is my Whoopee cushion.

I look around at our customers. To say the clientele does not look promising is a colossal understatement. They're all wrinklies: pensioners from the caravan site down the road.

"Local embalmers go on strike again?" I grumble to Sidney. "Looks like *Night of the Living Dead* in here. Tell them to keep moving, the local funeral home's taking inventory."

"At least they're paying customers."

I choke on a bitter laugh. "Paying customers?" I look around, counting off the drinks in front of each. "A pint of bitter, an orange

Britvic and the geezer in the cloth cap and braces with half a pint of shandy he nurses all night. Evaporation's faster."

"He's a regular."

"Yeah, a regular waste of space."

"Went well at the bank, did it?"

I glower at Sidney from under my brows. My bartender lolls with his back against the spirit bottles, sucking contentedly at his pipe. *No worries*, his big, stupid face says. No thoughts. No cares. And no wonder. He's in his forties and still lives at home with his partially fossilised mother. Never married. Never had a girlfriend as far as I know. And no, he's not gay, either. I think he's just too idle to be bothered with sex, with a real job, with anything relating to life. I've no doubt some day they'll find his badly decomposed corpse in a house with fifty-seven cats and ceiling-high piles of rubbish and old newspapers. His ripening carcass will be discovered only after the neighbours kick up a fuss about the horrible stink. The police will have to tunnel their way in like miners wearing respirators and biohazard suits.

"I'm gonna replace you," I say. "Get a dolly bird with long legs and big knockers. That'll bring the customers in."

Sidney makes a wheezing sound, which I finally realise is his cartoon dog laugh. "Never," he says calmly. "No one wants to work out here—too far from town. Especially for what you're willing to pay."

"Yeah, you're right. Besides, where would I find someone with such a low ambition threshold?"

He nods as if I've just paid him a compliment and repositions his pipe with a wet sucking sound like a dying man on a respirator. "I booked three rooms today."

My head whiplashes round so fast something cracks in my neck. "Three?" I say, struggling to claw back the hope rising in my voice and failing miserably.

Sidney ponders for a moment, pretend-puffing on his pipe. "No," he says, shaking his head, deflating me. "Sorry, not three." He ponders … ponderously. Can he see the exasperation squeezing out of my pores? "Mmmmn … four. Three for tomorrow. One beginning today."

Four bookings in one week? I goggle. I club my hopes senseless before they can rise again. "How long for?"

"Through Shunday," he slurs around the pipe like a bad Sean Connery impersonation. He yanks the pipe stem from his mouth, chewed and loathsome, and uses it to gesture at something. "There's the lady now."

She enters the room a little cautiously, eyeing for a place to sit. Though she's probably closer to forty than thirty, she is lovely. I know it's movie-corny cliché, but she seems to be lit by her own personal klieg light. Her skirt is a little too short for her age and for this early in the spring, but she has knockout legs and knows how to show them off. She clops her high heels into the snug, plonks down at a small table, snuggles her Prada bag beneath her chair and arranges a magazine in front of her. As she pages through it, a delighted smile whispers across her features. My crumpet-radar is set on full-scan. I can tell she's either never married (highly doubtful) or more likely has been divorced just long enough for the tan-line on her ring finger to fade.

I say, as casually as possible, "Get over there, Sid and see what she wants to drink. I'm just going to go change my shirt."

Sidney throws me a gormless look. "Get changed? What's wrong with what you're wearing? You just got back—" He flashes a cheesy grin, giving me an unwanted close-up of his nicotine-stained teeth. "Oh, I get it. Fancy your chances, do ya?"

"NO!" I say loud enough to creak a few arthritic necks around. "No," I repeat, lowering my voice. "I just want to . . ." I sigh. Drop the pretence. What do I care what a moron like Sidney thinks? "Answer one question," I say. "Did she register as Ms, or Mrs?"

Sidney stirs the pipe in his gob, thinks about it a moment, and finally mutters "Ms."

He says something else, but his words hang in the air at my back.

I am already gone.

When I dash back into the bar, five minutes later, she is still sitting at the table sipping a white wine, engrossed in her magazine. "How do I look?" I ask, catching my breath.

Sidney eyes me quizzically. "Is it Johnny Cash karaoke night?"

"Black's very slimming." I say, tugging the knit shirt down, smoothing the wrinkles and hoping it camouflages my paunch.

"You look like a sausage in a black casing."

"Remind me again, why do I pay you to insult me?"

"No one else would for the wages."

"And don't you forget it." I indicate our new guest with a nod. "What's she drinking?"

"Housh white," Sidney slurs around the pipe.

I make a face. The house white comes in gallon jugs which I have Sidney decant into bottles gummed with faux labels for French-sounding vineyards that don't exist: Chateau de la Wapping, Droitwich Chardonnay, Grimsby Riesling. Although I'm no wine expert, the house white has the gum-shrivelling tartness of antifreeze and the heady bouquet of cat piss. I reach under the counter and grab the bottle I keep handy for important people. Suitably armed, I pull my shoulders back, suck in my gut and saunter over.

She is engrossed in her magazine when I reach the table, but senses me hovering and looks up. Her eyes are large, sea green, and speak of soft beds piled with frilly pillows.

"Harvey," I say, introducing myself. "I'm the owner."

Her eyes take in the wine bottle. "Gillian," she replies in cut-glass syllables. From one word I can immediately tell that she is: Posh. Educated. Completely out-of-my-league.

Still, nothing ventured.

As she extends a hand, a gold tennis bracelet jangles on her tanned wrist. Her handshake offers only a clutch of fingers, which are long, slender and cool.

"Drink on the house?" I gesture with the bottle and she nods. I gurgle a generous pour in her empty glass, hoping my smile is coming across as suave host and not leering axe murderer.

She takes an experimental sip. "Mmmn," she says appreciatively. "That's much—"

"Better than the house plonk?" I jump in. "Yes, sorry about that. My barman's an idiot. We like to hire the mentally challenged—it keeps them out of the bus shelters."

Her expression falters and I realise my own petard has probably just hoisted me. I keep my smile clenched and wait to see how badly that un-pc comment has offended her.

Thankfully, she smiles after an awkward pause and gives up a chuckle. The laugh lines in the corners of her eyes ratchet up my estimate of her age up a few years; still, she's a handsome filly.

"So you're staying ...?"

"Until Sunday," she says, and then adds. "I adore your inn."

"Yes," I agree slipping into Mein host persona, "She's quite a place. If only these walls could talk, eh? A lot of stories . . . a lot of stories." I nod my head fondly although most of the stories I could share concern torn-up floorboards, short-circuiting electrics and leaky ball cocks.

"Really?" she says. "I'd love to hear some." She swivels in her chair and crosses her legs, flashing yards of creamy thigh. "Why don't you join me?" she asks, nodding to the empty chair across from her. "If you're not too busy?"

Too busy? I somehow manage not to inhale my tongue. Things like this do not happen to me.

Half an hour later, we've demolished the first bottle and I'm cracking open a bottle of cheap champers. The booze has loosened her up, but it's also loosening me, which is not good, since even fully wound stupid things have a tendency to fall out of my mouth.

"So," I say, "What brings you to Wiltshire? Fun, hopefully?"

"Business. I'm here for a conference."

"Ah!" I sigh sympathetically. "Boring, eh? Bloody conferences."

"They can be, but this one I'm rather looking forward to."

"Really? Great. Terrific. Still, all work and no play—"

She looks around at the inside of the pub and strokes her delicate hand along the knotty beam by her shoulder. I expect to hear a shriek and watch her snatch her hand away with a huge splinter in it. But it doesn't happen and she turns to me with eyes sparkling with enthusiasm.

"I love history. Old buildings. Don't you?"

"Oh ... gosh yeah," I lie, though for a moment I flash onto a mental image of me dancing with glee on the smouldering ruins of the White Hart, waving an insurance check printed with a number followed by a long line of zeroes. "Yeah, I love the old stuff, all right. Nothing like it."

"Has the inn been in your family long?" she asks, combing a silky strand of red hair behind one ear.

I laugh. "Not quite a year."

"Oh!" she says, surprised. "Must be a lot of work. But I'm sure it's worth it to preserve these old places."

"Definitely. Definitely worth it." I wonder if her opinion will change when she tries to flush the toilet in her room. "Definitely. Yeah ... definitely—" I ramble on, brain stuck in a groove.

She smiles archly. "You don't sound too convincing."

To change the subject I say, "Speaking of things historical, I did trace my family tree a few years back."

"Oh really?"

"Yeah, it appears that Braithwaite is a local name and that we Braithwaites have been a vital part of the town for centuries."

"Really?" the gleam in her eye tells me the fish is on the hook.

I nod. "It turns out that my great, great, great, great grandfather was— Go on, guess."

She purses her lipsticked lips—a fiery shade of red I would name *Begging to be Kissed*— and thinks about it. "Mayor?"

"No."

"Magistrate?"

"No."

"Sheriff?"

I shake my head. "Not even close."

"Oooh!" she says, sensing a titillating secret. "A famous criminal? A highwayman?"

"I wish. That at least would be colourful. Turns out he was the town shit cart driver. Used to drive his cart from house to house collecting people's … well, you know."

She chuckles into her champers. My God, it is a heart-skippingly wonderful laugh.

"Not something I normally tell on a first date," I add.

Gillian arches a razor-thin eyebrow she paid someone good money to pluck out then draw back on. "So this is a date?"

"No, I didn't mean to—" She lets me squirm for a moment before I can tell she's joking. "Sorry," I offer lamely. "I'm a little out of practice."

"Me too," she says and places her hand on mine. Just for a moment, but it's a first touch and she initiated it. I try to keep the smile from sliding sideways on my face like it does when I'm nervous. I don't think I quite manage it, so I tilt my head in an effort to compensate. Having shared that intimate moment I then torpedo everything by opening my big mouth.

"I mean history, culture, in the end it's all load of boll— I mean, er, rubbish, isn't it?"

"Why do you think so?"

For the next few minutes Mister Stupid hijacks control of my mouth. "Weeellllll, I mean, what's it got to do with how we live nowadays?" I happen to glance away at a young couple sitting at a table in the taproom. The nerdy guy is obviously a student judging by the sellotape holding his Harry Potter spectacles together and the *Will Power* t-shirt with Shakespeare's mug on the front. Unfortunately, this puts me onto the wrong track entirely.

"I mean, Shakespeare, for example."

I should see the iron portcullis slamming down behind her eyes, but I've drunk almost all the champagne without her help.

"What about Shakespeare?" she asks slowly.

I flash her my *you-know-what-I-mean-elbow-in-the-ribs* grin.

She responds with a *I don't-have-a-clue-what-you're-on-about* head shake.

"Weeeellllll," I say, leaning toward her and dropping my voice to a cosy whisper. "You know, people pretend to like Shakespeare because you're supposed to. It's art. Culture. But nobody *really* likes it, do they?

I think the average person, when they come home after a day's slog, they kick their shoes off and ... click, click ..." I mime using a remote. "What are they looking for? News? Naw, boring. Old movie? Repeat—seen it. American cop show—seen it, and it's boring. Oh look, here's a Shakespeare play." I throw my chest out dramatically, a hand pressed to my breastbone and mockingly intone: "Oh forsooth, I prithy. Hearken unto this." I toss her my best cherubic grin. I don't do rugged and handsome but I do a great cherub. "I mean nobody *really* likes that rubbish, now do they?"

She makes a face as if her sweet champagne just turned vinegar sour.

"Actually I do,"

I laugh. "Naw! Naw you don't, not really—"

"Actually, I very much do."

The floor has suddenly become an ice flow and I'm on the thin bit, which has cracked off and is starting to float away.

"It may interest you to know that I am a Professor of Shakespeare studies at Preston Polytechnic. So you see, I do like Shakespeare, really, truthfully, honestly, and no, I don't think it's a bunch of old rubbish or that people only pretend to like it!"

She holds up the magazine so I can see it and for the first time I realise it isn't a magazine, it's a glossy event programme. The cover says *Wexcombe Shakespeare Conference* and has a picture of some tarted-up bloke in a poncy jacket with an enormous lace collar. I admit I'm a bit slow, but even I can guess that this is supposed to be the Bard himself.

"I thought by conference you meant—you know—a *real* work conference." Immediately, I know I've just dropped a clanger. My brain scrabbles for a witty comment to defuse the situation. Something. Anything. But I'm no Oscar-bloody-Wilde.

She quaffs her drink and bangs the glass down so hard I'm surprised the stem doesn't snap—I'm clearly paying too much for these glasses. "Thank you for the drink," she says, obviously not meaning it. Her chair grumbles back from the table and she stalks out of the bar on her long, shapely, slender, delicious legs.

"That went well." The plodding voice behind my shoulder is Sidney's.

Of course, I need a witness to my humiliation and who better?

"I see you charmed her," he adds, twisting the stiletto a full three-hundred-and-sixty.

What can I say? He's right—sometimes I only open my mouth to change feet. I rise shakily. I can't feel anything because I'm numb from the neck down. I realise now that my first real conversation with a woman in a year has just gone very badly. I've managed to insult not only her, but also her entire profession in less than twenty minutes. Worse, she is staying here until Sunday, so I will have to avoid her for four more days.

Glasses clink noisily as Sidney clears the table. He picks up her wineglass. "Look at that," he says, waving it under my nose to show me the perfect lipstick print. "Can you imagine what those lips must feel like—? Oh ... I'm sorry," he smirks. "I guess you'll just have to."

"I'll be down the cellar," I mumble, and shove past.

CHAPTER 10: A SECRET PATH

"What do we search for?

"That which is hidden."

"What can be hid in this dark forest?"

Oswyn Scrope stopped and glared at Anthony Munday. "A path that Jesuits may travel by unseen." Scrope's dark eyes peered into the forest as if sopping up both gloom and shadows. His soldiers moved distantly among the trees where he had dispersed them for the search. "Sergeant-at-arms!" Scrope hollered.

"Aye, sir?" An armoured figure in the distance shouted back.

"Take your men in yonder direction. Master Munday and I shall search to the West."

The fringes of the woods, which received more sunlight, were verdant and lush with vegetation. The two pursuivants panted, breathing hard as they waded through hip deep grass and spiky ferns, tripping over fallen limbs, stumbling in rabbit holes, dragging their feet through snares of ankle-tangling vines.

As they stopped to snatch a breath, Munday said, "The woods here are wild and nigh impossible to move through. Would they not travel the roads by dark?"

Scrope scowled doubtingly. "They must needs carry torches to do so, which could be seen. Though dismal, these woods can be travelled by day with less fear of detection." He shook his head knowingly. "I'll vouch we will find a trail in these woods that leads back to the manor the unfortunate Father Pryce hid himself in. Following the trail in the contrary direction may well lead us to the house where his fellow rascals hide."

Scrope took another wading step and then threw his hand up to signal Munday to stop. "Look you!" he cried, pointing.

"I see naught."

"Those holly bushes over yon are dead, while others growing round here keep their green."

He stepped forward and grabbed the nearest holly bush. The bush had been cut free of its roots and was dead. It was one of four that had been lashed together by a few wooden spars. When he tugged on them they swung aside like a door, revealing a well-worn path behind.

"We have it!" Scrope exulted. He turned and shouted to the soldiers. "Sergeant Crugg, fetch your men!"

The trail they marched was worn by the feet of many travellers, testifying to frequent use. Accompanied by soldiers in clanking armour, the Pursuivants dogged a trail that wound through stands of giant oak. Here and there they surprised herds of grazing deer, startling them into flight. They marched for more than an hour, following the meandering path up and down, left and right. With no view of the sky beneath the green canopy of oaks, the pursuivants lost all sense of direction.

"How far have we come?" Munday asked.

"Miles.

"See, ahead the forest grows light."

"A clearing?"

They hurried on and a short while later heard the murmur of running water. Skirting a stand of holly bushes they stepped from gloom into twilight, and then splashed through a shallow brook. A few strides more and they emerged from the greensward and stood upon a dirt road baked brick-hard by weeks of hot sun.

"The Great West Road," Munday said.

"I had hoped it would lead us to a house," Scrope replied, grimacing with disappointment.

"This way is the more cunning," Munday argued, "for they may travel fast by way of the road, then switch to the path to reach their safe house, cutting through the woods to avoid the eyes of other travellers."

Scrope nodded in agreement. "A crafty Romish ploy. Much like—"

He was interrupted by the alarmed shouts of his soldiers. Sergeant Crugg burst from the trees and ran up to them, breathless.

"Pursuivant Scrope!" he said. "We have made a discovery most foul!"

CHAPTER 11: THE DIE IS CAST

When Shakespeare returned to his room, he found Richard Burbage sprawled across the bed, arms behind his head, a fat smirk upon his face.

"You do not dice?" Shakespeare asked, throwing a questioning look at his friend.

In reply, the big man chuckled. "I play a different game."

"Ah, the bounteous wife of our host inn-keeper?"

Burbage flashed him a wicked grin and said: "I'll wager a shilling I put the horns on him before morning."

Shakespeare folded the scented handkerchief and tucked it inside his doublet before Burbage could see it. The two men had a fierce rivalry to see who could bed the most women, and he did not seek to encourage competition when it came to this very special lady.

"I'll wager a shilling I take the maiden's maidenhead,"

"Done," said Burbage and the two friends shook on it.

"Your money is good as lost, sweet Will," Burbage gloated. "I have an assignation already agreed upon."

"With the pie-burner?"

Burbage nodded. "She has told me, come eleven of the clock every evening, the Inn-keeper and his Tapster retire to the cellar for an hour, sometimes two or more."

"Why so? Does the inn-keeper tap the tapster?"

"I think they take it turns. Anyway, I care not, so long as they stay gone. I will be in the kitchen with the pie-burner."

"Cooking up trouble?"

"I have the recipe here," Burbage chuckled, grabbing his crotch.

A fast, timid knock came at the door. Before they could answer, John Heminges burst in with a face that foretold the coming of the Doom Crack. "Have you any money?" he babbled. "A groat? A farthing? Anything?"

"I have but a shilling."

"A shilling and three pennies," Shakespeare offered.

John Heminges's face paled. His mouth opened, his lips quivered, but no words tumbled out.

"Your face speaks of calamity?" Shakespeare said.

"The money … " Heminge's voice had dried to withered husk, "… tis gone."

"What? The take?"

"Aye, the take. Gambled away. All of it."

"Tom Pope!" Burbage thundered. "I'll choke the rogue!"

The big man rolled from the bed and lunged for the door, but Heminges grabbed his sleeve and held him back.

"Nay, it was not Pope," Heminges said, shame burning in his face. "It was I."

Shakespeare gaped, incredulous. "You, John Heminges? You have gambled away our last groat?"

"I thought I had the trick of it," Heminges said, his hands fidgeting with each other, "for I won a little at first, but then fortune turned her face away."

"Rafe Foxe!" Burbage spat and Shakespeare nodded agreement.

"Here's a foxy Foxe indeed."

"Oh, I have ruined us all," Heminges wailed, covering his face with both hands. "We cannot pay the reckoning. We must steal away from here in the middle of the night, like rogues. Now the Chamberlain's Men shall never play in Marlborough!"

CHAPTER 12: A DEAD MAN WITH LITTLE TO TELL

The faceless corpse was dredged from the brook by Scrope's soldiers and dragged to the Great West Road where it could be better seen in the fading twilight. A halo of bloody water dripped from the clothes, staining the roadway crimson. Even the most jaded soldier, hardened in battle, winced to look upon a face shredded to red ribbons.

"A wealthy man from the cut of his clothes." Scrope. said.

"Most likely a merchant bound for Bristol," Anthony Munday speculated, "set upon by Highwaymen. The Great West Road is plagued with villains and footpads who prey upon travellers. He has been robbed of everything of value: boots, hat, gloves ..."

"And horse," Scrope added, and then in answer to Munday's questioning look he added: "There are a great many hoof prints in the soft mud of the bank. This man did not walk but rode here."

Oswyn Scrope squinted both ways up the road, and then looked back at the gap in the trees that led to the concealed path through the woods.

"A man murdered where the Great Road meets a hidden path used by Jesuits."

"Mere chance?"

"I doubt it much," Scrope said. "Plus, his murderer took much pains to scratch out his face. Why?"

"So his cold corpse may not speak who he was in life?"

"I think you have struck upon it, Master Munday."

Scrope squatted over the corpse and thrust a finger through every knife hole in the dead man's jerkin, counting wounds. He finished counting those on the front and nodded to Sergeant Crugg. The dead man gurgled and coughed bloody water as they rolled him over. Scrope's fingers probed the punctured jerkin counting more knife wounds on the back.

"He has been stabbed twelve times or more, front and back."

"Many knives?" Munday speculated. "A gang of murderers? He fought, but they surrounded him, each stabbing until he fell?"

"Or one murderer, stabbing many times, as in a mad rage." Scrope turned his warty face up to look at Munday. "Hand me your dagger."

Munday pulled the dagger from his belt and slapped it, pommel-first, in Scrope's gloved hand. Scrope pushed the dagger into one of the wounds until the blade would go no further. He drew the dagger out and handed it back to Munday, who looked at the bloodied blade of his own dagger with disgust.

"It was a dagger that killed him and not a sword." Scrope rose to his feet. "But no ordinary dagger. The blade was uncommon wide."

"Perhaps the murderer was a travelling companion? Perhaps a quarrel led to murder?"

"I think not," Scrope said. "Not a common robbery, nor a common murder. One man in a rage stabs another twelve times and then butchers the face and strips the clothes so that none may put a name to the corpse. I smell Jesuits behind this. I sense the workings of an infernal machine grinding out treason."

Anthony Munday looked up at a sky bleeding out its light. "The day is burned up. It will soon enough be night."

Scrope threw a look at the soldiers standing close by.

"Sergeant at Arms, cut branches to make a litter. We must carry the body back to the manor while we still have light to see our way in the forest."

The pursuivant threw a look to the west where the setting sun dipped behind the clouds and set the sky on fire.

"An auspicious sunset," Munday said. "Red sky at night, farmer's delight."

"Not auspicious," Scrope contradicted. "'Tis an augury of blood spilled now and more bloody deeds to come."

CHAPTER 13: THE DEVIL'S LUCK

Thomas Pope had gambled down to his last penny when Shakespeare and Burbage joined the other Chamberlain's Men crowded around the table. Pope threw a scowling look up at Shakespeare, saying, "I hope you fare better than we have done, Will. This fellow has the devil's luck."

Burbage positioned himself directly behind Rafe Foxe's shoulder so he could watch the action.

Thomas Pope licked his lips and timidly pushed forward his last coin. "That is my last penny," Pope said forlornly. "Win now and I will kiss every man in the room."

"Then I pray you do not win," Burbage muttered under his breath.

Pope shook the dice in the cup and rolled a five and a two: seven.

Rafe Fox pushed forward a coin from the towering stack at his elbow, scooped up the dice and dropped them in the cup. The dice rattled in the cup for a long time—seemingly long enough to wear the spots from the cubes—and then Rafe Foxe tossed them down. The die rolled across the table and came up double sixes.

Pope cursed and smashed a fist on the table. "'Tis unnatural! You are the devil's dam!"

"You have taught me well, coz!" Rafe Fox smiled. But as he reached across the table to take Pope's last coin, Shakespeare drew his dagger, and in one swift motion, drove the blade though the cuff of the fine leather glove, pinning Foxe's hand to the table.

"You have cut my glove, sirrah!" Foxe growled.

"And I will cut your throat, sirrah!" Burbage said, leaning forward and pressing the sharp edge of his dagger against Foxe's throat. Foxe made a choking noise, but knew better than to struggle with a blade to his windpipe.

"Tis a warm night, is it not, to be wearing gloves?" Shakespeare asked. "Even such a fine pair of gauntlets?" He yanked his dagger loose and snatched off Rafe Foxe's gauntlet. A hidden pair of dice rattled out onto the table. Shakespeare scooped the die up and rolled them. The dice came up double sixes. He rolled them again. Double sixes.

"Cheating dice!" Burbage shouted, pressing his dagger blade so hard that Rafe Foxe lifted from his chair.

"And look you all," Shakespeare added, grabbing Foxe's hand and pinning it to the table, "He bears the mark of a rogue."

The meat of Foxe's thumb was branded with a letter M for *malefactor*, an unerasable mark meant to warn others that Rafe Foxe had been found guilty of a crime before a magistrate.

"A Coney-Catcher!"[1] Thomas Pope spat. "The rogue is a Coney-Catcher."

"Inn-Keeper!" Burbage shouted. "I say, Inn-Keeper!"

Footsteps drummed up the cellar steps and then the inn-keeper bumbled into the room followed by his tapster, their eyes widening at the tableau before them: the great ginger beast Richard Burbage holding a dagger to another guest's throat.

"Gentlemen, puh-please!" the innkeeper stammered. "We are all friends in this house!"

"This man is friend to no-one," Burbage snarled. "He is a coney-catching thief, rogue and rascal!"

"Perhaps it was just an innocent mistake?" the innkeeper smarmed. "A harmless jape?"

"A jape lacking wit," Shakespeare said. "Look you, the fellow carries cheating dice." Shakespeare demonstrated with a deft roll. Double sixes came up on the die, and then in the Innkeeper's eyes.

John Thomas gave a nervous laugh, anxious to smooth thing over. "Verily, but there is no call for drawn daggers. I am sure the fellow will be happy to give your money back."

"It is not just our money," Shakespeare said. "Look at his fine cape, the fine hat, the fine gloves—the gloves of a nobleman. No doubt stolen. Have you ever seen their like?"

For the first time the Innkeeper's eyes fastened upon Rafe Foxe's garments and Shakespeare caught the flash of recognition in his eyes.

"I have never seen their like." The Innkeeper said, a little too quickly. "No . . . never." The piggy eyes looked around at the outraged players, clustered about Rafe Foxe. The sight of the fine clothes seemed to have suddenly changed the innkeeper's mind. "You are right. The fellow is a thief and must be held. Tomorrow morning I will send for the Constable, and then he shall be made to answer."

Burbage and the rest of the Lord Chamberlain's Men strong-armed Rafe Fox up the creaking stairs to the attic. The innkeeper unlocked the door with a heavy iron key and Foxe was pushed inside. The windowless space was little more than a cupboard: small, dark and bare of furniture. Stripped of his boots and finery, Foxe stood rubbing his bare wrists and glaring at his imprisoners as the door banged shut, sealing him in darkness.

"The attic room has no windows and I have the only key," the Innkeeper said. He turned the key in the lock, and then dropped it into the pocket of his apron. "This shall hold him secure until the Constable arrives."

"My friends," Rafe Foxe's muffled voice came from the other side of the door. "You treat me most unkindly—especially after I stood you supper."

Thomas Pope banged an angry fist on the locked door. "Silence, varlet! You made gulls of us once. See if you can pick the lock with your silver tongue."

Rafe Foxe cursed and kicked and pounded on the other side of the door for five more minutes, but then fell silent and was heard no more that night.

And with that, all dispersed for their beds ... or, after a discreet pause, someone else's bed.

CHAPTER 14: A SONNET FOR A MAIDEN

B urbage had vanished for his culinary assignation, so
Shakespeare took advantage of the quiet to work on his play by
the light of three quivering candle stubs.

He looked up at a gentle knock on the bedroom door.

"Come."

Constance, the innkeeper's daughter entered, carrying a shiny
brass warming pan.

"Sweet Conny?" Shakespeare said, standing up from the table.

"Can I warm your bed, sir? It costs only sixpence."

"Sixpence to warm a bed? Seems costly. Plus, it is a warm
summer's night ..." He felt at the brass warming pan and found it cold.
"... and there are no coals in your warming pan."

"I have my own way of warming a man's bed." She bit her lip and
looked up at him coyly, her hand stroking up and down the long
wooden shaft of the warming pan. "'Tis well worth the price."

Shakespeare swallowed, his mouth suddenly dry. "Six pennies?"

"A mere six pennies."

He took a step closer. "If you desire true riches I could pay you
with a sonnet."

She looked puzzled, but intrigued, "What is a sonnet?"

"Do you know what a poem is?"

She bit her thumb shyly and nodded.

"A sonnet is the most expensive kind of poem. Princes pay for them in gold."

Her face brightened with intrigue. "In gold? Then I shall have me a sonnet!"

"Then I will write you one."

"Now?"

"Aye, now, for you will be my muse and I will find the words in those pretty blue eyes."

Shakespeare took the warming pan from Constance's hands and placed it on the bed. He rested his hands on her hips and gazed deep into the girl's dazzled eyes.

"Shall I compare thee to a summer's day? Thou art more lovely and more temperate." He brought his lips close to her ear and whispered words into it.

"Rough winds do shake the darling buds of May ..." He pulled her slender form into his arms and began to unlace the back of her wimple. "... and summer's lease hath all too short a date;" She shivered as he kissed down her throat to the downy skin of her chest. "... Sometime, too hot the eyes of heaven shines ..." Her unlaced dress spilled in a crumple at her feet as he twirled his tongue around first one nipple, and then the other. "... and often is his gold complexion dimmed ..." He eased her back onto the bed and gently urged her legs apart. "... and every fair from fair sometimes declined ..." his kissing lips declined across the soft dome of her bellow, lingered a moment, then declined further.

"... by chance or Nature's changing course untrimmed ..."

Connie was breathing hard, her head thrown back, hands grasping at the sheets.

"But thy eternal summer shall not fade ..."

When he reached the special place, she sucked in a deep breath, and then sighed languorously.

"Nor lose ... possession ... of that ... fair ..."

The rest of the sonnet was rather muffled, for even Shakespeare, the master of words, could not speak with a mouthful of Conny.

CHAPTER 15: CULINARY DELIGHTS

The plump Mistress Maud was bending over the oven, stuffing in faggots for the morning fire.

Finding a ripe rump bent over and ready, Burbage crept up behind, grabbed two handfuls of her ample behind and squeezed.

Maud whooped with surprise and nearly leapt onto the hot stove.

"Master Burbage!" Maud laughed, turning to discover whom it was.

"Call me Dick."

"Oh, I like Dick."

"Did you enjoy your goose?" Burbage quipped. "A tad early for Christmas, mayhap."

Maud giggled as the two large people threw their arms around each other fell into a hungry kiss, her tongue wriggling in his mouth like a fresh-caught eel folded into a pie crust. When the two finally paused to snatch breath, Maud licked her lips like a cat done lapping cream. "I am pounding dough for the morning bread," she said.

"I am all for pounding," Burbage replied, "But I have a better recipe. Tis called rumpy-pumpy pudding!"

He tugged down the front of her dress so that her huge breasts spilled out. Burbage thrust his face into the yeasty warmness between them and shook his head from side to side, making happy blubbering sounds. When he pulled away, his ruddy face and red beard were dusted white with flour. Maud tittered with laughter.

Burbage blew flour dust from his lips. "First, we shall need some eggs ..." He grabbed two brown eggs from the table, cracked them into a bowl, and then poured them into her cleavage and squeezed her huge bosoms together. As the golden yolks dribbled between her breasts, Burbage thrust his face down there and lapped it up with relish.

Maud groped a hand down the front of Burbage's tights and seized his throbbing courter, which was swollen to the size of a rolling pin.

Clothes flew across the kitchen in slurred arcs of desire.

She tugged him backward by his rolling pin until they collided with the table and she sat down hard, loaves of rising dough squishing between her bare buttocks.

Maud breathed huskily, "I have a hot pudding you must stir with this!" She scooped a handful of soft butter from a bowl and greased his rolling pin with it.

Burbage slipped his loaf inside her oven with an effortless push. Maud threw her plump legs over the big man's shoulders and moaned with every thrust, until the table jogged across the stone-flagged floor with a scraping sound, both of them grunting and gasping.

They made love like a storm at sea: great waves of flesh colliding and roiling together. The air in the kitchen grew redolent with yeast and the funk of sex and sweat. The smoky light dimmed with swirling clouds of flour that made the candle flames flare dangerously. Soon, the floor, the table, and their skin grew silk-slippery with flour dust so that Burbage's bare feet could scarce find traction. He withdrew long enough to flip Maud over, face down on the table, her huge dugs mashing the rising dough and squeezing up between them.

Burbage grabbed a handful of flour, dusted her rump with it, and then slammed his hips forward, probing for the wet spot. The buttery wet slap of groin on arse beat time. Maud's breasts, belly and buttocks jiggled like jelly as his pumping intensified, and soon her moans grew louder and louder. Fearing lest Maud's howling awaken the house,

Burbage jammed a stale Banbury bun in her mouth, which she clamped between her teeth and screamed into as she climaxed.

By now, both were so dusted with flour so that on his final thrust, Burbage slipped from her sopping pudding bowl and plunged instead into the warm rising bread, exchanging one doughy fold for another, where he spent himself with a theatrically long groan.

CHAPTER 16: A GHOSTLY APPARITION

"I must creep back to my room. My father thinks I am still a maid."

Shakespeare gaped in astonishment at the naked girl in his arms, his mind reeling at her words. For the last hour the young woman had performed tricks the bawdiest strumpet in London would have blushed at. Constance pulled her dress back on over her head, blew him a kiss and crept out of the room. Shakespeare locked the door behind her and went to snuff out the candles on his desk. He pinched two wicks out and then a sudden movement out the window caught his eye. He stepped to the sill and peered out.

The night was moonless and impenetrably dark. An owl hooted from its roost in the gnarled oak outside the window. After a moment his eyes sieved from the darkness a pale blur in the trees across the road: it took the form of a woman dressed in white. But then he blinked and the image was gone.

Just the candle flame, he thought, *still dancing in my eyes.*

He jumped at a quiet knock on the door and went to answer; it must be Constance, back again.

"Who is it?"

"Thy father's ghost," a sonorous voice answered.

"My father is still among the quick. Answer again."

"Hieronomo. Falstaff. Richard the third."

He relaxed and turned the key, muttering, "Burbage . . ."

But when Shakespeare opened the door, he cried out in fear. A ghastly white face hovered in the dark hallway. A ghost? But no. The great thespian shambled in, dusted head to toe in flour.

"Where the deuce have you been?"

"Baking bread," Burbage answered and collapsed face-first on the bed. Within seconds, he was snoring.

Shakespeare pinched out the last candle and lingered at the open window, smelling the night air. A horned owl flapped by, silent as a dream, and vanished into the dark.

Feeling the ache of the long miles he had walked in the bones of his hips, he lay down in the shadow of Richard Burbage's snoring bulk. But despite his fatigue, Shakespeare could not stop the frantic play of images in his mind. He lay on his back, reflecting upon the dizzying distance he had walked from the son of a Stratford glover, to a player and poet with the Lord Chamberlain's Men, to this bed in a Wiltshire Inn. As he drifted through shifting veils of sleep, the smiling face of his darling boy Hamnet lit up, and then vanished behind a falling curtain of darkness.

His thoughts darkened with it. Though still not into his middle years, the Stratford playwright felt the cold clay of mortality clinging to his bones and could almost hear the soft, murmured insistence of the grave—yet to be dug—that awaited him. For with the death of Hamnet, so died the name of Shakespeare, a family tree rooted in an orchard grown barren and from which, in summers yet to come, no fruit would fall. He saw his own fame as a lighted squib that would flare and fade, and had no doubt that with time and the change of fashion the name of Shakespeare would no longer be bruited about the playhouse stage, and all the great words he had penned would die upon men's tongues. He tried again to conjure the image of his darling boy's face, but the mind—even a mind such as Shakespeare's—is a stage trod by unruly players with flubbed lines and lax direction. And though he would fain sleep in nightly scenes awash in profound meaning, in the end the greatest wordsmith of the world drifted into a narrow sleep and dreamed of sewing gloves.

CHAPTER 17: FROM MURDER TO ARSON

It was well past dusk when Father John Finch stumbled from the woods, hair and clothes dishevelled, his face branch-lashed and bloodied.

On the bank of the river that flowed under Wexdale Bridge, a hairy goblin crouched before a small fire and now he rose at sight of the approaching figure.

"Where have you tarried!" the man snapped, who was not much taller standing than kneeling. He had muscular arms and legs ill proportioned for his short, stubby body. He was a swarthy man of thirty-some years with a close-cropped black beard and black hair that still showed the tonsure from his days in the monastery.

"Father Thomas! Thank the saints!' Finch stumbled down the steep slope and slid to his knees in front of the dwarfish figure. His body quivered on the point of exhaustion.

Father Thomas Hyde scowled down at the younger man. "You should have been here hours ago!"

"The forest was dark. The ways strange to me. I became lost." Finch crawled to the fire where he held his hands close to the yellow flames, warming them. He looked at the dwarf and asked, "The others?"

"Left hours ago for the appointed place. I had just about decided your faint heart had failed and you had run away!"

"No, I told you. The way was dark."

In truth, running away is exactly what Father John Finch had tried to do. After losing his nerve, he galloped miles along the Great West Road heading toward London where he hoped to lose himself in a world of strangers. But when he stopped at a stream to wash the blood from his hands and face, a thief had stolen his horse and ridden away.

Now came the questions he had feared.

"And the woman? You killed her?"

Finch nodded emphatically, unable to look away from the fire, lest the dwarf's steely grey gaze catch the lie in his eyes.

"And the horse? The raiments?"

"I rode a good distance, then removed the saddle and drove off the horse." Now he had lied once, the lying came easier. "The garments I dug a hole and buried therein."

"And the vizard?"

For the first time, Finch remembered the Tragedian's mask he had worn. He had no idea what he'd done with it. "Buried," he lied.

The diminutive Thomas Hyde looked at him with lip-curled suspicion. But after a musing silence, he stepped over to where two horses stood tied to a log washed up on the river bank and fished a bundle from one of the saddlebags.

Even from ten feet away, Finch could smell food. His empty stomach clenched and gurgled. He eyed the bundle desperately, but Hyde made no move to offer it to him. "Did anyone see you? Speak to you?"

For a moment Finch flashed back onto the memory of barrelling past a rickety cart drawn by an old nag and crashing through a group of men who flung curses at his back. But instead he said only, "I passed a few homeless beggars on the road, but I rode the horse fast and spoke to no one."

Hyde did nothing for a moment. From his face it was clear he was turning over Finch's words in his mind. "Here!" he said, and tossed something which Finch caught. A cold cooked capon wrapped in a cloth. Finch unwrapped and tore into it with a famished moan. "I have not supped nor eaten all this long day."

Hyde walked over to where Finch gorged and handed him a stone bottle stoppered with a cork. Finch yanked the cork and sucked at the bottle. Cold cider chased down a half-chewed mouthful of chicken. He made a gasping sound of relief at the taste of food and drink, and hunkered closer to the flames. "Why so small a fire?" Finch mumbled around a mouthful of food, "I am cold and must warm myself."

The short man looked up at the living embers of fireflies skimming through the smoke. "Fires draw attention and we must not be seen. But come the morning, you and I will make a fire so large it will warm backsides all the way to London.

CHAPTER 18: WELCOME TO THE WHITE HART INN B&B

The next morning I stand in the micro-nook that passes for our reception desk and wait for Gillian to emerge from her room for breakfast. I am rehearsing my apologies and contrite looks when something large, loud and American crowds in through the front door.

"Ohmigod, this is sooooooooooo quaint!" The owner of the voice is a woman generously apportioned in every possible dimension including decibels. The door behind her swings wide and I watch a tiny Sikh taxi driver herniate himself dragging in a colossal suitcase. Between her and the bag I don't know how the aircraft got off the runway. She lumbers up to the counter and mashes a fleshy hand on the bell with a loud "ding" even though I'm standing right there.

"Emily," she booms, "Emily Hamm. I have a reservation."

I arch a questioning eyebrow at Sidney, who is just passing through, a stained bar towel thrown over one shoulder. He nods, which confirms that she's one of the bookings we received yesterday.

"Excellent!" I say, flipping open the register book on the counter and offering a pen. "If you'd care to sign in, madam, I'll give you your room key." Before my barman can skulk away I snap my fingers at him like I'm the concierge at the Ritz. "Oh, Sidney," I say. "Could you carry the lady's bag up to her room?"

Even though he's a big man, Sidney is soft and doughy as a bread pudding. Not exactly the physical type. He eyes the behemoth suitcase with a look of abject despair.

She tips the taxi driver too much—presumably to pay for the medical procedure he'll be requiring—before he limps painfully back to his cab. The taxi is just pulling away when a mini bus rumbles into the parking lot, the door flings open with a pneumatic sneeze, and passengers tumble out. I throw a puzzled look at Sidney as he hefts the lady's suitcase with a grunt.

"Four more bookings," he says in a voice that sounds like it's squeezing out from under a rock. "Came in last night when you were sulking in the cellar."

Five bookings? In one day? It's still early spring, a slow season. We're lucky to have one booking a week. What's going on?

The party from the mini bus troop in dragging wheelie cases behind them. Motley crew doesn't begin to describe them. Of wildly disparate ages, sexes and fashion sense, they look like the unsellable leftovers from a Church jumble sale. The tallest is a man in his early forties with a shiny bald dome the shape of a fifty-calibre bullet. The only hair on his entire head bristles under his chin, as if it crept there to thrive in the shadows. His pouchy eyes are darkly circled as if he's spent a week of sleepless nights hammering on the ceiling with a shoe, shouting at the upstairs neighbours to keep it down. I have this life-long habit of giving my guests nicknames and he instantly becomes "Spooky."

Next comes Mrs. Marple. Brittle and ancient, she has silver, regulation old lady hair, wrinkles and neck wattles and looks like that familiar actress they invariably cast in BBC Agatha Christy mysteries —the nosy frump who is always finding a dead vicar keeled over in the vestry when she arrives for tea and crumpets.

Crowding in behind is a small bloke with cropped black hair, probably in his late thirties and almost definitely a sufferer from short man syndrome. In his black polo neck sweater, black sport coat and black slacks, he looks like he just ducked out the back door of a Beat Generation reunion party. His dark eyes roll across me from behind thick, black-rimmed glasses thirty years out of fashion (which usually means they must just about to come back in fashion). He's dark and brooding, so that's what I'll call him: Broody.

"Welcome to the White Hart Inn," I smile, brain clicking into auto-smarm mode. "The finest Motoring Inn in Wiltshire. If you'd all please sign the register, I'll show you to your rooms."

Twenty minutes later I am showing the last guest to her room: Miss Marple, whose actual name is Beryl-something. "I trust you'll be comfortable in here madam," I say setting down her luggage next to the bed—by contrast with the American lady, Beryl's tartan cloth suitcase is so tiny and light it must only contain a spare pair of knickers and a tooth brush—although looking at her horsy, yellowing teeth...

"You'll find that this is one of our finest rooms ... " I say, which is a larf, because I say it about every room. Before I can escape she grasps my hand and pulls me close, her voice falling into a conspiratorial whisper.

"Is it haunted?" she asked, putting a lot of breathy "haw" into the first syllable.

"No, madam," I say, patting her hand. "Not to worry. It's definitely not *hawn-ted*"

"Oh," she says, looking crestfallen. "I imagined an inn so old was bound to have its ghosts." She sighed. "I was so hoping to feel a presence."

That could be a sexual reference but I doubt it. Then an opportunity occurs to me. I clear my throat. "Not this room. I mean, obviously, the inn has ghosts—the place is rotten with them. I do have one particular room that *is* haunted. Extremely haunted. Of course, it is a bit more expensive than this room ..." (I have in mind a cramped and airless closet in the attic that any person not strapped into a straight jacket would refuse to occupy.) ". . . it doesn't have a window," I continue, "but you will definitely feel a presence in there." I don't bother to tell her that the presence is mildew, which I refuse to kill since it's the only thing gluing the bathroom tiles to the wall.

"If it's still available," she says, squeezing my hand, "then you simply must let me have it."

Oh, I think. *I'll let you have it, all right.*

Later, I am stumping down stairs when I nearly collide with the lovely Gillian who comes bounding up. She is showing a lot of flesh, wearing short athletic shorts and skimpy singlet. From her quickened breathing and sexy pink glow I guess she's just come back from a jog —the running shoes are a bit of a giveaway.

She smiles. "Just went for a short run."

"I wondered why you weren't at breakfast. I hope … I hope I didn't offend you last night."

She laughs. "Don't be silly." She shivers. "I'm all sweaty. Must go jump in the shower. Could you be a love and bring me a tray up?"

"Continental breakfast?" I ask, figuring she must nibble on flat bread and carrot sticks to keep that figure.

"God, no!" she says. "Full English, with lashings of toast and fried everything. I could inhale a pig after I run."

Twenty minutes later I knock on her door and she shouts "come in" over the jet roar of a hair drier. I carry in the tray and back heel the door shut behind me. The bathroom door is slightly ajar and I glimpse a hazy figure looming in the fog. (Must get that bloody fan fixed.)

"Just a moment," she shouts. "I'm not decent."

I get a heart-stopping flash of nakedness as she flits past the open door. (What I glimpse looks more than decent.) When she sticks her head out of the bathroom, she is wrapped in a white terry bathrobe, her skin flushed adorably pink.

"Pop it down on the bed," she smiles, towelling her russety hair. "I'll be out in a tic." And plunges back into the swirling fog.

I set the tray down on the bed and rearrange the limp plastic rose in the vase, lingering. I'm not sure if her comment was an invitation for me to stay; luckily I got it right. She exits the bathroom, fluffing her auburn hair with both hands and flounces down on the bed. She eats with her hands, picking up a rasher of streaky bacon and crunching it.

"What I said last night—" I begin.

She dismisses it with a flourish of bacon. "Forget it," she says. "I tell you what I'd like."

"Name it, your majesty,"

"A tour of the inn. I want to see it all." She gives me a penetrating look. "Especially the secret places."

As the Inn has no "secret places" we start in the attic, where the roof beams are so low I whack my head now and then, and work our way down to the cellar, snooping into every room not currently occupied by a guest. Along the way I notice she appears to be searching for something, as she prods and pokes, raps her knuckles against beams.

"What exactly are you looking for?" I finally ask. We are down in the cellar. It's chilly in here thanks to the aircon, which is good for the beer. Our breath fogs the air.

"Ever found anything?" she asks, snooping in a cobwebby corner.

"Lots of things," I say.

She looks at me expectantly.

"Dry rot. Mould. Woodworm. Rising damp," I count them off on my fingers. "What were you expecting, a lost Shakespeare manuscript?"

She smirks, arms hugging herself against the chill. "It's not impossible. A workman discovered a Catholic testimony in the attic of John Shakespeare's house. These inns were often involved in smuggling and hiding contraband. Many of them have secret compartments, false cupboards, priest holes."

"We could try looking for secret holes in my bedroom," I say innocently.

She gives me an arch smile. "Naughty boy." She checks her watch. "I must dash off to Wexcombe House."

"I thought the conference started tomorrow?"

"There's a welcoming mixer. It's where we academic types reconnoitre the territory. Size up the opposition. You're welcome to tag along, if you like."

"Sorry. Couldn't abandon Sidney for more than five minutes. Like leaving a toddler on his own with a box of matches and a gallon of petrol."

"Are you sure? There will be a brunch—free food … and booze."

I think about it. What's the worst my idiot bar tender can do? Burn down the inn? That would be a boon.

I smile and say, "I'll just get my coat."

CHAPTER 19: AN ARGUMENT OF FLEAS

"Pissing in fireplaces breeds a plague of fleas," Shakespeare said.

"Pshaw!" Burbage scoffed back. "Tis a housewife's tale!" The big man stood, legs akimbo, directing a hissing yellow stream against the bricks at the back of the fireplace.

At the same instant, Shakespeare was pissing into a chamber pot on the floor between his feet. Having drained himself, he stepped to the window, carrying the chamber pot and fixed his friend with a disapproving look. "Nay, tis unhealthy and unclean, I tell you." and with that he tipped up the chamber pot and emptied it out the open window. From outside came the sound of urine splattering against something, followed by an angry cry.

Shakespeare looked below. He had just emptied the full chamber pot over Ned Smedley who was sleeping curled up against the inn wall after being put outside the previous night like the cat. But then something drew Shakespeare's eyes upwards and he glimpsed a pale form standing amongst the shadows of the trees on the other side of the road—The White Woman. The chamber pot tumbled from his fingers as he jerked back into the room. He heard the sharp crack of pottery breaking over a human skull followed by a dull wail of pain. When he shot another quick look down, Ned Smedley sat slumped in a puddle of piss and broken pottery, moaning as he rubbed the top of his skull.

Shakespeare looked back across the road, but the figure of the white woman had vanished.

His heart had not had time to slow its drumming when a howl of anguish shattered the morning stillness. A fist pounded on the door and when Burbage turned the key in the lock, John Heminges burst into the room, his face a mask of alarm.

"We are lost, gentlemen!" Heminges said. "Lost! Destroyed! Ruined!"

"Again?" Burbage demanded.

"Robbed!" Heminges blustered. "Robbed in the night! Everything gone! Not a groat remains!"

CHAPTER 20: A BURNING SEASON

The world was on fire. Their noses told them that. As a feeble dawn painted the sky with an anaemic, straw-collared light, a ruddy glow pulsed on the southern horizon, a pall of black smoke rising from it.

Oswyn Scrope, Anthony Munday, and their men had left Broughton House in the predawn hours and now they clopped their horses west along the Great Road, the detachment of soldiers trudging behind them. Bringing up the rear, four soldiers carried the butchered body on a litter wound in a sheet. All eyes were on the flickering fire glimpsed now and then in the break between trees.

"A great conflagration," Munday said, "Is it the Inn we journey toward?"

Scrope raised his hand to signal his men to stop and reached back to unfasten a leather map holder fastened to his saddle. He slid a map from its tube and unrolled it across the horse's neck, angling the map so the wan morning light made the dark smudges readable.

"No," Scrope said. "The inn we seek lies straight ahead. Whatever burns lies south of the Great Road." His eyes picked among a number of great houses drawn on the map. "It could be Stanton House, or Thorpe Manor, or Talbot Hall."

"A great pity, so whichever," Munday said. "This dry weather poses a great danger."

Scrope snorted at the comment and twisted in the saddle to throw a beetling glance at the horseman beside him. "Pursuivant Munday, you will ride to discover the name of the house that burns. I will continue on. We will meet at the White Hart Inn."

Scrope rolled the map and slid it back into its tube. "'Tis true, we are in a burning season, but in this fire I smell a whiff of Jesuit brimstone."

CHAPTER 21: FOXE GONE TO GROUND

"Does this bread taste odd to you?"

"They make it the country way out here."

Early risers, Will Kempe, Thomas Pope and young Samuell Gilbourne were already downstairs breaking their fast with bread and cheese washed down with ale. Not surprisingly, the bread was burned. The crust of the loaf, a heavy bread of leavened rye, was crispened to charcoal on three sides and the players were peeling away the blackened crusts and dropping the pieces on their trenchers as they ate.

Thomas Pope took a bite of bread and made a face as he chewed. "I say again. This bread has a puzzling flavour!" He suddenly choked on his crust as loud cries and shouts of alarm rang out from above and the remaining Lord Chamberlain's Men galloped down the stairs and caromed into the room trailed by the Innkeeper.

"Lads!" Burbage shouted. "We have been robbed!"

"Robbed?" Pope said, spitting crumbs. "How so?"

"That naughty rogue, Rafe Foxe!" Shakespeare said.

"But we locked him in the attic last night!"

"Gone!" the innkeeper said. "We found the door still locked but the room empty!"

Will Kempe crossed himself then licked his palm and touched it to the wood of the table. "Tis dark magic!" he said. "The man uses witch-craft to dissolve his bones into mist, then pours beneath the doorframe!"

"Check your purses!" Heminges said. "The churl has crept into every room even as we slept and stolen all. I keep the key to the chest that holds the take on a string around my neck, and yet he has emptied the chest and stolen everything within."

"He has even stolen my new play." Shakespeare said. "All my pages gone!"

"Not stolen." a familiar voice purred. "Merely borrowed, coz."

The eyes of all were drawn to the shadowed table next to the hearth where a dark figure sat with his boots propped up on the table. He was reading Shakespeare's new play.

"Thief! Rogue!" Heminges shouted, pointing his finger.

The Lord Chamberlain's Men surged over to confront Rafe Foxe.

"No thief." he countered, indicating the goods spread across the table in front of him with a lazy wave. "Here are your goods and money. If I did have it in mind to steal from you, I could have been long gone hours ago, while you snored in your beds. I held it in safe keeping, for the roads hereabouts are bedevilled by thieves and highwaymen."

In truth, Rafe Foxe had already tried just that. Waiting long enough for the house to fall quiet before he had picked the lock and escaped from the attic room. He had then crept through the house, jimmying locked doors, probing fingers into pockets, stealing back the noble-man's clothes as he visited each of the Lord Chamberlain's Men's rooms in turn to pinch everything of value. Then, in the grey light before dawn, Rafe Foxe had saddled the chestnut bay and galloped from the Inn-Yard heading east up the Great Road. But after ten miles he found the road ahead blocked by an enormous body of horses and wagons many miles in length. It did not seem to be an army, but from the dull flash of metal he could tell that a large column of soldiers rode at their head. He turned his horse and galloped back the other way, passing by the White Hart, where the black smoke billowing from the bakery chimneys showed that the Inn-Keeper's wife was busy burning breakfast. He rode five miles in the other direction before he saw more soldiers on the road ahead coming toward him, a smaller body of men, but no less daunting. Two of the three riders at their head were clad in the black clothes of Pursuivants. Behind them marched a small deployment of armoured soldiers bearing muskets and pikes. Rafe Fox turned the horse once more and galloped west, back to the White Hart Inn, where he turned loose the horse in the stables and slipped back inside. Like any good fox, Rafe knew there was a time to run and a time to go to ground.

John Heminges's shaking hands scrabbled among the loose coins atop the worn table, counting—it did all seem to be there.

"My pages, you pox-faced scullion!" Shakespeare said, holding out his hand.

"A goodly story, Master Shakepuddle." Foxe smiled as he rolled the pages into a tube and slapped them into Shakespeare's open hand. "I penned a few changes—a few places where the rhyme was weak, the couplets rusty—"

"A few changes?" Shakespeare spluttered with indignation. "You impertinent, dog hearted—"

"Naaaayy!" Foxe said, gesturing with a hand. "Hold your purse. I will not take coin for my pains for I, too, am a writer." He drew a crumpled pamphlet from his pocket and tossed it on the table. Shakespeare's eyes, despite himself, were drawn to look over it. The title read: *Coney-Catchers, Rascals and Cranks* and named the author as Gilbert Browne.

"You wrote this?"

"Aye, apart from those words I poached from others—as all writers do."

"You are Gilbert Browne?"

"A name some know me by."

"As others know you by Rafe Foxe?"

"As some know you as William Shakeshaft and others know you as William Shaxpeere."

As Shakespeare's face reddened further, Foxe smiled. He drew out his bulging change purse and banged it atop the table as he had done the night before. "But come! Let us all be friends again and I will stand you brave lads ale and eggs to break our fast. Your goods are all safe here. See. Count them. I have not stolen a single coin," He flashed a grin at Heminges. "Nor even one of your stones or nails."

"I'll break no bread with you!" Thom Pope said. "You are a coney-catching rogue! Let us call the Constable to arrest him."

"Thom! Thom, be quiet!" Heminges urged. He dropped his voice to a conspiratorial whisper. "We will do naught. We must away from here today for Marlborough. If called, the Constable will detain us."

As the others argued, Shakespeare was busy rifling through his pages, reading the many crossing-outs and changes that Rafe Foxe or Gilbert Browne or whatever his name really was had made. "You clot-pole!" he blubbered. "You surly, open-arsed barnacle!" But what stung worse was the fact that many of the changes were improvements, although Shakespeare was loathe to admit it.

"I say we tie the rascal hand and foot and toss him down the well!" Thomas Pope said. "Let's see him picklock his way out of that!"

Thom Pope grabbed Foxe by the scruff of his doublet, but the young man shrugged the grip aside and burst up from his stool, toppling chairs as he leaped onto a nearby table and vaulted out the open window.

As the Chamberlain's Men shouted angry cries, Foxe hit the dusty road, rolled, and then sprang to his feet. He ran toward the stables behind the Inn to recover his horse, but the Chamberlain's Men surged out of the inn door, blocking his way.

Foxe drew his gold-hilted rapier with a metallic schullliiing, but found himself surrounded by the players, who each flourished their daggers. The Coney-Catcher had the advantage of reach with his rapier, but the Lord Chamberlain's Men had the advantage in numbers. Bloodshed seemed imminent.

"HALT!" an imperious voice boomed. "Put up your blades! All of you!"

For the first time the men looked around to see a crow-beaked man clad in the black clothes of a Pursuivant. He sat on a black horse, glaring down at them. Behind him a phalanx of armoured soldiers threatened, muskets and wicked-bladed pikes held ready.

Oswyn Scrope's raven eyes swept the melee. "Drop your steel," he said. "I command you in the name of the Queen! Upon pain of your lives!"

CHAPTER 22: A PILLOW OF ASHES

Talbot Hall died with the groan and roar of a great beast suffering its death throes.

The thatched roof that flowed over the building's many gables, smooth as the topping of an over-risen cake, was the first to catch light and crackle away in a swirling vortex of fiery sparks. The rest of the manor, built of stout beams of good English maple and oak, would burn white hot for days.

Two figures watched the blaze from the nearby woods. Both wore disguises: one a hideous green goblin's mask, the other had improvised a vizard by wrapping a scarf around his face. But even behind their disguises, the fire was scorching hot upon their faces, so they could barely stand to look upon it. A loud crack split the air. The walls of the tallest gable shivered and buckled inward as the roof above caved in with a splintery crash, unleashing a dragon's tongue of flame and sparks that lashed and writhed high into the sky.

Once a handsome Tudor manor of three-storeys, Talbot Hall was now fully engulfed. From where the two Jesuits crouched, Father John Finch could hear a woman's lamenting wail and the crash and tinkle of window glass shattering from the heat. On the great lawn the household servants, the master and the mistress scurried about amid the swirling smoke and shivering heat waves, bearing buckets of water to throw into the flames. But from this distance the tiny figures seemed as helpless as woodland sprites tossing thimblefuls of dew into a conflagration. The house was already lost—Father Thomas Hyde had made sure of that by kindling the blaze at multiple points around the building's exterior.

A wicked chuckle escaped from behind the green mask "Feel warm enough, Father Finch?"

The scarf tied across his face revealed only Finch's eyes, flames reflecting in them as he glared at his fellow Jesuit. "God takes no glory in the burning of a man's house. And this man was one of our own—a Catholic!"

The Goblin mask turned to regard him. "No true Catholic, for he was prepared to open his house to the heretic bitch Elizabeth. There is but one King he should kneel to and that is our Holy Father in Rome. When this country is returned to the true religion, we shall burn more than just their houses. Pyres will blaze across England as every protestant cleric is rendered unto the flame! The streets will run hot and greasy with the fat of burning heretics!"

At that moment, a column of horsemen surged into the long drive and galloped toward the house, flags and pennants fluttering. Behind them crawled a ponderous snake of carriages, carts and riders on horseback

"Just in time!" Thomas Hyde chortled. "Elizabeth and her court are come. Sir Francis Talbot has provided the queen with a warm welcome."

They watched the soldiers dismount and run to help the figures trying in vain to put out the fires.

"I do not think Elizabeth will sleep here tonight," Hyde said. "Not unless she rests her head upon a pillow of warm ashes."

Finch shook his head and sighed. "I like it not. A man's house and goods burned? Tis a pitiful sight."

A mounted figure appeared and galloped past the stalled procession of carts and wagons to the cluster of soldiers. From where they stood, Hyde could see that the horseman was dressed in the black clothes of a pursuivant.

"Save your pity for us, Father Finch," the stumpy figure hissed through clenched teeth. "I know that devil's-spawn in black. He is Anthony Munday, a Pursuivant. He has spied upon and betrayed many good Catholics. I saw him speak honeyed lies to the crowd when our most holy brother Campion suffered death upon the scaffold. Munday is a liar, a bosom-viper, a dissembler, a double-tongued devil. Still it is not him I fear, but the companion who rode to join him of late: Oswyn Scrope, another slave of Richard Topcliffe's with a heart as dark as pitch. Now the game begins in earnest, as we hunters become the hunted."

CHAPTER 23: A PURITAN INQUISITION

"Remember, speak nothing about the dead man and all will be well," John Heminges whispered to his fellow players as Scrope's men marched them back into the inn at sword point. The Lord Chamberlain's Men and the Innkeeper and his family were all bullied into the taproom. Soldiers dragged forward a table behind which Scrope sat, while a pair of bellicose guards framed either side of the door with brawn and steel.

"This room will serve for our inquiry," Scrope announced.

"Inquiry?" asked John Thomas, the Innkeeper. He took a mincing step forward, the dangling strings of his apron grasped in both hands, like a giant mouse holding its tail, ready to bolt beneath the furniture at the slightest noise. "Inquiry?" he squeaked a second time. "Inquiry into what, sir?"

"Murder," Oswyn Scrope snarled. "And what may well be treason." The pursuivant's corvine gaze, uncanny and unblinking, swept the room, quashing further questions upon tongues where they trembled to be spoken aloud. "I am Oswyn Scrope, Messenger of the Queen's Chamber and servant to my master, Richard Topcliffe."

At the pronouncement of the most dreaded name in the land, the walls of the room seemed to suck inward at the collective drawing-in of breath.

Scrope made a "bring hither" gesture with his hand to the soldier standing guard by the door. The door flung open and four soldiers stomped in, bearing a litter. They set their burden down in the middle of the room, and then turned and marched out. The litter bore an unmistakably human form bleeding through the sheet it was wrapped in. Scrope rose from his bench and strode over to the body. "This man was found murdered by the Great West Road, but two miles east of here. Did any of you travel the road yesterday?"

The Lord Chamberlain's Men flashed alarmed looks at one another.

John Heminges quivered to his feet and spoke in a halting voice. "I … I … I mean we …" he threw a lame gesture to indicate the players sitting beside him, "did travel that very stretch of road yesterday, but, but we saw naught."

"The very road you travelled yesterday? Speak truth! Did you see this fellow, dead or alive?" Scrope carried a thin iron rod in one hand and now he pushed it into the winding sheet and flicked the sheet aside, revealing the oozing livid mass that had once been a face.

At the ghastly sight, a collective groan of horror squeezed from the lungs of all present. Young Connie looked away and had to be held up by her mother, who crossed her huge bosom repeatedly.

"Say nothing!" Heminges hissed in a voice only the players around him could hear.

When no one spoke, Scrope pushed more of the sheet aside and pointed to the clothes the corpse wore. "Note the fine blue doublet. This was a man of means."

The pursuivant's stony gaze scraped along the dumbstruck faces. That morning he had awakened to find a fresh carbuncle—a red growth swelling on his neck. The tight collar of his white linen shirt chafed against the carbuncle and he unconsciously yanked the collar down now and again to ease the pressure, an action which served only to chafe against the swelling and further provoke the irritation.

"Very well, then. Let us make a note of all present." Shakespeare's new play still sat atop one of the tables. Scrope walked over and grabbed the top sheet, then called for a quill and inkpot.

He threw a look at his sergeant at arms. "Can you write, Master Crugg?"

Fen Crugg, who at 32 was older and far less stupid than the rest of Scrope's soldiers, shifted his feet uneasily. "A little sir. Well enough. Names and such."

The pursuivant indicated that Crugg should take a seat beside him. He flipped the topmost sheet over to its blank side and banged it down in front of the sergeant. "I shall ask each here to speak aloud his name for the record." Scrope got up and paced the room for a few moments, not speaking but pausing at each person in turn and studying them with a look that could peel the shell from a boiled egg. At last, he returned to the innkeeper. "You, fellow, what is your name?"

The innkeeper deepened his cringe, "Ju-John Thomas."

Burbage began to snicker but Scrope stifled him with a seething glance. He nodded to Crugg to record the name and moved on. He paused before the tapster, recognising a rogue when he saw one. "Here's a man with the face of a devil. What is your name?"

The tapster made a face like a man swallowing a lump of dry poison, and then rumbled in a gravelly voice, "Walt Gedding."

On an impulse, Oswyn Scrope reached out and grabbed a handful of the tapster's hair at the side of his head, sweeping it out of the way. Where the ear should have been was just a chewed-looking red hole. "How lost you that ear?"

"I was nailed to the stocks[1] by it."

"Where?"

"In the north. Preston."

Scrope nodded knowingly, his suspicions confirmed. "What was your crime?"

"Adultery."

"Adultery?" Scrope questioned. "With another man's wife?"

"With another man's sheep."

Scrope recoiled at the words and let go the fellow's hair, his face screwed up in a moue of disgust.

"Tis the common practice up there," Gedding added, quite innocently.

"Make note of that, Sergeant Crugg," Scrope nodded. "Walt Gedding, a dissembling rogue and deviant."

"Aye, sir." But the Sergeant could spell neither, so he simply wrote down "bad man" next to Walt Gedding's name.

Scrope's lip curled further when his gaze fell upon Ned Smedley, who was slumped in his chair, head lolling. He poked Smedley brutally in the chest with his iron rod, tossing the old man's head back, which caused his bloodshot eyes to blink open. "Ancient fellow, speak your name and your living."

Smedley had just been dragged in from the spot he had slept all night. He was still paralytic drunk and slurred as he spoke. "My name is Ned Smedley. My profession was taken from me, but it matters naught, for I will soon be a dead man."

The Inn Keeper cringed forward and cleared his throat timidly. "Ned here was until late a servant at Wexcombe House. He lost his position and so has resolved to drink himself into his grave."

Scrope's face twisted with disgust as he stepped a little too close and got a whiff of Smedley whose hair was still wet and spiked up with piss.

"Pah! You reek like a midden!"

"Some villain broke a piss pot over my head as I slept!" Smedley shouted indignantly. Shakespeare coughed into his hand and averted his eyes.

"So you lost your living for love of strong drink?" Scrope asked.

"No!" Smedley bellowed, nearly falling from his seat with the force of his denial. "Never in my life did I drink. I was dismissed from service for following the old religion—even though I have been a protestant all my life!"

Shakespeare caught the Innkeeper and the tapster passing a worried look between them.

Scrope turned to the soldier. "Make a note of that. And of the man's drunkenness."

Scrope shook with irritation and moved onto the next man, which just so happened to be William Shakespeare.

"Here's a strutting coxcomb if ever I saw one. What is your name, sirrah?"

"Will Shakeshaft. I am one of the Lord Chamberlain's Men, London players on a tour of the provinces."

"Players?" Scrope spat out the word as if it were something vile whose lingering touch might burn an ulcer on his tongue. "So your name is Shakeshaft?" He puzzled upon the name for a moment and then stomped over to where the sergeant was writing down the name. He snatched up the sheet of paper and turned it over, reading. It was one of the pages of Shakespeare's play. The Stratford player had practiced signing his name several times in the margin—a nervous tic he often fell into while waiting for the muse to speak.

"Will Shakeshaft, indeed?" Scrope said in a doubting voice. He waved the page for all to see.

"And yet the signature on these pages reads "William Shake-speare?" Scrope slapped the page back down in front of Crugg. "Which is it, pray tell?"

In their rush to get out of his throat, words jammed against one another. Shakespeare put one hand on his hip, the other gesticulating vaguely in the air as he grappled to conjure an answer. "In the city I am known as William Shakespeare, but ... but in the country I am known as Will Shakeshaft."

"So you are known by two names?" Scrope said in a very unpleasant tone. "Why so?"

"Um, tu-tis a practice cu-common to the stu-stage," Shakespeare stammered.

"Yea," Scrope said. "'Tis also a practice common to rogues, vagabonds and cranks!"

John Heminges leapt to his feet and thrust out his chest with a little too much theatrical indignation. "We are no vagabonds, sir! We are men of property, players and sharers in the Theatre, the largest playhouse in London. And we have the Lord Chamberlain's patent to prove it!" By some miracle Heminges had the very document stuffed inside his doublet and now he pulled it out and waved it aloft. "This bears the seal of Henry Carey, the Lord Chamberlain himself."

Scrope stepped over and snatched the document from Heminges' hand. He dangled it over a candle flame as he read, so that the men of the Chamberlain's Men twitched and squirmed in their seats as the flame licked at the paper until it began to char and curl under. Just when they thought it would catch light, Scrope lost interest and tossed the document aside so that it fluttered to the floor at his feet. "So you are all good and honest men?" Scrope challenged.

"Yes, sir." Heminges reassured.

"Not tellers of lies?"

"No, sir. The Lord Chamberlain's Men are welcome at the Queen's court where we have performed for her majesty's pleasure many times."

"And yet I found you, daggers drawn, brawling in the road?" Scrope paced as he spoke, treading the patent underfoot, marring it with his boot print.

"Not brawling, sir, "Rafe Foxe said, standing up. "I was merely showing these stout lads the latest fencing techniques I learned in my travels."

"Indeed, so?" Scrope said.

Thom Pope had kept his churlish mouth shut until now, but could keep silent no longer and sprang to his feet. "Believe nothing this fellow says. He is a Coney-Catcher. A cheating, thieving, rogue!"

"I have not yet called upon you, sirrah," Scrope snarled. "Sit down."

Pope sank back onto his stool. Heminges tried to shush him with a look, but the younger man's dander was up. "Check his hand," Pope shouted. "He bears the mark of a rogue."

Scrope spun around, grinding a black heel-mark into the patent. For the first time he noticed the elaborate gauntlets adorning Rafe Foxe's hands. He nodded at them, saying, "Sirrah, remove your glove."

With obvious reluctance, Rafe Foxe started to pull off his left glove.

"The other glove!" Scrope interrupted. "And show your hand."

Foxe smiled as he tugged off the right glove and held up his right hand, as all defendants were required to do when brought before a magistrate.

John Heminges dropped his head and combed fingers through his greying hair. Pope's mouth had likely ensured that they would not be leaving for Marlborough that day—and perhaps many more.

Scrope saw the letter M branded onto the meat of Rafe Foxe's thumb. His eyes swivelled to the guards at the door. "Take this fellow and lock him up fast. We shall interrogate him further."

"The rascal knows the mystery of locks and how to pick them," Pope blurted out. "Last night we shut him fast in an upstairs room but he freed himself and broke into every room thieving our goods as we slept."

Scrope threw a look at John Thomas. "Have you a cellar?"

The innkeeper flinched. "Aye, but—"

Scrope nodded to his soldiers. "Lock the rogue in there and post a man on the door."

The soldiers seized hold of Rafe Foxe and dragged him to his feet, but he just snickered. "No, not the cellar!" He threw a laughing look at Walt Gedding and John Thomas. "I know what goes on in the cellar. There are dark deeds done in cellars. Shall I tell them?"

John Thomas whitened at the words.

"Away with this naughty fellow!" Scrope yelled as the guards dragged him from the room. They could still hear Foxe's shouts as he was roughly bundled down the cellar steps. Scrope scorched the Innkeeper and his tapster roughly. Both hung their heads like guilty men. Scrope knew what tricks tapsters and innkeepers practiced to mulct their guests: watering the ale, cheating on legal measures and dodging taxes on wines and sack, but he was neither purveyor nor inspector—he cared nothing about such petty crimes. "What a den of wickedness this is," he spat with Puritan zeal. "All the deadly sins served up in one place: greed, sloth, lust, drunkenness ... I have little doubt all of you are naught but idle rogues and ne'er-do-wells—patent or no patent. But I am here on a different mission." He fell silent for a moment, chewing the inside of his cheek before speaking again. "My business here touches on matters of greater import. Though villains you all likely are, I see no reason to hold you further. Go now, and pray that I never learn that any of what you have spoken here under oath prove to be lies." Scrope nodded to the soldiers guarding the door. At his signal, they snatched the doors wide.

Stool legs scraped as the Lord Chamberlain's Men rose as one, pushing aside their benches, anxious to put a day's fast walk between themselves and Oswyn Scrope.

Outside, young Samuell Gilbourne was running about on the Great Road, trilling with laughter as he chased the chickens and made them scatter. Scrope's eyes registered surprise when he saw the boy and he stepped quickly to the open door.

"That boy!" he shouted, pointing. "Is he not with you fellows?"

"Aye," Will Kempe said. "The lad is one of us."

"Sit!" Scrope barked, planting backsides on benches with a violent wave. "This boy has yet to be questioned."

The players threw anxious looks at one another.

"You there—boy!" Scrope bellowed. "Come hither."

Samuell Gilbourne tripped anxiously into the room where Oswyn Scrope seized him by the collar and pulled him close. Sam's eyes widened with terror as he found himself staring up at a gargoyle's visage of warts, moles and carbuncles. Held this close, Young Sam gagged on Scrope's foul breath and a body reeking of days of unwashed sweat turned alkaline sour.

"What is your name, boy?"

"Su-su-Sam Gu-Gu-Gillbourne."

"Who is your master? Are you apprenticed to an honest trade?"

"Nuh-no, sir. I am a pu-player, sir. Wu-with the Lord Chu-Chamberlain's Men."

"A player?" Scrope scowled. "What could you, a mere boy, play?"

"Sir, I play the ladies' parts."

"What's this?" Scrope said, hurling a disapproving scowl at the players.

"No, not like this, sir!" Sam scrabbled, anxious to explain. "I put on a wig, paint my face and wear a lady's dress so the other players may use me as they would a woman."

"Sodomy!" Scrope spat. "Most sinful lewdness!" The pursuivant threw a glowering look at the Lord Chamberlain's Men and then dragged Sam toward the corpse by the scruff of his neck. "Have you seen this man before?" Answer truly!"

But at his first glimpse, a terrified shriek ripped from Young Sam.

"The dead man! The dead man!"

"What dead man? SPEAK BOY!"

Young Sam strained to turn his face away from the bloody nightmare, but Scrope's iron fingers squeezed white grooves in the boy's neck. "The dead man we saw yesterday morning when the ghost chased us along the Great West Road!"

Scrope's hand relaxed on Young Sam's neck, allowing him to pull free. The Pursuivant turned and fixed the Lord Chamberlain's Men with a look that curdled the air.

Will Kempe pulled off his jingled bonnet and wrung it in his hands as his stared at the floor. "We are all for the Tower," he muttered and for once his fellow players nodded agreement with the clown's gloomy premonition.

"Aye," Richard Burbage said, casting a forlorn look first at Will Shakespeare and then at John Heminges. "There is no dodging it this time. We are all for the Tower."

CHAPTER 24: A SCENE SET FOR MURDER

"Surely they will kill us!" Shakespeare shouted.

"I can run no farther!" Burbage gasped.

Both men jogged behind two horses, their hands bound at the wrists and the ropes tied to the back of the horses' saddles. The horses' fast clop forced Burbage and Shakespeare to keep on the balls of their feet, jogging along at a pace somewhere between a fast walk and a slow run. Luckily, the distance was a mere two miles, for by the time they had reached the shaded place where they had seen the butchered body both were stumbling and ready to drop.

When the riders finally pulled up, both men fell to the ground where they lay gasping for breath. Oswyn Scrope dropped from his horse and stood eyeing them with cold fury. After the players had been caught in their own lie, the pursuivant had no enthusiasm for mercy. He nodded for Sergeant Crugg to untie their wrists, and then the hapless players were marched into the gloom beneath the trees. They plashed through the brook where Sam had watered the horse and followed it upstream until they came to a place where the bank was churned with footprints. Two muddy grooves marked where the faceless corpse had been dredged from the brook and hauled up to the road, heels dragging. During the trip, Oswyn Scrope had scarce uttered a word, but now he fixed the two players with his corvine stare and grunted a question, "This is where you saw the body?"

Burbage and Shakespeare nodded. "Aye," Shakespeare said. "But we ne'er ventured closer than some thirty feet away."

Scrope was wearing his wide brimmed black hat and in the shadows beneath the oaks his eyes showed as little more than a liquid gleam. "The boy spoke of a ghost?"

"Aye!" Burbage said, although Shakespeare said "Nay," at the very same moment.

"Aye or nay? Which is it?" Scrope spikily asked.

"We saw a woman—" Shakespeare began.

"I saw it clear," Burbage interrupted. "It was a ghost. It took the form of a gory woman. She had snakes for hair and her face was much bloodied. While we watched she tore the heart from the dead man and ate it. Blood drizzled from her lips as she chewed!"

The gleam beneath the hat brim moved to focus on Shakespeare. "And you saw the same thing?"

Shakespeare cleared his throat. He knew there was danger in contradicting Burbage's story, but he could not back up the fantastical tale the other player was spinning. "No." He shook his head. "In truth I saw her but a moment. Her face was much bloodied, but it could have been from injury. When she saw us, the woman sprang to her feet and reached out with hands as bloody as her face. Now that I think on it she may have been merely beckoning to us, but at the time her visage affrighted us all and ... and ..." Shakespeare's eyes dropped. "... we ran away."

"Scrope snorted contemptuously. "So you did not see her breathe fire nor fly after you on leathern wings?"

Shakespeare shook his head, keeping his eyes on his muddy shoes.

"Tis clear this woman was no ghost," Scrope said. "Mayhap she was companion to the dead man. Mayhap they both travelled the Great Road and were set upon by brigands."

Burbage nodded and said, "The highway is plagued with footpads and highwaymen. We keep our swords handy when we travel it."

"But this is no simple murder," Scrope said, "or robbery."

The pursuivant seemed to reach a decision. He strode off and threw them a curt wave to follow. They climbed the muddy bank and squeezed through a gap in the prickling stand of holly bushes. The forest was dim and filtered green by the canopy of oak leaves shivering overhead. Little light penetrated here, and the spongy loam they ambled through sported only a stunted clump of ferns here and there.

Ahead, a small opening in the canopy of trees spilled a shaft of light that slanted down and splashed upon the recumbent, mushroom-infested trunk of a storm-toppled oak. As they approached, Shakespeare noticed an object sitting atop it. "Look!" he said, and picked up a large hunting horn.

"No doubt left behind by hunters scrambling after a hart," Scrope said dismissively, "forgotten in their haste."

"'Tis a very fine horn to be so careless left behind," Shakespeare countered. "And left in a place sure to be seen. Not merely dropped in the nettles."

Scrope frowned and pursed his lips vexedly but said nothing further.

"Look at yonder tree," Burbage said, pointing ahead.

They converged on a tall oak where a rope had been wound several times around the trunk. The loose end lay among the fallen leaves. Burbage knelt on the forest floor pulling up the rope until he reached the frayed end. He found several short pieces of rope scattered nearby and showed them to Scrope.

"This rope was bound around something, then cut through with a knife." Burbage said.

"Bound around a person, I'll wager," Shakespeare said.

"How know you that?" Scrope asked.

"This forest," Shakespeare said, his voice dropping to a dreamy whisper. "This place. It is a stage whereupon some dread deed has been acted out, and these are the props left behind by the careless players in their haste."

"Stage, pah!" Scrope scoffed.

Burbage held up the rope. The cut ends were darkly stained. "Blood," he said. "He snatched up a handful of leaves from the forest

floor and held them under Scrope's nose. The leaves were also spattered with drops that appeared black in the sylvan gloom. Shakespeare spotted a strip of cloth on the ground and snatched it up.

"Look you on this," he said. The cloth was loosely knotted together and was also spattered with drops of blood. He slipped it on around his head. "A gag?" He asked aloud. He lifted the cloth higher and covered his eyes. "Or a blindfold?"

Scrope's demeanour instantly changed. He looked around for his sergeant-at-arms. "Master Crugg, we must search this area. Keep your eyes to the ground." The dark eyes swept over Burbage and Shakespeare. "My sergeant and I will search this area. You two take yourselves farther away and search over yonder."

The four men split up and began a slow sweep of the forest floor. Shakespeare spotted something white snagged in a thorn bush and stooped to retrieve it. Another strip of cloth, but this one torn and ragged—no doubt snagged in a thorn bush and ripped loose by someone who did not tarry to free it. The cloth was white, but of a very fine weave and Shakespeare instantly recognised what it was: the hem of a burial shroud. His eyes swept the forest about him. Scrope and his soldier searched with their backs to him. Burbage searched a dozen feet away. Shakespeare slipped the torn piece of cloth inside his doublet without saying anything and continued his search.

"Pursuivant Scrope!" Crugg stood with his hand raised, his eyes fixed upon something on the ground. The other men hurried over and looked. The pommel of a dagger protruded from the leaf mould, the blade buried to the hilt in the soft soil where it had fallen. Scrope stooped and drew the dagger from the soil.

"An evil-looking weapon," Burbage said.

"Used to cut the ropes and left where it was dropped," Shakespeare conjectured.

"No ordinary dagger," Scrope said. He drew his own dagger and held the two together, comparing blades. The blade of the dagger they had just found was half again as wide—which matched the wounds in the body. The blade was also unusual in that the tip was slightly blunt for it seemed to have been formed with a hollow tube at its centre.

Scrope sheathed his own dagger and, holding the flat of the blade with two fingers tugged and pushed experimentally. The blade, spring-loaded in its handle, moved back and forth slightly and as it pressed all the way in, a few remaining drops of liquid dribbled from the tip. Sergeant Crugg reached to touch it, but Scrope violently pushed his hand away. It was just as well, as the liquid hissed and white smoke tendriled up from where it spattered the leaves, curling and black-ening them.

"What wickedness is this?" Scrope asked aloud.

"A poison dagger!" Shakespeare said. "Filled with acid."

Scrope nodded his head. "Tis an assassin's blade. I have heard of such infernal devices." He handed the dagger to Sergeant Crugg. "There is cloth in my saddlebags. Wrap this carefully. A cut might prove fatal."

Burbage raised his face and made a show of sniffing the air.

"What do you nose out, Dick?" Shakespeare asked.

Burbage fixed his friend with a baleful stare. "Something dead."

Scrope and Shakespeare followed as Burbage's nose led him some thirty feet deeper into the forest where he stopped abruptly and threw a meaty forearm over his face to shield his nose from the smell. Fat flies with glassy green bodies swooped about their heads. The stink of rotting flesh fouled the air. The leaves on the forest floor crawled and seethed with the shiny black carapaces of scurrying insects devouring something.

Scrope pushed past the two players and knelt down, rummaging in the fallen leaves. He picked something up and stood, brushing away the beetles and ants that swarmed it. Up close it was a white and ghastly lump of flesh that had once been part of a human being, but neither player could guess what it was.

"A tongue," Oswyn Scrope said after a moment's scrutiny. He held his hand open to show them both, but neither man wanted to see. "And by the sharpness of the cut at its base, it was likely severed by the same dagger we just found."

Shakespeare's face had turned milk-pail white. Although he could write a grisly scene, the actual sight of spilled blood made him queasy,

and unlike most men of the time, he had no stomach for the cockpit or bear-baiting ring.

"So," Burbage said. "They cut the dead man's tongue out before they killed him. No doubt to silence his screams."

Shakespeare threw a look at Oswyn Scrope. "Does the dead man still have his tongue?"

The question vexed Scrope. He shook his head uncertainly. It clearly pained him to admit that he had not checked to see if the disfigured corpse still possessed a tongue. "I know not. We must inspect the corpse when we return to the inn. But then, if not his tongue, whose?"

"The woman," Shakespeare said. "The woman we took to be a ghost. Her mouth dripped blood, and her face was much painted with gore. It was not blood of the dead man we saw on her face, but her own blood after her tongue had been cut out."

"But why cut out a wench's tongue?" Scrope asked. "If this is the act of robbers, why not just kill the woman to silence her?"

Shakespeare's gaze had gone to the place that Burbage knew meant he was acting out a scene in theatre of his mind. "Have you ever hunted birds, Master Scrope?"

Scrope looked at Shakespeare as if he were mad. "Why ask a fool's question?"

"He is a country fellow," Burbage put in, "from Warwickshire."

"When I was a boy in Stratford, we used to hunt birds: woodcocks, ducks, pheasants, starlings—any bird was fair game to us boys."

"What care I of such nonsense?"

"The best way to hunt a bird is to use another bird. We would catch a bird, drive a stake into the ground, and tie the bird's leg to it. Then we'd conceal ourselves in a hide made of rushes." Shakespeare's liquid brown eyes gleamed with the picture he was painting. "The alarmed cries and flapping of the bird would draw its fellows. When the curious birds landed close to, we young lads would spring from our hide and catch them in a net laid upon the ground."

"And what does this childish tale—" Scrope started to say, but then a light went on in his dark eyes.

"Think on this!" Shakespeare said. He was using the same excited tone he employed when he sat the rest of the Chamberlain's Men down and told them the story of his newest play. And, likewise, he held Scrope and Burbage in his thrall as he unwound the events. "A nobleman comes riding down the Great Road. He hears the blast of a hunting horn. Curious, he draws his horse off the road into the shade of the great oaks. The horn sounds another trump and draws the man closer. He ties his horse to the holly bushes and ventures into the woods on foot. Here, he sees a lady, blindfold, tied to a tree. She cannot see who he is and neither can she shout a warning because her tongue has been cut out. Such a piteous sight draws him in, deeper into the forest, as he seeks to aid her."

"I would run away at such a sight," Burbage said. "I would not tarry to see if the rogues who did such a deed lay in wait for me."

"The woman is known to him," Scrope said in a voice resonating with conviction. "He is a wealthy man and the lady is likely someone dear to him: a wife, a daughter, a mistress. It is a trap carefully set for this man and this man alone. Afterwards, the villains steal his garments and finery and hack his face so that, should he be found, none will recognise him."

"But what of the woman?" Burbage objected. "Would they not kill her, too? Where is her body?"

Scrope compressed his lips to a straight line and furrowed his brow. "An apt question."

"We saw the maid," Shakespeare said. "The gory woman we mistook for a ghost."

"Mayhap she escaped her captors," Burbage speculated.

"Nay," Shakespeare said. "She was bound and blindfold. It takes more than one man to spring a trap such as this; I would think three, four or more. One villain was left behind to murder her, and convey her body from this place, so that the discovery of both corpses would not reveal whom they were. But the murderer they left behind could not fit his mind to such a vile task."

"How know you that?" Scrope needled.

"It is one thing to kill a man, who likely had time to draw steel and face his murderers. It is another to slaughter a helpless woman, bound and blindfold, with her tongue cut out. Maybe the murderers reasoned she could tell no one what had happened. Or maybe the slaughter of an innocent was so wicked a deed it shrove even the soul of a murderer."

Scrope had been studying Shakespeare's face the whole time he spoke. At first, he had dismissed the Lord Chamberlain's Men as little more than sturdy beggars too shiftless for real work, idlers who sought to escape an honest living by acting out displays of lechery and wickedness that fed the evils of the time. But there was something about this man, this Shake-scene-maker. He possessed an intellect that surprised Scrope and set him on his guard. The Warwickshire dandy was fox-cunning, but the pursuivant had yet to deduce whether he used that guile for Christian works or for wickedness.

"How do you know these things?" Scrope queried. "Do you claim occult powers of necromancy?"

"He is Will Shakespeare," Burbage interrupted. "The best writer of plays in London. This man's mind teems with tales of Kings and madmen, with noble enterprises and wicked ploys."

"And so he would be well-suited to devising such a twisted plot, would you not, Master Shakespeare?"

The Stratford poet shifted nervously at the question. "To what end, Master Scrope? We are a band of simple players on our way to play some of the largest houses in Marlborough. Poison daggers? This is the work of assassins, not simple robbers or cutpurses. You could find no proof that simple players would be behind such an act."

"Pursuivant Scrope!"

All heads snapped around at the shout. It came from Sergeant Crugg, who had gone to place the dagger in Scrope's saddlebags. "Pursuivant Scrope!" Crugg shouted again.

The three men rushed back through the woods. They found the Sergeant near the stand of holly bushes.

"What is it, Sergeant?" Scrope said.

The soldier pointed at something. "Look, sir," he said. "In the holly bush."

Hanging in plain sight, snagged about four feet up the boughs of the holly bush, was the tragedian mask Father John Finch had tossed away as he slipped on the nobleman's hat and cape. Scrope snatched it from the branches and shook it under Shakespeare's nose.

"I know who uses vizards such as these," Scrope said. "Players, such as the Chamberlain's Men. What say you now, Master Shakespeare? Can you look misty-eyed and spin me a pretty tale as to why a band of highwaymen would be wearing the guises of players such as yourself?"

"Wu-we do not," Shakespeare stammered. "Players no longer wear such vizards. It is an antique fashion. "

"ENOUGH, SIRRAH!" Scrope said, drawing his sword and levelling it at Shakespeare's throat.

"I arrest you, William Shakespeare, you Richard Burbage, and all the ne'er-do-wells of the Lord Chamberlain's Men for murder! You will be clapped in irons and transported to the Tower. There you may act a play for my master Richard Topcliffe. I hear he cared little for Ben Jonson's *Isle of Dogs*."

Scrope leaned his warty visage closer to Shakespeare's wide-eyed face. "I think in my master Topcliffe, you will find a critic most harsh."

CHAPTER 25: A BRUSH WITH GLORIANA

"Sergeant Crugg, rouse the other players and assemble them here! Oh, and fetch that rascal from the cellar. Then commandeer the biggest wagon you can lay hands on and bind these roguish players with chains. They are all under arrest and will be taken to the Tower."

"Aye, sir," The Sergeant at Arms slid from his mount and waved for the other soldiers to follow him inside the White Hart Inn. Shakespeare and Burbage, still tied behind the horses, flopped on the road to catch their breaths. Moments later, Scrope's soldiers marched the rest of the Lord Chamberlain's Men out at sword point.

"What are we accused of?" John Heminges shouted. He looked first at Oswyn Scrope and then at Burbage and Shakespeare. "We have done nothing. We are bound for Marlborough."

Scrope slid from his horse and shook his iron rod at the players. "I, Oswyn Scrope, do arrest you all for murder and treason."

"What?" Heminges said. "'Tis not so!"

A moment later, the Sergeant at Arms ran out of the front door of the inn, his face a mask of alarm. "Pursuivant Scrope!" he shouted. "The rascal we locked in the cellar has escaped!"

. . .

* * *

Scrope's boot heels thundered down the cellar's stone steps. A soldier stood post by the open door, which gaped onto darkness. Scrope shouldered past him and peered around the yeasty-smelling cave of the cellar. It was lit by only a solitary candle that sputtered enough feeble light to dimly sketch beer barrels and kegs sitting atop wooden cradles, a floor of stone flags, and walls of huge, oddly-shaped river stones. The room was deep underground and had no windows. There was no way of escape. Scrope stepped out of the cellar and flung his rage in the face of the soldier who had been posted to guard the door. "Speak you!" he barked. "Did anyone enter this room while I was gone?"

"Mmmn, nosir. Notheydiddun!" The young soldier, maybe sixteen, was a Somerset man with a rustic accent and all his long syllables slurred into one another.

Scrope narrowed suspicious eyes. "Did you leave your post at any time?"

The soldier shook his head a little too animatedly. "No, Marster Scrope. No ... oi ... once ... oi had me a great need to piss, but oi were not gone but a moment."

Scrope leaned closer and sniffed. The man reeked of beer. A slack smile hung on his face.

The first backhanded blow knocked the steel helmet from the soldier's head. The second blow caromed the back of his head off the wall and sat him down hard on the cellar steps.

"You are drunk!" Scrope bellowed. He kicked the soldier's legs as the man struggled to stand up. "Get up, you drunken fool! Get up those stairs!"

The Lord Chamberlain's Men, stood in a loose knot on the road outside the inn and now all looked up in fear as Oswyn Scrope drove one of his own soldiers out of the inn crawling on all fours, viciously kicking him the way a man would kick a mangy hound.

"Master Crugg!" Scrope screamed as he delivered kick after kick.

"Yes, sir!"

"Strip this cur of his armour and clap him in the pillory!"

"Yes, sir. Right away, sir."

Just then a horseman dressed in black galloped up. It was Anthony Munday, returned from reconnoitring the fire. "Pursuivant Scrope!" Munday cried with alarm. "What has happened?" Munday's eyes tried to take in all the action: the knot of men spilled across the road and his master, Oswyn Scrope, kicking the innards out of one of his own soldiers.

"These rogues are under arrest!" Scrope shouted, indicating the players with a wave of his hand. "To be conveyed to the Tower under suspicion of murder and treason. And this dog—" He gave the soldier a final brutal kick in the backside that launched the scrabbling man forward so that he ploughed the road with his nose. "This dog is drunk on duty and will be pilloried for it."

When Anthony Munday's eyes made a second sweep over the men standing in the road, he recognised familiar faces, even as they recognized him.

"Tis Anthony Munday, tis not?" Burbage muttered to Shakespeare.

"Aye, or his double!"

John Heminges threw an arm around the necks of Shakespeare and Burbage and pulled them close. "That fellow is Anthony Munday!" he whispered.

"Doubly-spoken," Shakespeare agreed. "We had just noted the same!"

"Why then we are saved!" Heminges said. "We have a fellow player to speak for us!"

"Be not so certain," Burbage muttered, his expression bleak. "I hear he has turned against the theatre of late."

"Against the theatre? Why so?" Heminges demanded.

"He was hissed from the boards."

"Aye," Shakespeare added. "Munday fancies himself an extempore player, but lacks the wit."

Extempore players were the bane of playwrights such as Shakespeare. It was not uncommon for players to forget a line or two and extemporise. Then there were players like Will Kempe who, as a clown, could extemporise effortlessly, though Shakespeare despised it. Anthony Munday thought that, he too, was a fine extemporiser; however, he was dreadful and his rambling speeches drew boos and catcalls from the groundlings.

"And yet he is a fine writer," Heminges said. "He has penned a goodly number of plays and ballads."

"Aye, and pamphlets railing against the theatre," Burbage said.

"A passing fair writer," Shakespeare grudgingly admitted. "But in truth, he is a dabbler in too many things."

"He is a twin-tongued Janus," Burbage warned. "He argues for leniency for Catholics, and yet it was he that brought Campion and other Jesuits to the scaffold. I trust him not."

"We may have little choice." Heminges said. "And I would choose him before Richard Topcliffe."

The drunken soldier was stripped of his armour and locked in the pillory. Before he walked away, Oswyn Scrope spat in the man's face.

Munday had dismounted and hovered at the shoulder of his master. "Pursuivant Scrope, I have intelligence of the house we saw burning."

For the first time, Scrope was able to pry his attention from the unfortunate soldier. "What say you, Master Munday?"

"I rode to the house that burned and found it greatly engulfed."

"Which house was it?"

"The seat of Sir Francis Talbot. And the fire, sir, it was no mischance. Deliberately set; the fire kindled in many places so there would no way of putting the flames out."

Scrope frowned as he puzzled over the news. "Talbot Hall?" He bit his chapped lips and tugged at the collar of his white shirt, causing the collar to chafe at the swelling carbuncle on his neck. "Francis Talbot? A known recusant! But why would Catholic spies burn the house of one of their own?"

"Sir, we may have the reason."

Scrope looked questioningly at the young pursuivant.

"While there, I witnessed the arrival of the Royal Court."

The news dumbfounded Scrope. "What? The Queen is abroad in the countryside?"

"Indeed, sir. She is on a Royal Progress across this part of her kingdom. It was planned for her to lodge at Talbot Hall for some three nights."

Scrope's eyes narrowed as he took in the information. "There is a dark purpose behind all this. What once I suspected, I now truly believe. I had not known the Queen would be in this part of the country, but now the purpose behind this plague of Jesuits becomes clear. A man murdered and his face scratched out. Today we found an assassin's poison dagger. We must puzzle out the meaning before the plot can be fully realized." He threw a searing glance at Munday. "Know you where the Queen's Progress travels to next?"

"Wexcombe House, just a short distance away. The queen and court will be the guests of Sir Richard and Lady Verity Wexcombe."

"When do they travel?"

He had no sooner spoken the words than trumpets pealed in the near distance.

Munday nodded up the road. "Look you. Even now they come."

A huge train of wagons and riders appeared in the distance headed by a column of mounted soldiers bearing pennants fluttering with the Royal standard. The Queen's train was so long it appeared to stretch all the way back to London. Scrope and his soldiers had to step clear of the road as the endless procession passed. The Innkeeper, his tapster and his wife and daughter came out of doors to watch. First there was a detachment of foot soldiers followed by courtiers on horseback. At the sight of the Royal Coach, a carriage open on all sides, drawn by four white horses fitted with white plumes atop their nodding heads, everyone bowed deeply. But as the cumbersome carriage rattled by, Shakespeare stole a quick peek up through his brows and saw that it was empty.

"She's not in it!" he announced, and everyone straightened up. Then more soldiers approached. Their colour standards proclaimed them as the Queen's Lifeguard. Trumpets sounded a brassy fanfare as the Queen herself appeared on horseback, riding sidesaddle in a heavy gown resplendent with jewels despite the heat of the day. Gentlemen Pensioners rode beside her: four tall men who formed a kind of body-guard-within-a-bodyguard, each holding a wooden pole that supported a white canopy of shot silk. Embroidered with the royal coat of arms, the canopy fluttered above Elizabeth, shading her from the rays of the sun.

Miraculously, as the Queen caught sight of the small crowd gathered outside the inn, she raised a hand and the ponderous train, all two and fifty carriages and nine hundred courtiers on horseback and in carriages, along with several detachments of musketmen and pikemen and bringing up the rear a retinue of servants, cooks, craftsman and scullery workers, stuttered to a protracted halt.

The appearance of Gloriana on a dusty road was a surreally celestial encounter, as if the radiant disk of the sun had abandoned its place in the sky and swooped down to hover low above the earth. And, in truth, it was almost as dazzling in is splendour. Elizabeth, even in her sixties, struck an audacious figure. The dress she was sewn into coruscated with mother of pearl; small gems and precious stones jiggled and caught the light. Her flame-red hair—an obvious wig—was topped by a gold crown glittering with diamonds and gems dug from the earth half a world away by poor brown people who laboured as slaves beneath the whips of the Spaniards and then in-turn purloined by English pirates and sailed back from the far side of the earth back to England. Beneath the crown, Elizabeth's face was painted like a porcelain doll's, the face with high forehead and receding hairline daubed ghastly white with lead pancake, the mouth a razored gash outlined in vermilion, gaudy circles of rouge dotting the knobby cheekbones. (Shakespeare had seen her from close quarters after performances at the palace and knew that, up close, the Queen's face, like many of the time, still bore the devastating marks of the small pox and was cratered and pitted like the moon's surface peered at through Galileo's telescope.) Still, from a dozen feet away, the illusion was dazzling as a saint's beatific vision, lit from above by the glowing nimbus of the silk canopy.

"Is that Master Shakespeare?" the Queen asked aloud. Her gaze swept across the rest of the players. "And Master Burbage? Heminges? Are all the Lord Chamberlain's Players here?"

Shakespeare shuffled forward dragging the chain, threw an elaborate flourish and bowed as low as he could. "The better half of the Lord Chamberlain's Men, your majesty!"

The queen's cool gaze took in the leg irons and chains but made no mention of them. "And what brings poets and players so far from the playhouses of London?"

Oswyn Scrope had held his tongue long enough, and could restrain himself no further. "Falsehood and lies!" he blustered, lunging toward the queen aggressively, a gesture sufficiently threatening that the Queen's life guards started to draw their swords until the Pursuivant thought better of it and took a prudent step backward. "They are wanton rascals here for the purpose of treason and sedition!"

Elizabeth's horse shied away at Scrope's loudness, but she pulled its head back with a snatch of the reigns. "And who are you, sir?" Elizabeth roared.

"I am—" Scrope began imperiously, but then caught himself and softened his voice. "I am Oswyn Scrope, servant to my lord Richard Topcliffe and your majesty's messenger of the chamber."

"If indeed you are the queen's messenger, Master Scrape," she began mildly, deliberately confusing his name, "then perhaps you would be kind enough to REMOVE YOUR HAT IN THE QUEEN'S PRESENCE!"

The last words rang like an iron bar dropped on a stone floor. The venom in Elizabeth's voice drew colour even from Scrope features and he hurriedly snatched off his hat. Suddenly his spine lacked sufficient articulation to bow and scrape low enough.

"Beggin' your pardon, madam," he said, making a clumsy, graceless attempt at a courtier's bow with a flourish. "I am Pursuivant to several Jesuits known to be travelling through these parts. I believe these men

—" he nodded at the players," To be murderous cut-throats and brigands embroiled in a traitorous plot aimed at your very person."

"Good Heavens," the Queen said, mockingly. "They do not look to
me so very dangerous to me."

"No, Madam, you are much mistook. I have proof —"

Scrope was about to say more, but Elizabeth cut him off with a
look that scythed through his words. No one ever told the queen to
her face that she was mistaken.

Never.

The tiny woman seemed to inflate like the sail of ship bellied taut
by a rising tempest.

"Do not presume to lecture me about my subjects, sirrah! These
fellows may be rascals but they aConey-Catchers rascals. They have
performed for my pleasure many times at court. The Queen of
England is a good judge of character and these players are her upright
and loving subjects and you molest them further at the risk of my
displeasure. Do I make myself clear?

Scrope vacillated, unsure what to do. "Yes, Milady, I mean madam,
I mean … your majesty."

"Good. Then unbind them at once!"

Scrope blinked rapidly, his mind stuttering. He turned and
scowled at his Sergeant at Arms, shouting for him to free the players.
Sergeant Crugg produced a heavy iron key and ran about, unlocking
the manacles that shackled the Lord Chamberlain's Men.

Elizabeth nudged her horse forward. Quixotic as ever, her voice
had changed, betraying amusement at how she had stricken terror
into Scrope. Now she spoke in a soft voice. "Master Shakespeare, a
change in fortunes sees our Royal Progress camped at Wexcombe
House a full five days. We are to have a Masque on Saturday, our final
evening. Could your players perform something for us?"

John Heminges, hearing her words, leaped forward, dragging with
him the Sergeant at Arms, who was trying to free him from the mana-
cle. "The Lord Chamberlain's Men would be honoured to perform for
the court, your majesty. Would you require us for just the one night?

We have many plays in our quiver and could entertain the court on other nights, should you desire."

The queen considered his offer for a moment. "Very well, then, a performance on the second night and another on the fifth night, so that we might conclude our stay with the masque."

Shakespeare bowed again to the queen. "Majesty What kind of play strikes your fancy? A tragedy or a comedy?"

"What are your players practiced at?"

"Richard the second?"

The queen's lips puckered in a sour face. "I think not. Never one of my favourites. And a bit crusty by now, think you not? Have you nothing new?"

Shakespeare searched himself. "A Midsummer Night's Eve?"

She smiled, flashing the black stumps of her teeth. "Yes. An amusing play. I like it right well. What shall we have for the fifth night?"

"Shakespeare paused, then decided to take a risk. "I have a new play. Very near to being done." When the queen's face fell, he hastened to add: "But it could be ready for Saturday night."

"What is this new play called?"

Shakespeare pondered. Suddenly, the title seemed obvious: "*Double Falshood*."

"A name that promises much. A comedy?"

"Nay. Tis a dark play. Filled with murder, betrayal, and double-dealing."

He saw uncertainty flash across her face and quickly added, "Aye, perhaps, it is not the best."

"Murder, betrayal and double-dealing?" The queen thought on it a moment and smiled sardonically. "Ever thus has been my life." Jewels rattled as she nodded. "Good then, Master Shakespeare, it will please us to have this new play of yours."

Shakespeare threw another elaborate flourish and bowed low before her.

As Elizabeth raised her gaze, she noticed the drunken soldier

Scrope had placed in the pillory. "Master Scrape, why is this fellow in the pillory?"

"Drunkenness, your majesty." Oswyn Scrope pronounced with puritan zeal. "He was caught drinking beer."

The queen frowned. "But it is no crime to drink beer. And is this not England, where we brew the best beer in the world?" She nodded at the Innkeeper. "You there, sir, in the apron, are you host of this inn?"

John Thomas dragged himself forward, cringing. He was too nervous to speak and merely nodded his head frantically.

"Are those not brew kegs I could smell for the last mile?"

The innkeeper nodded faster.

"Then be good enough to bring your queen a mug of beer. I am scorched in this frock!"

John Thomas fled inside and scurried back out a moment later carrying a frothing tankard. He bowed repeatedly as he stepped up to the queen and handed her up the drink. The queen quaffed deeply, draining the tankard in one mighty gulp before tossing it back to the innkeeper. A moment's pauses as she wiped her mouth on the back of her hand and then ripped out a long, elaborate belch. Her royal train burst into a roar of approving laughter. The queen was fond of shocking people with her earthy and unexpected shows of swearing and belching, and had a good laugh herself. "There's a good, honest glass of English beer!" she pronounced. "If you will be good enough, inn-keeper, I'd like a barrel or two of that beer delivered to Wexcombe House." She nodded at the soldier in the pillory. "Release the fellow, Master Scrape. Tis no crime to drink beer that good."

Scrope flinched. She was making him look like a fool, but he nodded and bowed in obeisance.

"Hurrah!" Shakespeare shouted aloud. "Long live the Queen!"

And everyone joined in.

The royal progress continued as the Lord Chamberlain's Men, the folk from the White Hart Inn and Scrope's own soldiers sent her on her way with a chorus of shouted "hurrahs." They all stood and watched until the last cart had clattered away, which took the best part of an hour. No one had ever seen that much traffic on the road in a lifetime, nor would they ever again.

By this time the many horses of the train, including the Queen's own mount, had sauced the road with so much fresh dung that blue-bottles swarmed and buzzed, and all scurried indoors to escape the maddening cloud.

CHAPTER 26: THE RELUCTANT SPY

The rest of the Lord Chamberlain's Men retired to the inn's great room to drink a celebratory toast. The wheel of fortune had turned and this time in their favour. While cups clashed and oaths flew amid bellyful laughter, Shakespeare took a mug of cider and slipped upstairs to his room. He needed to write. The Queen had commanded a performance of his new play and he had but four days to finish writing it and then a day to copy out pages for the players to learn their lines. To many writers this would have been daunting, but Shakespeare had been earning his crust for the past four years as a penny-a-page playwright. Writer's block was the prerogative of noblemen dalliers and university-educated bookworms such as Marlowe and Kyd, not the son of a Stratford Glover. If the Muse refused to speak then she went hungry, too. As he mounted the narrow, creaking stairs, he was already amending some scenes in his mind to shorten and simplify them.

In the room, he dragged the small table into the window so he could write for a good few hours without the expense of burning candles. Scrope still had the rest of his play, so he had been forced to take fresh pages and fresh quills and ink from one of the trunks. He would work on the new scenes until he could marry the new pages with the old.

Shakespeare's imagination was never more fired than when the queen herself made a request, and now his muse sang in her silvery voice. He dashed off pages, line after line, with scarce a crossing out or revision. Finally, knuckles rapping on the door tore through his reverie.

"Enter," he called out, but kept scribbling. He guessed that it was Connie knocking and smiled to himself. Behind him, the door opened. A floorboard creaked from a heavy tread.

"Sweet angel," Shakespeare said, not looking up. "Have you come so soon to warm my bed?"

"I have not."

The rumbling voice was a man's. The nib of Shakespeare's quill cracked, blotting the page with an inky black spot. His head whiplashed around.

The figure of Oswyn Scrope choked the doorway, a glowering presence so dark that he dragged a shadow behind him like a cape. The reek of overheated horse shimmered in the air around him. Even though the playwright felt as if he now enjoyed some protection from the queen, he knew the inconstant mind of Elizabeth to be fickle and unreliable. A dozen courtiers, flunkies, schemers and sycophants jostled and fought for Gloriana's attention every second of every day. Those not in the royal eye at all times were instantly forgotten and never brought to mind. She would elevate her favourites with titles and privileges, and in the next breath imprison them in the Tower and execute them. A man might risk body and soul fighting valiantly in a war against her enemies only to be boxed soundly around the ears upon returning, while another might be made her lapdog simply because he could caper and dance and had shapely calves. Shakespeare knew he had already tweaked Scrope's ire; a diplomatic approach seemed best.

"Pursuivant Scrope!" Shakespeare said. He noticed the papers tightly rolled in Scrope's fist. "I thank you for my pages!" He reached for them, but Scrope held back, and made no sign of giving them up.

"You are a fool who wastes his life with childish toys and the whisper of airy nothings." Scrope said, "I have read this," and rattled the papers in his face. "You write of wickedness and falsehood in men, both sinful and impious. If you are innocent of all stain, then why does this creature of your imagination follow so close the action of the last few days?"

"I take my plots from where I may," Shakespeare said calmly. His warm brown eyes met and held Scrope's unfathomable gaze.

Scrope snorted derisively. "I consider you a fool ... but a cunning and clever fool. Thus I will make use of you."

Shakespeare tried not to show fear. He held out his hand once again to take the play. "The queen herself has commanded my new play for this Saturday. I must have my pages."

Moments passed. When it became clear that Scrope was not going to hand over the play, he lowered his hand.

"You and your companion rogues have your living by distracting apprentices and base jibberwits with your so-called play acting."

"My plays put more than a thousand bums in seats at our playhouse and five hundred more groundlings at a penny a piece. Hardly insubstantial. Hardly nothing."

"And yet you quit your London playhouse to journey this far in a sweltering summer? I'd wager you couldn't make a fraction of that playing in the country."

"We had little choice. The London playhouses area all shut."

"Indeed? Why so?"

Shakespeare thought of *The Isle of Dogs*, Nash and Kyd's seditious play that had incensed the Master of the Reveals, but decided it was the last thing he would talk about. "The playhouses are shut because of the plague."

"Clearly, a sign of God's vengeance at your wanton displays of venal and wicked dealings."

Although he was bursting to refute Scrope's maligning of his livelihood, Shakespeare said nothing.

"Take me Master Shakeworth, are you a secret Catholic?"

The Stratford player visibly paled. "No sir, I am an observant Protestant."

"I am right glad to hear it. And where do you live in London?"

"On Silver Street. I room with a Huguenot family who were much abused by the Catholics of France."

"Silver street, eh? And so if I check the church attendance records, I will find the name William Shakespeare writ there?"

Scrope was venturing into deadly territory. His heart was beating so hard he was sure the pursuivant must hear it. "I, I . . . mayhap not. I have had need to change my lodgings several times of late . . ."

"Indeed. A ready excuse, as I would expect from a scoundrel who dissembles to earn his daily crust. But I think my master Topcliffe could reach down your throat and pluck forth the truth with a pair of hot iron tongs."

Shakespeare tried, but could not swallow the lump in his throat. .

"But enough posturing. Enough pretence. Here is what you will do. You will be my eyes and ears in the Queen's Court."

Alarm stretched across Shakespeare's face. Scrope clearly didn't understand the machinations of title and privilege when it came to matters of the court. "But I am a mere player, neither nobleman nor courtier. I have no license to be there—"

Scrope continued as if he had not heard a word of what Shakespeare said. "Exactly, to the Court you are a man of no account with neither wealth nor title and therefore … invisible. I will tell you what to look for and you will look. I will tell you what questions to pose and you shall pose them. There is something amiss about this affair. A plot is unfolding. As you said in the forest, someone is laying a net and 'ticing the birds to fly into it. You shall help me unravel this plot. And then—" He held the papers up. "Then you shall have your childish scribblings back. If not, I will burn them and you may eat the ashes."

Scrope turned to leave. "Make ready. You shall accompany Master Munday and me. We visit Wexcombe Hall. Oh, and bring that big ginger devil with you."

With that, the pursuivant swept out of the room. Shakespeare looked down at his pages, but it seemed as if Scrope's darkness had bled out into the room, staining the air, for there was no longer enough light to read what his own hand had written.

CHAPTER 27: WEXCOMBE HOUSE

A huge snoozer, that's how I'd describe Wexcombe House. Of course it's historical and grandiose. Great stuff if you're into vulgar displays of wealth built by decadent upper class oiks while the rest of the population lived in dirt-floor hovels scratching their arses. But if you've seen one old pile, you've seen them all. That's my attitude. Plus, it doesn't even have what every self-respecting stately home in England has these days: a safari park and a roller coaster for the kiddies. Instead, Wexcombe House has sold out by a classier rout —it's become a conference centre. I suppose that keeps out the Great Unwashed. Of course, I don't say this to Gillian as we traipse the creaking wood floors with the rest of the Geek Squad trailing behind us. And yes, it's architecturally splendid with this kind of Gothic arch and that kind of window and it's all so very old and the walls are cluttered with period paintings of ugly, fish-faced bastards in ridiculous clothes. Booooooooorrrrring. Still, I'm a good boy and do my best to smile and look interested every time Gill throws a look my way. She's the only thing I find fascinating and lights up every room she enters.

At some point we get separated from the rest of the tour and just the two of us drift into a small library. Like every other room the walls are lined with portraits of the Wexcombe family going back yonks. Most are dark and depressing, with creepy eyes that follow you around the room like in an old horror movie. One of them, white-haired old misery-guts in shiny armour positively gives me the willies. He seems to be glaring at me.

"Look at this!" Gillian says, drawing my attention to a series of framed pencil sketches. Quite frankly they're crudely drawn crap— easily the least impressive thing in there.

"Not very good, are they?" I say. "Looks like they were done by the children of Mrs. Arkwright's Form 1B at Wexcombe Junior School."

"You're awful!" She gives me a playful punch in the shoulder, which perversely I find strangely erotic. 'These are sketches from a Royal Progress that visited Wexcombe in 1597."

"When she sees I am clueless, she adds "Queen Elizabeth the first and her court stayed here during a summer tour of the region."

"Fascinating," I say and think *big deal*.

"Look," she points at the topmost picture. It shows two boats in the lake beside the house. One is shaped to look like a whale. The other one I have no earthly what it's supposed to be.

"These were part of the celebrations to welcome the Queen," Gillian says. "But what I'm really interested in are these." She points to another sketch hanging below. A number of figures stand on a stage. One's got a head like a donkey. The others are waving their arms about, apparently frightened by the appearance of the donkey-head man. There are names scribbled above each, but the writing is faded and the light is too poor to read them.

"This is believed to be a performance of A Midsummer Night's Eve that was performed by William Shakespeare and the Lord Chamberlain's Men for the queen. The figure in the asses' head is almost certainly William Kemp, the most famous comic actor of the time. Shakespeare may well be one of the other actors on stage, but we have no way of knowing which."

She moves to the second sketch. A figure in a monk's cloak, the hood drawn up, stands at the far right. In the middle, a group of masked figures armed with daggers attack a man in fancy dress—a plumed bonnet and cape.

"What this, then?" I ask.

Gillian has gone very quiet. She stands directly in front of the sketch, staring. Her fingers touch the glass, as if she's going to psychically suck out the information through her fingertips. "It appears to be another performance, but we don't know for certain which one. We do have a record of the Lord Chamberlain's Men being paid for two performances. The second was of a play called *Double Falshood*."

"Never heard of it," I say, which isn't saying much. How many Shakespeare plays could I name? Two? Three?"

"You've never heard of it," Gillian says, at last tearing those beautiful green eyes away long enough to meet mine, "because it's a lost Shakespeare play. No manuscript, not even a partial one, exists. Apparently, it was only ever performed once, for Elizabeth, here, at Wexcombe house, and never again."

Gillian's expression invites me to share in her sense of wonder.

I nod and try to look suitably impressed as I think to myself: *I'm bloody starving. I could eat the arsehole out of a pig.*

∼

I haven't worn these Italian shoes in years and they're too bloody tight. About the time I feel the burn of a blister forming on my big toe we are ushered into the Great Hall. Everybody oohs and ahhs and I have to admit the place is impressive. The oak-beamed ceilings are incredibly high. The room itself is vast, one of the largest in England, the tour guide drones, and blah blahs about the dimensions. Gillian and I trail at the back of the tour group. She's worn her hair in an up-do today and I'm more impressed by the soft downy hairs on the elegant curve of her neck, which I would like to nibble.

"My God," she says, her voice shivering with near-religious reverence. "We are literally walking in *his* footsteps."

It takes me a moment, but I finally get it: she's talking about William-bloody-Shakespeare. The giant forty-foot banners hanging from the ceiling with his mug on are a bit of a giveaway.

"He must have performed right there."

The stage she nods at is obviously a prefab job, dragged in and set up for the conference. Round tables with place settings for brunch occupy the main floor. There's an open bar at one side of the hall and the irresistible gravity of free booze draws me toward it.

"Champers?" I ask, before I wander away.

"Mmnn," she nods distractedly. She's in her own little world, so I toddle off.

On the way back from the open bar, I swipe a canapé from a passing waiter's tray and cram it in my mouth. I'm chewing ferociously, trying to choke it down, as I rejoin her, two effervescing flutes of champagne in hand.

"Ah, there are the others!" She points and starts to guide me toward a table. I recognise all of the guests I just checked into the White Hart and realise with terror that are we are supposed to join them. Perfect, I am going to break bread with a crusty bunch of academics. (Academons, more like.) Me, Captain Moron. My chances of looking like a complete pillock are one hundred percent.

Gillian touches my arm. "Before we go over, let me give you a brief intro to your guests. The man at the end is Professor Braxton," She nods to a teutonically–severe looking chap with a shaved, uglily shaped head so shiny he must buff it every morning.

"The lady next to him is Beryl Withers," she nods to the elderly Agatha Christie lady. If I don't accidentally call her Miss Marple before the week is up I'll be gobsmacked.

She continues around the table. The young pimply guy in the Will Power t-shirt is actually a graduate student named Kenneth and the young woman I took for his girlfriend is his fellow grad student named Penelope. The American lady, Emily Hamm, takes up her usual excess of space. Next to her is Broody Brendan.

We both mumble our hellos as we slide into the last two empty chairs. There's a period of silence, which makes it obvious we just interrupted an ongoing conversation, but then Emily Hamm pipes up, addressing her comments to me: "We know all about Gillian," she says, "But where do you stand on the authorship issue, Mister Braithwaite?"

I open my mouth and strain, but nothing comes out. She takes my hesitancy born of ignorance as an unwillingness to publicly commit.

"I myself . . ." she pressed a hand lavish with flesh and gaudy rings to her voluminous bosom, ". . . am a Baconian."

"More like a bacon sandwich," I mutter under my breath to Gillian, who pinches my thigh Smedley in reproach. "Ow," I yelp. They all look at me curiously so I clear my throat and say, "I think it was Bill ... Shakespeare . . . what wrote them—*who* wrote them. The plays, that is."

"Populist nonsense!" Broody Brendan scoffs. "It's preposterous that such works of genius were produced by a working-class nobody. An uneducated glover's son!"

"Marlowe was a shoe-maker's son." One of the others counters.

"Cobblers!" I blurt out in an attempt at wit.

The embarrassed looks hurled at me show that I am less than successful.

Gillian presses against my side thrillingly as she reaches for the water jug and fills her glass. "Brendan here believes that Christopher Marlowe is the true author of Shakespeare's plays . . . "She smiles as she slips the dagger in, "... even though fourteen plays appeared after Marlowe died in 1593."

In response Brendan smears his face with the insufferable smile of an intellectual giant trying to explain the workings of a digital camera to a tribe of savages who communicate mostly in grunts. "Gillian's read my book," he says, addressing me. "She knows full well of Marlowe's role in Walsingham's secret service. A time came when Kit Marlowe had to disappear for political reasons. In truth, he wasn't really dead."

"Didn't he go to live on an island in the Mediterranean?" I pipe up, chancing my arm. "Or was that John F. Kennedy ... or Jimmy Hendrix ... or Jim Morrison, I always get that story confused."

The whole table guffaws, except for Broody Brendan, who makes a face like I've just ladled a steaming turd onto his plate. His jaws bite down, displaying his atrocious overbite. He looks away, as if there's something tremendously interesting on the far side of the hall.

~

I'm waiting patiently in the hallway for Gillian, who has gone to freshen up in the Ladies' room, when Broody Brendan barges out of the door to the Gents and almost collides with me.

"Scuse me," I say, stepping back reflexively, even though he's the barger, not me. He looks me up and down and mutters through clenched teeth, "I'd be careful of Gillian, if I were you." He adds with a snarl in his voice, "Remember the Shakespeare line: a tiger's heart wrapped in a woman's hide."

"Shakespeare?" I say. "I thought Marlowe was the true author?"

His eyes startle wide. Hot half-moons flush in his cheeks. Thick I may be but I am quick on the uptake. He drops his head and shoves past, radiating fury.

Chew on that you bastard, I think.

Gillian appears, looking appropriately freshened. "Ready to go?"

I nod and we stroll toward the car park and the waiting mini-bus. I am smug having got one over on the pretentious prick. Still he's given me something to ponder.

As the mini-coach pulls out of the driveway to Wexcombe manor and trundles up the road toward the White Hart, I lean my head toward hers and whisper "Thank you."

She tosses me a look that says *what for?*

"A second chance."

She smiles and says mildly, "You're still on probation."

I smile too and my eye happens to fall on Broody Brendan. He's glaring at us and quickly looks away to pout out the coach window. I suddenly realise that there's some history between the two, but what? Between the pages, or between the sheets? I look back at Gillian and she's staring out the window, her lovely face relaxed and unguarded. The coach must hit a bump in the road because my heart goes weightless for a moment. I cup my hands and catch it as carefully as I would a dropped egg.

But all the while, Brendan's words ricochet inside my head.

A tiger's heart wrapp'd in a woman's hide.

CHAPTER 28: A ROYAL ARRIVAL

The driveway narrowed at a stone bridge over a stream where soldiers wielding halberds stepped into the middle of the road and menaced them

"Halt in the name of the queen!" a bearded man-at-arms gruffly demanded.

They had entered the long, wooded drive to Wexcombe House, Oswyn Scrope and Anthony Munday leading on their horses while Shakespeare and Burbage were forced to walk behind. Scrope shouted back the man-at-arms that he was Messenger to the Queen's Chamber and that the long-tongued varlet must yield the road or face the consequence of impeding her majesty's business. However Scrope had met his match in officiousness in the shape of a grizzled armada veteran who stonily refused to cede the way. The verbal arm-wrestling went on for a protracted period in the way that narrow men given a smidgen of authority grapple to exercise their power over one another. The sergeant that barred the way had a voluminous beard and droopy moustaches that hid his mouth entirely and made him look like a man chewing on a shrubbery.

"A Biblical scene," Shakespeare whispered sotto voce to Burbage. "This bush speaks, but does not burn."

"Would that I could amend that!" Burbage muttered back.

When fencing with tongues produced no victor, Scrope flourished a document with a daub of wax impressed with an official seal. Where neither words nor will could hold sway, the parchment won the day. The sergeant dropped his eyes and grudgingly ordered his men to step aside. As if in a final riposte, Scrope's horse lifted its tail and dropped a steaming pile on the driveway so vile in the sultry summer air that its stench coated the back of their throats.

They travelled along a drive lined on either side by handsome trees that screened the view and gave only tantalising glimpses of the large house that lay ahead. And then the tunnel of trees dilated and Wexcombe House sprawled in all of its mind-reeling majesty. In truth, it was more palace than manor: an immense pile of up to five stories in places, built not of wood but of pink brick and white stone, which was not local to the area and which must have been carted in at ruinous expense. Elegant chimneys festooned the tiled roofline, none of which were repeated in design, for some rose straight, some corkscrewed clockwise and others counter clockwise. But most astonishing were the windows. Glass windows were expensive and even the rich, when they moved between residences, would remove the window glass and haul it away with them. With Wexcombe House, that would have been impossible, for every wall of the great manse boasted floor to ceiling windows that glittered in the midday light, reflecting a thousand suns. No expense had been spared in any detail of the architecture, which embodied the latest trends from Europe including columns, pilasters and cupolas sporting gilded weather-vanes or flagpoles with fluttering pennants bearing the queen's colours and the Wexcombe coat of arms, a stag rampant upon on a field of red chevrons.

The first glimpse of Wexcombe House was so astounding it froze them where they stood and even Oswyn Scrope gaped in amazement before he remembered himself, shook his head and muttered, "All is vanity, wickedness, and greed." He turned his head and opined solemnly to Anthony Munday, "Here is house enough to hide every Jesuit in Christendom."

Vast grounds surrounded the house, stretching to the limits of vision. The front lawns swarmed with workmen and labourers hammering, sawing, raising huge marquee tents and banging together temporary wooden buildings to serve as banqueting halls, dormitories, stables. For even though the house boasted hundreds of rooms, the royal progress brought with it more than a thousand courtiers as well as their families, retainers, servants, and servants-of-servants, as well as two-and-a-half thousand horses. The beasts had been turned loose to graze on the grounds and were trampling through flowerbeds and sauntering through the orchards, nibbling flowers, stripping fruit from branches and churning up the vegetable garden, leaving nothing behind but chewed and splintered branches and everywhere malodorous piles of manure.

On the east lawn a large team of men hauled and strained at ropes, pulling up the canvas walls of an enormous banqueting tent: a huge pavilion four hundred feet in circumference made of thick canvas walls with a ceiling hung from massive ship's masts forty feet high. The eastern aspect of Wexcombe House looked out over a man-made lake created by damming the river and flooding three medieval fishponds. Even now a great crowd of people lined the lakeshore from which came strains of music and the hubbub of many voices. When Elizabeth reached a house or city it was common for her to be greeted with elaborate ceremonies and entertainments, which dragged on for hours. Something of the sort was even now playing out on the waters of the lake. Scrope and Munday guided their horses that way and the two players followed.

When the Royal train first arrived at Wexcombe House hours earlier, Elizabeth had clambered down from her horse and transferred into a fantastical creation: a fairy carriage drawn by six miniature ponies and driven by children dressed as fairies and pixies. The children, boys and girls less than six or seven years old and chosen for their comeliness, wore sparkling costumes with gossamer wings on their backs. The queen had laughed delightedly as she climbed into a miniature coach barely large enough for her to fit into. The miniature groomsmen shook the reigns, and the fairy coach trundled a road that wound around the circumference of the lake. At its northern most point, the coach stopped, and after more children dressed as pixies sang an especially composed welcome to her majesty, she transferred to a barge, which had been constructed so as to appear like a whale. As the whale set off from its dock it was accompanied by similar barge, this one a constructed in the form of a giant snail with a spiralling shell in which musicians, arranged in double-decker seats, strummed lutes and blew woodwinds as eight oarsman stroked the oars.

Scrope and Munday dismounted and handed the reigns of their horses to waiting pages, then strode to the edge of the lake where a congregation of men in black spilled along a wooden dock. The men were mostly time-worn gentlemen with white beards and constipated faces, heads balanced upon their white starched ruffs like melons on plates. Up close, Shakespeare recognized many of the dour faces from the times the Lord Chamberlain's Men had performed at court, for they always lingered at the edge of the queen's retinue like a reluctant shadow limning the halo of light cast by Gloriana's radiance—the Queen's Privy Council.

"Her Majesty, it seems, has been swallowed up in the belly of a whale," said a man who Shakespeare recognized as Lord Essex, the queen's current favourite and a contemptible, preening dandy. Once he had lounged on a cushion at her majesty's feet and prattled all the way through a performance of *A Midsummer's Night's Dream* in a voice so fond of itself that Shakespeare had been hard put to resist leaping from the stage and choking him senseless.

"I think the fellow that devised it hath ne'er seen a whale before," the Earl of Essex drawled, a lazy brag about his prowess as a seaman.

"Looks more like a giant cod to me," quipped another.

"'Tis clever, though. Very fishy looking."

"Another device of Thomas Churchyard, no doubt."

"And bears a keen resemblance, for Churchyard is a fishy-looking fellow."

The comment drew cruel laughter men from the rest of the Queen's Privy Councillors.

Burbage and Shakespeare stood at the back of the courtiers crowded around the dock where they could eavesdrop on their banter.

"Told you it was a whale," Burbage said.

"Aye," Shakespeare agreed. "'Tis very like a whale."

Propelled by four sets of oars decorated like fishy fins. An enormous whale head covered the front of the barge, complete with gaping mouth and huge eyes; a huge spiny fin raised from the whale's back and could be raised and lowered like a kind of lateen sail. The whale was skeletal from the head back, and within the giant ribcage, the queen and several companions could be seen lounging on cushions. The whale was fitted with some kind of mechanical device that made the fish-like tail wag from side to side and the huge eyes roll in their orbs.

The crowd gasped with delight and applauded as the whale surged toward the dock, its great mouth opening wide and a tongue extending to form a gangplank. The barge bumped into the dock and two of the oarsman leaped ashore to steady the craft.

"Her majesty, Queen Elizabeth," a herald announced. Knees cracked like musket shots as the entire crowd, including the old and arthritic Privy Councillors, went down upon one knee and bowed their heads.

At the back of the crowd, Burbage and Shakespeare, bowing low from the waist, had a clear view of the action.

"Welcome our most beloved Queen, Elizabeth Gloriana," announced the herald. Elizabeth stepped from the Whale's mouth onto the dock assisted by a richly dressed man, who held one hand to steady her.

"Our gracious host, Sir Richard Wexcombe."

Something about the man's face, the pompous tilt of his head and the sneer upon his lip struck Shakespeare as familiar and he suddenly remembered: the haughty-faced lord who rode past the inn. The man threw an impatient look behind him—the kind of *hurry-up* glare one uses upon a disobedient dog—as his Lady stepped onto the dock.

"Lady Verity Wexcombe."

It was the same lady he had seen from the inn window, the woman on horseback who had dropped her handkerchief. The crowd strained to bow lower as Elizabeth floated past on the arm of her host. Lady Verity followed several paces behind and Shakespeare could not restrain himself from staring as she wafted by. Her eyes met his for a moment, and then hurriedly looked away. But long enough for him to catch her flash of recognition. Gasps and murmurs followed the Lady as she passed, for her great beauty struck everyone. Even Shakespeare was stunned. From the window he had received only a sketchy preview. Up close, her pulchritude snatched the breath from his lungs.

"A comely wench," Burbage muttered.

"Aye, me!" Shakespeare breathed, "Is there a goddess walks the earth more fair?"

A tantalising whiff of lilac and rose petals swirled in her wake. Shakespeare closed his eyes and breathed it in. The same scent clung to her handkerchief.

The crowd surged forward, following the queen and her hosts and the two players drifted with it.

"Sad for her she is married to a whey-faced popinjay," Burbage grunted. He noticed Shakespeare's silence and threw him a cautious look. "Will, think not on it. This is not the Lady for one of your tortured affections. For your cow-eyed, dunce-brained, lunatic notions of courtly love. Put it from your mind. You have a play to finish for Saturday night."

But Shakespeare was already pondering a new drama—one of a forbidden dalliance between a great Lady and a humble player.

CHAPTER 29: VALENTYNE WINSTRINGHAM

"I s that Will Shakespeare Valentyne sees?" a girlish voice cried. "And Dicky Burbage with him?"

The two players had been quietly sloping toward the kitchen tents, trying not to draw attention to themselves amid a milling press of servants, workmen, local folk delivering live chickens and humping baskets of turnips and carrots. Now someone was shouting their names aloud. Heads turned. People squinted at them with suspicion.

A cart was drawn up to one of the side doors of the huge house. A pair of burly servants dragged luggage from the back of the cart and staggered inside with it. Standing beside the cart an extravagantly dressed man was halloing and waving a linen handkerchief at them. Even though they weren't close enough to see his face, both players instantly knew who it was: Valentyne Winstringham.

Known simply by his first name, Valentyne was the chief costume-maker in the employ of Thomas Churchyard, the courtier who had the plum position of designing the masques and entertainments put on for the Royal Court. Costumes were by far the biggest expense incurred by a troupe of players and the Lord Chamberlain's Men had purchased many of Valentyne's cast-offs over the years.

The two players grinned at each other and pushed through the milling press.

"Master Valentyne," Shakespeare said. "'Tis good to see a friendly face!"

Valentyne seized his hand with both of his and warmly rung it. "And so Valentyne is glad to see your handsome face, Master Shakespeare." He released Shakespeare's cool fingers and gingerly gripped the big, moist and meaty hand of Richard Burbage. "And you, Master Burbage."

Up close, it was understandable why the two players had not recognized him. The creatures of the court were obsessed with not just following fashion, but setting new ones, to a degree of excess that scandalised the rest of English society and drew scorn and outrage from the religious element. Valentyne was not a wealthy courtier and so could not bedeck his clothes with jewels and precious stones, but he made up for it in other ways. An enormous pearl earring dangled from either ear, and his large eyes were outlined with more black kohl than an Egyptian harlot. Long, auburn tresses spilled around his shoulders and the elaborate topiary of his beard was split into several braids at the bottom and dyed in black and yellow stripes. (As Burbage was to remark later, "like a bumblebee's arse.")

"The Lord Chamberlain's Men here?" Valentyne squealed. "In Wiltshire?"

"The better half of them," Shakespeare replied. "The playhouses are shut by order of the Master of the Revels."

"Valentyne has heard this." A pomander dangled from his wrist by a pink ribbon—a dried orange stuffed with cloves and other herbs. As the two players crowded closer, he raised his arm so that the aromatic pomander dangled close to his face, perfuming the air he breathed. For the first time Shakespeare realized that he had not washed his clothes in three weeks of slogging through the English countryside in the heat of a sweaty summer and that he probably did not smell too fresh.

"But we are to play for the queen," Burbage said, as always comfortable with his own stink. "By royal commandment."

"You have a Masque planned for Sunday evening?" Shakespeare said.

Valentyne clapped his hands together in excitement, a sound muffled by the purple velvet gloves he wore. "Indeed we have. A masque such as never has been seen before. This one will put a sturgeon in your cod piece!"

"Even better than the masque at Twelfth Night?"

The Masquer rolled his eyes dramatically. "This time, Valentyne has out-Valentyned himself. Tis called *The Masque of Herne the Hunter*. And the costumes?" Valentyne put a hand to his chest, sighed dramatically and then sighed a second time, deeper, as if he would swoon. "Such mad extravagance! Twill be a masque to out-masque all others, even though Valentyne has ransacked the treasury and ruined England to do it. In truth, I tell you, there is not a groat left. The finest silks. The richest satins." His voice rose to an excited squeal. "The ladies of the court shall be transfigured into angels. The gentlemen, heroes of legend!"

The two players exchanged excited glances. They knew Valentyne was likely exaggerating only a little. Masques were elaborate dramas, part pantomime, part-dance, in which every member of the court dressed in lavish costume and played a role in an elaborate musical spectacle. With close to nine hundred courtiers likely to take part, the cost truly must have been stupendous.

"Why chose you a hunting theme?" Shakespeare asked.

Valentyne pursed his mouth and widened his eyes, striking a ridiculous face. "Why hunting, sweet Will? Surely, you jest?" He tittered, setting his earrings a-waggle. "Wexcombe House has the finest deer park in England. The old girl has been chafing to visit for years. And though the Privy Council begs her not to, Gloriana is still mad keen to ride in the hunt, though she be sixty-four." He covered his mouth with a gloved hand and dropped his voice to a conspiratorial whisper. "You should see the Privy Council when she takes horse: they make faces like ostriches birthing elephants. In truth, tis terrifying to behold, for she is naught but a bag of sticks lashed to a saddle. I hold my breath at every jump for fear an arm or leg should snap off."

He grabbed Shakespeare's hand. "Have you seen the hall we are to perform in?"

Shakespeare shook his head. "We have scarce arrived ourselves."

Valentyne giggled. "Come, grab you a chest." he nodded at the sole remaining trunk in the cart. "I shall show the pair of you the greatest hall in all England."

The soldiers guarding the threshold raised their pikes and snatched open the double doors and Oswyn Scrope tromped into the room. Inside, the Privy Council, a baker's dozen of distinguished gentlemen in fine black clothes, sat around a long table strewn with scrolls and documents. Scrope eyed them all with disdain. He considered himself a man of action while the assembled group comprised mostly antique bureaucrats: a collection of wizened grey beards with ink-stained fingers. The Privy Council conducted the business of state that must be continued, even while the monarch enjoyed the hospitality of her new hosts. They were arguing an obscure point of law when Scrope first entered. Their conversation did not lull, nor did any so much as glance his way.

He tugged off his hat. His greasy black hair was plastered to his head and he combed the hair from a forehead lumpy with pustules and nascent boils. For ten full minutes he loitered there, unnoticed by anyone. Then ten minutes more. Finally he cleared his throat, at first discretely, a second time, louder, and when that gained no response, a third time in a thunderous clatter of phlegm.

The man seated at the head of the table was a short, crooked man with a large, hydrocephalic head and the wet, bulging eyes of a spaniel. His name was Sir Robert Cecil and his position at the head of the table reflected his rank as Secretary of State. (Although, because of his physiognomy, Elizabeth fondly called him "pygmy" or "elf," either of which nickname rankled him.) An involuntary frisson of distaste rippled across his irregular features when he recognized the pursuivant. "Yes, Master Scrope," he spoke with obvious authority. "What is your business with the Privy Council?"

The pursuivant straightened his posture. "The safety of her Majesty, sir. I believe there is a plot against her by Jesuits."

One of the other council members snickered: a longhaired man in his thirties who dressed extravagantly and slouched in his chair oozing boredom. Scrope had never met the man but had heard the description of a preening young dandy who played lap dog and licked the fingers of the ageing queen—Robert Devereux, the Earl of Essex. "There is always a Jesuit plot against the queen," Essex grumbled. "What of it?"

"I have taken a Jesuit Priest in a manor close by," Scrope explained, "one Father John Pryce."

"Well then," Cecil said, eager to be done with Scrope. "He must be conveyed to the Tower and put to the torture by your master, Richard Topcliffe. This is not a matter that concerns the Privy Council."

Scrope cleared his throat; his black boots creaked as he shifted his feet. "Unfortunately, the prisoner died during the arrest."

Essex tut-tutted at the news. His long fingers caressed his silky beard. He smiled archly and said, "Then there is little doubt the fellow will keep his silence."

Scrope continued undeterred. "We did learn, sirs, that there are a great number of Jesuits at large in this Bourne. I have little doubt they are come to plot treason, since of recent I made discovery of this."

He flourished the poison dagger and all eyes gravitated to it. Although armed guards stood ready outside the door, the production of such a weapon at close quarters set the Privy Council on edge. "'Tis a fiendish device, devised as to squirt poison into the victim. A single stab wound, even a scratch, is fatal."

With that, Scrope stabbed the dagger into the polished cherry tabletop so that the dagger stuck fast and quivered. A solitary drop of the poison remained in its inner chamber and now squirted into the wood, releasing a whiff of white smoke with an audible hiss.

A frightened silence was eventually broken by Cecil who drolly noted, "Master Scrope, you have greatly injured a table belonging of our host."

"And what of the other conspirators?" Sir Christopher Hatton spoke. The contempt in his voice made it obvious how much he hated Puritans such as Scrope.

"I have no knowledge of their whereabouts as yet, which is why it is imperative that I search this building. I am well-taught in the construction of so-called *priest holes* and hidden chambers."

"But this house is owned by Sir Richard Wexcombe," Hatton added with obvious irony.

Scrope tilted his head to one side to return Hatton's stare, a crow sizing up a tossed-away piecrust. "And is this man known to you?"

Cecil interrupted, deflecting the question. "The Wexcombe family has done loyal service to the crown and to the Protestant cause since Henry's day."

"There is his wife, …" observed a badly wrinkled bald man. "… the Lady Verity, a known recusant."

"Who never fails to pay the recusancy fines." Cecil countered.

But many of the Privy Councillors reacted with concern at mention of recusants.

One of the oldest members of the Privy Council, Lord Hastings, cleared his dusty throat and spoke: "The land this house sits upon was originally owned by the wife's family, the Mortlake's, until it was stripped from them by Henry because of their refusal to convert. It fell back into the hands of the Mortlake family during the reign of Mary, only to be lost once again, this time by marriage: ceded as a dowry to Sir Richard."

"My point taken," Cecil interrupted. "This house has been safely in the hands of loyal Protestants for twenty years."

"It is the wife's sister that concerns me," Lord Hastings added. Paper rustled dryly as his frail fingers rummaged the scattered documents and pulled a page free. He pursed his lips and squinted at a long line of tiny handwriting. "There is the vexing matter of Lady Verity's siblings, Lady Sybilla Mortlake and her brother Philip," he said, reading aloud. "Both are recusants and there is no record of them attending church at any parish. Nor is there a record of them paying the recusancy fines."

"They have already quit the house," Cecil said. "Left for their own estate before the Queen's arrival."

"No doubt to avoid embarrassment to the sister," Essex said.

"Or dodge the fines they owe the crown!"

Scrope fingered the brim of his hat, ears pricked like a terrier catching the scrabble of rat somewhere behind the wainscoting. "And where lies the Mortlake family seat?"

"North," Cecil said, searching the document in front of him and then finding it. "In Lancashire, three or four day's ride from here."

"Lancashire is a hotbed of recusancy." Scrope said. "A county where Jesuit priests swarm like fleas in a jezebel's bed!"

"A *hot* bed," Essex enunciated with relish. "Something I have not enjoyed since London." He guffawed at his own joke. When no one else joined in, he added carelessly, "'Tis a trifling matter, easily recompensed."

"As easy as capturing the fort at Cadiz?" asked another counsellor. This did raise laughter from the other councillors.

Essex's face blackened with rage. He ground his molars and hurled the man a look of pure death, but said nothing. "Aye," he spat, close to losing his temper. "Send a rider to the house and fetch them hence to face questioning." For the first time Essex turned in his chair to glare at the pursuivant. "Well? You have your orders, Master Scrope. Why do you tarry?"

Burbage heaved the chest from the back of the cart and dropped in on the ground at their feet. Shakespeare grabbed the iron handle on the other side of the chest and vertebrae cracked as he hoisted it up. "God's Wounds!" he grunted. "Surely this chest holds a dead horse and its rider!"

"Come along!" Valentyne shushed. "And peace!"

Even Burbage was sucking wind as they followed Valentyne's

mincing gait along a gloomy panelled in dark cherry and hung with family portraits of the Wexcombes. They passed a grand staircase and saw the two burly fellows step from a doorway up ahead.

"Ah," Valentyne said and lead the way into an enormous hall. Shakespeare and Burbage strained in after him, feet shuffling in baby steps as the enormous trunk strained to rip the player's arms from their sockets. They thumped the trunk down next to an accumulating mountain of luggage and stood looking around at the huge hall as they paused to draw breath.

"Tis … tis a … goodly space." Shakespeare panted.

"Very handsome," Burbage agreed. "And larger than any in London."

"Is it not fabulous?" Valentyne asked. "And come Wednesday, after I have performed my magic, you will rub your eyes and think you dream." Valentyne saw the puzzlement on their features and put two gloved fingers to his lips and went, "tee-hee."

Their chore completed, the players fled the hall. As commoners, they were not allowed to mix with courtiers and hastened to leave the building. However, as they skipped past the staircase, Shakespeare's eyes were pulled upward by the repeating yawn of steps and what he saw at the top of the stairs stole locomotion. Burbage continued on another twenty feet before he turned to say something to his friend and noticed he was alone.

"Will!" Burbage shouted. The big man threw his friend an impatient *let-us-be-gone!* wave. Shakespeare looked at him blankly for a moment, but then turned his gaze upward and vanished from view as something drew him up the stairs.

Burbage found his friend at the top of the stairs, staring raptly at two large portraits of the master and mistress of Wexcombe House. Like most portraitists, the painter was a flattering liar; but he had accurately captured Sir Richard's haughtiness, the sardonic narrowing of the eyes, and the cruel twist of the mouth, right down to the arrogance twirled tight into each waxed mustachio. Here was a shallow puddle of a man whose face hid nothing and who put on his pride and spitefulness every morning like a favourite shirt.

The players' gaze swept over Lady Verity's portrait. By contrast, hers was a face like a mountain lake, a blank mirror the eyes skipped off, reflecting all but revealing little of the dark currents roiling in its depths. The painter had captured nothing but the mask of beauty: the fine features, the slender, aristocratic nose, the full lips, and the limpid doe eyes.

"Aye me …" Shakespeare breathed. "Those eyes do beguile me."

Burbage studied the lady's eyes and frowned. "Drowning pools," he muttered. "And no doubt they have lured in many men before her husband."

"Nay," Shakespeare countered. "I'll not believe it. She seems a gentle and pious lady. See," he pointed to the portrait, "she wears a great cross of gold."

"As does the Archbishop of Westminster, and half the town is peopled with his bastards."

Shakespeare threw a look of irritation at his friend, but when he returned his gaze to the paintings, he suddenly noticed something. "These have been moved," Shakespeare said, his finger tracing the ghostly outline of a frame in the sun-faded panelling. "Larger portraits once hung here."

"They are the Lord and Lady of the house," Burbage said. "What else could have hung here?"

But Shakespeare had no answer.

CHAPTER 30: THE HANGING TREE

When our minibus jounces into the parking lot of the White Hart, there's a white estate car parked out front with an official seal of Marlborough County Council on the doors. The driver stands at the foot of the oak tree, examining it, craning his neck to peer up at the twisted snarl of branches, pen scratching on a clipboard.

Oh God, I think, *a man with a clipboard.* This cannot be good.

As Gillian and the Crusty Bunch scamper indoors, I fix my face in the sombre expression suited to a mature member of the local business community and stroll over to speak with him. Close up, I see that he's young, a kid really, probably mid-twenties, with the dishevelled mop of gelled-up hair that passes for a haircut these days and a shabby Mac over a cheap Marks and Sparks suit. Excellent, I think. I'll use my obvious authority to show him whose boss. "Can I help you?" I say, putting on my snooty voice. "I'm Harvey Braithwaite, the owner of these premises."

He glances at his clipboard, checking that my name tallies with what's written there.

"Mister Braithwaite," The morose youth does not return my smile as we shake hands. "My name's Pollard. I'm here about your tree.

At first I think he's having a laugh, giving me a joke name, but keep schtum just in case. "Yes. As you can see," I continue, "it's pretty dangerous. I'd like to take it down before it falls down."

The ironically named Pollard studies the decrepit oak for a few seconds, lovingly palming the scabby bark of the trunk, then throws a perfunctory glance at my treasured blue Jensen parked beneath, which is nearly white with bird shit. "This tree is ancient, Mister Braithwaite, but I can assure you, it is quite healthy. It will probably be here long after you and I have gone."

If I had a pickaxe handle in my hands he'd be gone in the next few seconds. Still, this is not what I was expecting. "No," I argue. "You can see. Look at that limb. It's ready to drop. I'm afraid that one of my customers will get—"

"The tree is a listed local landmark," he interrupts. "It was known as the hanging tree because it was used in executions. A number of famous highwaymen and criminals were hanged from it. There's even a reference to it in the Domesday Book.

"Don't think I've read that," I say. "Is that one of Grisham's?"

The council bloke makes a put upon face: even he can detect sarcasm.

"It's dangerous," I insist. "I'm afraid for the safety of my customers. If one of those limbs breaks off …"

He throws a conspicuous look around the parking lot. Not a single car other than mine. Then he eyes my Jensen Interceptor like it's made of pure shit, which it is starting to look like. The owl has evidently been on a purge. His glance ricochets between car, tree, and finally comes to rest on me. "You might want to park your car some-where else, sir. That might be the easiest solution."

"Look," I say, exasperation tightening my throat. "This is my pub, and my parking lot—"

"I'm sorry, sir. It's listed. You can't touch it."

I choke on my anger. "A local landmark . . ." I trail off, exasperated. "But it's a public bloody nuisance!"

He turns his back on my rage and climbs into his car. As he drives away I shout helplessly after him. "And this is where my bloody taxes go? Eh? Is it? This is supposed to be a free country! Property owners have rights, too!"

But I may as well shout up the exhaust pipe of the yobbo's car, because he is long gone.

"Yell a bit louder, he's almost out of sight."

I spin around at the slurred voice behind me. Of course, it's Sidney, pipe hooked in one corner of his gob. "The bank manager called," he says. "He wantsh chew to call him back."

"Sod the bloody bank manager ... and sod the bloody council." I start to walk away, but then a thought occurs to me. I stop and hurl a probing look at Sidney. "Do you know if they sell chainsaws at B&Q?"

CHAPTER 31: PURSUIVANTS AND PRETENDERS

"For what do we search, Master Scrope?"

"Hollow spots in the walls. Voids. Cavities."

Oswyn Scrope and Anthony Munday were treading one of the long hallways of Wexcombe Manor. They appeared to be on a casual stroll, dawdling along, except that Oswyn Scrope gripped a thin iron rod in one hand, which he casually rapped against the stonework, trying to gauge by its ring whether the bricks were solid or hid an empty space behind. In truth, it was near impossible, for the hallways bustled with noisy courtiers hurrying toward the banqueting tents where evening supper was being served. Their babbling talk and raucous laughter, and the constant need for the pursuivants to step aside, made the task nigh impossible.

At the end of the hallway, an elderly man, his white-bearded face creased from a life of worry, stood watching their progress. When they came close, he strode by the Pursuivants, barely pausing as he spoke quick words to Scrope. "I would share words with you privily, brother."

Scrope recognized the man as Lord Hastings, one of the Queen's Privy Council. He had made only one comment during Scrope's brief interview and scarcely rested his eyes upon the Pursuivant, so his stealthy approach was puzzling. Hastings continued on down the hallway as if nothing had been said, and paused to slip into a side room.

Scrope handed his companion the iron rod. "Continue, Master Munday" he said, and then followed after the councillor.

The room was a handsomely furnished library with many books chained to their shelves. Huge portraits lined the walls—likenesses of the Wexcombe family going back generations. The walls were decorated with elaborate floral wallpaper that irritated Scrope with its trivial gaiety. A band of golden mesh ran around the top of the wainscoting.

The elderly man lingered by the window, looking out. The library windows were the typical Tudor crosshatched glass but had the Wexcombe coat of arms, a rampant hart on a field of red chevrons in stained glass set into it. When Scrope joined the man at the window, his face glowed with red light.

"I speak to you now as a brother in the true faith," Hastings said. Like the other Privy Council members, Hastings dressed almost entirely in black, but the simplicity of his clothes and the lack of adornment, uncommon among other councillors, identified him alone as a fellow Puritan.

"I am your servant, sir," Scrope said.

Even though they were quite alone, Hastings stooped closer and lowered his voice. He was a cautious man who had survived to old age by mastering the art of whispering in shadows. "These are words I would share with none other, as they touch upon the very life of the Queen."

Scrope threw a quick look about the room, shifting uncomfortably under the scrutiny of so many painted gazes that seemed to eavesdrop upon their every word. He returned his eyes to Hasting's face and nodded for him to continue.

"There is more to the story of Lady Verity and the Mortlake family than was spoken of this morning."

Scrope's eyes narrowed like a deerhound catching the scent of game.

"The family is more of a concern than merely for dodging the recusancy fines. As you might know I am the only surviving Privy Councillor to have served under—I should say, survived—Mary's reign. Shamed as I am to admit the truth, I hid my faith back then. My fellow councillors who did not paid with their lives."

Scrope's eyes widened at the mention of Elizabeth's sister, Mary Tudor. Mary reversed her father Henry VIII and returned England briefly to Catholicism. It was a time when hundreds of Protestants were burned at the stake and earned her the name by which she was still known: "Bloody Mary."

"When the Lady Elizabeth ascended the throne, there was no end of plots, no end of pretenders to the throne championed by Catholics. Most were executed, but one family still has a claim, though distant, to the throne of England."

Scrope's heart quickened. "The Mortlake family?"

The old man nodded, the red light filtering through the glass kindling the memory of those crackling pyres of long ago.

Scrope licked his chapped lips and tugged at the collar that chafed the carbuncle on his neck. "So this Philip Mortlake—"

Lord Hastings shook his head. "Nay. Not he. Philip is but a half-brother, a bastard born of the family's serving wench—though tis not well known. The true blood line runs through the female side."

"Lady Verity, the wife of Sir Richard?"

Hastings shook his head, his grey beard rustling against his simple white collar. "Again, no, she is the youngest and last born. It is her elder sister, Sybilla Mortlake. Though born well into Elizabeth's reign, she is a Catholic and I have always feared that her place in the ascendancy—no matter how remote—could serve as a rallying point for Catholics eager to topsy-turvy this country. The Queen is sixty-four. She has produced no heir to the throne, nor can the Privy Council beg, bully, plead, or cajole her to name one. Her majesty will not be moved on this most prickly issue. But men such as you and I would not wish to live in an England squirming under a papist boot heel."

Scrope nodded. If a Catholic were to become monarch, then Puritans such as Lord Hastings and himself would be the first to burn in their fires.

"The Mortlake family was once wealthy," Hastings continued, "but were stripped of lands and property during Henry's reign. The lands were given to Sir John Wexcombe, a favourite of the king's. This proved a source of much enmity between the two families. To make amends, Sir John betrothed his son Richard at age nine to Sybilla, the first-born girl. But when Sir Richard grew to manhood, he broke his betrothal and married the younger daughter, Verity."

"I begin to fathom the weave of this tale," Scrope said. He thought he heard the ghost of a whisper and turned to throw a look over his shoulder. The painted stare of Sir John Wexcombe, a white-haired man in steely armour, glowered down at him. The sound must have come from another clutch of noisy courtiers passing in the hallway.

"That is all I have to say," Lord Hastings concluded. "I will leave now. Wait a moment before you follow. Tis safer we are not seen whispering together."

Lord Hastings shuffled to the door, opened it a crack and peered out, then slipped into the hallway and pulled the door closed behind him.

Scrope thought about the implications of this new piece of information. He knew the faceless corpse was somehow tied in with a Catholic plot, although he could not discover how the knot was tied. He had hoped to snare the conspirators in a neat bundle to be delivered to his master, Richard Topcliffe. Now he was beginning to think he might need to ask for his master's help, for as much as it irked his pride, when stakes were so high it was safer to ask for help than to fail.

When enough time had passed. Scrope stepped to the door, opened it quietly and stepped out.

The painted portraits of the Wexcombe family continued to stare blindly into the empty room. But just beneath the portrait of Sir John, the mesh screen darkened as the face that had pressed up against it was drawn away.

"Will Shakespeare, we have died and entered heaven."
The two players had crawled beneath the flap of one of the three huge kitchen tents. Elizabeth's court was a giant stomach, always needing filling. Feeding a thousand courtiers and their retinue was a thrice-daily war where a culinary army of cooks did battle with their own weapons: bubbling pots, sizzling skillets, hot ovens roasting joints.

Ignored by all, Shakespeare and Burbage wandered as if invisible through a melee of carving and chopping and slicing tender joints of mutton and beef before ladening them onto serving trays that the kitchen boys groaned beneath as they hustled them to the banqueting halls. A nimbus of steam rose from a long table where pies of every kind—beef, fish, fruit, venison, chicken—had been set to cool. Atop another table, log jams of boiled sausages, cooked leeks, roasted potatoes, turnips and meat, meat, meat everywhere. Every beast of barnyard and forest that could be skinned, flayed, plucked and broiled swung from cruel hooks dangling from the ridgepole.

Burbage and Shakespeare gorged their way along the tables, chomping pastry crusts, sucking the tender meat from chicken drumsticks, crunching manchets[1] of crusty, warm bread.

What they could not stuff into their mouths they shoved into their pockets and tucked into their doublets, reasoning they would share the booty with their fellow players once they returned to the Inn. They paused for breath when they reached the far end of the tent and stood in the cool breeze of the open tent flap, wiping sweat from their brows and the grease running down the corners of their mouths on the cuffs of their sleeves.

"Ah, if only the lads were here," Shakespeare lamented.

"Aye," Burbage agreed and belched volcanically. "If only—"

The two men looked at one another and chuckled like naughty schoolboys.

The kitchen tents stood close to a hedge, which served as a defacto borderline. This side of the hedge was for working folk: labourers and non-courtesans such as the two players. The other side of the hedge was for courtiers only, or servants to courtiers who had a good reason for being there. As part of the entertainments, a special fountain had been put up on the courtiers' side. The fountain was a figure of Diana, the huntress, ingeniously constructed so that white wine spurted from her right breast and red wine from the left. The wine splashed into two collecting bowls she held in either hand. A nearby ledge held goblets so that courtiers could help themselves to the drink.

"Hell's teeth!" Burbage said upon spying the statue, "If only such a woman were real. I would suck at those mammets for the rest of my life."

Just then a door on the side of the house opened and a female figure emerged. Shakespeare saw her and goggled. It was her—Lady Verity. She looked both ways, then stepped from the door and walked slowly but in a straight line toward the hedge maze at the edge of the knot garden.

"There goes a pair of mammets I would rather suck at," Shakespeare muttered. He shoved the pie he was eating in Burbage's hands. "Lay teeth to this," he said, wiping his hands on his breeches. "I have business anon."

"Business? What kind of business?"

"Hunting business. Gloriana came here to hunt the Hart. Will Shakespeare came to hunt a heart of a different kind."

Burbage followed Shakespeare's gaze of unconcealed lust to its object and threw him a doubting look. "The Lady Verity?" He gasped with exasperation and shook his head in disapproval. "Will, poach the hind in this fellow's deer park and you will be lucky to escape a whipping. Poach this fellow's wife and you will be broken on the wheel for it. Put such madness from your mind. The Inn-Keeper's daughter can be tumbled for a sixpence and you may forget her the instant you have groaned out your seed."

"Ah me, those eyes …" Shakespeare said. "I can think of nothing else." He flung aside the tent flap, hurried to the hedge, and slipped through an opening, making straight toward the maze. Lady Verity had entered by the northern end. He scurried to the southern entrance and ducked inside.

The hedges were nine feet tall. Screened from the setting sun, the inside of the maze was shaded and gloomy. He was safe from view in here, but first had to navigate the labyrinth to find his reward. In his haste, he made a dozen wrong turnings and several times ran face-first into a wall of hedge. He took turning after turning until his sense of direction became as tangled and knotted as a kitten's ball of wool. Finally, he turned a corner and stumbled into an open space at the maze's centre where water muttered in a stone fountain.

A single torch burned close by. The lady was there, but she was not alone. Surprised, Shakespeare dodged back from view. For a moment he thought the lady had seen him, for her head lifted. He stole a quick peek and saw she was speaking with a shadow that lurked behind her and which now stepped forward, revealing himself to be a nobleman.

Shakespeare's spine stiffened. The man was none other than Sir Richard Wexcombe, her haughty-faced husband. The two stood close together, engaged in intense conversation that did not look friendly. For a moment, Shakespeare puzzled why the Lord of the House would have to creep into a hedge maze to speak with his own wife, but then he tumbled to it. With the house swarming with eavesdropping courtiers, there was scarce a room, a closet, a private window nook one could speak in. And unless he was mistaken, it looked as if the Lord was speaking harsh words to his lady: an argument, no doubt, over something amiss in hosting the Queen beneath his roof.

After several long minutes, Shakespeare stole another peek and was in time to see Sir Richard speak a final harshness to his wife, and then curtly turn on his heel and stalk away, his back stiff with anger. The lady remained behind, her head bowed as if in thought. It seemed as though she could sense his presence. Then she reached out a hand and played her slender fingers in the fountain's gentle spray of water, deep in thought.

Shakespeare stepped from behind the hedge wall. Startled, the Lady gasped and flinched back; a hand reflexively flew to the large gold crucifix hanging around her neck. "Who lurks in the shadows?" she said. "Come forward so I might see your face."

Shakespeare drew off his cap and threw her a courtly bow.

"Forgive me, milady. I wear this cloak of shadows as the lonely moon wears its cloak of night, shamed by comparison to the radiant sun that turns night into day by its glorious presence."

As he took a step closer, light swept the shadows from his face. "Beg pardon," he said. "I merely wished to return this." He drew the handkerchief from his doublet and held it out to her.

Recognition lit in her eyes; still, her demeanour remained guarded. She looked at the handkerchief timidly, hesitant. "I assure you, sir, tis not mine."

Shakespeare drew the handkerchief to his nose and inhaled deeply. "And yet could there two such intoxicating scents?" He breathed deeper. "Lilac, rose petals ... and a pinch of lavender? A perfume such as sweet roses would swoon at?"

She shook her head. "No. I say again, tis not mine."

He held the handkerchief tantalisingly close, but just out of her reach. "And yet it is embroidered with the letter *V*." He paused before completing the thought: "*V*... for Verity?"

It took a moment and then realization flashed in her eyes. The embroidered *V* left no doubt as to the owner, and could be incriminating. Suddenly, she wanted it back. "Yes. Methinks I do recall dropping such a handkerchief. Are you the impudent rascal at the inn window?"

"Aye."

"You are with the court?" she asked, but from the way she appraised his clothing it was clear she did not think so.

"After a fashion. I am player and poet with the Lord Chamberlain's Men. We are to perform a play of mine tomorrow eve for the queen's pleasure."

"Ah," she breathed. "You are a poet. That explains the candied words that kiss my ears."

Shakespeare smiled handsomely. "I assure you, madam, my lips make far better attendants."

"Saucy fellow," she scolded, but her expression was playful. "You speak above your station. My husband is a strong and prideful man. He would slay you for speaking thus."

"Then call him back and let him slay me, before your beauty murders me."

She preened at his flattery. "I think your wit, master poet, is keener than any blade."

She reached out and grabbed the handkerchief. But Shakespeare held firm and would not relinquish it. "Might there be a reward," he asked, "for its return?"

The soft brown eyes dropped modestly. "I thank you, sir, for your gallantry."

She tugged again, but Shakespeare held tight. "There are many ways a lady might reward gallantry with more than airy words."

The two stood, their fingers almost touching, each holding the handkerchief while their eyes fenced. A mysterious smile floated to her lips and she relinquished her hold. Shakespeare was at first disappointed, but then she said, "I am sure the lady who lost this handkerchief would wish for its return, but perhaps at a more opportune time, when she might show her favour with a worthier demonstration of gratitude."

She smiled a final time, and then turned and walked away, leaving the turf maze by the entrance Shakespeare had used. Not wishing to seem as if he were following her, Shakespeare instead left by the other way in. It took several cursing minutes of wrong turns and then he spotted the entrance and flung himself toward it ...

... and almost collided with Sir Richard Wexcombe. Both men recoiled at the last moment and stepped back. Sir Richard looked startled.

"A goodly maze." Shakespeare said, patting the hedge wall as if he had been giving it his personal inspection. "Very ... er ... um ... mazy." He quickly bowed before the other man had chance to get a good look at his face and the two brushed shoulders as he barged past.

"Lucky to get away with that one, Will," Shakespeare muttered to himself as he scurried to reach the safety of the commoner's side of the hedge.

But he had not been lucky. Sir Richard had had chance to get a clear look at his face, as Shakespeare was soon to find out.

Burbage had disappeared when Shakespeare reached the other side of the fence, but then the poet spotted him, still on the safe side of the hedge, but fishing. He had stolen a long pole from somewhere— one of those used to hold a tent flap up. He had a goblet lashed to one end and was thrusting it through a hole he had knifed out in the hedge.

"If you're fishing, Dick, you would do better to stand closer to the stream."

"Indeed, I am close enough," Burbage spoke over his shoulder. "And to two streams: one white one red."

Burbage flashed an evil grin look and nodded at the hole in the hedge he had cut with his knife. On the far side of the hedge stood the fountain of Diana with wine spurting from either breast. Burbage extended the pole until the goblet hovered beneath the statue's breasts, holding the goblet beneath one of the streams as he filled it. He reeled the goblet back in and handed his fishing pole to Shakespeare. "The left tit gives white wine. The right tit gives red. Myself, I am a right tit man."

Shakespeare needed some wine after his recent encounter and quickly drained the goblet. Burbage pushed the stick back through the hole in the hedge and extended the pole toward the statue. "I think I shall have a mix of white and red," he said, moving the goblet back and forth, filling it with a little from each stream.

An outraged voice burst from the other side of the hedge. "Who dares steal the queen's wine? Rogues! Base thieves! This drink is for courtiers only!"

Shakespeare looked at Burbage. "I think you have been found out, Dick."

A quick peek through the hole revealed the owner of the voice: a servant, probably belonging to the household. He grabbed the goblet lashed to the pole. Burbage pulled back and a tug of war ensued, the pole sawing back and forth.

"Lend me your hand, Will!"

Shakespeare latched onto the end of the pole and the two men gave a mighty yank. A cry of distress came from the other side of the fence followed by the crash of falling stone. Suddenly, the pole came free and Burbage drew it from the hedge. They peered through the hedge to see the servant lying amid the toppled remains of Diana's fountain, which had broken in pieces. Wine sprayed freely into the air, soaking the man, who struggled to free himself.

"Fire the cannon," Burbage said. "'Tis time to go!" Choking with laughter, the two players scurried away. They ran around to the far side of the house where dogs frisked and gambolled on a large open lawn: big dogs of various breeds: deerhounds, mastiffs, wolfhounds. But these were not house pets that slumbered by their master's feet in front of the fire and looked up with soft eyes. These were working dogs bred and kept in kennels and taken out only to hunt. On the days they did not catch the deer, they would be cursed and kicked all the way home. If they caught a deer, they were often allowed to rip the dying beast until their muzzles were bloodied. Some courtiers had released the hounds from their kennels for exercise and now they bounded and tussled as they ran around the grassy lawn. As Shakespeare watched, he noted a small form in the midst of the barking clamour: a young boy. The boy turned his face and Shakespeare's blood froze in his veins. It was his Hamnet, his darling boy. Even from a distance he recognized the curve of the young neck, the tousled mop of brown-blonde hair, the slender bow of his young shoulders.

"Hamnet?" Shakespeare whispered and stumbled forward.

But then the boy turned his face full on, and Shakespeare saw that, though the face was fair, it was not his boy. A stab of familiar betrayal pierced his heart. In truth the boy was a peasant and he followed the dogs, picking up their turds and dropping them in a leather bucket. But a moment's extra observation revealed that the boy was not playing with the dogs—they were playing with him, as when a live rabbit is tossed to the pack to get their blood up before the hunt begins. The dogs' aggression grew. They snapped at the boy's legs and exposed hands. A hound barged into him and the bucket flew from his hands. He staggered.

Stay on your feet! Shakespeare thought, with rising panic. *Do not fall among the dogs or they will tear you.*

But then a giant wolfhound charged the boy from behind and bowled him over. The boy shrieked and went down in a snarling maelstrom of fur and snapping teeth, screaming as the dogs nosed and nipped him.

Shakespeare ran toward the boy, meat pies and drumsticks tumbling from his doublet as he ran. Burbage's shouted from behind, calling for him to come back, but he never heard it. He ploughed into the press of dog flesh, shouting and kicking and punching to reach the fallen boy. A tiny arm appeared in the scrum and Shakespeare grabbed it, hauling the boy to his feet. The wolfhound lunged at Shakespeare's groin, lips snarled back from the gums, flashing sharp teeth. The player clutched the only weapon to hand—a huge sausage tucked in his doublet and clubbed the dog atop its head. The sausage burst with the force of the blow, flinging chunks of hot meat in all directions. The wolfhound whined and leapt away while the other dogs rushed in to gobble up the sausage innards. A hole in the milling pack opened and Shakespeare carried the boy clear and set him down his feet. The small body was shaking with terror, the boy's eyes starred with tears.

"What do you mean, striking my dog, sirrah?"

Shakespeare looked around. A nobleman in fine clothes strode toward him; he had a rich cape thrown around his shoulders, a gleaming rapier jostling at his hip. As he drew closer, the form became recognisable: Sir Richard Wexcombe.

Shakespeare suddenly lost his words.

"How dare you strike Zeus!" Sir Richard's face purpled with rage. His hand flew to the handle of his rapier, loosening the blade. Shakespeare had no weapon other than the flaccid sausage in his hand.

"The dogs' grew overly heated, sir," Shakespeare explained. "They were set to savage this boy."

Sir Richard had not been aware of the boy until now, but discounted him with the briefest of glances before his eyes locked once again with Shakespeare's.

"Of what import is that? He is a filthy little peasant. We run down peasants here for sport."

"Surely, for the sake of Christian love—"

"Christian love be damned and you with it! Who are you, sirrah?"

Shakespeare hesitated, reluctant to give up his name but then Sir Richard's eyes narrowed with recognition. "Wait! I know you! The bumbling fool in the hedge maze. I think you were sniffing around my bitch." Sir Richard's hand flew to the pommel of his rapier and started to draw. "Villain! I'll make you crawl on stumps."

Shakespeare took a step backward, expecting the worse, but then Sir Richard's gaze fell upon something over Shakespeare's shoulder. He gasped. His eyes widened. His mouth fell open. He stared glassy-eyed, his head tremoring atop his neck. The hand atop the rapier shook. The grip loosed and the sword slid back in its sheath. Slowly, like a puppet with rusty iron joints, Sir Richard turned first his body, and finally his head, wrenching free his gaze at the last moment. He tottered away as if his knees might buckle. He reached the low wall outside the house and leaned heavily upon the wall for support. After a few moments, he finally gathered himself, and then stumbled the last few feet and fell in at the door.

Stunned, Shakespeare threw a look behind his shoulder to see what could have possibly caused the look of horror on Sir Richard's face, but saw nothing. Burbage remained where Shakespeare had left him, penned behind the barrier of the hedge and now he raised both arms and threw him a baffled shrug. Shakespeare looked a second time.

Nothing.

Just knots of courtiers idling about the grounds, sipping wine and conversing. Whatever had caused the look on Sir Richard's face was invisible, or was, perhaps, a phantom conjured by his mind.

But then Shakespeare noticed one of the courtiers eyeing him. The man seemed vaguely familiar. He recognized the clothes first: the plumed puce bonnet, the gold brocade cape, and the elaborately tooled leather gauntlets.

Rafe Foxe.

The Coney-Catcher loitered close enough to a knot of courtiers to be taken as part of their group, but a second look made it obvious he was not with them. He stood sipping wine from a glass goblet and now he raised it in salute to Shakespeare and flashed him a smile crammed with teeth.

Rafe Foxe, who had mysteriously vanished from a locked cellar outside of which a guard was posted—albeit a drunken one.

As Shakespeare strode back toward Burbage and the safety of the servant's side of the hedgerow, he puzzled over what was happening. Something strange was going on at Wexford House. Something very strange.

CHAPTER 32: GHOSTS

T he windows of the inn looked out like the dark eye sockets of a grimacing skull hunched in stony sleep. It was almost eleven o'clock when the two players fell in through the front door, stumbling with weariness. Burbage thumped Shakespeare on the shoulder, muttered "good night" and left him to climb the rickety stairs alone while he slipped through the shadowed darkness toward his nightly kitchen assignation.

Shakespeare slogged up the stairs, his shoulders sagging beneath a fatigue both physical and spiritual. With Scrope and his men billeted in the Inn, Kempe, Pope and Heminges had had to bunk together three a'bed with Young Sam sleeping on the floor. As he passed the room that had formerly belonged to Heminges alone, a sliver of light showed that the door was cracked and a candle burned inside. A floorboard groaned underfoot as he passed and a stern voice reached from behind the door and caught him by the ear.

"Master Shakespeare, come hither. I would share words with you."

He knew the voice instantly. When he pushed open the door, Oswyn Scrope knelt at his bedside, hands clasped in prayer, an open Bible on the floor before him. Shakespeare could not help noticing that he knelt on an iron rod set beneath his knees—part of the Puritan

CHAPTER 32: GHOSTS

The windows of the inn looked out like the dark eye sockets of a grimacing skull hunched in stony sleep. It was almost eleven o'clock when the two players fell in through the front door, stumbling with weariness. Burbage thumped Shakespeare on the shoulder, muttered "good night" and left him to climb the rickety stairs alone while he slipped through the shadowed darkness toward his nightly kitchen assignation.

Shakespeare slogged up the stairs, his shoulders sagging beneath a fatigue both physical and spiritual. With Scrope and his men billeted in the Inn, Kempe, Pope and Heminges had had to bunk together three a'bed with Young Sam sleeping on the floor. As he passed the room that had formerly belonged to Heminges alone, a sliver of light showed that the door was cracked and a candle burned inside. A floorboard groaned underfoot as he passed and a stern voice reached from behind the door and caught him by the ear.

"Master Shakespeare, come hither. I would share words with you."

He knew the voice instantly. When he pushed open the door, Oswyn Scrope knelt at his bedside, hands clasped in prayer, an open Bible on the floor before him. Shakespeare could not help noticing that he knelt on an iron rod set beneath his knees—part of the Puritan insistence on making even prayer an exercise in the chastisement of the flesh, the better to prepare the soul for the balms of heaven.

Scrope did not look up as he addressed the playwright, but kept his head bowed, hands together, and his dark eyes on the open Bible. "What have you to tell me?" Even the pursuivant's voice had the bruising texture of a stony road trod barefoot.

Shakespeare thought about the Lady Verity. In fact, he had thought of nothing else since his encounter with her, and her soft doe-eyes were all he could see when he looked into his mind. But he was not about to have the image of her soiled by brushing up against the malodorous Scrope. And yet, he must appease the pursuivant with something, if only the tiniest shred of information.

"The rascal you locked in the cellar, Rafe Foxe . . ."

"Aye?"

"He parades among the courtiers. Drinks the Queen's wine. Takes his ease there, bold as a midday moon."

"Does he, indeed? Saucy rogue! But he is not my concern. "What of the matter we spoke of?"

"Nothing . . . as yet.

"And nothing will be the pages I give back to you. I advise you to seek harder."

Shakespeare waited and when no more words were forthcoming, it became clear the interrogation had ended. He left the room and continued up the hall. As he passed a room where several of Scrope's soldiers had been billeted, he heard grunting and the creaking of a bed frame, testifying that young Connie was busy warming someone else's bed. Suffused with dread weariness, he pushed into his room and slumped at the table before the window. A candle flame fluttered, drowning in a pool of wax. He stared out the window. Minutes passed as darkness swarmed in his eyes. And then he saw an amorphous white shape drifting through the trees on the other side of the Great Road.

He blinked and looked again. Nothing. The white shape had vanished. Had he really seen something? No, it was nothing more than the candle flame's after-image, dancing on the back of his eyes.

His own words to Sam Gilbourne came back to him: *There are no ghosts in the forest. Ghosts cling to dark places: houses and castle dungeons where murderous deeds have been done and where they left their lives behind.*

No, he decided. *No one has died here of late. So how could there be any ghosts?*

CHAPTER 33: THE ROYAL HUNT OF THE HART

They found the dead man the next morning.

When Shakespeare dragged his feet downstairs, yawning, the rest of the Lord Chamberlain's Men were already at table, breaking their fast. The two pursuivants—Scrope and Munday—sat at a small table by the window. The common soldiers did not repast inside the inn, but took their meals in the open air with the farm animals.

"How comes the play, sweet Will?" Heminges asked. He affected a casual tone, yet the question irked Shakespeare, who recognized it for the prying nag it truly was.

"It comes well," the Stratford player said, "and it goes well, although as yet I cannot see its final destination."

"Your play must have an end, Will." Burbage said, tearing off a chunk of bread and chewing slack-jawed as he spoke. "We cannot extemporise a whole play, lest we be hissed from the boards."

Shakespeare cringed at the words, for Burbage said it loud enough for the pursuivants to hear—specifically for Anthony Munday, who turned and hurled a hateful look at the big man.

Connie bustled in from the kitchen and threw Shakespeare a curt-sey. "What might I bring you, sir?"

"Ale," Shakespeare said grumpily. (He had enjoyed only a few hours sleep.) The young maiden bent low over the table, wiping up an imaginary spills as she buried his nose in her cleavage.

"I missed your poetry last night," she whispered under her breath, wiping vigorously at the table with her cloth. "I missed your cunning tongue." Connie straightened up and tucked the rag in her apron. "I shall fetch your ale," she said, emphasising the word *fetch* and flounced away to the kitchens. She returned a moment later and set a tankard in front of Shakespeare.

"Wench!" Scrope called, snapping his fingers at her. She threw him a cutting look and tore herself away from Shakespeare's side.

"What might I bring you sirs?" she asked.

"Water," Scrope said, apparently ordering for Munday, too.

Connie wrinkled her nose. "Water, sir? Just water?"

"Aye, wench, water," Scrope said with irritation. "And be sharp about it!"

No one ever ordered water. It was a liquid often tainted and most people thought it a drink fit only for horses and beasts of the field. Small wonder that Puritans such as Scrope were not welcome guests at inns or taverns.

"I must go and draw it from the well," she said, and scowled out the door. A few moments later she scowled back in and banged two sloshing tankards down in front of the pursuivants.

"Your water, sirs," she said, sulkily and fled for the kitchen.

Scrope lifted his tankard and quaffed deeply, his enormous Adam's apple bobbing. He smacked his lips and made a sour face, then fished in his mouth with his fingertips and pulled something out. "A spider in my water," he snarled and hurled it to the floor. "He took a second sip and, once again, found something in his mouth. "Another!" But then he looked closer at what he pulled from his mouth. "Nay, tis an eyelash. A whole eyes' worth of eyelashes!"

Connie was just stepping back into the room when Scrope seized her by the wrist. "Wench!" he barked. "This water's befouled. Go and draw us some more!"

Connie snatched her arm free and glared at him, then stalked silently back into the kitchen. They heard her bang out the kitchen door and stomp toward the well.

Thom Pope leaned across the table toward young Sam Guilbourne. "How did you sleep last night, young Sam? No evil trolls peeking at you from the cupboard?"

"Tis not funny!" Sam snapped, face reddening.

"What's this?" Shakespeare asked. It was obvious he had missed out on an earlier conversation.

"Mock not the lad," Will Kempe said mildly. The clown looked at Shakespeare. "The first night we stayed here, Sam had a bad dream, that's all."

"Aye," Thom Pope interjected, "The lad said he saw a hairy troll climb out of the cupboard in the night. The troll danced upon the foot of his bed and pointed a finger at him."

Sam Guilbourne covered his ears with his hands. "Shut up! It was not a dream. I saw him. I did!"

"Screamed like a babe," Pope guffawed. "Woke us all up. You never heard such a carry-on!"

A piercing shriek from outside made everyone jump. It paused only long enough for the screamer to suck in a second breath and resumed, a high, jangling, nerve-ripping scream.

"Connie!" Shakespeare said, as the table of players jumped to their feet.

Everyone ran outside. Scrope's soldiers had been sitting in the shade of the trees at the far side of the road, and now they hurried over, swords drawn and ready. Connie stood by the side of the well, hands clamped over her mouth, staring down the dark shaft.

"What is it girl?" Scrope demanded.

Connie pointed a quaking finger. "A face ... in the well. I drew it up with the bucket!"

Men leaned around the low stone wall, staring down at the distant circle of flat calm water.

Nothing.

Scrope nodded to Sergeant Crugg to wind up the bucket. When he cranked the handle, the bucket came up and, just as it broke the surface, dredged up with it a drowned and bloated face. It was a corpse, the arm tangled in the bucket rope.

~

The morning chorus had begun a half-hour since and the chirruping of forest birds was clamorous. Dawn, not-yet-broken, stained the eastern sky blood red: a premonition of violence to come. In the still-dark forest, hunting horns blared in the distance, drawing nearer, as did the thumping of drums. The beaters, men and boys, some bearing torches to help burn away the morning mist, marched in a line abreast, driving the deer from the depths of the forest.

The Green Goblin crouched beside Father John Finch, who had his mask pushed up on top of his head. Both figures hid their clothes beneath buckram robes.

"By Jesu a tyrant bitch will die this morn," the Goblin said.

"I like this not," Finch worried, drawing the mask down over his face.

The Goblin mask forced its wearer, Thomas Hyde, to turn his entire head in order to look at his companion. Because Finch had left behind his Tragedian's mask in the forest by the Great Road where Scrope and his men had discovered it, he now wore a Fool's mask, with rolling-eyes and puffed-out cheeks. "I am no horseman," he whined.

Hyde drew a dagger from his belt. It was the twin of the poison dagger Shakespeare discovered in the forest. "If she still breathes, finish her with your dagger. Hyde seized Finch's forearm in a bruising squeeze. "Be absolute for death." The Goblin stepped from the shadow of the tree and waved his arms overhead. Two riders in buckram trotted forward from the tree line. One wore the mask of a fiery-faced Devil, the other a Satyr with tongue obscenely thrust out. The Goblin dodged back under cover. Already, they could hear the ragged barking of the staghounds leading the hunt, followed by the shouts of riders spurring their horses.

A huge stag burst from the forest ahead, followed by a hind and then another deer, and then another. The panicked deer ran in full flight, bounding in zigzags through the trees, eyes rolling, hooves kicking at the air. They flashed past in a blur of flailing hooves. Moments later, the lead pack of hounds howled by, yapping and barking.

Hunting horns blared as the first huntsman appeared on horseback.

The Goblin elbowed his companion. "Quick, to horse." Father Finch ran behind the tree to where his mount was tied. The horse whinnied and spun in circles as he struggled to catch a foot in the stirrup. Somehow he flailed his way atop the horse and careened away, fighting to stay upright in the saddle.

The Goblin flung an oath at Finch's retreating back and squeezed into the shadows beneath the tree. Then a single rider galloped past. It was the Queen herself, out in front. The courtiers had dropped back to allow her to ride unencumbered. The two masked riders recognized her and spurred away in pursuit. The Goblin made the mistake of poking out his head to watch, which attracted the attention of hounds trailing the main pack; several broke away and crashed into the brush growling and barking. An enormous black mastiff snarled and went for Hyde. The Goblin tried to stab his dagger into the massive chest, but the dog chested his arm away. As he flailed to stab again, the dogs set upon him, one high and one low. He screamed as bone-crushing teeth clamped down on his calf and arm.

Elizabeth rode on, oblivious, hanging low over the horse's neck, a small crossbow clutched tight. The lead deer was a hugely antlered stag. Now it broke left while the two other deer broke right. The Queen ignored the hinds and swerved her mount after the Hart, whose elaborate crown of antlers made it the bigger prize.

The masked riders followed. The Satyr broke left to pursue the

Queen, but the fiery Devil mistakenly followed the flashing white tails of the fleeing hinds and vanished into the forest.

The Satyr spurred his horse, gaining on Elizabeth. Soon he was just two lengths back. The blare of hunting horns from behind meant the pack of courtiers was fast catching up. The Satyr cursed and drove his heels into the horse's flanks, spurring mercilessly until it closed upon the Queen's shoulder, the two horses galloping side-by-side. The Queen was resolute on her pursuit of the Hart and looked neither left nor right. A simple nudge would send her sprawling to her death. The Satyr clutched the reins and leaned his body for a shoulder-charge to tumble her from the saddle.

But he had not been watching the Hart or the path ahead. The stag reached a steep and narrow ditch and sprang over it. The Queen vaulted her mount over it, too. But the Satyr's mount plunged into the ditch and the horse's front legs crumpled, pitching him over the long neck and flinging him into space. The horse crashed to the ground and cartwheeled nose-over-tail, flinging clods of dirt in the air. It came to rest on its side and did not move. Hurled from its back, the Satyr somersaulted into the top of a prickly holly bush. He landed heavily on his neck and shoulders amid a great cracking and snapping of branches.

Moments passed. The horse shook its head, snorted, and then clambered to its feet and lollopped away, dazed but unhurt. The Satyr hung upside down in the holly bush, legs kicking helplessly, groaning and cursing. A branch broke with a loud crack and dumped him head-first on the ground, the impact shoving the mask down his face, blinding him. He groaned and pushed the mask up until he could see, then crawled from the tangle of broken branches and collapsed on the forest floor, exhausted, sucking wind. He had little time to rest, however, as the rest of the hunt—riders and baying hounds—careened past seconds later in a cacophonous blare of horns. Shouting with terror, he barely managed to fling himself behind the shelter of a tree as trampling hooves thundered past.

Far behind, Thomas Hyde managed to kick loose of the dogs and had climbed high into the dangerously thin and swaying branch tops, where he looked down at the hounds that snarled and leaped up, snapping at him. He had been bitten a half-dozen times on the legs, buttocks, and arms. Now he spat down at the dogs below, cursing them as quislings of the devil.

Moments later, Father Finch trotted back on his horse. He had become lost the instant he set off and had ridden about the forest in aimless circles, the low hanging limbs whipping across his masked face. Now he pushed the Fool's mask up on top of his head and peered queerly at the Goblin perched high in the treetop.

With the arrival of the horse, the dogs lost interest, quit barking and trotted away.

"Is it done?" Finch shouted up. "Is the queen dead?"

There was an ancient bird nest lodged in the crotch of a nearby branch. Thomas Hyde tore it loose and hurled it earthward with a muttered curse. The nest smashed to twigs on Finch's head, toppling him from the horse.

Meanwhile, the Satyr lay crouched in the shadow of the tree trunk until the last horse pounded by. He crawled out, moaning and holding his shoulder. Moments later, the Devil appeared, illumined in a slanting shaft of morning sunlight.

"Help me!" the Satyr called, reaching out a hand in supplication. "I have fallen. I am hurt!"

The Devil sat atop its horse, staring, the fiery mask seeming to burn with rage. It made no move to help, and then silently turned and walked the horse away.

∽

"Ned Smedley," Thom Pope said, prodding the corpse with the toe of his shoe. "The old bastard's drowned like a ship rat!"

Pursuivants and players gathered around the drunkard's sodden form, puddles draining from his waterlogged clothes. It was clear he had been in the water for many hours.

"Who saw him last?" Scrope asked. His eyes scanned the group and then fastened on the tapster.

"I chucked him out at closing time," Gedding said. "Same as I always do. About midnight. In his cups as usual."

"He had vowed to drink himself to death," the innkeeper offered. "I never thought it would be with water."

Thom Pope scratched his beard thoughtfully. "It's obvious what happened. He came stumbling out the inn, pissed drunk, and fell arse-over-elbow down the well."

"Aye, seems likely," Scrope agreed. He threw a look at his Sergeant. "Master Crugg, fetch the Constable to bear the corpse away. I agree the fellow has murdered himself, an unredeemable sin. He must not be buried in consecrated ground." Scrope had little interest in the death of a drunkard and was anxious to conclude the business.

Shakespeare squeezed through the press of players and leaned over the body, examining it. "If the fellow killed himself," he asked, "then why are his bootlaces tied together?" He pointed at the dead man's feet and threw a questioning look at Scrope. "Did a drunken man hop to the well . . . or was he carried there and thrown in?"

The observation gave Scrope a moment's pause. But then he dismissed the suggestion with a contemptuous wave. "A childish fancy. Why would anyone bother to kill a drunken fool who is already tramping the road to his own death?"

Shakespeare had no answer to that, but he had also noticed that the innkeeper and his tapster seemed to be avoiding each other's eyes.

The dead eye stared up blindly. A deer fly landed atop the globe of wet jelly and perched, rubbing its hind legs together.

"Pierced through the heart, and yet the beast ran a quarter mile before it fell."

"It was honoured to be killed by you, Majesty."

The queen laughed broadly, her vermillioned lips drawn back, showing receding gums and the stumps of teeth rotted black from a fondness for sucking sugar sweets.

Lord Essex, as always, had been the first to arrive upon the scene where Elizabeth crouched over the giant stag she had dropped with a single crossbow quarrel through the heart. More riders appeared and drew up their panting mounts. To herald the Queen's success, one produced a hunting horn and trumped a loud blast, while the others burst into spontaneous hurrahs and applause.

Elizabeth acknowledged their diligent flattery with a wave, but her delight was real.

A horse and rider appeared from the forest and approached at a leisurely lollop. It was the Lady Verity, riding sidesaddle, a jaunty feathered-riding cap atop her head, her face demurely covered by a black veil.

Two of the male courtiers dismounted and ran to assist her. One held the reins while another lifted her down from the saddle. As her feet touched the ground, she rushed to the queen's side and dropped into a deep curtsy, bowing her head.

"Oh, well done, Majesty!" she gushed. "Surely you are Diana incarnate!"

The queen laughed gaily and taking her hands, lifted Verity to her feet. Although the young woman seemed a timid dormouse, Elizabeth found herself beginning to grow fond of Verity, unlike the husband, Sir Richard Wexcombe, who Elizabeth found to be a contemptible, preening boor.

"I thank you, child," Elizabeth said, for once the poisonous jealously she always felt in the presence of a younger, prettier woman forgotten. "But where is your lord?"

Lady Verity put a hand to her lips and looked about, struck by sudden remembrance. "Why, I know not, majesty. We set off together." She leaned forward and lowered her voice into conspiratorial tones that all the courtiers could plainly hear. "Do you know," she said. "I believe he has become lost. He has no sense of direction and sometimes wanders these woods for hours with no clue of the way home."

"Lost, in his own deer park?" the braying voice belonged to Lord Essex. "Now there's a foolish fellow!"

The hunting party burst into gales of laughter at such a ridiculous notion.

Wracked by mirth, no one noticed the slender white shape, diaphanous as smoke, gliding through the nearby trees. It paused, watching from a gap in the greensward, and seemed to take the form of a woman, face pale as death, dressed in her own tattered burial shroud.

CHAPTER 34: A PAUCITY OF PLAYERS

"Line, Master Shakespeare! Line!"

Shakespeare looked up from his pages. John Heminges and the rest of the Lord Chamberlain's Men glared at him. The players had lashed together their temporary stage in the yard of the White Hart Inn. Shakespeare used a barrel top for his writing desk while they rehearsed *A Midsummer's Night's Dream*. For audience they had the ostler and his dogsbody who were mucking out the stables. They also had Maud, who paused from time to time in her kitchen labours to hang her huge dugs out the open kitchen window and make gooey eyes at Dick Burbage. He, in turn, threw Billy goat looks back. Daughter Connie, who had chores she should have been tending, loitered in the open doorway, biting her thumb and batting her eyelashes every time Shakespeare looked her way. Even John Thomas and Walt Gedding had stolen away from what they should have been doing to watch the proceedings, for few had ever seen a play put on by a professional troupe of players before. Less obviously, they also had Anthony Munday, who lurked in the shadows of the stables, so as not to be obvious.

But it was not going well. Tasked with performing two and sometimes three roles, players missed their cues, forgot lines, or blundered into irresolvable conflicts upon discovering the need to be onstage twice at the same time. Shakespeare himself was of little help, as he had planned to merely speak his lines from where he stood on the ground, but his constant distraction was dragging the rehearsal to a standstill.

"Master Shakespeare, will you speak your line, sir?" Heminges growled.

Shakespeare snatched up his copy of the play, eyes skimming down the page, searching for his line. He had given himself the role of Theseus, Duke of Athens. After a moment he sighed and looked imploringly at Heminges. "I am lost. Where are we, Thom?"

Heminges cleared his throat and yelled: "Here, mighty Theseus—"

Shakespeare's eyes plumbed the scribbled lines until he found his place. "Say, what abridgement have you for this evening? What masque? What music? How shall we beguile the lazy time, if not with some delight?"

A silence. Moments passed.

Heminges bawled, "Speak your line Philostrate!"

Silence.

"Thomas Pope," Heminges screamed. "Speak!"

"I thought I was Demetrius?"

"Aye, as you are Quince, too!"

Pope slapped his pages against his thigh. "God's wounds! How may a player show two, even three faces to the world and keep each straight?"

While the ostler shovelled shit into a barrow, the dogsbody, a shabby fellow in holed stockings, scratched his arse and opined within Shakespeare's hearing. "These fellows are poor players, are they not?"

The Ostler paused, flies orbiting his steaming shovel load. "I once saw Lord Strange's men perform *Tamburlaine* at Bristol. Now *that* was acting!"

John Heminges grabbed his hair with both hands and threatened to pull it out. "This is impossible. Tis my profession, but I cannot labour under such conditions!"

The Pursuivant drifted from his hiding place and approached the playwright. "Master Shakespeare."

Will looked up.

"I could help," Munday said. "As you know, I have played upon the stage and could read a player's part or two."

Shakespeare bit his lip as he mulled it over. The Lord Chamberlain's Men performed twenty odd plays in weeks. The players were masters at fast memorisation. Still, many lines were often forgot and players would extemporise. But as playwright, the mangling of his words was anathema to Shakespeare and Anthony Munday had a reputation as a profligate extemporiser. But then he thought, *it's just for a rehearsal already going badly.* He thrust a sheaf of loose pages in Munday's hands. "Take you the part of Theseus that I may employ my time in writing and I thank you."

Munday smiled, and sprang up upon the stage. Thomas Pope and the other players threw scowling looks at one another. Heminges broke the inertia by clapping his hands together and calling out: "Once more, gentlemen!"

Free to concentrate upon his play, Shakespeare scribbled lines, trying to catch the fast flow of words in his mind. But after only ten minutes a shadow fell across the page. He looked up. Oswyn Scrope stood at the edge of the stage watching his underling's performance with a disapproving scowl. "Master Munday," he spoke at last.

When Anthony Munday saw the Pursuivant, lines shrivelled in his throat. The action stuttered to a halt. "Aye, Master Scrope?"

"Leave these toys. I have need of you."

Munday handed his pages to John Heminges and jumped from the lip of the stage. The two pursuivants wandered away, heads together. The Lord Chamberlain's Men shared an ominous look.

It could be nothing good where Oswyn Scrope was involved.

* * *

.   .   .

The two pursuivants left the yard and walked to the front of the inn. Scrope did not speak again until both stood upon the Great West Road, where they could not be overheard.

"Crave you again the nonsense of play acting?" Scrope asked.

"No, master—" The words caught in Munday's throat. It was bootless to lie to Oswyn Scrope. "Aye. Upon occasion, my fancy strays back to those days."

"Put such toys and childish fancies from your mind, Master Munday. The business we are about is the only one of merit."

The younger man answered with a curt nod.

"I have a task for you. The brother and sister of the Lady Verity, the mistress of Wexcombe, one Philip and Sybilla Mortlake, quit the house shortly before her Majesty arrived. Both are unrepentant Catholics with no record of paying the recusancy fines. You will ride to their Manor, arrest them, and fetch them hence for interrogation. While at the Mortlake house you may search the place for priest holes and Romish devices."

"Where lies this Manor?"

"North … in the county of Lancashire."

The destination came like a gut punch and Munday gasped. "Lanc — but that's … two hundred miles north!"

"You will ride post, changing steeds every ten miles. I warrant it will take no more than three days."

"But when shall I sleep?"

Scrope grimaced at the question. "You must abjure such luxuries while on the Queen's business. Until these Jesuits are locked in the Tower, I care not if the world lacks dreams!"

* * *

"We are doomed," John Heminges said gloomily, shaking his head: "We are doomed."

"Tis an ill omen," Kempe added.

They had a stage to practice on, but lacking players, the rehearsal continued to go poorly. The play, though well known to the players, was too much for too few. The performance would be a disaster. Even Burbage was downcast. "This profits us not," he moaned. "Even the better half of the Lord Chamberlain's Men cannot act for the whole."

Just then, they heard the slog of heavy footfalls and several dusty figures trudged into the Inn-yard, weary and footsore. "Huzzah!" one shouted. "We are back, lads! Rejoice!"

The action stopped. The players on stage gawped at the intruders, as no one recognized them. And indeed, they were unrecognisable. They looked like an army of mangy, crow-pecked scarecrows and the briars tangled in their hair and the pickers snagged in their clothes told a tale of miles trod and weary nights spent sleeping under hedgerows.

Burbage teetered on the edge of the stage and cast down a scornful look. "Begone beggars. If it's food you seek, go nose you with the pigs at the trough."

"Nay tis us, good master Burbage," William Sly bleated. Sly was always thin and his loose clothes showed that the miles had rendered him skeletal. "Do you not recognise your brother players?"

"Aye, tis us!" shouted John Sincler, Richard Cowley, Henry Condell and Augustine Phillips as one man.

"You remember me, sweet Dick," said George Bryan standing at the lip of the stage. "I stood you cakes and ale last time we supped at *The Witch's Tit*."

Burbage squinted down at the fellow as if he could not recognise him. "True enough, you have a look of a rogue I once knew. And yet you cannot be George Bryan. He has gone back to London, for he has an honest trade."

"Aye," Shakespeare added. "He is an honest doorkeep at a swiving house!"

The players on stage burst into raucous laughter and it finally dawned on the starvelings that their fellow players knew full well who they were and were making fun of them.

"What say you, Master Heminges?" Shakespeare said. "Shall we forgive these mutinous rascals?"

"No! Begone with them!" the manager blustered. "They should be whipped from the parish like all sturdy beggars and vagabonds!"

The former mutineers clutched their caps, looking crestfallen and despairing, but Shakespeare urged Heminges to reconsider. The manager folded his arms upon his chest and stared up at the cloudless blue sky, tapping his foot upon the boards as if giving the matter great consideration. Finally, he dropped his arms and breathed a heavy sigh, saying, "Ohhhhhhh, very well then! You are all unworthy sons of whores, but you may rejoin the Lord Chamberlain's Men."

A cheer went up that all joined in.

The long walk quickly forgotten, the returned players surged upon the stage where they rummaged through the trunks and found their costumes. But the practice recommenced only after the truth had been extracted from them: a sorry tale. The journey back to London had been harrowing. They were turned away at the city gates because of rumours of plague in the surrounding towns. Upon entering Oxford they attempted to raise money by performing in the city square and were arrested as wandering vagrants and whipped from the city. Along the road they had been stoned by farmers and chased off time and again. They caught news of the Queen's Progress while performing a scene (more accurately, begging) in St Albans' market. It was the meagrest glimmer of good news, but it brought them hobbling back along the Great West Road to Wiltshire.

The reunion celebration was interrupted by a hulking fellow who tarried at the lip of the stage. Shakespeare recognized him as one of the burly servants they had met unloading luggage at the house. "I have word from my master Valentyne," the man said. "He bids you come see his work and be amazed."

"Amazed?" Shakespeare asked. "How so?"

A smile fought its way to the surface of the burly man's thick beard. "He has done what Merlin himself could not do. He has brought the Forest of Arden to Wexcombe House."

· · ·

* * *

The noisy rabble of players spilled in through the side door of Wexcombe House. Only Burbage and Shakespeare had been inside the house before and all babbled in amazement at a great mansion that made the Queen's palaces seem unimposing. The players crept quietly along the corridor and passed an open door on the right. Shakespeare threw it a quick glance and what he saw made him shush the other players with a harsh word and a fierce look. The door opened onto a small private chapel. More important, a figure knelt at the altar, praying—the Lady Verity. She knelt on the cold stone flags, head bowed, eyes closed, both hands wrapped around the gold crucifix that hung from a chain around her neck.

Shakespeare bade his fellow players continue on, and then darted back outside. He went straight to one of flowerbeds that edged the knot garden, drew his dagger, cut a single red rose, and hurried back inside. The lady was still praying when he crept up to the altar and silently laid the rose on the stone flags before her knees. If she heard his stealthy tread, she never opened her eyes or turned her head, although he thought he saw the tremulous ghost of a smile on her lips.

Shakespeare's mind was still full of thoughts of Verity when he stepped into the Great Hall, and so he was unprepared for what he found.

Overnight, and somehow magically, the Great Hall had been transformed into a forest. Giant oak trees soared to the lofty ceiling where they spread branches wreathed with mistletoe, hung here and there with glowing lanterns and huge candelabras waiting to be lit. To complete the illusion of being in a forest, cagefuls of songbirds had been captured and loosed inside the hall, and now they perched and flitted among the branches, filling the airy space with the chirrup of sweet birdsong.

Valentyne truly had brought the forest of Arden to Wexcombe House.

Shakespeare gaped, mouth open. Girlish laughter pulled his eyes to a stage that had been built along the north wall. Standing in the glow of many candles was a garishly dressed elf conjured by a magic spell: Valentyne Winstringham.

"Did I not say you would rub you eyes and think that you dreamed?" Valentyne shouted.

"Aye, me!" Shakespeare said, looking around in amazement as he wandered toward the stage. "What sorcery is this?"

"Tis for our Masque, as Valentyne told you. Herne the Hunter must have his woods."

Burbage gave Shakespeare a hand up onto the stage. The playwright stomped the boards, testing them. The stage was as sound and handsome as the Theatre's or any London playhouse.

"Tis a goodly stage to play our scenes." Shakespeare said, and clapped Valentyne on the shoulder. "Truly, you are Merlin's equal in magic."

Valentyne tee-heed like a schoolgirl.

"Enough!" John Heminges shouted and clapped his hands for attention. "We have much to practice, gentleman!"

The rehearsal went much better than the disaster of the inn-yard. Shakespeare stood at the edge of the stage. He had taken the role of Oberon, a part that did not require much stage time and which allowed him time offstage to work on the new play. Henry Condell was playing Titania: a poor choice but Young Sam was already playing the role of Hippolyta, which required him to be on stage most of the play.

"Ill met by moonlight, proud Titania" Shakespeare said, striding out onto the stage wearing a battered, tin-plate crown and wrapped in a gold-spangled robe of the King of the Fairies.

Henry Condell's slender and willowy Titania turned and struck a dramatic pose. He had only a crescent moon headdress to signify his role and so looked like a man with man with a scythe blade stuck in his head. "What, jealous Oberon?" he cast a look at Burbage and Heminges, who were doubling as very unlikely fairies. "Skip hence. I have forsworn his bed and company." The two big men lumbered off the stage more like draft oxen than fairies.

From the corner of his eye, Shakespeare noticed a figure at the far end of the hall. Someone was watching them rehearse. He made the mistake of stealing a quick look. It was the Lady Verity herself. Words, cues, lines, flew from his mind.

A ponderous silence pooled around him and dilated.

John Heminges, acting as prompter, hissed the line from the front of the stage. "Tarry, rash wanton—"

The words reassembled in Shakespeare's mind and tumbled from his mouth. "Tarry, rash wanton! Am I not your lord?" Shakespeare's demeanour had suddenly gone from lazy read-through to full-on dramatic thunder and caught the other players by surprise.

"Thu-then I muh, must be your lady!" Condell stammered, trying to come up to speed. "But I know when you have stolen away from fairy land, and in the shape of Corin sat all day, playing on pipes of corn, and versing love to amorous Phillida. What art you here …"

Trying not to be obvious, Shakespeare turned his head slightly and searched from the corner of his eye. She was still there. Still watching. He drew himself up to his full height. Thrust out his chest. Good posture always impressed. Then he snatched his mind back to the action. "… to Theseus must be wedded, and you come to give their bed joy and prosperity."

Shakespeare stepped so close to the lip of the stage that Burbage and Pope feared for a moment that he would walk into thin air. He flung out his arm in a fiery gesture. "How canst you for shame, Titania, glance at my credit with Hippolyta, knowing I know thy love to Theseus? Doest you not lead him through the glimmering night from Perigenia, whom he banished? And make his with fair Aegles break his faith with Ariadne and Antipa?"

Burbage furrowed his brow as he watched his friend strutting and fretting upon the stage. He hurled a dubious look at Thomas Pope and muttered sotto voce, "A bit over the top, think you not?"

Pope nodded back, and lifted an ironic eyebrow. "A performance more stuffed with bombast than John Alleyn's cod piece."

But the next time Shakespeare stole a look, the lady was gone. His fiery tone fizzled to vague disinterest, which raised more eyebrows amongst his fellow players. When his scene ended and he stepped backstage, Shakespeare could think of nothing but the Lady Verity. He leant with his back against the wall, softly banging his head against it. Soon, he became aware of someone looking at him. The backstage door to the hall had been left open. Framed by the doorway, the Lady Verity stood watching him. To his joy and amazement, her hands cradled a red rose, and now she lifted the bloom to her face and breathed in its perfume. She flashed a heart-cracking smile—gentle, yet bold, demure, yet enticing. (Oh, how a world of delightful implications could be read into that carelessly studied expression.) Having thrust cupid's arrow through his heart, the lady turned and glided away. Shakespeare vacillated for a moment, uncertain what to do. His scene was coming up.

John Heminges's voice nagged from the hall. "Flute! I say Flute! Master Shakespeare, are you awake, sir?"

But Shakespeare could hear nothing—deafened by the blood pounding in his ears. He leapt from the stage and dodged into the hallway. The lady had gone, but up ahead, on the stone flags, he spotted a single red petal. He ran to snatch it up and then saw another forty feet ahead. He pounced upon that one. Around the corner he found two more. It soon became obvious that she was laying a trail that he would most willingly follow. Even though he was not a courtier and had no license to be in the house, he stalked the trail up one staircase and then another. The petals led him along a third floor hallway, around another bend and then into a turret stairwell that wound upward. He leapt up the stairs and reached the door of what must have been the highest place in the turret. A few petals lay scattered upon the threshold, the door of which was cracked slightly. When he pushed open the door the Lady Verity leaned against the wall, waiting. The windows were all open to chimney hot air from the house and the swirling breeze lifted her hair and rustled her skirts. A loose strand of hair blew across her eyes and she brushed it aside.

His hands clenched fistfuls of gathered-up petals and now they slackened, spilling their redness across the floor. Only one petal remained on the rose he had given her. As he watched, she plucked it loose and placed its redness between the crimson pillows of her full lips. He strode across the floor to her, gently drew the petal from between her lips, and then planted his own lips upon hers. A shock jolted through him as he felt her tongue slip between his lips and press against his own. They kissed for a short eternity, a brief lifetime. Finally, they broke apart to snatch a breath.

"Would you be my Oberon," she said in a husky voice, "and I thy mistress Titania?"

"Aye," Shakespeare replied. "And in a fairy bower we would make our love nest."

He went to kiss her again, but she turned her face away, a hand pressed against his chest. "No. Stop!" she said. "Our love makes us mad. I have my marriage vows … even if my husband be a base brute."

Shakespeare stopped and regarded her seriously. "He treats you ill?"

She dropped her eyes, lower lip quivering. "I am less than a slave, for I am his wife, a chattel he may dispose of as he is wont. Unhappy in a marriage I had no choice in. My husband is a bad man. A wicked man … and wicked jealous." The huge brown eyes softened, welled, and streams ran down her cheeks. "If he saw me so much as look at another man, he would beat me. And so I tremble at what he would do to you."

He drew away slightly, his mind spawning second thoughts, but she hugged him close. "Oh, if only my husband were dead and I was your mistress. This great house—all this could be yours —and me with it."

Shakespeare stiffened. He could see the precipice she was enticing him toward. Still, he yearned to take that fatal step and fall forever.

She pulled her face to his, so that his vision was filled with nothing but the soft, doe-eyes and he drowned in them. Before he could gasp another breath, she pressed her soft lips to his. They kissed so deep it left him dizzy.

"I have a request …" she whispered in his ear.

"Ask and it is yours."

But when his lips sought hers again, she pushed him away. "Come to my rooms tonight, when the clock strikes eight. My husband will be at dinner, filling himself with sack like an old wineskin." She saw the hesitation in his eyes and continued, "Do you think only men lust? Then come tonight and I'll show you how hot a woman's blood can run." She planted a soft, warm kiss upon his lips, then tore herself from his arms, and flitted from the tower room.

For a dizzying moment, Shakespeare found himself transported back to Stratford when as a young man barely beyond his schooldays, he had first kissed Anne Hathaway, a full-ripened woman eight years his senior. He looked around in wonder. From the turret room it was possible to look out over the immense house and the vast estate that stretched around it. *All this could be yours.* The words echoed in his mind and reminded him of something he could not quite summon from his mind. Had not most of the blood in his body surged to his lower extremities, he might have recalled a similar situation from his Bible studies in a Stratford grammar school—of Jesus being taken to a high place where the devil tempted him with visions of greatness.

As it was, he floated down the stairs as if his body were a bladder buoyant with hot air and he the lucky boy holding its string. *Tis madness,* he thought. *I am no boy. I am no man's fool. Nor any woman's. I am a gentleman, a man of property. Soon to be a sharer in a great endeavour. My fortunes are rising.*

But he could still feel the soft pillows of her lips on his and his mind drowned in the limpid pools of her eyes. Still, he was not a boy of eighteen but a man of thirty-two, a fox with enough grey hairs to know how to steal the bait from a trap without sacrificing a limb. *Good sense be damned,* he thought, *though I will likely hang for this anon. If the world must burn then let it burn.*

He was resolved. When chance presented itself, nothing in the world, not even his new play, would keep him from the Lady's bedchamber.

∾

A fter the court had finished gorging from the many platters of extravagant food the cooks had slaved to create and had belched their way out of the giant banqueting tent, those of lower rank: servants, servants-of-servants, and the motley performers such as tumblers, acrobats and players took their place at the great tables to scavenge whatever morsels their betters had left. In truth, there was still an embarrassment of food—enough to have fed every citizen in a town larger than Stratford. As he gnawed the bones of a lamb shank, Burbage grunted and elbowed Shakespeare in the ribs. "That dark beauty is making eyes at you, Will." He nodded to a diner on the far side of the table. Seated amongst the tumblers was a woman who performed dances of the east: a dusky beauty whose eyes, heavily accented with kohl, lurked with witchcraft. The Stratford player met her gaze and smiled. The woman did not act coy nor demurely look away, but devoured him with a look that smouldered.

"The lady is on fire for you," Burbage said. "See how she burns."

"One of the wandering tribe of Egypt, as are her fellows," Shakespeare noted." Her long days under the sun have left her brown and sweet as a nut."

"The lady smiled, flashing perfect white teeth, but Shakespeare tore his gaze free, looking down at the table. "Aye me!" he exclaimed. "I drown and you offer me a cup of water!"

When the players had eaten their fill, Shakespeare and Burbage toured the former mutineers around the grounds. (On the courtier's side of the hedge, workmen were carting away the broken remains of Diana's magical fountain—much to Burbage's disappointment.)

"Tis a marvellous house," Henry Condell remarked.

"Tis no mere house, tis a palace," William Sly said.

"Nay," Pope countered, always the contentious one. "Tis finer than the Queen's palace at Richmond."

"I knew not you had played the palace," Condell said.

"Aye, I have played it twice." Pope insisted. "Once when I was with Lord Strange's Men."

They strolled to the southern end of the lake where Burbage described the mock-whale that ferried the queen to the dock.

Thom Pope nodded at a work still under construction, a large palisade made of wooden pales fifteen feet high. Inside, carpenters sawed and hammered, busy at work on an elevated wooden platform surrounded by a railing.

"Tis for the morrow," Heminges said. "For her majesty's drive hunt."

"*Drive* hunt?" Shakespeare snorted derisively, and made a disapproving face. "Tis not a style of hunt worthy of the name."

The first hunt Elizabeth had taken part in was a pursuit hunt, where riders chased deer through the forest, covering many miles, sometimes even spanning counties in their pursuit of the wild hart. Designed for the gentility, the drive hunt was a less strenuous affair where deer were rousted from their forest hides by gamekeepers and beaters blowing horns and pounding drums. The stampeding deer were then herded into a fenced palisade. Once inside, large gates would swing shut, sealing them in. The royal hunting party could then pick off the deer at their leisure, shooting from the comfort and safety of the hunt stand.

"Drive hunts are the parvenu of lily-livered courtiers and apish fops," Shakespeare spat. "Tis a hunt where deer are slaughtered by wine-addled fools too drunk to wield a bow." It was a sore subject with the Stratford player, and he would gnaw on it for hours like a dog with a chew rag. The other players, all city boys who had never hunted, exchanged glances and rolled their eyes as Burbage led them back toward the house.

By now the hour had grown late and a surreally magnificent sunset was drawing people out of doors. Faces pressed against every glass window. Courtiers spilled from doorways. Servants ceased their labours—unsaddling a horse, scrubbing clothes in a tub, hauling ropes to raise a tent—to turn and look. Cooks and scullery boys crept from their tents to steal a gander, leaving pots to boil over and unturned joints to char black on their spits.

On the southern side of the great house, tall glass doors flashed open and the Queen, Sir Richard, Lady Verity and the royal retinue glided out and took a position at a low wall where they could marvel at the spectacle. The world trembled in a weird twilight that stretched the shadows of trees and people into gangly, unnatural shapes. On the western horizon, the sun was a fiery phoenix settling upon a burning nest of clouds. Directly overhead, the blue skies had thinned to black and stars already shone brightly. The clouds finally swallowed up the sun, which burst and ran everywhere like a yolk split open, releasing snakes of silvery fire that wriggled through the clouds. A collective gasp arose from the watchers. Suddenly the clouds stuttered with pulses of light, and after a long, long, long delay, a loud crack and a pursuing rumble shook heaven and earth. The booming din brought musket and pike-bearing soldiers at a run, clanking-clanking, boots thudding across the grass as a Sergeant-at-arms shouted at his men to set up a defensive line at the perimeter of the grounds. Then a succession of concussive booms broke across the land, like the slow, rumbling collapse of mountains. Awe was replaced by anguish as terror whiplashed through the crowd. Courtiers, men and ladies who had moments before paraded the grounds in genteel grace, now turned and ran, their faces stretched with terror at what cold only be the roar of cannon fire from an approaching army. To all it seemed as if what had been feared for years had finally transpired—the Spanish had landed a huge army. Either that, or it was another rebellion where malcontent lords had gathered together a force of men under arms which and was even now bearing down upon the Queen and her court. The tall doors flung open again as Elizabeth and her retinue scurried back inside.

Then the world sucked in a huge breath and breathed out a gust of sultry air that blew hard into the faces of those who stood and watched, blowing off men's caps and lady's henniers, whipping the pennants straight atop the cupolas of Wexcombe house and flapping the leaves of tents like flags. Moments later, a second gust hit, a gale-force blast that ripped loose up one of the giant tents still being erected and flung it free of the ground. Several of the labourers struggling to put it up became entangled in the canvas and the snaking lines that lashed in all directions. The wind snatched the canvas octopus and twirled it forty-feet in the air, then whisked it along until it crashed into a smaller tent in a clumsy embrace. Then both tents catapulted high in the air where they danced, spitting out screaming men and tent poles. Those on the ground cried out in fear and dodged as falling bodies and tent poles thumped down around them, giant spars impaling themselves in the ground mere feet from where the players stood. In a moment, five were killed and one badly crushed so that he died later in the night of his injuries.

And then, after the tempest, came a sudden and preternatural calm.

The day died quickly as light bled out of the sky. The stars crowded forward against the dome of night—cruel in their steely glittering. Those who remained on the great lawn looked around, dazed and stunned—storm survivors spit up by a malevolent sea.

Shakespeare and the rest of the Lord Chamberlain's Men clambered to their feet and looked around in shock at the destruction of a few moments. Only one member of the royal party lingered on the veranda. He was a tall man in a black robe with a long pointed beard that dangled to his waist. Shakespeare had seen the ancient fellow on occasion at court, and gleaned from the whispers that chased after his retreating back, that he was called Doctor Dee and that he was a magician and the Queen's Royal astrologer. From where Shakespeare stood, it was hard to make out the man's features, but they seemed familiar. He stood at the veranda's low wall like a sea captain at the prow of his ship. His eyes, lit only by the glitter of starlight, seemed to be looking straight at Shakespeare and his mouth moved, speaking inaudible words that resonated in his mind: *The tempest is massing, Will Shakespeare, and it comes for thee.*

CHAPTER 35: A GHOSTLY ENCOUNTER

The wooden bench was bone-bruisingly hard. The blanket they had given him was scratchy and stank of wet horse. He was certain it had just been snatched from the back of a sleeping nag and tossed to him.

Anthony Munday had ridden post since the early morning, changing horse every ten miles or so. He had stumbled into this inn an hour after dark, when his eyes could no longer make out the road in front of him. During the last three hours of riding he had thought of nothing but a soft bed and hot food, but the inn he arrived at, which was called *The Anchor*, or *The Tabard*, or *The Pecock*—he had changed horse at so many times he could not remember which—had no rooms to let.

His dinner was a lump of mouldy cheese and a stale manchet. Afterward, he was given the choice of sleeping on the floor or on a wooden bench. He chose the bench, which was in the inn's main room where a knot of merchants journeying to Bristol market crowded around a backgammon board as they wagered with loud oaths, banging the pips down at each man's turn. And so he spent a restless night plunging in and out of ragged shreds of sleep. Still, he had made good time, and was more than half-way to his destination, though his thighs and back ached from the hard day's ride and he could not fathom how he would be able to climb back onto a horse come the morning.

～

The doorknob rattled and then Burbage, dusted with flour, stumbled in around midnight. He collapsed onto the bed, farted a prolonged fart, and was droning within seconds.

Shakespeare hunched at the small table over a growing stack of pages. Unable to sleep, he scribbled by the light of two smoky candles. Out the open window, endless flashes of dry lightning lit the night sky and set the window shutters and the table beneath to rattling and vibrating with each rolling percussion. After weeks of dry weather, violent storms raged over the Welsh Mountains some hundred miles distant, where cold sea breezes warred with hot, inland winds parched of moisture.

Shakespeare happened to be staring into the black rectangle of the window, his mind tripping iambically over fresh-penned soliloquies, when the skies pulsed, washing the road and the trees beyond with flat white light. A figure stood at the edge of the forest—a woman in white, her face ghastly pale, and a mane of wild hair swirling about her head. The light extinguished and darkness surged in, leaving purple after-images cascading before his eyes. Moments later, a second flash lit the world outside the window.

But the White Woman was gone.

The candle flame threw his quivering shadow against the walls as he crept down the stairs and blundered along the narrow passage that led to the great room. As he passed the narrow steps that plunged down to the cellar, he paused a moment. A quiver of candle-light glimmered beneath the crack of the closed door from behind which came the low murmur of men's voices. It could only be the innkeeper and his tapster. But counter to Burbage's speculation, it did not sound like an amorous assignation. He could not pluck a single word from the rumble of consonants, but the speech had the dissonance of argument. He lingered a moment longer and then carried on.

In the kitchen, the air was still hazy with settling flour. Lifting his candle, Shakespeare saw the floor tracked with phantom footprints in a variety of positions, testifying to the amatory cavortings of Burbage and the Innkeeper's wife. Atop a fibrously grained pine table he found a wicker basket and placed inside it a hunk of cheese and a leftover wedge of game pie still drooling gravy.

He left the candle in the kitchen and navigated through the inn by the touch of his inky fingers to the front door. The key had been left in the lock. He turned it and slipped outside. By now a half-moon, late rising, floated low over the trees and whetted the shadows sharp as an axe blade. Eyes sieving the shadows, he crossed the road and set the basket down in the shadow of the trees. For a moment he are stood still, ears pricked, looking, listening.

Mute lightning flashed in the distance and the twisted shadows of trees leaped up and then toppled back. A fretful wind hissed in the treetops. Somewhere branches rattled. He had sent himself on a fool's errand. There was no White Lady.

A sudden flash. A spectral shape rose up from the ground.

"God's Blood!" he shouted, heart banging. He wanted to run but his legs would not obey. Although the flash left him night-blind, he could perceive an amorphous white shape drifting closer. Terror arced through him.

"If you be damned," he spoke aloud, "blast not my immortal soul! Speak, ghost!"

A double flash of lightning. The White Woman stood an arm's length away, her eyes rolling and wild. She lifted both hands to her mouth and mewled pitifully.

The scream was entirely his.

He found his legs and turned to run, but a skeletal hand grabbed his ankle and he fell—a tree root. He scrambled to his feet and sprinted to the safety of the inn. Reaching the doorway, he looked back. Another flash. Nothing. No White Woman. The trees were empty.

A phantasm, spun by my fevered brain, he thought. It took a while but he forced himself back, slowly, haltingly, across the road. He stooped and picked up the basket, stunned at its sudden lightness. When he snatched the lid off, moonlight revealed only a shadow curled asleep inside.

The food was gone.

CHAPTER 36: AFTER THE TEMPEST

Sections of palisade had blown down during the storm. Now carpenters hammered and sawed, replacing or setting upright the broken pales which spanned the height of two men—tall enough that a deer could not vault over them.

Oswyn Scrope stepped through the open gates into the palisade. As the servants had informed him, the Lord and Lady were inspecting the repairs, as the postponed drive hunt had been rescheduled for the following day. Finally, he saw them on the shooting platform. The previous day they had constantly been in the presence of the queen where he could not question them. Now was his chance. Scrope climbed the wooden ladder to the platform. Lord and Lady each cradled a crossbow as the Lord conversed with a scraggle-bearded fellow in the green doublet and hose of a gamekeeper.

"Good 'morrow, Sir Richard, my Lady Verity," interrupted Scrope, bowing stiffly.

Sir Richard tossed him a curt look, unable to keep the curl from his lip. He could, no doubt, guess by Scrope's simple clothes he was neither nobleman nor courier. "Who are you, sirrah?"

"I am Oswyn Scrope, messenger of the Queen's chamber."

Lord and Lady exchanged the briefest of looks. "Load the bows,

Harold," Sir Richard said, pushing his crossbow into the gamekeeper's hands. The gamekeeper put a foot into the crossbow's metal stirrup and strained to draw back the bowstring. He handed the crossbow back to his master, cocked and ready to be loaded.

"What is your business?" Sir Richard asked while the gamekeeper cocked the Lady's bow.

"Until recent you lodged two guests here: Philip and Sybilla Mortlake, brother and sister of your lady wife."

Sir Richard's sour face made it clear that he did not care for this line of questioning. He drew a quarrel[1] from a leather quiver the gamekeeper offered up. "Drive in the quarry," Sir Richard muttered to his gamekeeper. He did not look at Scrope as he spoke. "As I told Lord Cecil, the Mortlake's have quit the house and returned to Lancashire."

The gamekeeper raised a small hunting horn to his lips and blew a quick blast. Scrope looked up in surprise as an odd-looking deer galloped drunkenly into the palisade. Sir Richard raised his crossbow and sited. When the deer, which was very slow, galumphed alongside the hunting platform, Scrope saw it ran on two legs, not four. It was no real deer, but a man in a deer suit running for all he was worth.

"Sir, you shall cause great injury—" Scrope began to say, but at that moment Sir Richard fired. The quarrel hit the faux deer in the front shoulder with a THU-WHAP sound and bounced off—the arrows had been fitted with blunt metal tips. Still, the force of the shot staggered the man in the deer suit whose ankles clashed together, making him stumble and scream in pain.

Oswyn Scrope looked at Sir Richard with alarm.

"Be not afeared," Sir Richard said blithely, handing the crossbow back to his gamekeeper to reload. "Tis just a peasant. I would not waste a deer so cheap." Sir Richard took the loaded crossbow back and said to his gamekeeper. "Have the villain run faster this time."

Scrope pursed his lips. Like many puritans he did not condone the slaughter of God's creations except for food—not amusement or sport —but he had matters of greater import. "Can you tell me, sir, why the parish register shows no record of the Mortlake's attending church, and yet they did not pay the recusancy fines?"

The two-legged deer was making another pass. Sir Richard drew a bead, aimed, and fired. The bolt missed by several inches and glanced off the hard ground. The nobleman's face tightened with fury as he handed the crossbow to his gamekeeper. "We have our own chapel. Tis a tedious long ride to the church at Marlborough."

"There is still the matter of the fines."

"You must take up the matter with the Mortlakes, sirrah. It is none of my concern—"

"I do intend to broach the subject with the Mortlakes. My lieutenant is even now riding to Lancashire to fetch them back to face questioning. He should return in three days."

Sir Richard's faced turned black at the news. "Three days?" He laughed scornfully. "You are ignorant of the roads to Lancashire—in sad disrepair after the floods of winter. Plus brigands haunt every bridge and ford, lying in wait. Three days? I'll wager a sack of gold he never returns."

The faux deer was making another pass. Lady Verity stepped between the two men, breaking their eye contact and interrupting the conversation. She raised her crossbow and fired a shot. The quarrel thwacked the deer squarely between the antlers and stuck, striking with such force that the peasant staggered and sprawled on the ground.

"Madam," Sir Richard said with amusement in his voice. "You have chosen the wrong quarrel. That arrow had a broad head on it."

The lady gasped in mock surprise and put a hand to her mouth. For his part, Sir Richard's smirk showed his amusement. "A great fortune the ruffian was not killed, but then again, he is only a peasant."

Amid a great deal of cursing the peasant struggled to unbuckle the straps holding him into the deerskin. "My lordship!" he shouted up at the hunting stand. "I wish humbly to resign! I am not being paid to be killed of my life!"

"Be warned, Master Scrope," Sir Richard said with cheerful malevolence. "Never pick a quarrel with my lady wife."

CHAPTER 37: MORTLAKE MANOR

The road had begun as a little more than muddy sheep track. Through years of use, broken and pocked, it meandered crazily, forcing the horse to a walk. The rider, sweating through his black clothes, drew up at a field where two rustics stood waist-deep in golden barely, swinging their scythes in unison.

"Good day to you, fellows," Anthony Munday called to them from horseback.

The scythes ceased swinging and the men shouldered through the tall barley to speak to the horseman. The day was sweltering and Anthony Munday's mouth was parched with the heat and miles of swallowed dust. He could barely talk. "I seek the manor house of the Mortlake family. How far?"

The two men exchanged uneasy looks.

"There is no manor, sir," the elder man said. Both had curly ginger hair and faces strawberried with freckles from long days in the sun.

"Never has been," added the other labourer, a younger version of the first, clearly his son.

"Aye," agreed the father. "But the Mortlake *house* stands yonder."

Munday followed the point of the man's calloused finger and his eyes fell upon a handsome thatched house, surrounded by a wooden fence.

Munday thanked the men and rode up to the house, tying his horse at the gate. But, up close, he found a house desperate for mending: the thatch was balding at the roof's crown, many windows were missing their glass panes, and the fence hung crooked from broken posts and was holed in places. Chickens spilled through the gaps and milled about the road while sheep had pushed through the other way and were nibbling the green tops of the vegetables in the root garden.

When Munday dropped from the saddle he had to hang on to the horse for several moments. He had been riding nearly twenty hours straight and his numb legs nearly buckled beneath him. With pins and needles tattooing his thighs, he shambled stiffly to the front door. He tugged the leather gauntlets from his hands and wiped sweaty palms on his doublet, then rapped at the door which swung open slackly, for it lacked even a latch to hold it shut.

He hallooed into the house a half dozen times, but no one responded, and so he stepped inside. As he strolled through the echoing interior, he walked through rooms stripped of furniture. Only dust marks on the walls remained as a ghostly witness to where a sideboard had stood, a portrait hung, a hutch leaned. In the sitting room fireplace, the legs of a chair, half-consumed, protruded like a forked tongue from a mouthful of cold ashes, testimony to the inhabitants' desperation for firewood the previous winter. Other rooms told the same story of a bankrupt house, slowly cannibalising itself.

When he stepped into the kitchen, a woman of past-middle years was making pies and singing to herself. His sudden appearance surprised her, for she looked up, whooped with fear, and dashed out the open back door.

"Madam," he called after. "Be not afeared!"

The woman ran and hid behind a man who stood at a chopping block the middle of the cobbled yard: a big, bearded brute in a bloody apron. As the woman rushed up, he pinned a chicken to the wooden block and whacked off its head with one blow of the cleaver. The woman jabbered to him excitedly. The brute straightened and looked up under his bushy brows at Munday. He loosed his grip on the chicken. The headless bird tumbled from his hand and continued to flap about on the ground, thrashing in its death-throes. Never taking his eyes off the pursuivant, the brute turned his head slightly and boomed: "Thomas." In answer, the barn door squealed open and an even bigger fellow slid out, a hulking peasant clutching a crude wooden pitchfork. Moment's later, footsteps crunched at the side of the house as the father and son he had spoken to in the barley field arrived, still wielding their scythes.

"This fellow be lookin' for the manor house," the elder redhead explained.

Munday said, "I would speak words with your masters Richard Mortlake and Lady Sybilla."

The woman stayed hidden behind the bulk of the brutish man but now she stood on tiptoe and whispered something in his ear.

"And who are you?" the giant grunted.

"I am the Queen's Messenger," Munday said, casually resting a hand on the pommel of his rapier. Anthony Munday was neither large nor physically imposing and he was outnumbered four to one. Worse, they all had weapons. Crude though the pitchfork may be, the wooden tines were wicked sharp.

The Brute's eyes watched Munday's hand slide to the pommel of his weapon. "You have ridden a long way from London for naught."

"My lord and lady have gone to market," the woman interrupted, her voice taut and nervous. "They did not say when they would return."

Munday's eyes scanned the yard, taking in the tumbledown barn, the collapsing chicken coop and the overall dishevelment of the house. In the corner of the yard, three grubby children giggled as they tormented a large hog, pulling its tail, dangling from its ears, and climbing upon its back as the hog squealed and threw them off.

The truth was obvious. These masterless servants were squatters in a house they did not own, and had been so for some time. They were working the farm as the Diggers were said to do, selling the furniture and fittings as need be to pay the local tithes, confident the true masters of the house were never coming home.

Displaying a fearlessness he did not feel, Anthony Munday drew loose the gauntlets he had tucked beneath his sword belt, slapped the knee of his breeches to knock loose the dust and pulled them on. "Hear me now. I am Anthony Munday, the Queen's Messenger and servant to Oswyn Scrope, pursuivant to recusant Catholics and those who would harbour Jesuit Priests. If you do not answer me true, soldiers will come after and drag you to the Tower in chains. There you will be put to the question by my master's master. You will have heard of his name … Richard Topcliffe."

Their faces paled at his words. Even people in the backward and benighted county of Lancashire knew of Richard Topcliffe, for word of the dark doings of the queen's torturer were whispered in taverns across England and spread faster than the plague. It was a name to frighten children into behaving. With adults it was often enough to pry loose the truth from tight-closed lips.

The woman stepped from behind the brute, hands fidgeting with her apron strings. "My lord and lady are not here," the woman confessed. Since the Mortlake fortune is gone they have removed to lodge with their sister and her husband, Lady Verity and Lord Wexcombe."

"I have information they returned here a week hence."

The woman looked stunned. She shook her head. "Nay, sir. We have not seen them nigh on two years."

He believed her instantly. The house's slow collapse into ruin provided all the proof he needed. Munday nodded sagely. "Then it seems I have been sent on a fool's errand." He attempted to make them all relax by striking a pose of relaxation himself. It did not work. They watched him tensely. A wrong move could provoke violence at any moment. "I pray you, Goodwife, a drink of cool water before I take horse again."

In the kitchen the woman's hands shook as she sloshed water in a tankard from a stone pitcher. Still suspicious, the brute lurked at the threshold of the kitchen door, the cleaver gripped in his sweaty hand.

As Munday quaffed the water, his eye fell upon a series of tiny portraits hanging on the wall in the other room. He clomped across the splintery boards to look. Three miniatures hung above a fireplace, almost the only furniture remaining in the room besides a lopsided chair and a broken wooden chest. The portraits were of three young people, a male and two females.

"My young masters and my young mistress ..." the woman explained, "... painted in their youth. Their parents died of the plague some three years ago."

"Tell me their names."

The housewife pointed to a beautiful girl of sixteen with blonde locks curling around her face. "That is Verity, the youngest and fairest. It was she who married Sir Richard, though her dowry took the last of this great house's fortune. The other two are Philip and Sybilla. He is an indolent wretch, overfull of himself. The red haired girl is Sybilla, the eldest daughter. Though I raised them all, Sybilla is a basilisk, all vanity and spite. She was betrothed to Sir Richard from birth, but when he came courting and saw Verity, he broke his vow and married the younger sister, taking the dowry with her. I was glad on it at first. But then the plague took the master and mistress before their time and now we live as we do."

Munday took the three miniatures down and tucked them into his doublet. "Should any come after me," he said, "speak nothing of this." And with that he tromped out of the house. Moments later he took horse again, riding fast to Wexcombe House, the miniature portraits tucked safely in his saddle bag. At last he had his answer. Though they had been painted a decade ago, the likenesses were masked but a little by their youth. The current mistress of Wexcombe House was a redhead, not a blonde. It was proof that revealed who the corpse with the ruined face was. The Lady Verity and Sir Richard Wexcombe he had met were imposters—Sybilla Mortlake and her brother Philip had usurped their places.

Oswyn Scrope's suspicions were proven correct. A wicked plot was being hatched. He had to return to Wiltshire as fast as possible.

Queen Elizabeth was in mortal peril.

CHAPTER 38: NOTES FROM UNDERGROUND

After closing time I stump down the cellar steps and latch the door open. The light switch clacks on and the overhead fluorescents stutter into life sending shadows skittering back into their hiding places. The cellar air lays a clammy hand on my forehead, which is flushed with all the thoughts grinding through my overheated brain: *the bloody tree, the bloody town council, the bloody bank . . .*

I try not to think about the lovely Professor Gillian Ryecroft, but of course it's impossible. I had my hopes up after she was so chummy at the conference opener. But since then we've only exchanged a few neutral greetings at breakfast. This evening, she came in late from the conference and barely mumbled a "Goodnight" at me before slinking up to her room with a brandy. It's a good thing this inn doesn't have any secret passages.

I might be tempted to pay her a midnight visit.

To occupy my thoughts I busy myself checking the stock, tapping on the aluminium beer barrels. They're all depressingly full. Looks like I won't need to place an order with the brewery anytime soon. I'm getting so desperate I wonder if I should just quietly pour some of the beer down the grid out so I can place a new order. If the brewery drops me, then it's goodnight Mr. Chips.

A brewery calendar lies atop one of the beer barrels, pages curling in the soggy air. I don't have a calendar and reason it could come in handy—if only so I don't miss Sidney's birthday. (That was a joke.) When I snatch it up I see that the photograph for May is of a thatched roof inn with a familiar face swinging from its pub sign. It's called—cue the crippling irony—*The Shakespeare*.

Like I already said, Life is my Whoopee cushion.

I rummage in a corner toolbox, dig out a hammer and nail and step to the wall. I figure I should be able to pound the nail into the soft mortar between boulders. I give it a first gentle tap to get it started. The nail bites with a solid "chink" and peppers my face with a stinging spray of stony bits. I pull the hammer back ready to really whomp it when I hear a sharp metallic *crack*. My hammer is raised, fingers still clutching the nail, when the stone floor drops from beneath my feet …

… and I plummet into darkness.

CHAPTER 39: MURDER IN THE PANTRY

"I saw the ghost last night."

"What? Burbage asked. "The White Woman you keep chundering about?"

"Aye," Shakespeare nodded. "In the trees beyond the road. While the heavens burned with fiery lightning and the winds shrieked of graves robbed."

Even though he was not a religious man, Burbage crossed himself and said: "God's blood! Did it speak to you?"

"Not in words. But it put its hands to its mouth and made a most piteous sound."

The two players had just raided the kitchen tents and were breaking their fast on sausages and crusty bread hot from the oven. As they chewed, Shakespeare related the story of the food basket, which magically emptied itself.

"A hungry ghost, then?" Burbage speculated, wiping the grease from his lips on the sleeve of his jerkin.

The playwright shook his head. "I think it was no ghost or unearthly spirit, but the same woman we saw with the murdered nobleman. The gory woman we took for a ghost. I think she has gone mad, driven from her wits by suffering."

Burbage ripped a prolonged belch, complete with trills and flourishes, and made a sour face. "Such matters are not good fare for morning conversation, Will. You disturb the labours of my stomach."

Just then a surly-faced man passed the kitchen tents leading a pack horse laden with baskets of fruit: rosy-skinned apples in one set of baskets; tawny pears in the others. A white-haired lady traipsed behind. She seemed strangely familiar and then Shakespeare recognized her. He sprang to his feet and fell in step with her. "Sweet Mistress," he said in greeting. "I think we have met before. I am Will Shakespeare."

The woman looked up and met his eyes. It took a moment, but then she smiled. "Aye, I remember you: the kind player we met on the road. I am Winifred."

"How do you fare, Winifred? You were much distressed when last we met."

The old woman shook her head, ruefully. "I had nowhere to go, so I moved in with my daughter and her husband, an orchardist." She nodded to the man leading the horse. "They dwell in a small village not five miles from here."

They reached the house kitchens. Winfred's son-in-law, a gruff, balding man called Jack, tied the horse's reins to a rosemary bush that grew outside the pantry door. "I must present the reckoning," he grumbled, and indicated the bushels with a nod. "Unload the horse, old woman. I pay you to work, not gossip to shiftless idlers." He lavished the player with an angry glare to show whom he meant and strutted away.

"Truth is he does not pay me at all," Winifred confessed when he had gone. "He is my son by marriage only. He treats me like a slave. Yet it is better than starving or begging on the roads as many do in these times. But how do you fare, Will?"

"Our fortunes ride upwards. We are to perform two plays for the Queen and court."

"I am right glad to hear of your good fortune." The woman grabbed a heavy basket from the horse and struggled to carry it into the kitchen. Anxious to help, Shakespeare unloaded a basket of pears and followed her in. The room they entered was the larder, a narrow storage place for vittles next to the kitchens. They thumped their heavy bushels down on a long table.

"Have you seen the Lord and Lady of the house?" she asked.

"Aye, I encountered his Lordship last night: a haughty, proud-face man, much overfull of himself."

"Nay," Winifred said. "Sir Richard is a kind man. Had he not been gone away on business to Bristol, we should not have all been cast out, I know it."

"The lady dismissed you?"

"Nay, Verity is a gentle dove and showed us all much kindness. It was her sister, Sybilla. She thinks herself the mistress of the house and plays the tyrant when the lord is way. It was she who dismissed us all. She is poison—both she and her brother."

"Brother?"

"Aye, Philip Mortlake, a contemptible and lazy rogue. Both are house guests who long since wore out their welcome."

"Did you not know? Brother and sister have quit the house. Talk has it they fled before the queen arrived. They were of the old faith but would not pay the recusancy fines."

Winifred's laugh was tinged with bitterness. "Old faith, indeed? In truth, neither are godly folk of any persuasion. A pair of leeches, more like. Sybilla was spiteful and envious of her sister. Her and her vile brother idled here two years, eating their fill and paying nothing. Indeed, they have no money. If they have quit the house, then I am right glad of it."

They stepped back outside to finish unloading the horse. On the second trip, Winifred wasn't strong enough to lift the heavy bushel onto the larder table. Shakespeare hurried to set his basket down so he could help. Winifred was pale and panting with effort.

"Tarry a moment and rest," Shakespeare said. "I shall bear the rest in."

"You are kind," puffed Winifred, leaning heavily on the table and wiping sweat from her brow. "I am an old woman and not as strong as I once was."

As Shakespeare stepped outside to fetch the remaining bushels, Winifred happened to glance through the open kitchen door and froze at the flash of gold. It was the light glinting off a large crucifix that hung around a lady's neck. Winifred looked up at the face and blanched. It was Verity's sister, the Lady Sybilla. At that same moment Sybilla looked up and their eyes met. Sybilla's eyes widened for a moment in surprise, then she swept into the larder and banged shut the door to the kitchen behind her.

"You are dismissed from this house. I told you never come back!"

Winifred trembled as the lady approached. "I am here to deliver these apples, these pears …" Winifred paused, her eyes roving over Sybilla. "That is one of my lady's favourite frocks. Did she give it you?" The older woman's eyes continued to crawl over Sybilla. "And those rings upon your fingers . . . those are my Lady Verity's!" The old woman's eyes widened with dread realisation: her lady would never give up her wedding ring, or her betrothment ring. "What wickedness is this? What have you done with my Lady?"

Sybilla's face darkened. She stepped to the outside larder door and closed it, then shot the bolt, locking them in. "I warned you, crone, to quit this house and never come back." Her voice was sharpened steel. "Now you shall repent your foolishness!"

Winifred cringed as Sybilla stepped toward her, fingers caressing the base of her gold crucifix.

"Wu-where?" Winfred stammered. "Where is my good lady?"

"Where she belongs, in a grave, as you shall be soon enough!"

Verity thumbed a hidden catch at the base of the crucifix, which unlatched, and drew out of the base, revealing the cross to be a miniature of the poison dagger Shakespeare and Scrope had found in the oak forest. Winifred's eyes widened. She backed toward a curtain that screened the doorless opening of a walk-in cupboard.

"Come," Sybilla said. "You owe God a death, old woman. Of all my sister's wretched slaves I hated you most. If I had time, I would cut out your wagging tongue."

Winifred began to shout out: "Help! Murder! Oh help me!"

Sybilla clamped a hand over Winifred's mouth and shoved her

head back so hard it cracked against the wall." I feel your heart flutter like a little bird trapped in a cage!" she taunted. "How shall I set it free?" Sybilla drove the dagger upward into the old woman's chest, slipping the keen blade under the ribs, into the liver. Winifred's eyes flashed wide with terror, her drawn-out scream squeezed between the fingers clamping her mouth. As the caustic poison burned through her veins, the old woman shuddered. A horrible, convulsive wave rippled across her face. Sybilla trilled with laughter to see it.

"The coldness of the grave steals through your bones," Sybilla taunted. "'Tis the poison, old hag. Struggle not against it. Die and let the ghost slip out."

The outside pantry door rattled. Knuckles rapped against wood. Someone was trying to get in.

Winifred gripped Sybilla's wrist. Years of hard work had given her strong hands. Sybilla let go of the dagger stuck in the old woman's chest and tried to pry the tenacious fingers from her forearm, but could not.

"Winifred," a man's voice called from outside. "'Tis Master Shakespeare."

The door latch clanked up and down impotently, for the door was securely bolted. When she could not pry the fingers from her wrist, Sybilla sank her teeth into the wrinkled fingers biting down until teeth grated bone. Winifred moaned with pain, but her grip did not slacken. Sybilla pushed her through the curtain into the pantry cupboard. Dark and deep, the cupboard was a niche set into the heavy stone walls of the building. Wheels of cheese wrapped in muslin sat on the shelves. A large knife sat atop one. Sybilla snatched it up and slashed the blade across Winifred's fingers, severing muscle and tendon. Her fingers loosened and Sybilla hurled her backwards. The old woman crashed into the shelves and crumpled to the ground. The impact dislodged several heavy wheels of cheese, which tumbled from their shelves and clubbed her about the head and shoulders, stunning her senseless. Sybilla pulled the dagger from Winifred's chest and wiped the blade on the old woman's dress, then slipped the needle-like blade back into its crucifix sheath.

The knocking became hammering. Sybilla stepped from the cupboard and drew the curtain shut.

Shakespeare heard the bolt being slid aside. He was shocked when he saw who answered the pantry door. "Milady Verity!" She grabbed the front of his doublet and dragged him inside. "Methinks, I—" he began to say, but she banged the door shut and silenced him with a passionate kiss. They crashed into the pantry table, knocking over one of the bushel baskets. Apples rolled across the table and thumped to the floor.

The Lady shoved Shakespeare against the wall. His arm hit the curtain and it flapped open. Inside, Winfred was still not dead. Worse, she was trying to crawl out of the cupboard and pull her self up by the curtain. The old woman reached out with a flailing arm, her fingertips brushing Shakespeare's ankle. Sybilla stamped on her hand, grinding it beneath her heel until it went limp, and then kicked it away. She snatched the curtain closed and pushed Shakespeare farther along the wall.

Sprawled on the floor of the cheese cupboard, Winfred twitched in her death throes, choking and gurgling. Shakespeare broke from the kiss, breathing hard, his eyes wide. "Methinks I heard something stir in yonder cupboard!"

"Tis but a rat in the cheese. We have laid down poison."

She silenced him with another thrilling kiss.

Breath spilled from Winifred's lungs in a drawn-out wheeze, her heels drumming the cupboard floor in a final, spastic kick.

Shakespeare broke from the kiss again. "Methinks it must be a giant among all rats!"

To silence him, she pushed her tongue in his mouth and cupped a warm hand on his crotch. "Milady!" he gasped. Even Shakespeare was unused to such an aggressively wanton woman.

A fist pounded. "Who locked this door?" a gruff voice shouted from the other side of the pantry door. "Open varlet or I shall box your ear!" It was Jack, Winifred's surly son-in-law and now he hammered on the door with his fist.

"Go to," she said breathlessly. "We must not be seen together. But come you to my chamber tomorrow night, after your play."

"But, but what of your husband?"

"He wastes half the night in carousing. By then he will be pouring himself full of sack."

She dragged him to the door and shot back the bolt.

"Go, now, my love!" She kissed him quickly and pushed him out the door. He turned to say a final word but she had vanished.

Shakespeare banged shoulders with the gruff son-in-law as he pushed past. The orchardist was carrying the last bushel of apples and thumped it down on the table. When he saw the toppled bushel and the apples scattered about the floor, the orchardist cursed Winifred. He strode back outside and shouted at Shakespeare.

"Where did the old witch go?"

"Winifred? I know not, sir."

The gruff fellow yanked off his cap and ruffled an angry hand through the lank wisps of hair straggling his baldpate. "Wife's mother or no, the drab shall share our roof no longer!" He stalked back into the pantry, grumbling and cursing under his breath.

"Who was that fellow?" Burbage asked, as Shakespeare rejoined him in the shadow of the kitchen tent.

"An onion-eyed eunuch, a peevish and lousy knave," Shakespeare spat, but then smirked at his fellow player.

"Ah," Burbage said, noting the expression. "I spy Will Shakespeare's devil smile. That smile can mean only one thing."

"Aye," Shakespeare agreed. "Tomorrow night, while you are pounding dough in the kitchen, I will be pounding in a Lady's chamber."

The hidden door opened and Sybilla ducked in through it into a secret passage that ran behind the fabulous bedroom built for Elizabeth. John Finch and Thomas Hyde sat at a small table eating from wooden trenchers and now they both rose.

"We have a dead rat in the pantry," Sybilla announced.

Hyde wiped greasy fingers on a cloth. "Why tell us? Have a kitchen boy fetch it away."

"This rat walked on two legs."

The priests stopped chewing and exchanged frightened looks. "How mean you?" Finch asked.

"The old woman, Winifred, one of Milady Verity's servants. She came back, delivering fruit. She saw me."

"God preserve us!" Hyde said, crossing himself.

"Peace! Tis done. She is dead." Sybilla nodded at the luggage stacked against the wall. "Take a trunk to the pantry. Put her aged corpse inside and hide it in a closet. Come nightfall you shall toss it in the river and we will be rid of her forever."

"But we cannot be seen," Hyde said. "We both are sought after. Scrope and his men are everywhere. Finch may not attract notice, but my foreshortened stature invites stares."

Sybilla ruminated upon it. "Then you," she said, her eyes fastening upon Finch. "You must go alone."

"I cannot by myself carry a trunk with a dead corpse in it!"

"Put the body in the trunk and lock it. Then have a servant, a labourer, anyone, help you carry it."

Finch hesitated; he threw a frightened look at Hyde.

"NOW!" she screamed. "Hye you away! If the old hag is discovered then this knotted skein shall come unravelled!"

Finch rose uncertainly, hesitated a moment, and then brushed past her and stepped through the hidden door. When he had gone, Sybilla put a hand on Hyde's shoulder, hovering close to his ear as she dropped her voice to a conspiratorial whisper. "You, I trust," she said. "But this fool and Philip ..." She said nothing further, but her meaning was clear in the look she gave the Jesuit.

"Weak men who would betray our cause," Hyde ventured.

"They must be the first Catholic martyrs of a new age for England. I have ensnared a man, a fool player. I can fan his lust to do aught I bid. I will have him kill Philip. You must lie for Finch."

Hyde said nothing for a moment, and then nodded his dark head in agreement.

The horse lamed itself on the broken-back road an hour's ride from Chester. Anthony Munday dropped from the saddle and tried to lead nag on, but it limped a few steps and then tossed its head and refused to move. The pursuivant looked about him. The land here was flat. Beyond the hedgerows, rills of shadow pooled in the ploughed furrows of a farmers field. Dusk rushed on. Bats flitted in dizzy circles overhead. The next post inn was fourteen miles distant. He scanned the horizon for the meagrest glimmer of candle light, but the land was sparsely populated and the folk who lived hereabouts, mostly farmers, got up with the sun and went to bed with the sun. Few had coin to waste on luxuries such as candles.

He tugged at the horse's reigns, and though it whinnied and tossed its head, dragged it from the stony road to the grass verge. Talking gently to the mare and stroking its neck, he finally enticed it to lie down.

Here he lay back against its stomach, pulled his doublet up around his neck and tucked his hands into his sleeves, like a bird roosting for the night. The heat of the day spiralled up from ploughed fields into darkened skies lighting up with fiery stars. The sun had been down less than an hour and already a dank chill seeped into the air. Munday shivered in his doublet and hugged himself, squirming against the horse for warmth.

He would pass the long night with his mind skimming in and out of fretful dreams of treason and treachery.

Though he snatched at it, sleep was a silver-winged moth that flitted through Shakespeare's fingers. On the bed beside him,

Burbage snored like a rutting boar. A thousand thoughts raced through Shakespeare's head. A curtain teased open in his mind and the events of the last few days played out as if upon a stage: the bloodied man; the white shape flitting in the trees; the double sixes of the rattling dice reflected in Rafe Foxe's eyes. How had the rogue escaped? As the soldiers dragged him off, Foxe had shouted about dark deeds being done in the cellar. What did he mean by that? Who or what was the white woman he kept seeing? And then, again, like a massy wheel turning, his thoughts returned to the limpid brown pools of Lady Verity's eyes.

The cycle repeated, again and again. Finally, Shakespeare sat up on the lumpy mattress. Sleep would not come until he had answered at least one of the questions that vexed his mind. He swung his legs from the bed.

For several minutes, he stood at the top of the cellar landing, straining for a sound. Nothing but the tick and creak of the Inn settling about him. He crept down the stone steps and paused with his hand upon the rough iron latch. It lifted silently beneath his thumb and he eased the door open slowly to forestall its creaking. Inside a candle guttered, drowning in a puddle of wax.

No one and nothing. The room lay empty save for casks of sack and ale cradled on trestles or stacked against the stony walls. The Stratford player walked around the gloomy space, slapping the walls and rapping on the casks. All was solid. Immovable. Maybe Will Kempe was right, maybe Rafe Foxe did practice dark magic and could dissolve his bones and pour beneath the crack of a door. But Shakespeare, although he often invoked the supernatural in his plays, was not a believer in magic, faeries, or such like—at least not during the hours of daylight.

A sudden thought struck him.

Following the needling stir of instinct, he crept back into the kitchen. Once again, the bare footprints of Burbage and Maud wrote a bawdy play in the flour dusting the kitchen floor. A moment's searching produced Maud's flour sifter. He snatched it and crept back into the cellar where he sprinkled the stone flags with a light, barely perceptible sifting of flour. He pulled the cellar door closed as quiet as he could and began to creep up the cellar steps. He paused at a heavy thump from within the cellar and then voices seemed to ascend as if from under the earth. Men's voices. He could make out Walt Gedding's churlish snarl of consonants and John Thomas' nasal whine. The voices approached the cellar door, so he scampered up the stone steps and ducked into the kitchen where he crouched beneath the table. The cellar door screeled open and thumped shut. He heard two pairs of feet pad by the kitchen door: the innkeeper and his tapster heading to bed. Most nights, Walt Gedding slept in an attic over the brew kegs while John Thomas lay eclipsed in the shadow of his moon-sized wife. Shakespeare waited until the house fell silent, and then crawled from beneath the table.

In the cellar, two sets of footprints walked from the far wall to the cellar steps. Shakespeare lifted the candle and followed them. The footprints appeared to emerge from the solid stones of the cellar wall, as if they were ghosts who could pass immaterial through earth. He lowered the flickering candle flame and studied the floor slab. It was large and rectangular, but the edges were sharp and not caked with dust or dirt—as if it had been recently laid. He stepped onto the slab and it pitched down beneath his weight. He leapt off and the slab lifted and thumped against an invisible stop. He pushed again and this time the slab, pivoted at its centre by an iron rod and balanced perfectly, swung open and thumped against the back wall. A hidden door. The shuddering candle flame showed a wooden ladder that descended ten feet to a stone floor. A glimmer of light showed that candles burned down there. He replaced the dying candle atop the barrel. How to erase the flour marks on the floor? He spotted a cask on its side with a cork protruding from its rotund belly. He snatched up the mallet atop the barrel and whacked the cork loose with one stout blow. Sweet-smelling sack gurgled from the barrel in a steam and splashed onto the stone flags. As the pool of sack dilated, it washed away the tell tale flour trail.

A waste of good sack, he thought, stopping the flow by pushing the cork back in. Screwing up his courage, he peered down into the hole in the floor. A chill breeze rose from the tunnel's throat. Shakespeare had always hated crypts, caves, low cellars and such dark, enclosed places, but he had to find out where the secret passage went. His heart was softly thumping as he probed with a foot until he felt the ladder's top rung. Seconds later he had clambered to the bottom. The tunnel stretched off into unfathomable darkness. Candle stubs flickered on a waist-high ledge than ran the length of it. Shakespeare had heard tales of such secret passages and underground tunnels—the town of Nottingham was said to be riddled with them—but until now he had taken such stories for wives' tales and the ale-fueled bombast of tavern idlers.

And then he saw it: a light hovering in the far distance. But, no, it was moving. Bobbing. Swaying. And then he realized what it was.

A human figure, stooped over in the low tunnel, shuffling toward him.

He looked back up at the opening.

"Walt, you jolt-head," a voice came from the cellar above. "You have left the door agape!" The voice belonged to the innkeeper, John Thomas, dangerously close. Shakespeare threw a quick look back up the tunnel. The bobbing candle was much nearer. He could just make out the faint shape of a man in the halo of light. Angry voices hissed at one another from the cellar above. "Nay, I closed it!" the raspy voice was clearly that of the rough tapster, Walt Geddings.

"Well, it is open now and the wind did not blow it open!"

"I tell you I closed it." From the closeness of the voices, the two must be standing directly above. Any closer and they would see Shakespeare at the bottom of the ladder.

"Lack-wit, we will all be undone!"

Suddenly, the heavy slab in the cellar floor slammed shut above the player's head. Panic surged through him. He opened his mouth to shout out. To let them know he was there, trapped below. But then strong arms grabbed him from behind, and a gloved hand clamped over his mouth, imprisoning his shout of terror so that it thrashed in his throat like a bird trapped in a chimney.

CHAPTER 40: A LONG JOURNEY THROUGH A SHORT DARKNESS

M ole Man is gone for what seems a very long time, but is probably only twenty minutes. Eventually we hear his laboured breathing and then the scrape of boots on wooden ladder rungs. Then mole man's helmeted head pops out of the opening in the cellar floor, eyes blinking at the light like something dug up from the garden.

"So," I say, unable to contain myself. "What? What did you find??"

The cyclopean eye blazing atop his hard hat focuses its retina-searing beam on me. He snaps off the headlamp and I blink my eyes tearfully, ugly yellow after-images cascading before my eyes.

"Bloody brilliant!" he says, clambering spryly out of the hole. The human mole rat tugs off his hard hat and wipes a hand across a face smudged with dirt.

"What?" I say.

"Bleedin' amazing!"

"What is?"

"You'll never guess where it comes out."

"I'm not paying you to guess!" I yell. "Just tell me."

He's still puffing hard and it takes him a moment to catch his breath. "It must be five, six hundred yards long!"

I hurl an angry scowl at Sidney. "He's your cousin. Will you please kill him!"

"Yeah, all right. All right!" Moleman says, raising a hand. His real name is Mike something and he's related to Sidney. I'm trying to keep this whole discovery on the QT for the time being. I don't want the Police, the Local Council or any government officials poking around or telling me I've got an unmarked medieval sewer running under my pub and so I have to shut down. One whisper and they'd be in here like a shot with their high-vis jackets, fluorescent orange traffic cones and yellow caution tape.

Moleman Mike sits down on the stone flags beside the hole and chugs a mouthful of water from a plastic bottle. Sidney and I crowd closer like children at story time.

"I've just been inside Wexcombe House," he says as a gleaming grin breaking out on his filthy face.

It's not what I'm expecting to hear. A dumbfounded silence hovers in the air.

"Wexcombe House?" I share a disbelieving look with Sidney. "Impossible!" I say. "Wexcomb is half a mile away—"

"Yeah," he agrees, "a half mile *if* you take the road and go in through the driveway. This tunnel runs straight as an arrow about four hundred meters. It comes out in a secret passageway inside the walls of the house. I didn't go any further. There's a lot of trash and debris in there. Probably hundreds of years' worth of rubbish. Plus I know the hall has all the high tech kit: motion-detector burglar alarms, video cameras. The lot. Didn't want to set them off. That'd bring the Rozzers and sharpish."

"I don't believe you."

He takes off his orange plastic hard hat and offers it to me. "Don't believe me, go have a shufty yourself."

"Surely it's not safe!" I say, back-pedalling furiously. I'm very claustrophobic. Hate tight spaces. I can't even stay in the car when it goes through a car wash—gives me the heebie jeebies. Having barely recovered from the half hour I already spent down there, in the darkness, shouting for Sidney, there's no way I'm going back down. "You must be having a laugh," I say. "Go poking around in some musty old medieval tunnel? Probably cave-in if a mouse farts."

Mike the mole shakes his head dismissively. "Nah. Safe as houses. Whoever built this tunnel really knew what he was doing. I'll bet it was built the same time Wexcombe house was built—as a bolt hole. It's got a drain running down the middle to siphon away rain water. The sides of the tunnel have niches for candles. The slab you stood on was originally a secret door. It had an iron bar drilled right through the middle to act as a pivot. The slab was precisely balanced so it would swing open under a slight push."

"Then why did it give way under me?" I ask. "And please, no comments about my weight."

"Iron rusts. Corrodes. Gets brittle. After four hundred years of exposure to moisture, including the odd beer spill, it rusted through."

"So you didn't find anything down there?" I ask. I try to sound casual, but I'm no poker player. (The only card game I was ever any good at was Snap—played against myself.) I'm sure my every look, every gesture, is a tell.

He shrugs. "Old candleholders holding puddles of melted wax . . . I wasn't really looking for anything. Just following where it went. I could go back down, if you like, and have a good nosy around—"

"Now, that's quite all right," I quickly interrupt. My hands are shaking as I peel a fifty-pound note off my roll and dangle it under Moleman's dirt-smudged hooter. "Well done," I say. "Thanks for your help, and, er, this is just between us, right?"

"Oh yeah," he says, sounding very unconvincing. "You wanna come down yourself and have a look?"

"No," I say. "I've already had a look."

Sidney chuckles around his pipe. "A good long look. He'd been down there for half an hour before I found him. Should've heard him yelling and carrying on.. Screaming like a school girl." Sidney makes his voice go all whiney: "Help! Help! Get me out!"

"Yes, thank you, Sidney," I say and realise the obvious at the same moment. "What the hell are you doing here, anyway? Who's minding the bar?"

254 | DOUBLE FALSEHOOD

Sidney takes the hint and shuffles back up the cellar steps, chuckling around his pipe.

I clap Mike the Mole on the shoulder. "Cheers, mate," I say. "Keep this schtum, right? I don't the want the health inspectors nosin' around here."

Mike is an amateur spelunker, unemployed and—most important —an ex-con. He used his underground skills to tunnel out of the remand home he was sentenced to a few years ago. Of course, the law caught up with him a day later, having a pint in his local pub. Prat.

He frowns at the fifty-pound note in his hand as if disappointed with the portrait of the poncy, bewigged bloke on it. "Fifty quid?" he mutters dully, syllables sagging with disappointment. "I rode my bike all the way from Marlborough for fifty bleedin' quid? Do you know how much petrol costs?"

Actually, I do know how much petrol costs. It pains me but I figure an investment in his silence would be prudent. I peel off another fifty and slap it in his hand.

A smile lights up his filthy face. "Cheers." Once again he tries to hand me the hard hat. "Sure you don't want a look around—"

"No!" I say. "That's fine." Yes, I'm scared of the dark, of narrow tunnels, of being underground. But mostly I'm scared of what Sidney or Mike the Mole might find if left to their own devices. I'm scared, you see, because I already found something down there. I put my hand on it in the darkness. I don't know what it is. I haven't told anyone about it yet, not even Gillian.

Especially not Gillian.

But I've a feeling it could be worth a lot of dosh.

CHAPTER 41: THE HIDDEN WEXCOMBE

"Peace, Shakeword. Keep your wits. Call out and I'll snap your neck!"

Shakespeare's eyes bugged in the darkness. He could not draw breath, let alone shout. The gloved hand smothered both his nose and mouth. He quit struggling, relaxed, and the hand clamped over his face pulled away.

A hot chuckle licked the bowl of his ear. "So, coz, you have tumbled to the secret of the cellar?"

Shakespeare knew the owner of the voice before he turned to look: Rafe Foxe. "So this is how you escaped when Scrope locked you in?"

"Aye, a simple trick—a door in a stone floor where none would look for one. Fools believe their eyes. Tis how I make my living." Foxe had been dragging a sack behind him as he crawled and now he thumped it down. The sack spilled opened and a solid silver candlestick rolled out. Other objects of gold and silver caught the candlelight and gleamed back.

"You have stolen these things!"

Foxe laughed at Shakespeare. "Stealing is how I make an honest living, coz. But I confess I cannot carry the larger things, such as the furniture and house fittings as many of the Queen's own courtiers do."

Shakespeare knew it was not an exaggeration. He had heard tales of courtiers on the Royal Progress where they descended upon a great house as rapacious as two-legged locusts. They would hunt down and slaughter every deer in the deer park, and strip whole rooms of furniture, going even as far as dismantling the wood panelling on the walls and hauling it away in carts.

"I'll steal nothing," Shakespeare said, squinting into the darkness where Foxe had just come from.

"You may at least steal a look. Tis wondrous. Come, I'll show you."

The tunnel was just tall enough to allow a man to duckwalk, crouched over. Shakespeare forgot to bend quite low enough at several places, and incurred a painful whack atop the noggin. Moving in the darkness, just fast enough to prevent their candles from blowing out, the trip seemed to take forever, but they finally arrived at a set of narrow stone steps that rose steeply. By the time they summited the steps, both men were breathing hard. At the top of the steps they entered a long, dark passage so narrow their shoulders brushed either wall.

"Where are we?"

Foxe turned to throw a grin back at Shakespeare. "Within the walls of Wexcombe House. Hidden passages run both length and breadth. Follow and be amazed."

They continued on as the passage turned a corner.

"Who could have built this?" Shakespeare whispered.

"I reckon it was fashioned before the present house was built." Foxe slapped a hand across the bricks to his left. They were uneven and crudely cut compared to the fine mason-work of the outer wall. "Wexcombe House is built upon the bones of an old manor house."

"Aye, but why build such a tunnel to the Inn?"

Foxe turned his head to look back, his smile gleaming in the candlelight. "Can you not guess, coz?" Ten feet on, Foxe stopped and fumbled with something in the wall. Hinges creaked as a door swung open and candlelight spilled out, stretching their shadows against the wall behind. The two slid into a small room where votary candles burned, filling the small chamber with an otherworldly light. Shakespeare's eyes widened. The heady scent of incense burned in his nostrils.

A chapel. Small. No bigger than a monastic cell. An altar stood at one end of the room, a jewel-encrusted cross on the wall above. A priest's vestments hung on another. The chapel was decorated with all the trappings of Catholic Mass. In the reign of Elizabeth, the sacramental objects, the chapel, all were proscribed by law as treason, a crime punishable by the worst possible death—to be hung, drawn and quartered.

"'Tis not wondrous to behold?" Foxe said. "Back in Henry's day, the house belonged to the Mortlake family, secret Catholics despite the King's proclamations."

Shakespeare trembled just to be there. "We must leave this place."

But Rafe Fox strolled about, calm and unafraid. "So a travelling priest may take a room in the Inn and magically vanish by next morning, smuggled into the house through the tunnel. Right under the noses of the pursuivants."

Shakespeare said nothing. He had no doubt Rafe Foxe was correct, which meant that the Lady Verity had been living in peril of her life for years.

The Coney-Catcher approached the altar slowly, reverently, then dropped to one knee and crossed himself. Shakespeare lingered in the shadows. The danger of even setting foot in such a forbidden place was giddying. Foxe rose slowly, smiled, and then started to help himself to the candlesticks and the gold crucifix, stuffing them into a sack he pulled from his belt.

"Stop!" Shakespeare cried. "To steal from a holy place is wicked blasphemy!"

Rafe Foxe raised an eyebrow and smiled. "And are you such a godly man, coz? A praying man? Tell me true, how long since your knees felt cold stone beneath them? Peace, and I will show you the most wondrous room in all the world."

They left the chapel and groped farther up the narrow passage, eventually emerging into a wider chamber. A number of large chests lay neatly stacked. Next to them, two huge paintings in elaborate gilt frames leaned against the wall. The uppermost was a portrait of a man posed next to a globe. He regarded the viewer with an open, charitable face of obvious good humour. Something about the figure seemed immediately familiar.

"Do you know who this fellow is?" Shakespeare asked.

But Foxe ignored the question for he was busy fiddling with something in the wall. Shakespeare moved closer and watched him slide a hasp holding shut a narrow panel in the wall. When Foxe opened the panel, light spilled into the dark space filtered through a mesh screen.

A secret spy hole.

"Look upon this, Master Shakescribble."

Shakespeare put his face to the screen and peered out. The spy hole looked into the ornate chamber that had been prepared for the Queen. He could see a corner of the huge four-poster bed, marble sculptures, and a room filled with silk cushions and the most handsome furniture and fittings he had ever clapped eyes on. As he watched, a pair of maidservants was helping a lady into a fine dress. She held out her arms as they lowered a farthingale of rich satin over her. The dress whispered onto her shoulders and Shakespeare drew in his breath when he saw the lady's face.

Verity.

Shakespeare yanked his face away from the screen.

"She cannot see you," Foxe chuckled. "In this dark chamber we are quite hid behind the mesh."

The Stratford Player could not help but look again. The lady held her arms out as the two maids, using needle and thread, sewed her into the dress.

Rafe Foxe's hot breath snickered in his ear. "Tis not marvellous? The house is warrened with passages such as this. Oh, the things I have seen through these peepholes! I tell you, the queen's court is a hot, sweaty press of lewd license and bawdy bangings."

"But not this lady," Shakespeare insisted, hackles rising.

"No, but I tell you this—the lady's husband does not frequent her bed."

Just then the door opened and Sir Richard swaggered in. "Madam!" he said in a stern voice. "The queen had summoned us to dance. Why tarry you?"

"I am dressing, sir!"

Sir Richard's face purpled. He glared and turned away, pacing the room impatiently. After five more minutes, he grew even more impatient and sank into a chair. He grimaced as he put an arm to his shoulder and massaged it.

"Have you hurt your arm, husband?" the lady asked as her servants fussed.

Sir Richard answered with a hateful look.

"How came you by that injury?" she asked. "Playing at cards? Dancing the volpe? Is that what you shall tell the queen?" Her voice was ironic, taunting.

Sir Richard's jaws clenched as he spoke. "You know full well how I came by it."

The maids finally finished tying the cuffs of her sleeves. "Leave us," she said, dismissing them with a gesture. The women curtsied and scurried from the room.

Sir Richard rose creakily from his chair. "Come, *Madam*, Gloriana awaits."

The two walked to the door. Before they opened it, the Lady Verity held out her arm primly and Sir Richard took it. He opened the door and they left together, the very picture of a devoted couple.

"She likes him not!" Shakespeare breathed. "Nor he her."

Foxe tapped his shoulder. "Come, coz, and I'll show you more."

Foxe touched something in the wall, a metal latch retracted and a man-shaped doorway swung inward. As Shakespeare followed the Coney-Catcher through it, he noted the door's odd shape. On the other side he looked back and saw the reason. The wall they had just passed through was painted with a giant fresco in a Biblical theme: the expulsion of Adam and Eve from the Garden of Eden. The camouflaged door was the exact outline of Adam. Foxe pulled it closed behind him. The latch clicked shut and the door melted into the immense fresco and vanished.

"See?" Foxe taunted. "Fools believe their eyes—especially where beauty is involved."

Shakespeare looked around in wonder. He had never seen the like of the room they were in: the huge bed, the ornate tapestries hung on the walls, the trickle of a fountain in which rose petals floated. Foxe busied himself wandering about, stealing objects small enough to stuff into his doublet: a fine silver bell, a pewter snuff dish, a silver hand mirror.

"Enough, rogue!" Shakespeare chided. "You will be hanged, and me with you!"

Foxe tossed the Stratford player the scantest of looks. "We all must all hang for something, Master Shakebag. I will at least hang for goods of quality."

Shakespeare paused, looking dumbstruck at the great clockwork mechanism in the ceiling. The moon in its phases and all the signs of the zodiac turned slowly about the sun, a smiling fiery orb at the centre. Its movement was ingenious, mesmerising, its slow revolution drew Shakespeare's mind into it and scattered the dizzy pieces among the painted stars.

Both men froze at voices outside the door. The Lord and Lady were unexpectedly returning.

Foxe darted back to the fresco and seemed to pass through it like a ghost, so fast did the hidden door fly open and bang shut behind him. Shakespeare ran to the where the door had been, but it did not open to his push. He pushed and prodded the portrait here and there as he had seen Foxe do, but could not fathom the trick of how it opened.

Stranded.

The door of the room flung open and Lady Verity entered, followed closely by Sir Richard. Shakespeare had time only to run and dive beneath the bed—where he banged his head into something cold, hard, and iron.

"… cannot sit to supper in this heat without my fan …" the Lady was saying.

"We are late already. The Queen will be much offended!"

The player had collided with a great mechanism beneath the bed, a massive thing of iron gearwheels and cables.

"Tis hot summer and I swelter in these skirts. I'll not go without my fan."

"Should we fail to appear—!"

"Speak not of failing after *you* failed this very morn."

"Chance yet remains. At the Masque. We have waited this long—"

"I am tired of waiting … as I am tired of you."

"Then I am doubly tired of you!"

"Milk-livered fop!"

"Churlish witch. When this enterprise is done—"

"What? What then? Choose your words wisely."

"Things will be different. I shall say no more."

"Aye. Indeed, sirrah. Things shall be very different. The world will change on that day."

The door banged shut. The contentious voices, muffled by the door, receded. Shakespeare crawled from beneath the bed rubbing his throbbing head. He raced to the Biblical fresco. The Creator floated on a cloud in the top right hand of the portrait—an angry God, smiting his flawed creation with a scornful finger pointing the way, casting them out of the Garden. Adam's terrified eyes showed the whites. He cowered, arms thrown up, shielding his head. Shakespeare's gaze traced down the body, nude but for the fig leaf that preserved male modesty. What was it Rafe Foxe had said? *Fools believe their eyes.* He reached down and put a finger on the fig leaf. It depressed beneath his push. Somewhere a latch snicked and Adam became a door once again and swung inwards.

Inside the secret chamber, Rafe Foxe knelt at one of the chests, probing the lock with a pick.

"Roguish, ill-bred varlet!" Shakespeare said, stepping inside. "You abandoned me!"

"All's well that ends well, coz," Foxe chuckled as the pick turned in the lock and the tumblers rasped open. The Coney-Catcher smiled and was just lifting the lid when both men froze at the sound of whispered voices approaching. The glow of a lantern appeared at the far end of the passage, floating toward them.

"We are discovered! Shakespeare hissed. "Someone approaches!"

Foxe leapt to his feet. "Fear not, Shagpaw. Once before I encountered a rascal. He was white as a cave grub. It was obvious he hides from the day within the walls and creeps out at night. When I came upon the fellow, pale as he was, he took me for a ghost and ran away."

Shakespeare set the candle down on one of the chests, an idea for a bit of stagecraft quickly forming in his head. He shoved Foxe farther away, in the darkened passageway beyond the candle's meagre light. "Pull down your cap so your face is masked in shadows." Shakespeare backed himself into a dusty corner where he disappeared into the darkness. "I shall be your voice and together we shall out ghost them."

Father Thomas Hyde and Father Finch strolled together, both men carrying lanthorns, the horn shields closed so as to put out no more than a feeble glow. As they entered the chamber, the Coney-Catcher stepped forward, looming over the candle that lit his face from below, his eyes appearing as nothing but dark pools beneath the white glow of his brow.

Both Jesuits froze at the sight of him, their eyes widening in terror. The puce bonnet, the cape, the boots, the gloves—it was the ghost of the man they had murdered: Richard Wexcombe.

"Richard's ghost!" Hyde whispered. "See, he troubles us!"

Crouched in the shadows, Shakespeare pitched his voice down low, into its lowest register and spoke with his face to the wall, so that the sound resounded in the small chamber, disembodied from the form looming in from of them. "Ohhhh. Ohhhhhhhhh! Murder most wicked and bloody. I died unshriven of my sins, and so am bound to walk the earth until my death is avenged!"

"Tis he!" Finch said. "As I have seen before. A visage I tremble at!"

Finch began to back away, but Hyde stood his ground and raised the simple wooden cross that hung around his neck.

"Most foul spirit!" Hyde said. "I exorcize you by all the saints in heaven."

"From purgatory's flames I come to chide you. I will summon devils to grasp your limbs and drag you screaming into the bowels of hell!"

Foxe put out his arms and lunged toward the two Jesuits, who howled with fear and then turned and bolted, running as fast as their feet would carry them.

"Come," Shakespeare said, grabbing Rafe Foxe's arm. "We must away." Shakespeare began to run back the way they had come, back to the tunnel that led to the inn, but after only a dozen steps, realized he was on his own.

"I'll see you anon, coz!" Rafe Foxe shouted from the darkness. "I have more to steal—before I steal away."

CHAPTER 42: TREASURE TROVE

I fight the urge to look until I'm sure everyone is asleep.

Half an hour ago, Sidney wiped down the bar and draped towels over the beer taps, then weaved away on his rickety bicycle toward Marlborough chasing a wan disk of light thrown by the bike's feeble headlamp. The Shakespeare conventioneers have all tossed back their nightcaps and turned in for bed. I circuit the Inn listening for the mindless babble of left-on televisions. Looking for a crack of light glimmering beneath any of the doors—especially Gillian's.

All quiet. All dark. All right.

Back in my office I glance up at the clock: 12:30 a.m. The inn is quiet. Deathly still.

I hold my breath at the subdued roar of tires on macadam—a car driving by on the road outside. The sound rises and recedes. An owl hoots close by—no doubt the same cheeky bugger who perches in the top of the oak and shits all over my car. (Beware my feathered friend, Harvey's revenge is coming!)

My hands tremble as I sort through my jailer's ring of keys and select the tiny brass key. The strongbox holds the day's take and springs open. I reach in, take out the sheaf of papers and set them down carefully on the desk before me. The pages are old, brittle and scrawled with surprisingly straight lines of ye-olde-writing. While I was stumbling around at the bottom of the secret passage, blind and terrified in the darkness, I accidentally put my hand on them. Someone had placed something cold and heavy atop the pages as a kind of paperweight—in the darkness I never saw what. Whatever it was my flailing hand knocked loose hit the stony floor with a thunk. Then, as I groped blindly along the wall, I felt and heard the crackle of papers beneath my fingertips.

I snap on the desk lamp, then get up and lock the office door—just to be safe. I settle back into my chair and hunch over pages turning brown and crispy at the edges and try to decipher the cramped lines of handwriting scrawled across them. I strain for ten minutes, eyes blurring in and out of focus, but the handwriting is migraine-inducingly tiny. I drag open the desk drawer and grab my glasses. I rarely wear them; they're just for reading, which I don't do much of. Plus they make me look like a nonce. I pull the glasses on and the tiny script sharpens, but it's still illegible. Now and again I think I can make out words, but the whirly-twirly handwriting is all flourishes, scrolls and loops. I seem to recognise several small words like "to" and "the" and "of" and "by," which makes me think it's written in English. But the long words all seem to start with S or two Fs and I have no bloody clue what they're supposed to be.

I snatch off the glasses and massage the bridge of my nose. I'm tired. My eyes are sore. It's too late to decipher this gibberish. In the bottom of the box is the day's take, a sad handful of notes and a scattering of coins. I scoop the pages back into the strong box, lock it, and then tuck it behind the leather couch in the corner of my office. I've been meaning to buy a proper safe since the day I moved in. Now I'm kicking myself that I never got around to it.

I am heading toward my room when I hear a thump and see a light in the kitchen. I flip the light switch for the hallway but the bulb is burned out. When I pop my head in, Mrs. Bramsworth is spatuling mashed potatoes atop a tray of Shepherd's Pie. Mrs. Bramsworth is in her early sixties, heavy-set, and a more than a little dotty. She does the pub food and comes in early mornings to serve breakfast. Still, so much for my careful reconnoitre of the Inn. I'd completely missed her presence.

"Mrs. Bramsworth!" I say. "You gave me a start. You're rather late, aren't you?"

She has a lit ciggy dangling between her lips and never removes it as she speaks. "'Allo dear. Just making Shepherd's Pie for the rest of the week."

A blob of ash topples from the end of her cigarette and lands in the meat filling. I say nothing as she smears mashed potato over it.

She finishes with the mash and barges open the door of the large commercial fridge with a well-padded hip and slides inside the Shepherd's Pie. I know it's a long shot—Mrs. Bramsworth is hardly the Brain of Britain—but she seems like a safe person to ask the question I have burning in my mind. "Do you know anything about Treasure Trove?" I ask as casually as one could possibly ask a question like that.

She slams the fridge door and puffs on her cigarette a few times, clouding the air before answering. "Treasure Trove? Isn't that one of those game shows on the telly?"

My smile buckles. I should have known better. "No ... no it's not a game show on the telly."

"Oh, wait," she says. "Yeah. I think I have heard of that, now. *Treasure Trove*. It was in the local paper a week ago. Some chap with one of those mine detectors—"

"Metal detectors?" I interrupt.

"Yeah, one of those. He found a pot of gold coins in a farmer's field, just at the top of our road. Roman, they were—the coins."

"And what happened?"

She puffs her cigarette as she pulls on her leather biker's jacket. "I'm not sure. I seem to remember the government said they were Treasure Trove and took them off him."

An icicle spears through my heart. That's exactly what I feared.

Mrs. Bramsworth pulls on a shiny black motorcycle helmet and yanks aviator goggles down over her eyes. With the lit ciggy hanging out of her mouth, she looks like *the granny from hell*.

"Toodle-oo," she says, letting herself out the back door. "I'll be here in the morning to do the breakfasts."

A moment later I hear the throaty roar of her Triumph motorcycle fire up. She revs it mental for a few seconds and then roars off. As the motorcycle drone fades into the distance, I snap off the kitchen light and plod toward my bedroom.

Treasure Trove.

I'm not sure if a found document falls into the same category as a cache of Roman coins, but I'm not going to chance it. I need to find out from a less-than-official source.

I'm going stealth on this one.

CHAPTER 43: A HANGING, A WHIPPING, AND WORSE . .

I could not pen such a twisted plot, Shakespeare thought as he lay next to the snoring Burbage. The goings-on had become a noose tightening around his neck. He had a planned dalliance with a lady whose husband would happily kill him should he found out. He was being forced to spy on the self-same lady by Oswyn Scrope. Worse, thanks to the coney-catching rogue Rafe Foxe, he was now privy to secret that could land them all as guests of Richard Topcliffe: Lady Verity was a secret Catholic and Jesuit priests were being harboured in the very house that hosted the Queen. If sleep had proved elusive before, it was now impossible. He had hoped this tale would end a comedy, with the wicked punished and the lovers escaping, but now it seemed more likely to end in tragedy, with the stage of affairs groaning with bodies … his among them.

The secret door opened with a squeal like a tortured soul. Rafe Foxe paused, cursing its noise and making a mental note to steal some lard from the kitchen to lubricate the hinges before he next used the secret tunnel. The door opened into the back of the cupboard that sat in, of all places, Oswyn Scrope's room. Foxe knew that the best place to hide something from a canny enemy was under their nose and in plain sight. The cupboard door had been left slightly ajar and he peeked out through the crack. A candle glimmering on the table let him know that Scrope was still awake, despite it being in the early hours of the morning. Scrope's broad back faced him as the puritan knelt beside his bed, hands clasped in prayer, an open bible on the worn floorboards. As usual, Scrope knelt upon an iron rod to chastise his wicked flesh.

Foxe sank to his haunches in the closet and sighed. This could take hours. But after only twenty minutes, Scrope staggered to his feet, collected the rod, and set it aside. He stepped to the table and pinched out the candle flame, pitching the room into darkness. He heard the mattress chuff as Scrope lay down. As part of his puritan sense of vigilance, the Pursuivant always slept fully clothed, right down to his creaky leather boots. He chose this in order to be ready at a moment's notice. Scrope breathed out a heavy sigh and then, after ten more minutes, fell into a steady nasal breathing that skimmed the edges of a light snore.

Slowly, and with infinite patience, Foxe eased the cupboard door open. The chest he had been hiding all his swag in sat against the wall beside the bed, literally under Scrope's beakish nose. He reasoned that when he had accumulated enough, he would steal a horse and cart and make good his escape. Wexcombe was the richest house he had ever robbed and the many fine things he had purloined would make him a wealthy man. He toyed with the idea of using his filched wealth to buy a handsome new wardrobe and present himself at Queen Elizabeth's court where there would no end of things to steal and rich fools to gull of their fortunes.

The door swung wide and Foxe crept out, holding in one hand a sack bulging with gold candlesticks and jewel-encrusted crosses he had stolen from the chapel. The room was black and unfathomable to the eye, but Foxe could navigate through darkness with the grace of a cat. When he was sure he was clear of the dresser, he paused a moment and listened to Scrope's sonorous respiration as air spilled from the mossy caverns of his nose.

Asleep.

Foxe brushed between the wall and the bedside, careful not to let his sack bang against either. He stooped slowly and groped for the lid of the chest he knew must be there. In the darkness, he did everything by touch and was well practiced in such arts. The lid pulled open and he rested it against the wall, and then lifted in the sack of booty. But as he took a half step forward, his foot hit an unseen object—a chamber pot—and it toppled with a crash. In truth, it was but a small sound, but in the silence it seemed deafening. Foxe held his breath and listened. Scrope's breathing did not alter. After five more minutes he decided it was safe. Hoisting the sack in both hands, he started to gradually lower it into the black maw of the open chest.

In the darkness, a hand seized his wrist in a bone-crushing grip.

"So," Oswyn's Scrope's voice boomed, "we meet at last, Master Foxe."

CHAPTER 44: A ROGUE IS HANGED

The next morning, breakfast was accompanied by a hanging. When Will Shakespeare stumbled down the inn stairs, late and blinking at the light, he found the body of the Lord Chamberlain's Men along with the Innkeeper and his family assembled outside in a semi-circle about the great oak tree.

Thomas Pope was chomping an apple as Shakespeare joined them. "What is it, Thom?" he asked. "What's happening?"

Pope nodded and spoke around a mouthful of apple. "A villainous rascal about to come to the end of his rope."

Shakespeare's mouth gaped. Rafe Foxe stood on the back of a wooden cart. He had been stripped of his purloined nobleman's clothes and wore only a white death shroud. His hands were lashed behind his back, a noose looped around his neck. The other end of the rope was tossed over one of the oak's stout limbs. The local Constable stood holding the bridle of a sway-backed nag hitched to the cart.

"Thievin' rogue!" Pope cursed and hurled the apple core, which whizzed over Foxe's head.

"Hello, coz," Foxe said, seeing Shakespeare's face in the crowd. "It appears you must write me out of your play. But as I make my exeunt,

I pray you, put clever words into my mouth, for I would fain be remembered as a crafty Foxe."

Oswyn Scrope stepped forward and raised his voice in address, "Rafe Foxe, you are a conconney-catcherey-catcher, a thief, and a villain. For the crime of burglary and theft, I sentence you—"

"Wait!" Shakespeare interrupted. "Is this man to have no legal council? Is he not afforded even a trial?"

Scrope's face clouded over. He made a face as if swallowing a cupful of bile, and continued. "As these crimes have been committed within *six miles* of the royal presence they constitute Treason. I thereby sentence you to death under my authority as Messenger of the Queen's Chamber. Prisoner!" Scrope enunciated. "Have you any final words?"

"Aye," Foxe said. He cleared his throat, waiting patiently for silence from the crowd, and then began his litany: "I regret that I stole not more, whored not less, lied not more, mocked not more the church, ate beef during lent—"

Foxe's irreverent reply drew scandalised chuckles from the crowd.

"Enough!" Scrope shouted in disgust. He gestured to the Constable. "Sentence is carried out. Lead on the horse."

The nag chuffed, tossed its head, and the cart stuttered forward. The rope sizzled over the rough oak branch and drew taut.

"There is no God!" Rafe Foxe shouted. "And none are saved—" But then the rope jerked tight, choking off his words. His feet kicked at the air as he was hauled upward, his face purpling.

For a man who had been so brash and boisterous, he died a brief, pitiful and small death. Foxe's feet gave a final, spastic shiver and hung still, his corpse swaying with the sudden accumulated mass possessed by all dead bodies.

Thomas Pope spat a gleaming wad of phlegm that landed in the dirt beneath the cooling corpse. "Good riddance!" he muttered, and shouldered his way through the remaining players and back inside the inn. The rest followed until only Burbage and Shakespeare remained, watching as the cart was backed up and Rafe Foxe's body was laid in the back and covered with a canvas scrim.

"A rogue to the end." Burbage said. "And yet I take no comfort in his death."

"Aye," Shakespeare agreed. "He gambled with death, but could not use false dice."

Burbage clapped a hand on Shakespeare's shoulder and the two men went inside.

As the cart bearing the coney-catcher's body clattered away, Sergeant Crugg stepped over to join his master. "A hasty trial, sir?" Crugg's questioning tone raised Scrope's warty eyebrow.

"My haste has a purpose." The pursuivant stood staring down the Great West Road as if looking for something.

"Expect you Master Munday, sir?"

Scrope chewed his chapped lips and shook his head ruefully. "I expected him back yesterday." He shrugged and tapped Crugg on the shoulder. "Come you and look at this."

Sergeant Crugg followed Scrope upstairs to his room where the Pursuivant flung open a chest nestled against the wall, hefted a bulging sack and emptied it out onto the bed. "This is but part of what the villain had stolen."

Crugg's eyes trailed over the assorted treasures spilled across the bed: a silver hand mirror, a gilt ladle, and a fine clock.

"Handsome wares," Crugg said.

"All, no doubt, stolen from the great house nearby." Scrope reached under the bed, dragged out another sack and upended it. A pair of heavy gold candlesticks spilled out, accompanied by an ornate gold crucifix sparkling with gems.

Crugg's eyes widened. The objects were all vestments used in Roman Catholic Mass. "Came these from the same house?" Crugg asked.

Scrope's lips compressed in a mirthless smile. "The villain would not confess to it, but I have little doubt. His thievery has given me better intelligence of what happens inside Wexcombe House than a spy among the servants. It is clear that Romish Mass is being celebrated, which means there are Jesuits hidden within."

"Then we must ride to the house and search it."

"The Privy Council would forbid it, not without irrefutable proof. Three days since, I sent Master Munday to the Mortlake house in Lancashire to arrest the sister and brother and bring them back for inquiry. He has not returned, and now I think it likely he never will."

The news shocked Crugg. "Never, sir?"

Scrope shook his head for answer. "I think it is time I brought in greater powers than mine. Do you know Westminster, Master Crugg?"

The sergeant's face betrayed his surprise. "Westminster? I know it passing well, but I am a London man."

Scrope produced a tightly rolled paper tied with string. "I have a letter you shall deliver."

"To a house in Westminster?"

Scrope nodded. "I shall draw you the streets in words. Once there, you must ask the way. Folk will know the house. The windows are often shuttered during the daylight hours."

Fen Crugg's stomach lurched. Acid filmed his mouth. He knew of the house. All London knew of the house in Westminster with the shuttered windows. His hands trembled as he took the letter from Scrope. "Shall I await a reply, sir?"

"No," Scrope said, shaking his head. "The reply shall accompany you back."

CHAPTER 45: SITTING ON THE FENCE

Sidney is pulling a pint of mild for one of the caravan site fossils when I enter the taproom. I pause to straighten the beer towels having from their rail and drift closer to where he lurks, pretending to carefully scrutinise the levels in the spirit bottles behind the bar—got to keep him on his toes. At last, I edge up to him and say as casually as I can, "That mate of yours who got me the mobile phone, what's his name again?"

Sidney freezes with his hand mid-pump and eyes me suspiciously. "Why do you want to know?"

"Why do you always answer a question with a question?"

He nods in agreement—I've got him there. "He's not my mate."

"Whatever. What's his name?"

"Hedgehog," he grunts after a pause.

"Yeah, that's it. Do you have his number?"

Sidney keeps the punter waiting for his pint. "Why do want his number?"

"Nothing," I say. "Just curious."

Sidney finishes pulling the pint, and slides it across the bar. He takes the money and rattles the handful of coins into the till. "You found something, didn't you? Down in that tunnel?"

"Shush!" I mumble with barely restrained fury. The old gent judders away from the bar, slopping beer as he goes. "No, I was just . . ." I don't want Sidney to guess why I want to talk to the local fence. So I lie. "He got us that case of cheap Chinese whiskey a while back."

"Yeah, which you said tasted like paraquat."

I laugh dismissively. "It wasn't that bad."

"You poured it all down the sink. Said you didn't want to risk being convicted of poisoning."

"Now you're exaggerating—"

"What did you find?" Sidney won't let it go. I need to fob him off with some kind of explanation.

"Just some old papers."

"Papers, what kind of papers?"

"I don't know what kind of papers. Nothing important. Might be of historical interest. For the pub, I mean. That's what I need your friend for."

Sidney sucks at his pipe for a while before rummaging in his pocket. He hands me a worn-smooth scrap of paper with a phone number inked in shaky ballpoint and a one-word name: *Hedgehog*.

CHAPTER 46: A PLAY WITH NO ENDING

The courtiers whooped with laughter as a man with the head of an ass stepped upon the stage and Will Kempe's muffled voice came from within. "If I were fair, Thisby. I were only thine."

The Lord Chamberlain's Men were on stage, performing *A Midsummer Night's Dream*. Will Kempe was playing Bottom the weaver, one his most famous comic roles. The other players, taking the parts of the tradesmen, reacted to his transfigured appearance with terror.

"Oh, monstrous," cried Henry Condell, playing Quince, "Oh strange! We are haunted. Pray masters! Fly masters! Help!"

The shoulders of the courtiers, including the Queen, heaved with laughter as the astonished players fled the stage.

Shakespeare, watching from back stage, was struck by the similarity of the scene to when they all ran screaming from the appearance of the ghastly woman in the forest.

The queen sat close to the stage on the portable throne that travelled with her on her Royal Progresses. Essex, her fawning lap dog, lounged beside her, stroking her wrinkled hand, the fingers of which flashed and twinkled with jewel-studded rings. Lady Verity sat close by. The seat reserved for her husband, the po-faced Sir Richard, was notably empty. His absence encouraged Shakespeare. But then the boor appeared, sidling through the seated courtiers to his place. From his tense posture, he seemed to have injured his shoulder. He shuffled to his chair and settled into it gingerly, wincing. Lady Verity did not so much as glance his way as he sat down.

Shakespeare was playing the double roles of Theseus, Duke of Athens and Oberon, King of the fairies. Every time he stepped onto the boards he played as if for the Lady alone. Never before had his voice sounded so powerful, his posture so regal, his bearing so poised. He saw her liquid eyes pool with delight as he boomed out his lines from the very lip of the stage and at times nearly forgot his words, for he was burning with lust.

~

The play over, the courtiers departed, Shakespeare and Burbage lounged against the luggage backstage, watching while the other members of the Lord Chamberlain's Men packed costumes into trunks and stowed props.

Burbage ruffled through pages hieroglyphed with Will Shakespeare's spidery handwriting. He finished reading and turned over the final page, looking for where the story continued. "Will," he said, "your play has no ending. You are short the fifth act."

"The fourth act shall end with a masque."

Burbage raised his head and glared. "Aye . . . And then?"

"And then . . . and then the action shall resolve itself."

Burbage cleared his throat with a noise like a bear stirred from hibernation by the jab of a pointed stick. "Will, we have but two days. A day to copy each player's lines and set them to memory; another day to practice."

Shakespeare looked away, his face despairing. "I know. I know. Yet I have not the ending."

"Then you must look for it!" It was rare for Richard Burbage to raise his voice to his best friend, but they had never been so poorly prepared to perform a play—and this would be in front of the Queen and the entire court.

Burbage raised an eyebrow as Shakespeare rose and buttoned his doublet.

"Tis near eight of the clock. Where do you go?"

"I must look for the end of my story." Shakespeare paused, put a hand on his crotch and threw Burbage a lascivious grin. "Or the story of my end."

The Lady Verity raised her arms. The maids stepped forward, each armed with a pair of scissors, which went *snip, snip* as they cut the threads of her bodice and pulled it away. Next they disassembled her dress in the reverse order it had been put on: farthingale, kirtle, bumroll. The ladies-in-waiting whisked each piece away and stored it in a large chest at the base of the huge four-poster bed. When the Lady was naked, she bade the girls sprinkle her with rose water, before slipping on a hooded, red silk gown. Lastly, they undid the many brooches and jewels fastening her hair and let the long russet waves spill down around her shoulders.

"Fetch me the glass," she said, nodding to her youngest maid. The serving maid curtsied and swished over to the table, but though her eyes searched the marble top again and again she could find no hand mirror. "Tis not there, milady," the maid said.

"Look again, foolish girl. I used it before I went down for supper."

The girl's eyes scoured frantically, but the tabletop was bare. Rafe Foxe had taken the silver mirror, along with the silver bell and a pair of candlesticks.

"Nu-no, madam. Tis not!"

"Idiot child!" Lady Verity snapped and strode over to the table to look for herself. The table was bare. Everything was gone. She glared at the young maid. "You have stolen it!"

"No, madam. I have stolen nothing! I am an honest girl!"

Lady Verity slapped the girl across the face. "You lie, strumpet. Get you gone from my service!"

The young maid's face collapsed in misery, tears rolling down her cheeks. "Bu-bu-but—no! My good lady! Do not dismiss me for I am innocent!"

The word "innocent" flushed the Lady's face red with anger. She grabbed the maid's wrist, sinking in her nails until the girl screamed in pain. "You heard me. You are dismissed! Collect your rags and quit this house!"

"But, but … no! I am—"

"GET YOU HENCE!"

Sobbing, the girl rushed from the room. Her companion looked at her lady with wide eyes, both hands covering her mouth. By her expression, she expected the same.

"You … leave me."

The servant curtsied and fled from the room, head down.

A moment later a quiet knock came at the door.

The lady turned her back as she composed her face, and then spoke in a warm and sultry voice: "Come."

The door opened and Shakespeare slipped in.

Lady Verity had her back to him, the hood of her red robe drawn up.

"I am here," he said.

The lady turned, pushing the hood back. Her disarrayed beauty made the poet catch his breath. "O Venus! O Aphrodite! Methinks I am in the presence of a goddess more rare—"

"I have heard your pretty words," she said. "Now is the time for deeds."

She glided to him, grabbed the hair at the back of his head and pulled his face to hers, drowning his words in a deep, wet kiss. After some time he pulled away to catch his breath, but then she took it away again by placing a hand on the front of his breeches to rub his throbbing erection. They fell to another kiss, more passionate than the first as she pushed him toward the bed and her nimble fingers tore loose the buttons of his doublet.

Sex with the lady was more like wrestling a spitting, hissing wildcat than making love. She raked his back and arms with her sharp nails until his many scratches bloodied the sheets.

And she was a biter.

She bit his neck, his chin, his right shoulder—until he cried aloud and her white teeth stained red with his blood. Their lovemaking was like a Tempest: two warring clouds of hot and cold colliding. It was both pain and pleasure—a cup of sweet wine spiced so that it burned the tongue. Desperate to stop injury, he fought to capture both her arms and pin them above her head as he plunged into her. He thought himself spent after the spectacular first act, but her soft hands would not let him rest and stirred him to a second act, more violent than the first, and them teased him back for a short encore. Finally, they lay in each other's arms, panting, the bedclothes tossed in disarray, rills of sweat cooling on their bodies. "That was, perhaps, my greatest performance," he said and turned to kiss her forehead.

She stopped him with a hand on his chest and asked, "Would you be a great man?"

He smiled a fool's smile. "For you I would be Hercules, Agamemnon . . . all the heroes as one."

"No, greater than that."

"I may seem to you a humble player, but my star is ascending. I am a gentleman with a coat of arms. Soon I shall be a sharer in the Lord Chamberlain's—"

She put a hand to his lips to silence him. "Speak not of lords unless you would be my lord."

Fear tightened his chest. His mind vaulted back to Stratford, his wife Anne, his girls, Susanna and Judith. He had not told her he was married. He wore no wedding band. Before she could read the truth in his eyes, Shakespeare hid behind a mask of puzzlement. "But how could that be? For while your lord lives—?"

No longer the cooing lover, her voice hardened as she said, "You could have me *and* this great house."

The words tumbled in his stomach like a jagged chunk of ice. His heart thudded. He said nothing, his mouth dry as parchment.

And then he felt something cold upon his naked belly. It was a dagger, the tip of which she traced slowly upward, scratching a fine red line in his pale skin, pausing at his heart, and then continuing upward, until the dagger's point nestled in the hollow of his throat. He tried not to swallow, but did so in spite of himself and the blade pricked his Adam's apple.

"A moment's bravery," she hissed. "A moment's resolution is all it takes."

"I understand you not."

"My husband is a bad man. He plots a terrible action. You could be a greater man. A single dagger thrust in the dark. A deed easily done. Then all this ... and me. You could be the master of all you behold."

Now his heart was pounding. Nay, I cannot," he said, but the dagger point pricked deeper.

"Not for love of me?"

Not for love of you? He thought. *Nay! Not for all the gold in England!*

The pressure of the dagger tip increased and for a moment he though she truly would plunge it deep into his throat. But then it eased as she pulled away.

"I see the answer in your coward's eyes," she said. "It seems that I am forever cursed by faint-hearted and weak-kneed boys who can only play act the role of men."

She flounced out of the bed, leaving behind a wisp of sweat and sex commingled with rosewater. He untensed and laid back, slack limbs swallowed up in the soft vastness of pillows.

Will, he thought, close to despair, *this time you shall not escape a whipping, for all your deeds have braided a whip for your own back.* He heard a door creak open and bang shut. He looked, but was alone in the room. The lady had gone. No doubt fled to some nearby chamber. *Good,* he thought. *Better to make good my escape now, rather than face such a fiery woman's wroth.* But before he could move the bed shook mightily and then he heard a thump, a bang, and the ascending howl of metal gears. For a moment it seemed as though the brass Fleur de lis of the bed hood had turned to spear points falling toward him, and then he realized the truth. The bed canopy was in fact plummeting toward him, the barley twist legs revolving like screw threads drawing the canopy down to crush him.

He barely had time to roll and fling himself free before the massive canopy crashed down, the brass Fleur de lis impaling the mattress with a dozen sharp points

He began to snatch on his clothes and only then did the realisation hit him—the heavy iron gears he had collided with beneath the bed were not just to animate the cupids, but were designed to crank down the canopy and murder a sleeping victim. This was no accident—the bed was an infernal device built so as to ensure a sleep that none would awaken from. And in the next minute he realized who the room was originally intended to host:

It was meant to kill the queen.

Shakespeare pulled his stocks and shirt on, and then snatched up his cap from the floor.

The door to the room banged open and Sir Richard entered. "I heard a great tumult! Who have you killed?"

Their eyes met for moment, Sir Richard' widening with surprise. Shakespeare's arched brows rising with fear. Sir Richard recovered first, his hand flying to his sword pommel as he started to draw.

Shakespeare sprinted for the fresco. His hands shook so badly it took several attempts to depress Adam's fig leaf. Finally, the door flew open and he toppled into the hidden chamber and banged the door shut behind him. A robed figure knelt at one of the chests stacked against the wall and rose as he entered. It was the Lady Verity, the hood of her red silk gown drawn up.

"Milady!" Shakespeare panted. "Your husband lurks without!"

The lady said nothing, keeping her back to him."

"I pray you understand," Shakespeare said. "I would do ought for you, but that which endangers my immortal soul." His mind galloped. He simply wanted a chance to slip back to the White Hart and alert Oswyn Scrope. These matters were beyond him.

She spun at his touch. He gasped, for the sweet face was gone, replaced by a hideous devils mask. He turned to run back to the hidden door, but someone blocked his way: a short, swarthy man with muscular arms and legs. The man's hands clamped upon Shakespeare's throat and began to squeeze. Shakespeare tried to pry the fingers loose, but the dwarf's grip was crushing. A deafening hammering sounded in his ears, and then he realized it was his heartbeat, flailing to pump blood to his dying brain. The dwarf snarled, showing white teeth amid the curly black beard. As the grip tightened even more, colour drained from the world and the dwarf's face receded, sucked away down a long dark tunnel.

It was the last thing he remembered.

CHAPTER 47: HEDGEHOG

As soon as he walks through the door of the Marlborough *Costas*, I know why they call him *Hedgehog*.

He's a big bruiser. I'd guess he's over six-foot-six tall and almost as wide. And he's bushy with it. He's about my age with a mop of greasy black hair down to his shoulders, huge mutton chop whiskers and eyebrows like an overgrown wisteria bush. Despite the fact that it's a warm spring day he's wearing a voluminous brown army-surplus great coat. He orders a cappuccino and pays for it, then lingers by the counter for a moment, black eyes scanning the tables, looking for me. I raise a hand and toss him a quick wave. He nods and lumbers toward me, squeezing between tables, knocking chairs aside with his thighs. Other customers throw him hateful looks as he bumps their tables, spilling coffees. He shambles up to my table in the corner, sets down a frothy cappuccino, snatches a chair out, and thuds his bulk onto it.

"Mister Braithwaite, I take it." His accent is local: Wiltshire farm boy. Apt, since he smells like an overheated tractor.

What am I supposed to say in return? *And— if I don't miss my guess —you would be Mister Hedgehog?* But I don't say that and instead simply mumble, "That's right."

He scratches the bristles on his thick throat with filthy fingernails —rasp, rasp—and rumbles, "Whotcha got for me?"

"Some kind of document. Old papers. Don't know what." I casually set a twenty-pound note on the table. "Thought I'd hire your expertise. You know, for an evaluation," and quickly add: "A *discreet* evaluation."

I don't actually see him take the twenty but it vanishes, like a magic trick.

"So ya reckon it might be worth some dosh?" he says. "Bit outta my line. I deal mostly in modern retail goods. Previously owned goods— if you know what I mean."

I know exactly what he means. Nicked. Hot. Stolen. Thieved from someone's house and flogged off at the nearest car boot sale before the owner even notices it's missing.

He slurps his cappuccino, his little finger curled in a jarringly dainty fashion, and smacks salami-sized lips. Jarringly, the cappuccino foam ringing his pie hole momentarily transforms the hedgehog into a rabid dog. He sets the cappuccino down, smacks his lips and says, "Let's have a dekko, then."

I throw a quick glance around to make sure no one's watching, then snap open the briefcase at my feet and gingerly set the sheaf of papers in front of him.

He furrows a brow the size of a cliff face, jaw jutting stupidly as he studies the top page like a Neanderthal pondering a calculus equation. He finishes and flips to the next page. As he reads he sips his coffee, then sets down the cup atop the flipped over top sheet. To my horror, I see cappuccino pool around its rim.

"Hey!" I yell. "Watch out!"

"What?"

"Look!" I say, pointing.

He lifts the coffee cup and blinks at the brown ring staining the page. "That was there already."

"No it bloody wasn't!"

"Well, I wouldn't get too excited if I was you. Pretty sure I know what this is."

"You do?"

He nods, knowingly. "Some kind of legal document. You can tell. It's written in Latin or Greek or some silly, foreign-fuck language. Plus it's signed in half a dozen places. Look," he stubs a thick finger down on the parchment. His grubby digits look like he's just finished changing the oil on a fleet of taxis—filthy. He's leaving black finger-prints on the white manuscript clearer than the ones they take at the police station—every whorl and line is defined. "Willulula Shogsffffff-ful." he reads. "Funny bloody name. But there you are. Like I said, it's probably worth bugger-all, but if you like I know a bloke who knows a bloke who could give it the once over."

He makes to tuck it in his overcoat and I know I'll never see it or him again if he does.

"No!" I stretch a hand out. "I'll keep it, thanks." He stops, reluc-tantly uncoils his arm and I snatch it back. "You rattle your mate's cage and see what he says."

"No worries," he replies, fumbling a mobile phone out of his jacket. "One photo," he says, "so my mate can have a shufty. That way he can tell if it's worth anything."

I tense. Alarms klaxon in my head. Still, I can't figure how someone having a blurry mobile phone picture of the manuscript could possibly hurt. I carefully set the pages back down on the table, avoiding coffee slops. The mobile appears toy-like and tiny in his massive hand. He holds it over the page and snaps a single shot. All done, he jams the mobile back in his coat pocket, grabs his cappuccino and slurps it down in three noisy gulps.

"Right," he says, towering up from his chair. "I'm a busy man . . ."

"So what if it's worth something?" I ask.

His smile breaks loose from its thicket of beard scraggle, showing a mouth crammed with gold teeth. I have a queasy notion they're stolen, too. "Then I'll find you," he says. "Don't worry, I know where you live."

Maybe I'm paranoid, but the last statement sounds like a threat.

CHAPTER 48: HUNTING THE HART

The Stratford poet opened his eyes. He was still in the small chamber: the secret room hidden behind the fresco of God expelling Adam and Eve from Eden. A tingling numbness surged in his hands—he was tied to a lopsided chair. A wan candle burned on a small table. He blinked the shadows from his eyes and looked around. Several trunks were stacked against one wall—the same trunks that contained the devil mask Sybilla wore. Next to the trunks, two large portraits leaned against the wall. The first was of a handsome man painted leaning against a globe of the world. Shakespeare recognized the one he had glimpsed when he first entered the chamber with Rafe Foxe. He looked again, and this time noticed something familiar. The man in the painting was wearing gloves. Worked into the leather cuffs was a stylised letter W. And then he recognized the gauntlets and the gold brocaded cape. They were the clothes Rafe Foxe had been wearing. The next portrait was of a woman. The face could have been that of Sybilla in her younger years, yet the complexion was fairer and the hair a honey blonde, not red.

Shakespeare now realized who the portraits depicted: the murdered Sir Richard Wexcombe and his wife, the true Lady Verity, the white woman he had taken for a ghost and who now wandered the woods in a fit of distracted madness. These then were the portraits that had originally hung at the top of the stairs until their place was usurped by the images of the pretenders who had supplanted them.

Voices stirred in the distance, moving closer. Shakespeare dropped his head slackly and feigned unconsciousness.

The footsteps of several people entered the chamber and stopped before his chair.

"Who is this fellow?" Father Finch asked.

Philip Mortlake grabbed Shakespeare's hair and roughly tilted his head up. "I recognized the rascal: a player, a poet, a madman. A base fool of no count." He let the head drop.

"How came he here?" Thomas Hyde asked.

Shakespeare cracked his eyes a sliver until he could make out the quivering image of four human shapes circled about him.

"Indeed!" Philip Mortlake said, throwing a dark look at Sybilla. "Why, pray tell, is he here, sister?"

"The fellow is a spy for Oswyn Scrope. The innkeeper and his man have heard them whispering."

"That Puritan buboe!" Hyde spat. "'Tis past time Scrope died!"

"Aye," Philip agreed. "And this fool, too!"

"He must," Sybilla agreed. "He shall." She touched the heavy gold cross around her neck, thumbing the catch and drawing the slender blade in one motion. She held out the poison dagger to Thomas Hyde. "Here, dispatch him, then drag his corpse to the river and toss it in as you did the old wench."

But Hyde would not take the dagger. "I am a priest," he said mildly. "I cannot kill this man."

"You have killed already!" Sybilla argued.

Thomas Hyde bristled with anger. "Not *I*," he spat, meeting her stare. "*You* murdered Richard. *You* murdered the old lady in the pantry. *You* cut out your sister's tongue. There is no stain upon my soul."

Philip Mortlake gripped the smaller man by the shoulder. Hyde hurled a glowering stare that made Finch snatch his hand away. "But *you* are a part of a plot to kill a queen!" he said petulantly. "Tell us—is that not murder?"

Hyde shrugged at the thought. "The Pope has expressly said tis no sin to kill Elizabeth. But this touches not upon that action. I will gladly kill Oswyn Scrope, for he is a heretic foot soldier in Elizabeth's godless cause, but I'll not kill an innocent."

"False rogue!" Finch snarled. "You left me in the forest to murder the Lady Verity, and she unequalled in innocence!"

Hyde's smug calm never wavered as he met Finch's indignant stare. "Each man acts according to his own conscience. I did not hold your dagger hand as you slit her throat."

Lady Sybilla stamped her foot in anger and thrust the dagger out to Philip. "Take it, brother. You must do it!"

"Nay, I'll not. I alone did not strike a blow against Richard, and yet …" Philip Mortlake's face changed, became ghastly pale. His voice quavered as he spoke. "Yet I have seen Richard's ghost, in full daylight. It smiled at me and raised a glass in toast."

"You have seen Richard?" Sybilla's voice thinned to ice skimming a winter puddle.

"His ghost," Philip nodded, a hand covering his eyes.

"Aye," Finch murmured in growing fear. "As we have, too. He haunts the dark passages of the house. He spoke of burning in purgatory and of murder before he had time to confess his sins. He came to drag us both to hell and we fled!"

Philip let out a squeal of terror. "Oh, God!" he moaned, clutching his hair. "Oh, God!"

"What of it?" Sybilla said. "The dead cannot do us physical harm, though they smile upon us or howl the night long and gnash their teeth."

Philip glowered at his sister. "If you had seen Richard, you would not speak so easily."

"Nay," Sybilla interrupted, "I have not seen Richard …" Her voice became shrill. "… but I have seen my sister …"

A dread silence.

All faces turned to Sybilla, whose eyes emptied as she looked into the darkness of her mind and drew forth a terrible image. "I happened to look out my window one morn. Verity stood at the forest's edge, clad in her bloody shroud of death, staring at the house. Her eyes met mine, and my guilt gushed forth like an overflowing fountain of blood."

At the mention of Verity, Father John Finch looked away into the shadows to hide a face wretched with fear. He had never confessed to the others that he had failed to carry out her murder.

As she spoke, Sybilla acted out the gesture. "My sister's ghost raised both hands to her bloody lips as if to chide me for cutting the tongue from her mouth." Sybilla's fierce gaze returned. She looked at the others with eyes wet and gleaming. "That sin is mine alone. Mayhap she will be revenged upon me when I am in hell. But burn though I may, I regret not killing Richard Wexcombe. That foul, base, double-speaking liar. If we meet in hell, not even the devil himself shall hold me back." She raised both hands, nails bared, teeth clenched in anger. "For I will fly upon him and gouge out his eyes with these nails!"

Philip moaned and covered his ears. "Speak not of hell, I beg you!"

"Something is amiss," Hyde muttered bitterly, shaking his head. "If we are plagued by walking spirits, unnatural storms and foul portents, our cause cannot be a holy one."

"We are all cursed in the eyes of God!" Finch cried out. "What we do is cursed! We have gone too far! We shall be damned for it!"

Sybilla backhanded Finch across the face, a stunning blow that shocked and silenced him.

"We had already gone too far when we began this fatal action," she said in a voice trembling with anger. "One dark deed gathers another like a great and massy wheel rolling down a hill. Once set in motion, one can only run before it ... or be crushed beneath it." Her voice became choked with scorn and disdain. "Oh, what a milk-livered rabble of school boys you are! Is there not even one of you with the spleen of a woman?" She walked away from the cowed men, who hung their heads in shame. They looked up at her soft laugh. Sybilla turned and floated back, her eyes lambent in the candlelight. "We need not shed his blood, brother." She smiled off-kilter. "Why should we trouble, when the Queen herself shall do it?"

She rested her hands on Shakespeare's shoulders. He flinched slightly at her touch, but she failed to notice, caught up in her own thoughts.

"How so?" Philip asked.

"Tomorrow morn is the drive hunt. The Queen and her favourites will shoot the hart from a hunting stand. A hundred deer will be driven to slaughter. Who would notice if one of those deer runs on two legs, not four?

CHAPTER 49: LOOSE LIPS

It's Friday night. Tomorrow is the final day of the conference, a half-day goodbye wind-up before everyone goes home and the folding chairs are stacked. The *Academons* are all in my taproom, sitting around one big table, yakking about, what else?

William Bloody Shakespeare.

All except for Broody Brendan, who sits on his tod in the snug, pounding down Johnny Walkers' and hurling baleful stares at Gillian, who just keeps looking lovelier, as if on purpose.

I linger behind the bar just to look at her, wanting her, grinding my molars into dust. Maybe I should tell her about the manuscript. What could it hurt? But then I realise that she represents everything official and above-board. If it really is worth something, then she's bound to inform the authorities. My libido wars with my few remaining shreds of common sense. Meanwhile the bank has been calling so often I've unplugged the telephone. I need money and I need it quick.

I cannot afford to bugger this up.

"Don't I know you?" A strangely familiar voice asks.

I look over. Spooky stands at the bar, a five-pound note in his hand. He's asking the question of Sidney who looks his usual baffled self as he pours Spooky a scotch and soda.

'Don't think so," Sidney says.

"No," Spooky insists. "I know you from somewhere. Didn't you used to teach?"

Sidney hisses with laughter. "Not me."

"Have you worked here long?"

"Seven months," Sidney says, which I know is a lie. When I bought the pub he told me he'd worked here for two years … or maybe that was a lie.

Before I can get too nosy a sexy voice interrupts my eavesdropping. "You look unhappy," Gillian is standing at the bar. "Sad to see me go?"

"Devastated," I say, ab-so-bloody-lutely meaning it.

She drops a tenner on the counter. "I'll have a brandy. And buy yourself a drink. You look like you need to drown your sorrows."

I throw a glance at the spirit bottles behind the bar. "We've nothing deep enough to drown my sorrows. There is an old well outside. It's capped, but I pry the lid off and chuck myself down it."

She gives me one of her heart-tremoring smiles. "Problems?"

"Longer than a jam on the M4," I say. "Mostly money."

"We've all got those."

For some reason, Spooky hasn't buggered off with his drink and is still pestering Sidney. "You sure we've never met? Your face looks very familiar."

"I've jusht got one of those fayshes," Sidney slurs around the pipe.

Spooky throws him one last unbelieving look and then saunters back to the table with his drink, shaking his shiny bonce.

"Poor Ambrose," she says. "It's his final night here and I think he was hoping to get lucky."

That makes two of us, I think, but say nothing. It takes a moment, but then it registers.

"Oh, so you mean he's—"

Gillian laughs. "Oh, God, yes. Ambrose was gay decades before queer became trendy."

"With Sidney?" I guffaw. "He's barking up the wrong tree there."

"Are you so sure?"

I toss a quick glance at Sidney. He's at the end of the bar, stealing peanuts from the dish of complimentary bar snacks I put out for the punters. I keep my voice low, but as usual he's dopily oblivious.

"Naw. You've got that wrong. Not Sidney."

"People's sexuality is often kept hidden."

It's impossible not to read a thesaurus full of filthy innuendos into everything Gillian says. "Might be so. He could have a kink for glove puppets and stuffed animals for all I know. But I've never—in the six months he's worked for me—ever seen the slightest clue that ..." I lose my thread, trail off.

Two years, he told me. Why lie about that?

"Well," she says. "You can't blame him. Everyone gets lonely. We all need to be touched now and then ... fondled ... caressed ..."

Oh God, why did she have to say that? It triggers something deep. Too bloody deep. I've got hidden rooms I've kept locked for years, a busload of cackling skeletons pressed against the other side of the closet door, waiting to tumble out. My secret bursts out me before I know it, before I even have time to reconsider.

"I found something."

Her smile tautens. The green eyes widen just a fraction. "What do you mean?" she tries to sound casual, but even she can't quite pull if off. I've done it now. There's no going back.

"I found something. In the cellar. A secret passage."

"A secret passage?" Her voice is straining at the leash, a wolfhound on the scent.

"I fell through the floor. A secret trapdoor thingy ..."

Her eyes continue to widen. She puts a had on mine and squeezes, milking the words out of me.

"In the tunnel I found some papers ... old papers ... with writing on them. A ... a document ... or something."

She says nothing for a full minute, which I know is dangerous, because she's thinking. And like a Russian chess master, she is sixty-five moves ahead of me. I've barely pushed my pawn to Queen four and she's already at checkmate.

She drains her full glass of brandy in one swallow and sets the glass down on the bar. I try not to look but can't prevent the downward tilt of my eyes. The glass is rimmed with a perfect lipstick kiss.

"I'd like to take a look at it . . ." she says with thrilling ambiguity, and then finishes her thought with the line that brings the theatre curtain crashing down ". . .. in bed."

I grip the bar to stop from floating through the ceiling.

I am such a goner.

CHAPTER 50: THE HUNTER AND THE HUNTED

The tavern tales and rumours were only half right. The house had been blinded. Not just shutters: the window glass had been painted black.

Every window.

An act of madness. Inside the house, it must be perpetual night. But then Fen Crugg thought of the stories he had heard and shuddered at any man's reason for painting out the world.

It had been a long day's ride. Changing post horses every ten miles, the sergeant had stopped for neither for food nor drink. His stomach groaned. His throat was a riverbed in late summer, dry and cracked. The letter, tucked inside his doublet, chafed against his chest the whole long ride. He simply wanted to hand it over and be rid of it, but doubted he would be released so easily. As his horse trotted into Westminster, he stopped to ask locals the whereabouts of the house. However, just the mention of the owner's name made them avert their eyes and quicken their step. Finally he had accosted a drunken man reeling out of a tavern.

"The house that screams?" the drunk said, sobering at the description. "Why seek the way there? Better to seek the way from it." Despite his answer, the drunk eventually accepted a handful of coins to point the way to an unassuming brick house of three stories. Once great, the house had fallen into disrepair: a blinded war veteran that jostled shoulders with its newer neighbours. He heard no screams from within, but the house gave off a sense of hopelessness. Even the trees growing outside leaned and twisted away from its walls, as if seeking to escape the darkness that radiated from it.

Sergeant Crugg knuckled a front door weathered almost to splinters and listened to the echo of his knock rebound hollowly as it wandered from room to room seeking the master. After an interminable delay, footsteps shuffled to the door. He heard several bolts being shot, and then the door was dragged open by an ancient man with a shock of white hair and a horribly disfigured face. The man had one good eye—the left. The right eye was shrunken to a glaucous white marble. The hallway behind him was dark as midnight. Not surprisingly, the tremulous hand clutched a candle in a holder.

Crugg held up the letter for the man's one good eye to focus upon and said: "I have a letter for your master."

The ancient fellow shuffled back from the door and beckoned the Sergeant in with a wave. Fen Crugg stepped into a space where the light of day had not intruded for years. A bad smell hovered: dust, mould, a butcher shop reek of dead flesh, and something else, which the Sergeant could not quite place—a sharp smell like vinegar. He sniffed deeper and his stomach lurched at the acid tang of vomit.

The ancient servant limped to a large double door and knocked. A muffled voice bade him enter and he dragged himself inside, leaving the door slightly ajar. The door hung crookedly and under its own weight groaned a little wider. The Sergeant could see one bare wall of a large room. The room squirmed with candlelight and the shadow of a man slumped in a chair was thrown large upon the wall. The man's arms rested upon the chair arms, although his head teetered unsteadily atop his shoulders. Then it lolled and sagged and Crugg's skin irrupted with gooseflesh at a long, drawn-out moan of suffering.

The ancient servant returned, followed by a short man with a salt and pepper beard and grey, receding hair. The man wore the clothes of a nobleman: a black doublet and black hose over legs skinny and knob-kneed as a stork's. A butcher's leather apron, greasy and stained, stretched over a paunch. As he followed the servant from the room he was wiping, wiping, wiping his hands on a rag.

"You have been sent by my servant Scrope?" the man's voice was a deep, ominous bass that seemed overlarge for such a body.

"Aye sir," Sergeant Crugg had been nervous before, but now that he was *in the presence* his knee tremored.

Richard Topcliffe was a surprisingly slight man for one who cast so large a shadow. Delicate hands. Thin wrists. In his sixties. Frail-looking. His deep-set eyes darkly socketed in the poor light. The butcher shop odour swirled about him. The queen's *Grand Inquisitor* kept wiping and wiping his hands, as if he could not get them clean enough. Finally he said: "You have a letter for me?"

The Sergeant's hands shook as he pushed the rolled correspondence into the torturer's delicate hands. Topcliffe slipped off the string and unrolled the letter. The servant lifted the candle so that his master might read and in the quivering light the torturer's features melted and reformed. He had baggy, pouchy eyes and wet, raw-red lips that thrust from a thicket of greying facial hair. As Topcliffe read, a drawn-out moan pulled Sergeant Crugg's eyes back to the room. Evidently, the man in the chair was not well, for the shadow head lolled, lifted momentarily, and then toppled to one side.

"Have you read this?" Topcliffe asked.

Crugg dragged his eyes from the grotesque play of shadows. Topcliffe's gaze was a spoon scraping the brains from the back of his skull. The Sergeant swallowed. "No, sir, I have not." It was the truth. He had been tempted to read it all the way to London but had resisted the urge and now was profoundly glad of it.

"My servant Scrope writes that my skills are needed in Wexcombe to dismantle a plot that touches the very life of the queen. I have a very special relationship with her majesty." The wet red lips quivered. "One might say … intimate." His lascivious tone, a bawd's wink-and-elbow-in-the-ribs, shocked Crugg speechless.

Topcliffe grew serious. He handed the letter to his servant. "Ready my coach and make sure to have all my devices loaded." The beady eyes fixed upon the Sergeant's face: two hermit crabs peering from their shells. "You may ride in my coach should you wish."

The sergeant could think of nothing he wished less. "I have my horse, sir. I will follow you." Fen Crugg did not look forward to the one-hundred-and-fifty mile ride back to Wiltshire, but when he finally saw the eldritch monstrosity Topcliffe called a coach, he was happy to sweat in the hot sun and choke on the dust thrown up by its wheels.

~

The gamey reek of tanned hide awakened him. Shakespeare could smell his own breath, moist and hot. He opened his eyes but it was as dark with his eyes open as closed. The bag was still over his head, though he no longer lay on cold stone. He squirmed a little. His arms were tied together at the wrists. Straps of some kind with hard metal buckles. Tight leather bands squeezed his waist and constricted his chest. He squirmed some more. The ground was soft and yielding beneath his knees. He ceased his struggles and listened. Bird song. And then in the distance, a hunting horn blared. He could smell grass. Ferns. Feel the tickle of pollen in his nose. He was outside. In the forest.

He moved his legs and found they were not bound. Grunting and straining, he managed to drag his feet together and finally wobbled upright. He tensed, expecting a blow or worse—a knife blade. He stood still, trying to quiet his breathing. Something was tied to the bag that weighed mightily upon his shoulders so that his neck muscles strained to keep his head upright. And then he realized what it was. He was not in a bag, but in a deer hide, such as wealthy landowners trussed peasants in to exercise their dogs.

"Halloo!" he shouted, but the deerskin muffled his voice.

Another blast of the hunting horn. Louder. No. Closer. He could hear the bark and yammer of deerhounds fast approaching. It was a drive hunt. Dread gripped him as he grasped the dire truth of his predicament: he was strapped into a deerskin and the hunt was bearing down. Gamekeepers would be marching through the forest, beating drums and blowing horns to roust the deer from their sleeping places, panicking the herd into flight. There would be a few riders, steering the fleeing deer, but the hounds would likely reach him first …

… and rip him to bloody ribbons.

He turned this way and that, feeling the ponderous rack of antlers swaying atop his head.

He tugged and heaved at the straps binding his arms, but it was useless. They were cinched numbingly tight. He must try to hide. Looking down, he could just make out his feet and the forest floor. Half-blind, he stumbled over every fallen branch, every tussock. And then he heard the terrible yap and snarl of hounds drawing near. He tried to hurry but the antlers snagged a low-hanging branch, wrenching his head back painfully. He backed himself loose of the tree and shuffled away as fast as the deerskin would allow, although he could not guess which direction he moved in.

If I could but see, he thought. A second later the first arrow hit the deerskin with a THWAP, puncturing the neck. He veered left, stumbled on something, barely kept his feet beneath him. The arrow snagged on something and tore out. Now he had a hole to look out of, though it was low down. He could see the base of trees and the ferns he was crashing through. More hooves. A second arrow thunked into the deer head and lodged. He kept moving. A third arrow whished through the neck and lodged. He shook the ponderous head from side to side. The arrow could not fall out as the feathered fletchings held it in place. He crashed head on into a thorn bush and he struggled to free himself, the arrow snagged and yanked out. He now had a flapping, palm-size hole in the deerskin's neck. He spun and looked. Just in time to see the hounds. A giant mastiff saw him and veered away from the pack. Shakespeare turned and ran, stumbling, weaving, falling to his knees and scrambling back to his feet. He crashed headlong into something that yielded and then sprang back. He tried to pull away, but couldn't—he had run blindly into a thorn bush and the horns were stuck fast. His legs buckled and he sank to his knees, then froze at an unexpected touch: a hand on his arm. He heard and felt someone struggling to pull the antlers free of the thorn bush, but with little success. He thrust his bound together hands as far out of the deerskin as the straps would allow.

"I beseech you, loosen my bounds!" he shouted. He felt hands tugging at the straps, loosening them. The strap around his chest slackened and then the second strap around his waist. Without waiting for his wrists to be unbound, he shrugged his head and one shoulder loose of the deerskin, and looked to see whom his rescuer was.

The White Woman.

A thunderous *wooooooooooof!* jellied his insides. One of the dogs had scented him. He looked to see an enormous wolfhound—no doubt, Zeus, Sir Richard's dog—charging through the trees toward them. They both would be savaged.

As the dog seemed ready to spring, the woman stepped forward and raised both her arms. The wolfhound slid to a halt and barked thunderously, slobber flying from its wicked teeth. The dog barked ferociously as the woman slowly stepped toward it.

"No gentle lady!" Shakespeare cried out. "The beast will tear you!"

But the woman knelt and threw her arms around its great neck, rubbing her face against the dog's, which stopped barking and wagged its tail. The woman then made an "away" gesture. Zeus looked at her a moment longer, its face alert and eager, then sprang away and ran off to join the rest of the pack.

Hunting horns blared. The last of the riders approached.

"Come!" Shakespeare said. "We must hide ourselves. These fools will loose an arrow at anything that moves." The woman took his arm and the two dodged into the trees as more dogs burst from cover.

"Run!" he said to the woman. "Leave me!" But she would not. They kept running as the hounds devoured the distance between them. Shakespeare finally shrugged loose from the heavy deer hide, but a final strap caught around his ankle and nearly tripped him. He kicked with his tangled foot until the deer hide came loose. Legs burning, he put his hands in the small of the woman's back and pushed her along as the snapping dogs closed on their heels. But as they jumped through a stand of dense ferns, the ground fell away beneath them, and they tumbled into empty space.

~

"A good morning to hunt," Lord Essex said. He put a foot in the metal stirrup of the crossbow and gripped the bowstring with both hands. He grunted as he drew back the string until it caught on the nut and then handed the weapon to the Queen: a small, lightweight crossbow made especially for her. She took it from him and rested the wooden stock upon the railing, shouting in a laughing voice: "We shall gorge ourselves on fresh venison tonight!"

Lady Verity did not wield a crossbow, but stood next to Sir Richard whose weapon was cocked and loaded with a quarrel, ready to fire. "We need only to kill one beast," she whispered into his ear. "Be sure to hit the mark."

Sir Richard threw her a lazy look of contempt. "The fool will never make it thus far. The hounds will run him down in the forest and rip him bloody. If he is unlucky enough to survive the dogs, he will prove a pincushion for arrows."

The first wave of deer careened into the paddock and thundered past the hunting stand. Elizabeth raised her crossbow and fired a quick shot. The arrow hit a doe in the flank, but it continued to run, dragging its wounded leg. The queen laughed with delight. "First arrow and I have drawn blood!"

"Oh, excellent shot, majesty!" Essex gushed. She handed him the crossbow and he handed her a bow freshly cocked and loaded. By this time the milling herd of deer had reached the far side of the paddock and turned back, galloping the other direction, confused and terrified. The queen fired a second shot. The bolt pierced the deer's chest, a full-grown stag, and dropped its front legs. A second later two more bolts hit the beast and it trumpeted in pain and keeled over, legs flailing.

The Queen laughed gaily to see its death throes. "Quickly Essex, another bow."

Sir Richard had not fired a single bolt thus far. He and Lady Verity's eyes followed every deer that galloped into the palisade, searching for a peculiar beast that ran on two legs.

CHAPTER 51: RUMPY-PUMPY AT LAST!

S ex with Gillian isn't the erotic apotheosis I has hoping for. She drags me into my bedroom. Whips her knickers off. (Doesn't even bother to remove her blouse.) Throws me down on the bed. Yanks down my pants. Then hops on and rides me like one of those mechanical horsey-rides you put coins in at the supermarket.

It's been a long, dry spell for me. I try to hold out, to savour it, but ….

… I last three seconds.

She rolls off and wipes herself on the sheet, and is instantly all business.

"The manuscript," she says, "where is it?"

"That's it? I don't even get a cuddle?"

Her look says *no*. So much for romance. I sigh and clamber out of bed. The strong box is tucked in the bedside chest. I haul it out and drop it on the bed. The lid springs open to my key and I take out the manuscript. She snatches it before I can offer it to her.

"Ohmigod!" She says. She sits on the bed and wraps herself with the duvet.

"You won't be able to read it," I warn. "Not unless you know Latin or Greek or whatever it is."

"It's neither!" she says, her voice rising an octave. "It's written in secretary script, which Shakespeare and most of his contemporaries wrote in!" Her eyes skate all over the page—so excited she can't focus on any one point. Finally, she sets the papers down in front of her, sucks in a deep breath and cups both hands over her mouth, trying to stop from hyperventilating.

"I don't believe it! I don't believe it!" Her eyes well up. Real tears trickle down her cheeks and she wipes them away with the back of her hand. Somehow I doubt a human relationship could have as profound an effect on her as this pile of yellowing papers.

"It's real!" she says in an awed whisper. "I'm holding a lost play by William Shakespeare!"

Now I tear up as I'm seized by visions of me caught in the crossfire of photographer's flashguns. I'm holding a large novelty cheque inked with a long row of zeroes. This is going to save my worthless arse.

Her eyes race down the first page then suddenly stop.

"This ... this looks like a coffee stain!" She glares at me with horror.

I play dumb. "Really? I didn't know Shakespeare drank coffee."

She hurls me a look that is pure poison, then dives back into the page, reading on. "My God!" she breathes. "These are the foul papers!"

"Waitaminnit!" I say. "You can't blame me for that. They're just as I found them—"

"No, you dolt! The *foul papers* are Shakespeare's handwritten first draft. They contain cues and stage directions. From these foul papers a *fair copy* would be made by a professional scribe. Do you know what this means?"

"Well yes, of course," I say, then shake my head and admit, "No, I don't have a bloody clue."

"It means this is Shakespeare's own handwriting! Do you know how rare that is?"

I nearly choke with joy. The novelty cheque just gained another line of zeroes.

"This is not just an original manuscript. Not just a new play. It's a *Rosetta Stone*, a key to unlock the mind of Shakespeare. Look at the handwriting. I can see the rhythm of his thinking. Here he seems to rush, as if he's hurrying to pour everything out before it evaporates. Here it stutters and stalls. Look at the ink drips and blots He's stuck, quill hovering over the paper. I'm not just reading his words, I can feel his mind working, like fingers stretching out in the darkness, groping for the way ahead. "

I've never seen anyone read so fast. She is silent for the next hour as she rips through the pages. She turns another page and squeals. "Ohmigosh! His signature! In the margins, he's practicing signing his signature: "Shakespere … Shakespeare … Shakespeer …!" She flips to the last page. I watch her eyes flicker left to right, sucking words from the paper. She reaches the end and lets out a startled gasp. She turns the page over and over again, searching. Finally, she looks up at me with an unreadable expression.

"Wow ending?" I venture. "Teaser for a sequel?"

"*No* ending. It's incomplete!" she says in a voice sucked flat of air.

"What?"

"There's no fifth act!"

"Maybe he didn't write one?"

"Of course he bloody well wrote one! This play has no ending!" She throws an accusatory look at me. "Where are the rest of the pages? Tell me you have them. Tell me!" She grabs my forearm, claws digging in. "Where are they?" Her voice is a drill bit biting into steel.

"Ow!" I yell. "That bloody hurts—"

"Tell me!"

"I don't have it! That's it! All of it!"

She lets go of my arm. Once the blood rushes back in, it really starts to throb. I massage half-moon nail-marks welling up with blood. *Tiger's heart wrapp'd in a woman's hide?* Broody Brendon wasn't jesting. Once the cool intellectual façade cracks the madwoman in the attic leaps out howling and frothing. I realise it's the first time in my life I've been physically afraid of a woman.

"I want to see this tunnel! This secret passage!" she says, pacing the room half-naked, agitated and frantic. "I want to see exactly where you found the manuscript. We have to look again."

I'm about to argue, but she gives me a psycho-eyed-Betty Davis-as-Baby Jane look that shrivels the words in my mouth. I'm embroiled in yet another disaster my dick has led me into. That's what I get for thinking with the auxiliary male brain. But it's not like she's giving me a choice.

We are going underground.

CHAPTER 52: DARKNESS APPROACHING

The coach was a hideous monstrosity. Most of the scabrous black paint had peeled down to the wood. Stranger still, the window shutters were raised, barring the admittance of fresh air or light. Topcliffe's lumpen man-servants rode atop the carriage, jostling about on the wooden bench. Both men were worn and threadbare as an old rug. With their dark, liquid eyes, there was something of the feral about each, as if they had begun their lives as something small and squeaking scurrying in the shadows, only to have grown monstrous, fed on a diet of tidbits snipped from living victims. They had not a full set of teeth, eyes, ears or fingers between them, for they had begun their careers in torture through a hard apprenticeship as victims. Meanwhile, inside the coach, ensconced in his own private darkness, rode the Queen's personal interrogator, Richard Topcliffe.

Sergeant Crugg rode in the coach's wake, choking on its dust plume. He had a rag tied around his mouth and nose, and lifted it occasionally to spit a mouthful of dirt. The brilliant day was cloudless and hot and the hapless Sergeant broiled like a lobster in his breastplate and helmet. Still, he was grateful to be riding behind the coach and not in it. His flesh crawled at the thought of being confined in that dark airless space with the lugubrious Topcliffe.

The coach jounced and swayed over the rutted road. Lashed to its outside was a rattling jumble of grotesque carpentry formed of rough, splintery word fitted with crude ironwork: screws, manacles, chains, iron spikes—infernal devices of suffering borrowed from Topcliffe's personal torture chamber at Westminster.

The coach wheels brushed against a milestone scratched with an arrow and a rain-worn inscription: *Marlborough, fifty miles*. They had many grinding miles yet to travel, but Richard Topcliffe, like a solitary black cloud staining a blue summer sky, drifted inexorably closer to the White Hart Inn.

～

Shakespeare and the white lady tobogganed thirty feet down a steep, mud-slick slope and skidded into a bog. The bog, which was a deep pond during times of rain, was all but dry. Now they sat in a circle of muddy soil covered by desiccated weeds and dead leaves.

"God's wounds!" Shakespeare gasped, wiping clammy sweat from his face. From above came the snarl and whine of hounds ripping the deer hide to shreds.

His eyes fell upon his companion and for the first time he had chance to examine his rescuer up close. It was the ghost, the gory woman that had terrified the Lord Chamberlain's Men that day in the forest. She knelt on the muddy ground, swaying slightly, her fists thrust between her thighs like a child. Her head sat tilted, eyes staring vacantly into the forest. She seemed to have already forgotten him and was making a low noise in her throat. Shakespeare recognized it as a nursery rhyme of the type sung to babes. She wore nothing but a burial shroud, although by now it was torn to rags, and streaked with forest green and filth. Her face was grubby, her once glorious mane of blonde hair matted and snarled with briars.

"Milady," Shakespeare ventured. Her eyes turned to his. "I thank you. You have saved me from a cruel death."

But the stare that met his eyes resonated emptiness, and he could not tell if she understood a word he said. But even beneath the grime, the familiarity of the limpid eyes could not be mistaken. They were the same doe-eyes as the Lady Verity's, although these were cerulean blue instead of brown. But instead of the cunning that sparked Verity's eyes, her dreamy gaze showed a mind that had been called away somewhere.

"Who are you, madam? Can you speak?"

Focus returned to the eyes for a moment and the woman mumbled a slur of indecipherable consonants.

Shakespeare shook his head, baffled. "I understand you, not." The woman opened her mouth to show a tongue cut to a stub, and then tittered with laughter. Shakespeare could only guess at what this poor woman had experienced. Under the horror of her ordeal her mind had retreated back through the years to a time when such terrible deeds were unguessed at. She was mentally five or six years old. He picked up a stick and then knelt and brushed away the leaves to reveal a blank slate of muddy soil. He grabbed her hand and pressed the stick into her hands.

"Can you read? Cipher?" He had no idea if the woman was literate. But if she was who he suspected she was, she could no doubt read and write English and maybe even French or Italian.

The woman looked blankly at the stick in her hand, then put it in her mouth and champed her teeth upon it while she growled like a dog trained to fetch.

"No!" Shakespeare said, gently pulling the stick from her mouth. "Your name, sweet lady. Look you, this is my name." He scratched out his name in the mud: WILL. "I am Will." He grasped her hand and pushed the stick into it. "Can you scribe your name upon this muddy page?"

Her eyes showed that his words echoed only distantly in her mind. She thought for a long time and then leant forward, the end of the stick hovering over the mud. In the distance a frenzied blaring of horns signalled that the hunt had concluded. Slowly, as if teasing the words from a far away place, the woman touched the end of the stick to the ground and started to draw it through the mud. When she had finished Shakespeare leaned forward and saw the words written in a shaky hand, before the soft mud oozed back together, partially erasing her name:

VERITY.

The name reefed the knot in Shakespeare's chest tighter.

"It was your husband, murdered in the forest?"

She clamped a hand over her mouth and squeezed her eyes shut. Hot tears trickled down her cheeks.

"Sweet Jesu." Shakespeare said. "The lady of the great house calls herself Verity—" He stopped as the woman had begun to write again.

SYBILLA.

She mumbled something to him that, even though the words were unintelligible, he could tell by the rhythm what she said. "Your sister? You are the Lady Verity. Sybilla is your sister?"

She nodded.

"And the fellow who calls himself Sir Richard?"

She smeared the flat of her hand against the mud to erase her sister's name, then took up the stick and wrote again.

PHILLIP.

The name upset her. She stabbed the stick into its middle and stirred the mud angrily, growling. Shakespeare rose to his feet, knees quaking. It was a darker deed than any his own febrile brain could spawn: a brother and sister plotting to murder and supplant. He wondered what to do and soon the answer became clear. His eyes scanned the forest. The hunters and the hounds had by now retired back to the house. The way to the inn was clear. He had but to find his way through the forest.

He finally had intelligence for Oswyn Scrope that would buy back his pages and then some.

~

In the palisade, more than a hundred deer lay dead or in their death throes, tongues lolling in slack jaws, legs twitching. Elizabeth and the hunting party descended from the hunting platform, bloodying their shoes as they strode past heaps of slaughtered animals, smiling and laughing at a happy day's carnage.

Sir Richard paused before the largest hart, a magnificent stag. Several crossbow bolts stuck jaggedly from the beast, which was not quite dead and tried to rise, but then the great antlered head fell back.

Philip Mortlake looked around. The Queen stood quite alone. Essex and the other courtiers were strolling about, laughing and kicking at the dead deer. The wheel of fortune had turned in his favour. He touched a hand to the dagger in his belt and walked slowly and resolutely toward the queen. She looked up at him as he drew closer, puzzlement on her face. He walked toward her like a man in a dream and drew the dagger. One quick thrust and the world would change forever. There was no one to stop him.

"Well done, majesty!" Essex brushed past him to reach the queen. He grabbed her gloved hand and kissed it. They both noticed the drawn dagger in Philip's hand.

"Sir Richard?" Elizabeth asked, questioningly.

Philip fell to one knee before her, offering up the blade.

"Your majesty," he said. "Truly you are Diana incarnate. Milady has requested that you do us the honour of taking the great hart's life."

The queen smiled, took the dagger from him, and crouching as much as her skirts would allow her, slashed the stag's throat. Hot blood fountained from its jugular, spraying the Queen's face and the front of her frock. Seeing her majesty so despoiled, the courtiers gasped, but the Queen merely wiped her face with the back of her glove and laughed gaily, and the rest of the hunting party joined in the laughter.

CHAPTER 53: A DAGGER IN THE DARK

The niche is empty now, save for an old candleholder. Over the years, it has held a succession of candles, judging by the accretion of melted wax that dribbles down the walls in waxy stalactites. Gillian and I are down in the secret passageway. It's freezing down here, but that's not the only reason I'm shivering.

"Right there," I say, flushing shadows from the niche with the beam of my torch.

She runs a hand around the cobwebby opening as if overlooked pages might somehow be invisibly lurking.

"And that was all? Just the manuscript?"

"It was pitch dark. I'd just fallen through the floor. I was flailing about, blind as a bat, and my hand hit something hard. I heard it fall to the floor—something heavy set on top of the pages to hold them down."

The gleam of Gillian's torch sweeps the floor of the narrow tunnel. An object glints in the torch beam. She stoops, and picks it up. "Oh my God!" she says. She takes out a hanky and wipes away four hundred years of accumulated dust.

"What is that?" I ask.

"What does it look like?" The object is long and slender and flashes dully in the torch beam. A second look confirms what I thought the first time I saw it.

"A dagger!"

"Yes," she agrees. She strokes the tip of the dagger with a fingertip.

"Careful," I say. "Could get a nasty cut."

He eyes flare at me, lambent in the torch beam. "No ordinary dagger," she says, her voice stretched tight as the skin of a snare drum.

"What?" my own voice has crept up a few octaves as I realise she is blocking the only way back to the Inn. I feel my head inflate, ears buzzing as claustrophobia squeezes my chest. Alone and deep underground. My eyes are riveted to the dagger as she turns it over in her hands.

"Poison." She says it so quietly at first I think I can't tell if I just thought it or she said it aloud. In the torch beam, her smile twists a little, the weird play of light and shadow stretching the corners of her mouth into a Joker's leering grin. Why is she acting so strange?

"A dagger with a hollow tip." Her fingers caress the base. "A reservoir in the handle for poison." Her eyes hold mine. "An assassin's weapon, just like in *Double Falshood*. My God! We do have quite the story here, don't we?"

"How interesting," I say, trying to sound casual. Which is a big laugh—I'm practically wetting myself.

"Don't worry, I doubt there's any poison in it after all these years. Of course, there's only one way to find out." Her tone is suddenly very different. Distant. Cold. She turns the pointy-end my way. I suck in a breath and step back. "You have the fifth act, don't you, Harvey?" She says it flatly, calmly. More of a statement than a question. "I know how you think. You've hidden it somewhere, haven't you? As insurance?"

My right knee starts to tremor. I clamp a hand on it and try to calm its shaking. "No," I say, then realise it may not be wise to admit that I have nothing left to bargain with. "I, I mean . . . I might have," I quickly add.

"When you found the manuscript, why didn't you call in the authorities?"

Despite the subterranean chill, I'm sweating. "Too much bother. You know . . . red tape. Bad for business. I'd just as soon we kept this on the Q.T."

"Some people know how to lie, Harvey. Some Don't. You're a very bad liar. I'm sure your ex-wife could see through you as easily as I can."

"Treasure Trove," I blurt.

Given the situation, her trill of laughter is actually quite creepy.

"What? Treasure Trove?"

"Yeah."

"You silly man. Treasure Trove only applies to precious objects, not to papers, or manuscripts, or books. The manuscript is yours. It was discovered on your property. The Government has no claim—"

"Then I can sell to who I like?"

"Well ... yes. And it is literally priceless. However, I want to be the first to announce its existence. At the conference. Tomorrow. I think it will make a lasting impression. Give all the attendees something to think about on the long drive home. Is that something you could agree to?"

The glare from the torch beam stretches her face into a grotesque mask of shadow and light. She gives me a good long look. I mean a loooooong look. As if deciding what to do. I can almost hear smoothly greased gears whirring in her brain. What course of action would leave her the most advantages? A simple push of the dagger and she could leave my stiff down here for the next generation of archaeologists to discover. Another murder mystery.

She doesn't move. "So?"

"Yeah. No problem," I say. "Whatever you like."

"Good."

I clear my throat. "We should get back. Sidney must be wondering where the hell we are." Of course, that's bloody ridiculous and we both know it, but I'm desperate.

She smiles, and this time it looks normal, not off-kilter. She lowers the dagger and says: "You lead the way, Harvey."

She squeezes against the side of the tunnel to let me pass. I hesitate, and then cringe by her. I grab the rung of the ladder and climb like a monkey with his arse on fire, my back tensed, waiting for the knife blow that I am sure will come at any second.

Of course, I keep my promise until I'm safely out of the tunnel.

CHAPTER 54: AN ASSASSIN'S BLADE

He did not want to kill Oswyn Scrope while he prayed, for then the Pursuivant's soul would fly straight to heaven. But yet it may be less dangerous to do so, for Scrope's rapier stood propped against the wall, just feet from where he kneeled at the bedside before the open Bible set on the floor before him. The cupboard door creaked as Hyde eased it a little further open. Scrope's head turned slightly at the sound and the Jesuit snatched back into the shadows. A poison dagger dangled on his belt and now he drew it from its sheath. Of all the flashpoints of religious strife, the hatred between Puritans and the Catholics was the strongest. As a pursuivant, Scrope had persecuted Catholics across the country, and had personally sent many of Hyde's fellow Jesuits to the scaffold. Although he was doing God's work, killing this man would be a pleasure close to sinful.

Hatred welled in Hyde's heart. Finally, he could restrain himself no longer. His dagger begged to be plunged into this man's flesh. The cupboard door made no sound as he eased it wide and stepped out. He slipped the dagger from its sheath and crept forward. At the last moment, Scrope seemed to sense a presence behind him. The pursuivant's eyes flew up from the pages of the Bible and he started to turn his head.

"Burn in hell!" Hyde hissed and lunged.

~

The country boy in Shakespeare did not fail him. They followed a deer trail through the woods that emerged from the trees directly opposite the White Hart Inn. He had hoped to find the way clear, but several of Scrope's men idled by the Inn door, smoking clay pipes and spitting in the road.

Shakespeare took the lady by the hand and gently pulled her with him. "Come," he said. "If I tell them we have business with their master, the soldiers shall let us pass unmolested."

But the armed men frightened Verity and she jerked back. Shakespeare tried several times, but she grew more fretful and reluctant with each attempt. Finally, he told her to keep herself hidden and promised he would soon return.

As he emerged from the forest, Shakespeare felt the soldier's curious stares fall upon him. But he sauntered across the road with a smile and nod to them and passed unchallenged through the front door. Inside, as he stepped into the great room, the Innkeeper emerged from the kitchens carrying a tray of tankards. When John Thomas saw Shakespeare, he started so violently the tray slipped from his fingers and crashed to the floor, slopping ale against the walls and the shins of two travellers who sat at a table awaiting their drink. "Walt!" he bellowed, never taking his eyes off Shakespeare. "Walt! Walt!"

The Innkeeper's reaction did not bode well; the Mortlakes must have told him that Shakespeare was dead. The Stratford player hurried on and vaulted up the stairs. "Master Scrope," Shakespeare called, knocking and flinging open the door at the same instant.

Scrope was at his prayers, kneeling by the bedside, hands clasped, eyes fixed upon the Bible before him. "Scrope. Sir. A plot. I have news. The work of devils. The lady. She is not. Tis not she. The real she is without ... I mean, outside. Double-dealing. Danger ... danger to the queen. A foul plot. Come, I have much to tell you." And with that,

Shakespeare rushed out the door. He was bounding down the stairs when he noticed that Scrope wasn't following. He ran back upstairs. "Sir, I beg you, forswear your prayers. Tis a matter of much import. Foul murder and treason!"

Still, Scrope did not flinch, did not twitch. Did not blink.

"Sir, do not ignore me," Shakespeare said. "I jest not."

The pursuivant, hands folded in prayer, stared glassily at the Bible on the floor before him. Shakespeare took a timid step closer and touched the pursuivant's shoulder. "Sir, we must hasten—" At his touch, Scrope rocked forward on his knees … and toppled face-first to the floor. It was only then that Shakespeare saw the pommel of a dagger thrust into the back of his neck. Scrope's legs, stiff with rigor, kept the same fold they had assumed while he knelt. The poison in his veins had contracted his limbs in a rigid paralysis.

Something bumped behind him. Shakespeare looked around. Fierce eyes stared back from the crack of the cupboard door: a hairy face, that of the dwarf who had throttled him. The door creaked open and Thomas Hyde slid out. Shakespeare reached for his own dagger, but it had been taken from him. He reached down and drew the dagger from Scrope's neck. The dwarf looked at the knife, but only laughed and kept coming.

"Master Scrope! I am returned!" the voice and footsteps pounding up the stairs was the Sergeant at arms, Fen Crugg.

Alarm flashed across the dwarf's face. He jumped back into the cupboard and banged the doors shut behind him.

The bedroom door slammed wide as the Sergeant at Arms and one of his soldiers crashed in …

… and froze at what they saw: Oswyn Scrope, dead, slumped face-down on the floorboards in a grotesque posture of death. William Shakespeare standing over him, clutching a dagger dripping blood. For a long moment of astonishment, no one spoke nor moved.

"It was not I," Shakespeare quickly said. "I brought intelligence to Master Scrope. There is a hairy little fellow, a dwarf. He killed your master with this very dagger. I saw him plain. He is hiding in the cupboard."

The two soldiers looked at each other sceptically. Then Sergeant Crugg drew his sword and levelled the tip at Shakespeare's throat. "Empty your hands," he threatened. Shakespeare complied, tossing the dagger on the floor. The soldier pushed past and snatched open the cupboard door.

The cupboard was empty.

Crugg scowled at the playwright. "Nothing. I see no dwarf!"

Shakespeare's mouth dropped open. "But I just. A small fellow. He was but yea high," Shakespeare insisted, indicating Hyde's height with a gesture.

"Perhaps he was a pixie or an elf?" The soldier mocked. "Did he fly away on gossamer wings?"

"No. I tell you, I speak true."

The Sergeant snatched up the dagger and glared at the playwright. "William Shakespeare, I arrest you for murder of the Queen's Messenger, Oswyn Scrope, a treasonable offence."

"Shall we put him to the question, sir?" the soldier asked.

The Sergeant shook his head. "No. My master's master, Richard Topcliffe, will soon arrive and he shall put him to the torture. Then all mysteries will be revealed."

The men banged out. Shakespeare heard the rasp of a key and the deadbolt tumbling in the lock. His knees buckled and he sagged back on the bed. Oswyn Scrope remained where he was, facedown on the open Bible. On the verge of hysteria, Shakespeare wondered if the pursuivant was still reading in Heaven. He threw a fearful look at the cupboard, half-expecting the dwarf to burst out, screaming and lunging at him with a dagger, but nothing happened. He stood up and pulled the cupboard door open, pushing and prying at the boards. It seemed solid. Where had the hirsute murderer gone? Had he really seen a dwarf?

A cry from outside drew him to the window. The White Woman, the real Lady Verity, must have shown herself, for she had been captured by the soldiers and the Constable was lashing her wrists to the back of a wooden cart. Desperate to help her, Shakespeare hung out the window and shouted down. "Stop, I beg you. Stop. What are you doing?"

The constable flung up a scowl of irritation. "This mad woman is to be whipped from the county as is the law for all lunatics, cranks and sturdy beggars."

"No, you are mistaken!" Shakespeare shouted. "She is no madwoman. She is distracted by great suffering and cruel murder plotted against her."

But his pleas were ignored. The Constable cracked the whip on the haunches of a sway-backed dray horse and the cart trundled forward. The woman looked up at him and let out a great wail of despair. "Nooooooo!" Shakespeare shouted, helpless and ineffectual. A great knot tightened in his chest as he watched until the cart was too small to see and Verity's moans could no longer be heard. Suffused with despair, he fell back on the bed, tearing at his hair and smiting his own chest with his hands. The woman had saved him from the hounds and he had repaid her with yet more suffering. He was a fool, an arrant bumbling fool, and he lacerated himself for it.

When he finally opened his eyes, he noticed a pile of dog-eared papers atop a pile of nobleman's clothes—the same apparel Rafe Foxe had paraded in. He picked up the sheaf of papers. It was his work-in-progress: *Double Falshood*. A laugh, bitter as poison, escaped his lips. The play had come back to him, only now he realized it was a cursed piece of writing that brought only bad luck. The wheel of fortune had turned weighty as a millstone and he was being pressed to death beneath it.

∼

At last, the stone bridge at Wexcombe loomed ahead. Anthony Munday had slept a few miserable hours in flea-ridden bed in Derbyshire, a stinking coaching Inn called *The Tabard*. The horse he now rode was fresh; he had exchanged mounts just six miles back at *The Green Man*. His thighs were chafed raw. He was dizzy from thirst and hunger and hallucinating from lack of sleep. Just five miles beyond the bridge hot food and his bed awaited at the White Hart Inn— though he would likely have to first make report to Oswyn Scrope, who had no patience for human suffering when the Queen's business was to be done. As the horse clopped over the arched stone back of the bridge, a rider broke from the trees and blocked the road ahead. Munday blinked and wiped the sweat trickling into his eyes from beneath the brow of his hat. Another hallucination? The rider wore a buckram cloak and hood, his features hidden behind a scarf tied across his face. Munday heard a noise behind him. Several shabby men spilled from the bushes and fanned out across the road. Each was armed, mostly with crude weapons: pitchforks, cudgels, a broken sword.

Highwaymen.

Munday had feared running into a band of brigands at some point on his long ride. He had not expected to do so a few miles from his journey's end. He drew the rapier from his side. The figure ahead flung aside his buckram cloak and drew a rapier at the same moment.

"I am the Queen's Messenger on royal business," Munday announced using a herald's voice he had once used on the stage. He hoped he was able to keep the tremor of fear from his syllables. "Yield the road, or you shall draw down the Queen's army upon your head; she resides a few miles away at Wexcombe House.

"You shall be the one to put up your steel, sirrah!" the High-wayman yelled back. "The Queen and her court are rapacious beasts that steal and cheat the honest folk of these parts of all their labours. There is not a chicken, not a turnip, not an egg to be had in three counties hereabouts. Our children starve so that the Queen and her court may glut themselves."

Munday looked hard at the rider ahead. "I am sorry for your hard-ship, but molesting me is treason against the crown. I say again, yield the road."

Like all desperate people with nothing left to lose, the rider was unimpressed by Munday's threats." Our fields are enclosed. Our tillage hedged in by rich men to fatten their purses. We have levied a toll on this bridge. And the toll shall be your horse, your sword and—"

he pointed with his rapier. "Whatsoever fattens those saddle bags." The armed rabble behind him chuckled and shouted curses of encouragement.

Munday sheathed his sword. He reached behind him, loosened the straps holding the saddlebags and pulled them free.

"Wise fellow," the Highwayman said. "Now here is what we shall yield you—your death!" The highwayman soured his mount and galloped toward him. A shout went up from the rabble behind and they charged forward with a shout, levelling their pitchforks and swords.

Munday did something totally unexpected. He dropped from his horse, vaulted up on the wall of the bridge and leaped into space, legs windmilling. The stream was twenty feet below and he splashed down hard, throwing water high into the air.

The highwaymen reached the top of the bridge and stared down in wonder at the pursuivant's black hat floating in a circle of bubbling water. None could swim, and most avoided water of any depth, so Munday's plunge seemed suicidal.

The bubbles finally abated, leaving only expanding ripples of water.

"The fool has drowned himself!" grunted one of the shabby robbers.

The leader of the highwaymen scowled down from the bridge. "Aye! And thus drowns our prize,"

CHAPTER 55: THE WILTSHIRE PAPARAZZI

F lashes strobe in my eyes as I hold up the manuscript, showing it off. The Press turnout isn't exactly what I'd hoped for: five reporters, four from local rags in Marlborough and Chisbury, one stringer for the *Daily Mail*, and some rustic type from Radio Wiltshire who normally does the farm reports.

But it's a beginning.

When I called the bastards at the *BBC* regional office they just laughed and hung up. We'll see if they're still laughing a week from now.

Shutters click and strobes pulse. Reporters shout demands. I must admit it's a thrill—my own personal paparazzi.

"Could you hold it higher?"

"Can you tilt it slightly?"

"Can you suck your gut in?"

My smile is going glassy by this point, but I hold the manuscript close to my face and grin cherubically, which coaxes another flurry of flashguns.

"Can you make sure to get the pub sign in the background?" I ask them.

There's about a half dozen of us assembled in the parking lot outside the White Hart. I waited a full ten minutes after Gillian and the *Academons* left for the conference. Then I started phoning the local media.

"Has the document been authenticated?" one of the local reporters has the moxie to ask.

"Yes," I answer. "It's been thoroughly vetted by Gillian Ryecroft, a Professor of Shakespearean ... er ... thingies," I waffle. I can't remember what her official title was.

"Is that a coffee ring?" One the reporter asks, pointing with his pen. His observation produces guffaws.

I rotate the dial of my bullshitometer to its maximum setting: 11. "No, that is actually a mark left by a beer tankard—of the type used in Shakespeare's time."

"And you claim that Shakespeare's signature appears in several places on the document?"

"Absolutely. William Shakespeare. Dead clear. No doubts."

"Can we see?" another shouts.

"No, sorry gents and, uh, ladies. "I quickly add, noticing the scornful look from the lone female reporter. "This is just a preview. I can't exactly hand a precious manuscript around while everyone has a quick gander, now can I?"

A car door slams and I notice faces watching from the edge of the parking lot. The middle figure is familiar: Hedgehog. He's flanked by two younger and even hairier versions of himself, obviously his sons —although they could just as easily be human-animal hybrids escaped from the Island of Dr. Moreau. *Why the hell is he here?*

But my troubles are only beginning. Displaying the worst timing imaginable, Gillian's black BMW squeals to a halt in the parking lot. She jumps out and hurls a look of pure death straight at me.

Oops, time to vamoose.

"Thank you gents, that will be all for now," I say, anxious to wrap things up,

"What will you do with the manuscript, Mister Bracewell?"

"Braithwaite! Harvey Braithwaite!" I snap, correcting him. I know they're only reporters, but shouldn't they be able to at least get my name right?

"I'm considering my options, but of course, the manuscript of an unknown Shakespeare play is incredibly rare. Worth tons of money. Priceless, actually. As soon as I've spoken with my solicitors we will be contacting Sotheby's for the auction."

I make this up on the spot but have to admit it sounds like a good idea.

Gillian shoves through the reporters and stalks up to me, her face an interesting shade of livid. "Auction? What auction?" She's crowding me, getting in my face, but I try to keep my attention on the reporters. "Thank you. Thank you all for coming." I pull away and plunge into the safety of the inn but she follows, stepping on my heels. "I thought we had an agreement?" she demands, grabbing my arm.

"We did?"

"You made me look like a fool. I never even had a chance to make my announcement when the news came on the radio—"

"Blimey! That was quick!"

"You bastard! You selfish little horror. I hope you choke. I hope you bloody well die!" She leaves by the front door, slamming it on her way out. I hear an engine roar and the tires of her BMW squeal away.

"I think you've made an enemy, there." It's Sidney, as if you needed telling.

"That's okay," I say. "I had enemies before, only now I can afford them."

CHAPTER 56: A PLAY TO CATCH THE CONSCIENCE

"Master Shakespeare taken by Topcliffe and bound for torture," Richard Burbage lamented. "We have lost our poet and the best man among us."

"Tis an ill omen," Will Kempe agreed.

"Tis the blackest," Burbage said. "We must tell the Queen our play cannot go forward." It was unlike Burbage to give up, but things looked bleak.

The players were assembled in the road outside the White Hart Inn. In a few hours, the royal court would finish their supper and assemble ready for the evening's performance of a play both unfinished and scarcely rehearsed.

"Will!" Burbage shouted up at one of the windows. "What of your play?"

Shakespeare appeared at the open window, holding a stack of pages. "Here!" he shouted and flung them. Pages fluttered down and players dashed about, gathering them up. "Tis all I have writ," he said.

The players handed the pages to Burbage, who riffled through them, putting them in order. He slipped the last page into place and threw a doubting look up at his friend. "Will, have you still no ending?"

"Nay, I have not!" Shakespeare called back. "You must play it extempore."

"Extempore!" Burbage grumbled. "A new play and the ending we must play extempore? Who does he think I am, Anthony Munday?" He looked at the other players and rumbled: "The Warwickshire fool's gone mad!"

"Fortune turns against us," Thomas Pope wailed as the players turned their backs on the White Hart and trudged toward Wexcombe Hall.

"Aye, this effort is doomed," Will Kempe added, nodding his head so that the bells on his hat jingled. "We all shall be whipped at the cart's tail!"

~

The black coach rattled to a halt outside the White Hart Inn and vanished for a moment inside its own swirling dust cloud. When the dust settled, one of the burly manservants folded down the step and held the carriage door open. Richard Topcliffe stepped down from the coach and looked around. Satisfied, he walked to the front door of the inn, followed by his two rough servants, who lumbered after.

Shakespeare was in the open cupboard, frantically trying to find the secret latch when he heard the key scrabble in the lock. He yanked the cupboard doors shut and jumped on the bed. The door opened and a short man with a salt-and-pepper beard entered. The man flailed the room with an excoriating gaze, and then fixed his eyes upon Shakespeare.

"I am Richard Topcliffe," he said mildly. "You will have heard of me." For someone whose name inspired dread, the man was physically unimposing. Slightly stooped with a deeply lined forehead reaching back to a receding hairline of salt and pepper curls. But it was the eyes that revealed who and what he was. They were a washed-thin grey. Unalive. Peculiarly dead eyes. They fixed Shakespeare with an incurious gaze, as if he already knew all there was to know about the player. As if the Stratford Player had already confessed every dark secret.

"Shakespeare leaped to his feet," Master Topcliffe, I have dire news. There is a plot to kill her majesty. I can tell you all."

He was about to continue but Topcliffe silenced him with a gesture. "Others may, should they choose, listen to any tales you have to tell. I am not here for that," he said quietly. "I am here to extract a confession of treason."

The two heavy-set thugs crowded the doorway behind him. "Remove the bed," Topcliffe commanded without looking at them. The largest of the two, a fellow with long greasy hair and an apish jaw barged into the room, grabbed the bed and tipped Shakespeare out of it. He flung it on its side and dragged it from the room.

"Fetch the chair," Topcliffe said to the other. "Then light the brazier and find my iron tongs." The thugs left on their errands. With tedious deliberation, Topcliffe began to pull on a leather apron over his clothes. Shakespeare noticed its stains with horror, his heart thundering in his chest.

The large men moved fast as a nightmare. They carried in a hideous square chair and thumped it down in the middle of the room and then grabbed the struggling Shakespeare and crammed him in it. Iron bands snapped close around his feet and arms. A solitary band snapped shut around his throat, keeping his head pinned to the back of the chair. They set up a brazier, opening the window wide to let smoke escape, and kindled the coals until they glowed red. Finally, they presented their master with a cruel set of iron tongues, which he plunged into the flames, stirring the coals until red sparks spat from the brazier. Watching the long, drawn-out ritual, hopeless terror surged inside Shakespeare.

Finally Topcliffe sighed a long, languorous sigh and fixed the player with his dead gaze.

"We shall have a long, long talk, you and I, wherein we may learn many strange new things."

CHAPTER 57: LOSERS AND LEAVERS

By noon all the guests are trooping out to the shuddering mini-bus, dragging their suitcases. As they pass the reception desk, each looks at me with murder in his or her eyes, rather like the cast of characters from *Cluedo*: *in the library with a lead pipe*; *in the drawing room with a rope*; *in the kitchen with a revolver . . .*

Broody Brendan is the last nerd out. He pauses by the desk to say, "A lot of people hate you right now."

"Really? Most guests find me so lovable they want to smuggle me home."

"You've just undone a lifetime's work—for me and the others."

"Not my fault you lot backed a losing horse."

His expression tightens. "Still, I imagine Gillian is a happy camper. As a Stratfordian, you've just made her day."

"Not quite. I'm afraid I didn't release the news quite the way she wanted me to—"

"Yes, you did rather steal her thunder." His smirk swims in a puddle of grease. "Someone heard the news on the radio—local farming report, of all things. Word spread like wildfire. Rather upstaged Gillian who was just beginning her remarks. In seconds the whole conference fell into an absolute bloody shambles as people scrambled to find what they could learn on television and the Internet. I'm afraid you left Gillian with a rather a lot of egg on her face."

"Yes, I thought I detected a note of upset."

He gets in my face and it's clear he forgot to brush: "Be afraid, little man. Remember, *there's no fury like a woman scorned.*"

"Shakespeare? I ask, "or is that one of Marlowe's?"

He shakes his head. "Congreve."

"I thought that was a double glazing firm?"

He gives up a grunt of exasperation and heads for the door shaking his head and muttering: "What she ever saw in a buffoon like you—"

I can't let the bastard have the last word so I yell after him: "Probably all the filthy, nasty, pervy, rampant sex we had last night" He freezes when I say it, his back all tense and furious, and so I pile on the agony: "Said it was a relief to meet a real man, after all the limp-willied academics she's been with."

Bingo! I've found Brendan's pressure point and pinched the nerve with a Vulcan Death Grip. He spins around, chin quivering like a spoiled child about to boo-hoo. "You'll regret saying that," he hisses, hurling a look at me that says: *in the cellar with a poison dagger.* And then he's gone.

Well, I think I've pissed-off enough people for one day. Or maybe not. For hours, the phone rings itself stupid: calls from the BBC, calls from overseas news agencies, calls from investors, calls from famous television presenters. But I have enough savvy to let things build. Pick up momentum. The longer I wait the higher the offers will go.

After the first dozen calls, I get bored and stop answering. I let the answering machine pick them up until the memory chokes. The calls keep coming but they're sporadic now. By eleven o'clock they've pretty much stopped, except for one that sneaks in and takes me by surprise. It rings a bit then stops. Thirty seconds later it rings again.

Intuition tells me it's Gillian. She's still mad at me, but she probably wants access to the Shakespeare play and is willing to swallow her pride in order to get it. Maybe I'll get something more out of it. After all, even though my driving ban still has a day to run, I'm in the driver's seat now. I reach for the phone but it squawls into silence as I lift the receiver. If it is Gillian she'll call back. Sure enough, a minute later the phone rings again. This time I snatch it up and hold it to my ear.

There's a moment's silence, long enough for me to hear the faint, ghostly sounds of distant relays tripping, and then a metallic voice crackles: "I'm going to kill you!" and hangs up.

I stand there for several long moments, phone clamped to my head, dial tone squalling in my lughole. I've pissed off a lot of people in the last few days. More than I usually manage to piss off in a year. But I've just crossed over into unknown territory.

Something bad is going to happen.

CHAPTER 58: THE TONGUE TORN FROM MY MOUTH!

Eyes wide open, Anthony Munday sank until his boots touched down on the rocky bottom of the stream. The water was glass clear and shockingly cold. He strode off downstream, clothes billowing and spilling a trail of air bubbles. Lungs straining to burst, he climbed the tumble of round river stones until his head broke water in the cover of the cover of tall reeds crowding the riverbank. Anthony Munday spat water and sucked in a lungful of sweet-smelling air.

Keeping his head low, he moved deeper into the cover of the reed bed, and almost collided with a corpse: eyes wide and staring, wet hair plastered over a ghastly white face busied with flies.

It was the corpse of an old woman. The Jesuits had carried Winifred's body to the bridge and tossed it into the river. The current had swept it to the bank where it hung up in the reeds. Munday lingered in the corpse's vile company for half an hour, listening to the robbers rail and curse at one another. Despite the heat of the day, the water was frigid so that that his teeth chattered. When the churlish voices grew distant, he ventured a quick peek above the swaying pussy willows. The figures on the bridge had gone.

The riverbank was steep. It took several exhausting attempts before he found a section with solid enough footing to drag himself from the water. He clambered to the top of the bank, feet skidding in his sodden boots and slogged back to the stone bridge where he sat atop the wall, shivering as the hot sun dried his clothes. The thieves had made off with his horse. Worse yet, in his leap from the bridge he had lost the saddlebag containing the miniature portraits—his proof of the plot and the reason for his two hard days of riding stripped from him in the moment he splashed down on the river.

His head jerked up when he heard men's voices approaching. For a moment he feared the robbers were returning, but then he saw a straggle of men plodding toward him, and instantly recognized them by the ginger-bearded giant that trudged at the head of the group.

The Lord Chamberlain's Men.

Burbage threw out his arms to halt the players as they climbed the curving backbone of the bridge and spotted Munday. "How now!" Burbage cried. "A drowned rat!"

"Master Burbage!" Munday said. "I am right pleased to see you!"

"Would that I could say the same, traitorous rogue! You and your fellows are the reason we are short our best man!"

"What mean you?"

"Will Shakespeare, taken for murder."

Munday's jaw dropped. "Murder? Murder of who?"

"Your master, Odious Scrope."

"Oswyn Scrope, dead?" Munday could not believe his ears.

"Aye, stabbed with a poison blade. And our Will Shakespeare taken for the crime and soon to be put to the torture by Richard Topcliffe!"

"Topcliffe is here?" Munday gasped, much amazed.

"Aye, and two of his personal devils with him."

"And our play has no ending and we are to perform it before the Queen!" Heminges added.

"We are sure to be hissed from the stage!" Kempe said.

"And worse yet," Heminges came back. "Not paid for our pains!"

CHAPTER 59: THE VOICE OF DOOM

Hedgehog throws a quick look around the inside of the Marlborough *Costa Coffee* to make sure no one's looking, then flips aside the cloth covering the heavy object he just set in the middle of the table. It is huge and shiny—bigger than I thought, a cruelly machined chunk of metal. Even though I don't pick it up, I can guess at its steely mass.

"Smith and Wesson 32 calibre revolver," Hedgehog says. "Six shots. Very accurate. Very reliable. Drop a Rhino at fifty paces—"

"Of which there are very few in Wiltshire."

Hedgehog grunts and asks, "What did the voice on the phone say?"

I do my best to reproduce the mechanical Dalek voice, "I'm going to kill you."

"Just like that? With the funny voice?"

"It was disguised somehow. Makes me think it's someone I know." I throw Hedgehog a look of deep suspicion, but it just ricochets off his dense skull.

"Dodgy. Very dodgy. Sounds like you've pissed off some dangerous nutter. If I was you, I'd buy it." He nods at the artillery piece on the table between us.

I shake my head. "This is daft. I'm not trying to be Dirty Harry. I just want a gun for the off chance—"

"The off chance that the bloke who keeps ringing you up threatening to kill you isn't going to show up with a loaded shotgun some dark and stormy?" Hedgehog throws me a twinkly grin.

"I never said it was a bloke. Like I said, the voice was disguised. Might be a fella. Might be a woman." Even as I say it I can't stop thinking of Gillian: *A tiger's heart wrapp'd in a woman's hide.*

Hedgehog snatches the gun off the table, finding a home for it in one of the many voluminous pockets of his great coat. "I've got a buyer for that document of yours. Very interested. And this way there'd be no income tax and no V.A.T. involved."

"Too late. I've already announced it to the world. I've gotta go legit, now. Don't want the taxman banging on my door. And especially not the V.A.T. bastards. Worse than the cosa nostra."

I don't share in Hedgehog's throaty laugh.

"Is that all you got?" I demand.

He digs in the opposite pocket, pulls out something considerably smaller than the Dirty Harry Cannon. He opens the wrappings to reveal a compact pistol. Even though I know almost nothing about guns, it looks familiar.

"Beretta 418 automatic," he growls.

The James Bond gun. I knew I'd seen it before. The weapon is tiny and invites me to pick it up. It fits my small hand perfectly. Even though it's small, holding the gun makes me feel big. Powerful. Debonair. Like I should be wearing the pistol in a shoulder holster underneath a black tie and tux, lounging by a swimming pool full of bikini babes, ordering a dry martini shaken, not stirred.

"How much?"

"Naw, I don't recommend it. You don't want this piddly little thing. It's old. Unreliable."

"So is my barman. How much?"

He guffaws sceptically. "It's a ladies' handbag gun—no stopping power."

"It might be a lady with a handbag who's threatening to kill me."

"No, mate. Trust me. The Smith and Wesson will drop a charging Rhino—"

"What is it with you and Rhinos? When you were a child, did a rhino break into your house and kill your entire family? I want this gun. How much?"

"He names his price. I peel off a half-dozen fifty pound notes and drop them on the table.

Hedgehog sweeps them up with his filthy tractor mechanic's hands. "I'll throw in the bullets free," he says setting a tiny clip of bullets atop the table.

"Huge of you." I snatch up the tiny clip and slap it into the butt of the gun to load it like I've seen in a million American movies.

Hedgehog's huge hand flies across the table and grabs the gun. "Be bloody careful!" he says. He yanks the Beretta from my grip and deftly removes the bullet clip before setting both back on the table. "Don't ever do that!" he barks. "The, uh, the safety ain't so clever and this gun's got a hair trigger. Don't load it until you mean to use it."

"My old Dad used to say that, but he was talking about a condom."

I scoop up gun and clip and slip them in a jacket pocket. I can't wait to get home and practice my DeNiro in the mirror: *Are you lookin' at me? Are you lookin' at me?*

"My buyer is still very interested in your Shakespeare."

"Tell him to get in the queue. Anyway, I'm off. Gotta see a man about a chainsaw."

I hate *B&Q* with a passion. I never remember this fact until I'm actually in the store, and then I find myself overwhelmed by towering aisles of cheap and nasty tat manufactured in the People's Republic of China and shipped halfway around the world for consumption by the great-unwashed masses of the People's Republic of Swindon.

After being misdirected several times by clueless staff in shapeless nylon smocks, I stumble by chance into the gardening area, which features lawn mowers and, ta-da!, chainsaws. I pick the biggest, machoist, shoutiest, petrol powered something-or-other they have and then set off toward the impossibly distant tills two time zones away.

"I'm going to kill you!"

The voice freezes me on the spot. It's the voice from the telephone, with almost the exact electronic rasp to the syllables.

"I'm going to bash you up!"

I'm passing the kiddie toys and the sound pulls my gaze down one of the aisles. A tyke of maybe seven or eight is holding some kind of futuristic microphone to his mouth. When he talks into it, his little boy's voice is digitally garbled into a giant robot monster. He puts one arm out, wobbling back and forth in a kind of robot dance as he talks.

"I am the robot monster from Mars. I can crush you!"

"Give us that, kid," I say, snatching it from him.

"Hey!" the little boy says. His momentary bravery evaporates when he sees that his toy has been taken away by a scary, middle-aged geezer holding a chainsaw. I experience the momentary exultation of the playground bully as he scampers away, presumably to fetch his mum.

I examine the toy. It's garishly coloured in fluorescent pink and orange. A large sticker on the microphone spells out: VOICE MORPHER 2000.

I put the microphone to my mouth and speak into it: "I'm going to kill you." No, not quite right. I find a big black adjustment knob and twist it. "I'm going to kill you!" Almost. "I'm going to kill you!" Nearly. I tweak the knob a bit more. "I'm going to kill you!"

That's it. Perfect. Identical to the voice on the phone.

"I'm going to kill you! I'm going to kill you! I'm going to kill you!"

I happen to look up see the kid standing at the end of the aisle. His mum is with him and they're both staring at me in wide-eyed horror. "Come along, Brian! Mummy says it's time to go!" The woman snatches her tyke away so quickly his feet leave the ground

I march toward the distant tills feeling invulnerable; feeling like Bruce Willis in that movie where everything explodes at the end.

What's the expression Americans use? *Loaded for bear.* Yeah. Not quite sure what it means, but yeah! Too bloody true! I'm fully kitted out: a gun, a chainsaw, and a kiddie's toy voice changer. Let's see the wanker on the phone try something now.

Harvey Braithwaite's coming and he's bringing the pain!

CHAPTER 60: THE TONGUE TORN FROM MY MOUTH!

W hen removed from the brazier, the iron tongs glowed cherry red.

"Before I left London," Topcliffe said. "I sent for intelligence of you. You live on Silver Street."

"With a good family," the Stratford player quickly offered. "French Huguenots. I am but a lodger."

"And yet you are not registered at any church?" The hooded eyes swerved up from the brazier, impaling him. "There is no record of your attendance."

The wordsmith had none to offer.

"Which are you, William Shakespeare? A secret Papist? A recusant who refuses the Queen's true religion? Or a God-cursed atheist like the sodomite villain Marlowe? He is suffering all the torments of hell, having taken a dagger in the eye."

Before Shakespeare could speak, he first had to pry his tongue from the roof of his mouth. "I had heard it was tavern brawl ..." he croaked dryly, "... over the reckoning."

He was answered by Topcliffe's dark laughter. "Aye, it was a costly reckoning."

Dread surged through the Stratford player. He would end his life as Topcliffe's dancing bear, twitching with every application of the master's rod.

"Mu-my lu-lord," Shakespeare stammered. "My trade as player means I must travel. Plus I have a wife and babes in Stratford and journey there many times a year."

Topcliffe licked a finger and touched it to the iron tongs. It made a sizzling sound. "Aye, You have two girls, Susannah and Judith. Your son, Hamnet, died a year hence."

Shakespeare nodded. That blessed name in this man's mouth seemed defilement. "As player with access to the court, Master Scrope employed me as his spy. I came here to present him with urgent news of a plot that touches the very life of Elizabeth—"

"I have touched the Queen myself," Topcliffe interrupted. Shakespeare paused, not knowing whether to continue.

"Aye," Topcliffe smiled, his deep-socketed eyes gleaming. "She has very fair skin, and soft. Oft I have stroked her belly . . . and sucked upon her cherry paps."

Words jammed in Shakespeare's throat. He did not know what to say. Or whether to say anything. Was it a test? Should he raise a protest at the Queen of England being spoken about in such scandalously familiar terms? He was a man lost on a barren moor, walking through a blasted landscape with quicksand on all sides.

Topcliffe turned arthritically. He walked around behind Shakespeare and rested his hands familiarly upon the younger man's shoulders. Then he leaned down and the player's skin crawled beneath the unwelcome lick of hot breath in his ear. "I have touched her majesty in her most privy parts," Topcliffe continued, warming to his subject. "Indeed, I have knelt at her feet, and tickled the fine hairs of her cunny with my nose, as she rested the back of her thigh upon my shoulder."

Shakespeare could feel his face reddening, his heart banging. Such talk was high treason; even hearing someone else speak the words aloud was dizzying. When Richard Topcliffe slid from behind Shakespeare, he had a hand thrust beneath the leather apron and was groping himself.

Shakespeare threw a quick look at the faces of the lumpen henchmen. They lounged against the wall with lazy leers on their slack faces. They were not shocked because this behaviour was clearly not new to them. Topcliffe paused at the brazier and lifted the iron tongs from the fire. They smoked hot, but had not yet begun to glow red. He thrust them back in, agitating the coals, which crackled and spat fiery sparks.

"And her majesty hath many times leapt upon my rampant courter, so as to summon her sweet flows of honey—"

An icy sweat trickled between Shakespeare's shoulder blades. Topcliffe was not just evil, not just sadistic, worse, he was clearly mad —but then what sane man could do his work?

"… and her majesty and I were in the heat of a full swive and she cried out, and bade me not to slow my thrusts—"

Topcliffe drew the tongs from the brazier. The ends glowed cherry red. The wet red lips pulled back from his teeth as Richard Topcliffe advanced toward the helpless poet. "Now, master player, you have a tongue known for its wit. I intend to stretch that tongue further than you could believe possible." He threw a glance at his henchmen. "Hold fast his head."

The two lackeys lurched forward and seized Shakespeare's head. Massive hands pried his jaws open. Shakespeare choked out a moan of terror as Topcliffe loomed over him, the heat from the tongs singeing his beard. Helpless, he pressed his head against the hard back of the wooden chair, his eyes wide, a scream coiled in his throat, ready to spring out.

An impatient fist hammered upon the door. Topcliffe paused for a moment, as if he would stop, but then continued. The hammering resumed. And then a voice, Anthony Munday's called through the door. "Master Topcliffe, I have need of you."

Topcliffe's eyes showed recognition and he straightened. "I am never interrupted in my home in Westminster," he said with irritation. He flung the tongs back in the brazier to reheat and nodded at one of his men to unlock the door.

"Master Topcliffe," Munday said, entering breathless. He threw the quickest of glances at Shakespeare. "The Queen has summoned you."

The dark face displayed an unfamiliar expression: surprise. "Her majesty? She asks for me?" Topcliffe looked excited.

"There is to be a play and a masque tonight. "She has expressly asked for you to attend and sit by her, for you are a great favourite of hers."

Topcliffe needed no further encouragement. He snapped his fingers at his two henchmen. "Come, leave him. We shall resume where we have left off anon. For my queen has summoned me!" Topcliffe hurried from the room and his men bumbled behind. Munday waited until their footsteps banged down the stairs before closing the door and rushing to Shakespeare. "We must be quick!" He released the bands holding Shakespeare's ankles, and then worked on his wrists. "I stretched the truth a good deal farther than it will hold."

Munday unlatched the metal band about Shakespeare's throat and he rose shakily from the chair.

"I have seen proof of the deception," Munday said. "I visited the Mortlake home and took three miniatures, painted when they were in their youth. The Lady Verity is in truth the Lady Sybilla; Sir Richard is her brother, Philip Mortlake."

"If we have proof, then, all is well!"

"Nay, I was robbed by highwaymen. Our proof is lost, drowned in the river. Still, we must contrive a means to stop this foul plot." Then a sudden realisation struck Munday. "But we are not courtiers. We have no license to mix with the court. With our rude dress they shall bar our entry!"

Shakespeare thought on the problem. Then his eyes alighted on a pile of clothes stacked on a chair: a rich brocaded cape and a puce bonnet, a pair of gloves and a riding boots—the nobleman's clothes Rafe Foxe had worn. Shakespeare grabbed the clothes and handed them to Munday. "Put on these raiments," he said "I know of another way we may enter Wexcombe House."

He opened the cupboard doors wide, his eyes scanning the insides.

"Why tarry you?" Munday asked as he dressed. "There is nothing in that cupboard!"

Now that he had time to look, Shakespeare closely studied the frame of the cupboard and noticed a fine, almost invisible diagonal cut through the wood. He grabbed it and tugged, pushed, pulled. Nothing. Then he pressed down and sideways. A section of the frame rotated about a pivot: a hidden catch. A mechanism behind the wall snicked and the back of the cupboard swung open onto a shaft hewn into the bricks of the wall. A wooden ladder, fixed to one wall, descended into darkness.

Munday gawped in amazement.

"Come," Shakespeare said, climbing onto the ladder. "Follow and be prepared to be amazed."

CHAPTER 61: IF A TREE FALLS IN THE WOODS

"This is a bad idea."

"Shut up," I say to Sidney. "No one asked you."

"The bloke from the council said—"

"Bugger the bloke from the council. And bugger the council. Things are different now."

Obviously, I haven't actually got the money yet, but even the Bank Manager has read about the Shakespeare manuscript and his tone has undergone a sea change overnight. The phone hasn't stopped ringing. It's only a matter of time before even more news crews and looky-loulooky-looss converge on the White Hart Inn. I want to be ready.

"It's a listed landmark. You'll get a whopping fine."

I flourish the chainsaw triumphantly. "Brilliant. Now I can afford it."

"We're both in the parking lot in front of the White Hart. I grab the handle of the starter rope and give it a mighty jerk. The chainsaw clears its throat with a grumbling cough, but doesn't fire. I thumb the choke switch wider and give it another snatch. Again, it chuffs and whiffles but won't start. I give it two more yanks, but my hair's falling into my eyes and I'm starting to sweat.

"Do you want me to try?"

"No Sidney, I don't want you to try. You're already very trying." I heave the starter rope again, and again, and again …and again and again and again and again …until my arm is ready to fall off.

"Why don't you let me—?"

"Thank you, Sidney, but I'm quite capable. I give the starter a mighty heave—and something pops in my shoulder.

I set the chainsaw down on the ground, forcing a smile, trying to conceal my agony. "Why don't you have a go, Sidney?"

I look up as the chainsaw snarls into life. "First pull," Sidney shouts over the roar, then adds: "You didn't have the ignition switch turned on,"

Now do you know why I hate the bastard?

"Gimme that!" I snatch the chainsaw back and gun the throttle. It roars savagely and bucks in my hands. I feel myself respond in the primal way that all men respond to power tools. *Righto, where's that bloody tree?*

The whirring blade bites into ancient bark and glides through like its butter, spitting sawdust. Yes, I'm not a complete idiot, I did think ahead and have moved the Jensen a good twenty feet away. I've never cut down a tree before and only have a vague sense of what to do. But how difficult can it be? However, the trunk is enormous, too big to make one cut. I make a v-shaped cut on one side of the trunk, and then move around to attack from the other side.

"Move back!" I shout to Sidney over the roar of the motor. "I'm going to drop it so it falls away from the inn."

Sidney shakes his head and keeps backing away until he's almost in the next county. I gun the chainsaw and make a downward slanting cut from the back, ready to jump clear when it starts to go. As the blade is almost through, the trunk lets go with a mighty crack. I kill the motor, and leave the chainsaw where it is, stuck in the trunk, backpedalling until I'm well clear. The cracking gets louder. The oak starts to lean, farther, farther, farther . . . A final loud snap and it starts to topple, but then the top of the tree cracks and falls in the opposite direction. The lower half crashes to the parking loud with a ground-shaking WHUMP. The top half falls the opposite way . . .

. . . and crashes down on my beloved Jensen. The windows explode as the massive limb flattens the roof, pinning the car to the parking lot and triggering the car alarm into a fit of howls and wails, the head-lights flashing manically.

I cannot think of a thing to say.

Tires squeal as a white estate car swerves into the parking lot and a young man jumps out. He stares disbelievingly at the ancient oak, broken in two halves, and then hurls an angry look at me. Of course, it's Pollard, the young man from Marlborough council.

I can almost hear the novelty cushion's plaintive whoop.

CHAPTER 62: THE GREAT ESCAPE

F resh candles burned at intervals along the tunnel left by the conspirators so that, after murdering the queen, their escape route would be well lit.

"You were right, Master Shakespeare," Munday said, breathing hard as the two men duckwalked, stooped over. "I am amazed!"

"Wait till we reach the house. Then you will see the work of Thomas Hyde, the dwarf I told you of. Tis wicked ingenious."

They continued on in the darkness of the tunnel.

"How is it that you renounced the stage?" Shakespeare asked. "I have read your ballads and poems. You have fine skills."

"Not as great as yours," Munday said. "Your fame shall live for an age. No one will mourn the loss of my scribblings. I took the post of Queen's messenger to make my fame there."

Shakespeare scoffed at such a notion. "Aye, I have fame—such fame as snow in May. Much marvelled at but soon melted."

They reached the end of the tunnel and climbed the steep steps up into the warren of hidden passageways that honeycombed Wexcombe House. Shakespeare showed Munday the spy holes that looked out onto the library and many of the private rooms. Finally, they entered the hidden chamber behind the fresco of the Queen's chamber. Here,

Shakespeare took down a candle and shone its light so that Munday could examine the two portraits.

"Ye gods!" Munday said, pointing. "These are the same raiment's I wear, the clothes of a nobleman! So, this is the true visage of Sir Richard Wexcombe, the man we found in the forest with his face so barbarously hacked."

"And this is the true Lady Verity," Shakespeare said, holding the candle before the next portrait. "She still lives. I came upon her wandering in the forest, her mind greatly distracted. She saved me from the hounds, but the Constable took her for a madwoman and whipped her from the parish. I despair to think what has become of her."

"Oh, this is wickedness worse than Marlowe's *Jew of Malta!*"

Shakespeare flipped open one of the trunks that lined the wall. "Look you!" he said drawing something out of the trunk.

A devil mask.

"Ill warrant these are the vizards they wore that fateful day," Shakespeare said. "We found one snagged in a holly bush." The Stratford poet thought a moment. "And I have an idea how we can use these same vizards and buckram robes to devise a play that will scorch the souls of the murders who see their foul crimes acted out before the Queen and Court!"

"We must kill Will Shakespeare," John Thomas said to Walt Gedding as the two watched Richard Topcliffe's coach clatter away.

"The player locked in the attic room?" Gedding asked. "Why?"

"To leave no witnesses." John Thomas nodded to Walt Gedding and the two thumped up the stairs to the room Shakespeare had been locked in. The paused a moment outside while each drew a poison dagger, then John Thomas turned the key in the lock and the two burst in.

Topcliffe's cruel chair sat in the middle of the room.

Empty.

"He has escaped!" Gedding said. "But how?"

John Thomas stepped to the cupboard and swung the door open. The two players had failed to close the hidden door behind them.

"Fetch candles!" Thomas said.

"There are enough lit that we may see our way now," Gedding complained.

"For the way back, lackwit!"

"Tis not the plan!" Gedding snapped. "We are to remain here until the deed is done and then ride with the Mortlakes to our safe house in Derbyshire before the hue and cry can be raised."

"The plot is unravelling, coz. It will be a struggle from here on in. The rascal Shakespeare has escaped through our own tunnel and gone to warn the Queen. We must catch and kill the interfering rogue before he can raise the alarm."

CHAPTER 63: HISSED FROM THE BOARDS

"A poison dagger!" Thomas Pope shouted, raising the wooden dagger aloft. "Oh, what wickedness is ..." he trailed off and snatched a look at the page in his left hand, reading. "Oh, what wickedness is this we plot?" He dropped his arms in exasperation. "Our plot is plotless. Tis nonsense!"

"Oh, what disaster is this," Will Kempe mocked. "That has entangled a sorry troupe of players!"

On the stage in the great hall, the Lord Chamberlain's Men were reading from their pages and practicing lines.

"Silence, rabble!" John Heminges bellowed, stepping to centre stage. As business manager, he saw the tragedy strictly in terms of lost money if the troupe failed to perform. Less important to him was whether that performance was good or bad. "Rouse yourselves, sluggards!" Heminges encouraged. "Are we not players? We have played sweet love scenes in stinking inn-yards ankle-deep in horse shit. We have spoken poetry in leaky barns with a tempest sluicing down upon our heads. Aye, things may seem ill. We are one act shy of a play. Two players shy of a company. We are to perform a play as yet strange to us. Pah!" He made a dismissive gesture. "Tis nothing. The Queen and her court expect a performance and by Christ's bones we shall fulfil our contract." He threw a hard look at Henry Condell. "Henry, you shall perform Will Shakespeare's role."

"But . . . but, I know not his words," Condell complained.

"Then mouth your own!"

"I could play a part," called a voice from backstage.

The players looked around to see who had spoken. Anthony Munday had been lurking behind the scenery, watching, and now he stepped forward. "Give me pages, I can fast set them to memory. And those I cannot recall, I can extemporise."

Burbage threw a *don't-you-dare* look at Heminges and spoke only one word: "Dangerous."

But Heminges cared less about the quality of the night's performance and more about the contractual obligations of not having a performance. He loved to take money, and hated worse than the devil to give it back. "Fortune favours us not, Dick. We must play the cards she deals us." He thrust pages in Munday's hand. "Here are your lines. Do your best Master Munday and contain your extemporising. No bombast lasting longer than a minute of the clock, or we will all be hissed from the boards."

"And what of Will Shakespeare's lines?" Burbage demanded.

A figure in a buckram cloak stepped from behind the scenery. "I shall speak them." All eyes fixed upon the strange figure. He stepped to centre stage and flipped back the hood, revealing familiar features.

"Will!" the players cried.

"I thought Topcliffe had you?" Burbage asked.

"He does. He did. I escaped him."

"You escaped Richard Topcliffe?" Burbage said, incredulous.

"We are all for the Tower." Will Kempe moaned.

Thomas Pope and the others began to squabble among themselves about the best course of action to take, but Shakespeare raised a hand to silence them. "Listen to what I say. We have but little time. The Lady Verity and Sir Richard are false fellows. In truth they are Philip and Sybilla Mortlake, brother and sister. The mad woman we saw in the woods is the true Lady Verity. The much abused corpse we stumbled upon in the brook was the real Sir Richard Wexcombe, his face hacked to conceal his true identity."

Heminges said. "What was the purpose of this dread action?"

"A serpent's plot," Shakespeare said, "which uncoils even now. A bloody stratagem to murder the Queen."

The players gasped and threw astonished looks at one another.

"Hell's teeth!" Thom Pope uttered.

Burbage said, "This is beyond us, Will. We must alert the Privy Council and the Queen's lifeguard. These traitors must be taken—"

"We have no proof," Shakespeare interrupted. "Plus we are mere players and I am the prisoner of Richard Topcliffe. We will be arrested. Instead, we must goad the conscience of the murderers. When their dark deeds play out in the light of day, they will know they are discovered and confess or flee." Shakespeare tugged up the hood of his buckram robe, hiding his face. "Come fellows, we have but two scant hours to practice. If you be true players, play your part as if your lives hang by it, for if not, we shall all hang together."

Burbage stepped closer, still not convinced. "But Will, this play has no fifth act!"

"True, but it must needs write itself upon the page of history. We will act all that is written. The fourth act will end with the masque. If all is still not resolved by that time . . ." Shakespeare paused a moment, his face grave but resolute. ". . . then I will step upon the stage alone and speak a soliloquy, either of my death or proof of the plot."

CHAPTER 64: FROM BAD TO VERSE

"Yes, ten o'clock tomorrow works fine. No, I won't be here, I'm driving into London. My barman, Sidney will be here. No, the tree is already down. That's right. Yes. Yes. Yes … yes …. thank you."

I hang up the phone. I've spent the last twenty minutes talking to a tree removal service. I realise I won't be driving into London—at least not in the Jensen, which is still smashed to the axles beneath half an oak tree. Bugger. That leaves the train or a hire car. The first day my driving ban expires and I'm carless. Oh well, I can afford an Aston Martin with what I'm going to get for this play. I'm going to London to meet with the people at Sotheby's.

Mrs. Bramsworth didn't come in today—a poorly aunt in Marlborough—so I'm all alone. Sidney wobbled away on his pushbike an hour ago. I'm moving through the Inn, flipping off lights, getting ready to lock up. I pause to pour myself a scotch. Why not? After all I've been through a lot. I need a bit of a restorative.

I take the first sip when the phone rings. I look at the wall clock: 11:30. It's late for the press to be calling. Another potential buyer? For some reason I think of Gill. She left a message on the machine yesterday saying she'd like to talk to me. I haven't called her back, mainly because I know she's only interested in the manuscript, not in me. The phone keeps ringing and ringing and I can't understand why the machine isn't picking up until I remember—the memory's choked on all the calls. I set the scotch down on the bar and hurry to my office as the phone jangles for attention. I hesitate a moment and then pick up the receiver and lift it to my ear.

Nothing. Silence. Nada.

"Hello?"

"I'm going to kill you!"

It's the merry prankster. Luckily, I've got the Voice Morpher 2000 standing ready on the desk and snatch it up. "I'm going to kill you, you stupid prat!" I snarl back, giving whomever it is a dose of his own medicine. The line clicks into silence. I smile to myself. Got the bastard. But then I notice the phone has no dial tone. I tap the receiver and hold it to my ear. Dead.

Ah.That's a bit worrying.

I remember my mobile and fish it out of my pocket, but when I try to dial the Police the screen flashes "NO SERVICE."

Bugger. I'd forgotten. The Inn sits in a hollow. I can never get any service on my mobile out here. I'm not panicking yet, but I am starting to feel a bit cut off. I go to the window, pull back the curtain and look out. It's dark outside but I can just make out a car parked in the lay-by up the road. It doesn't have its lights on. It could just be a break-down, but then I hear the motor start up and the car creeps toward the inn.

WITH THE HEADLIGHTS OFF.

Okay, no reason to panic. But then I hear the crunch of tires on gravel as the car pulls into the parking lot. I grab the strong box and quickly unlock it. On top is the manuscript. As I snatch it up, something tumbles loose and thumps to the ground. It's the dagger Gill found, wrapped in a cloth. I pick it up and stuff it in a pocket. The Beretta lies in a nest of loose banknotes. I grab the gun and the clip, hands shaking as I slip the clip into the gun and slap it home with my palm.

The *Bang!* makes me jump. Surprisingly, it's not that loud—like the world's biggest Christmas cracker. I stand there for a moment, stunned. The air spools with the bitter tang of cordite. I look down and there's a neat hole in the front of my cardigan. A moment later a red stain radiates out. I take a breath and feel a sharp pain in my chest.

Ohmigod! I've been shot.

Then I notice the smoke curling from the muzzle of the Beretta and think: *Ohmigod! I've just bloody well shot myself.*

The sound of shattering glass brings me back. Someone's breaking in! I dither for a moment.

It's the murderer! Can't let myself go into shock. Got to keep moving.

There's a panic button next to the desk drawer. I press it to trip the silent alarm to alert the police. But then I realise, if the phone lines have been cut . . .

I hear the crunching of glass underfoot. Someone's climbing in through a window. I grab the Shakespeare manuscript, bang the strongbox shut, locking it and wobble from the room.

I n the Great Hall, the babble of impatient courtiers grew louder. The Queen fanned herself with an ornate fan inlaid with pearl and gold while Essex sprawled on a cushion at her feet guzzling wine from a golden goblet. Their false hosts—Sybilla and Philip Mortlake— sat to their immediate left. Both now exchanged tense glances. The fateful hour had arrived.

On stage, a figure stepped out into the light of a dozen giant candelabrums: a monk in a buckram robe, his face hidden in the shadows of a deep cowl. The monk crept to the edge of the stage. He raised a finger to his cowl in a "shush" gesture. Such was the monk's ominous presence, that the chatter and mindless babble drained away and silence prevailed.

A full minute passed. The silence deepened. Ripened. Just when it seemed as if the monk would never speak, a voice rumbled from the cowl and resonated outward, filling the Great Hall. It was a voice that spoke of graves robbed, of madmen stumbling across a blasted moor, a voice that would someday resound from the ghost of Hamlet's father.

"Here we set our tale of vile murder and wicked treason in an ancient oak forest, once sacred to the Druids ... still greedy for the blood of innocents." The monk raised his arm and pointed to the wings. "Behold who comes. Four murderers, bound together by wicked ambition, their faces hid by vizards."

Four players lurched onto the stage—Burbage, Henry Condell, Thomas Pope and Thom Heminges. In their seats, the Mortlakes, brother and sister, stiffened, their eyes widening in disbelief. The players were dressed in buckram cloaks and wore their very own masks: a Goblin, a Fool, a Satyr, and a fiery-faced Devil.

"The murderers do not come alone," Shakespeare continued. "With them, a pure and innocent Lady kidnapped from a great house." The body of players parted to reveal the slender form of a woman hidden in their midst—Young Sam Gilbourne in a blonde wig and a burial shroud, his hands tied and eyes blindfolded.

Philip threw a look of pure terror at his sister. He began to rise from his seat in an involuntary contraction of muscles. Without ever looking at her brother, Sybilla put a hand on his shoulder and shoved him back down.

"The murderers come with a hunting horn, but today they hunt not the Hart, but the heart of a great man—the Lady's husband, Sir Richard. The innocent maid is to be used as bait, but before they can set the snare, the villains ensure that she has no voice to call out a warning."

"Come," William Sly spoke in the high-pitched voice of a woman, his face hidden by the Devil mask. "Bind my sister fast that I may cut the tongue from her mouth!" The murders swarmed their victim, two holding her wrists while the one in the devil's mask flourished a dagger to cut out her tongue.

"Speak not our guilt, vile tongue!" the she-Devil cried and slashed with her dagger.

Sybilla had her hand on her brother's hand, and now her nails dug in until they drew blood, but neither noticed, their eyes wide with fear as they watched their heinous crime being re-enacted before the entire court.

The Queen and her courtiers, even the military men hardened in battle, flinched in their seats at Sam Gilbourne's piercing shriek catapulted to the highest rafters of the hall. The Devil reached in, snatched something, and held it aloft.

A severed tongue.

In truth it was merely a length of red ribbon, but the effect was horrifying. Lettice Knollys, one of the Queen's Ladies in Waiting, fell over in a swoon and had to be held up and fanned by the other ladies. The court gasped at such wickedness. The Queen herself snickered behind her hand and thought it all good fun.

Philip Mortlake doffed his cap and fanned a face white as parchment, sweat beaded on his forehead. The action continued and what happened next drove icy terror, pure and naked, into his bowels.

The murderer in the green Goblin mask blew his hunting horn. Moments later, a nobleman stepped onto the stage. It was Anthony Munday dressed in the clothes Rafe Foxe had stolen: the puce bonnet, the rich cape, the gold-hilted rapier and the leather-riding boots.

The murderers went rigid. Philip looked like a man ready to choke up his last breath.

"What naughty fellows dare poach in this, my family's ancient deer park?" Munday said. "I'll follow the horn blast. When I find you, you shall be whipped for it, be you poets or knaves!" The nobleman advanced and suddenly the four murderers, their faces hidden behind vizards, stepped from behind the trees and menaced him with drawn rapiers.

Even from backstage, Shakespeare could see Philip's head quiver atop his neck. Once again, he tried to rise from his seat, but Sybilla clutched at his sleeve and dragged him down. Oblivious, the Queen reached to the table beside her, selected a sugar sweet from a golden box lined with red velvet and popped it in her mouth.

"Who are you," Munday cried, "that hide your faces behind dissembling vizards?"

The Devil-masked murderer crept up behind the nobleman and

plunged a dagger into the small of his back. Anthony Munday screamed and fell to his knees. He reached behind and yanked out the knife, staring at the bloody blade with horror. "What wickedness is this?" he cried out. "A cold river flows in my blood. The dagger is poisoned!" He reached out a hand to the blindfolded maiden. "Oh, my beloved, I am slain. Oh, most wicked and godless murder!"

Philip Mortlake shrieked and leaped to his feet, hands clawing at his own throat. The play stopped. All eyes in the room—the Queen's, the courtiers, even the players on the stage—fastened upon his horror-stricken face.

Sybilla stood up, put an arm around her brother's quaking shoulders and settled him back in his seat. "My husband is not well, majesty." she said. "He is much fatigued from the hunt. Perhaps such bloody plays are not fair meat for the court."

"Nonsense, girl!" Elizabeth snapped, clearly irritated. "Your Queen is enjoying this. Tell your husband he must groan a little lower or leave us." Elizabeth's eyes returned to the stage and she waved for the players to pick up where they left off. "I command you continue, sirs."

The action recommenced. But as the plot unfolded, it became clearer that the story was one of assassination involving a figure clearly meant to be Elizabeth. Courtiers threw uneasy looks at each other. It seemed scandalous and seditious material to be uttered in the Queen's presence.

Throughout the performance, Philip Mortlake sat collapsed in his chair like a broken puppet, his eyes downcast. He never once looked up, but seemed a man turning upon a spit of guilt, for he was being rendered in a puddle of his own sweat.

The rest of the court began to throw lingering stares at the couple, for the intimation of the play's meaning—treachery, double-dealing and treason—was becoming scandalously obvious. Even Elizabeth turned in her throne and hurled a curious glance at her hosts. For her part, Lady Sybilla watched the action with a face set in an unnaturally frozen smile that never betrayed her unease or growing sense of doom. In truth, it was the smile of a woman climbing the steps of the scaffold.

Backstage the players, who knew they were about to act themselves off a cliff, confronted their poet with panic and dismay. For their five-act play had no fifth act.

"Will," Heminges said. "What shall we do? You said the action would resolve itself, and yet we are out of words!"

"Aye!" Burbage said. "Come, Will, how shall we unveil this poisonous plot?"

Shakespeare looked helpless. "I know not," he said. "I have been watching Philip closely. He is a man being stretched upon a rack. A few minutes more and he must surely break!"

"We have no more minutes!" Heminges whined.

Shakespeare's eyes alighted upon Anthony Munday, still dressed in Sir Richard's nobleman's garb. "Master Munday," he said, grabbing his rival poet by the shoulders. "We have need of your skill at extemporising."

"Oh, fie, no!" Burbage groaned and stepped away, shaking his head.

Munday's wide eyes betrayed his own fear. "But what shall I say?"

"You must play Sir Richard's ghost. Speak of your murder. Of foul deeds done in darkness. Of wicked plots."

Before Munday could protest, Shakespeare spun him around and propelled him on stage with a shove. Munday stumbled into the light, aware that all eyes were now fastened upon him.

"Ohhhhhh!" he began in a weak voice.

"Louder!" Heminges prompted from backstage.

"OHHHHHHHH!" Munday groaned. "He stumbled a few steps more. "I am naught but a ghost, my mortal corpse stripped of its life …"

"Good start!" Shakespeare whispered to his fellow players. "That's very good."

Munday continued his ghostly soliloquy, speaking of graves robbed, of bloody murder. But after a few minutes he ran out of words and began to repeat himself. "I am but a ghost. A ghostly ghost … for I have given up … the ghost …"

"A ghostly ghost?" Burbage rumbled. "What the hell does that mean?"

Meanwhile the crowd, who at first had hung upon Munday's every word, became restive and began to fidget and murmur.

Munday strutted stiffly around the stage, as if looking for his lost lines. "For I am a dead ghost, being dead and most ghost-like …"

The courtiers became a pit of hissing snakes.

"Hissed from the boards!" Burbage exclaimed. "I told you!"

"We are doomed," Will Kempe lamented.

As the hissing turned to scattered boos, Shakespeare snatched up the buckram robe and pulled it on, drawing the deep cowl over his head to hide his face in its shadows. He glided back onto the stage and stood before Munday. "Go, spirit," he said, pointing a finger to the wings. "Get you to purgatory where the sins of your life may be burned away."

Munday scuttled from the stage in a most un-ghostlike haste. Shakespeare stepped forward and addressed the crowd, keeping his cowled head down, his face masked in its shadowy depths. "The conclusion of our play is hid behind a mask. And so we adjourn for our own masque. After this measured interval our plot should be unwound and double-speaking treachery unbound."

From the balcony at the back of the hall, violins and cellos groaned into life. As the Queen rose from her throne, the court stumbled to its feet, turned and bowed as one. Elizabeth paused long enough to fix her hosts with an accusative stare, but said nothing and glided to the doors, trailed by Lord Essex and her ladies-in-waiting. Philip and Sybilla Mortlake bowed deeply, although Philip had to be supported, or his knees would have buckled.

"We have failed!" Burbage said to Shakespeare as the court filed out, heading for fitting rooms where they would don their masque costumes. "Our plot is done. Now we must quit the stage with the villains free to end their plot."

The Queen's Lifeguard, soldiers in armour, mounted the stage and shooed the players into the hallway outside. They would not be allowed back in the Great Hall until the masque was concluded.

"What shall we do, Will?" Burbage asked as they trooped out.

Shakespeare looked desperate, but then his eyes alighted upon a flamboyant figure directing courtiers to their respective tiring[1] rooms. As usual he was decked out in the most outrageous costume— a fantastical creation plumed with ostrich plumes in a rainbow of colours.

Valentyne Winstringham.

"Valentyne!" Shakespeare shouted above the hubbub, and waved frantically. Valentyne heard his name being called and craned to look over the heads of the courtiers milling around him. He smiled and yoo-hooed back, waving a handkerchief.

"Come," Shakespeare said. "Valentyne will have masque costumes we may borrow."

But then a door opened behind Valentyne and Richard Topcliffe and his two torturers stepped out and looked about, clearly furious. Shakespeare quickly turned his back on them and ducked down. "Go!" he said to Burbage and the others. "I shall join you, anon!" The Bard dodged around a corner, only to find the innkeeper and his tapster loitering at the end of the hallway. They saw Shakespeare and drew weapons from their belts—poison daggers. He ducked back around the corner but was spotted by Topcliffe and his men, who shouted and ran toward him.

The door to the backstage area was still open and he sprang inside

. . .

. . . colliding with a yeoman of the guard. "Get you hence, sirrah." The man barked, barring the way with his pike. "Only those of the court may stay."

Shakespeare bowed obsequiously. "Beg pardon. I am a player, come to retrieve my costume." One of the prop chests stood close by. Shakespeare flung it open, grabbed the asses' head that Will Kempe wore when he played Bottom in *A Midsummer Night's Dream* and jammed it on his head. As he stepped back into the hall, Shakespeare bumped into Richard Topcliffe, his henchmen close behind. Walt Gedding and John Thomas converged upon them at the same moment.

"Murderers!" Shakespeare shouted, pointing at the innkeeper and his tapster. "Assassins!" It must have presented an odd sight, a man with an asses' head pointing and denouncing treason, but Topcliffe and his men saw the blades the two men were carrying and recognised them as the same poison dagger that had been used to murder Scrope. The innkeeper and his tapster turned and ran, and Topcliffe and his men ran after them.

Meanwhile, the ladies and gents of the court had finished attiring themselves and the music for the masque had already begun playing when Shakespeare caught up with Valentyne and the rest of the Lord Chamberlain's Men. The players were got up in woodland costumes with Green Man vizards pushed back onto the tops of their heads.

"Burbage!" Shakespeare shouted.

"Will? You present yourself a bigger ass than usual!"

Shakespeare pulled off the asses' head. "We must get inside the hall and stop them. The assassins will strike when the Masque reaches its conclusion."

"But the Queen's Lifeguard stands at every door and will not let us pass."

Valentyne spoke up. "There is a hidden way inside. I have constructed a secret door so that Herne may enter upon the appropriate cue." Shakespeare followed Valentyne into a tiring room where a huge man sat at a table quaffing wine from a metal goblet.

"Toby," Valentyne said. "You shall not play Herne tonight. We need your costume!"

At the news, Toby banged his goblet down so hard that wine sloshed in the air. He stood up … and up … and up … until his head brushed the ceiling beams, for Toby was a giant of a man, seven foot tall and built like a bull. "Who says I shall not play!" he boomed. "Toby is to perform for the queen!"

"Nay, gentle friend," Valentyne said, patting the giant's arm. "You shall not."

Toby banged a fist on the table so that the goblet jumped and toppled. "I play before my queen or I'll break the bones of any man who says nay!"

Valentyne shared a worried look with Shakespeare.

"A draft horse would not say nay to this fellow," Shakespeare whispered.

Valentyne snatched out a purse and poured coins into the giant's hand. "I'll pay you double what we bargained on."

"I would play for naught for my queen!" Toby boomed and flung the coins at the wall.

"What would you have, then? Name your price."

Toby furrowed his huge brows for a moment, looking stupid as he scratched his ponderous jaw. "A strumpet," he rumbled.

Valentyne threw a despairing look at Shakespeare. "He wants a strumpet. This is not Eastcheap, wherever shall we get a strumpet?"

Shakespeare frowned and thought a moment. "Have you a spare frock and wig," he asked.

"Aye, Valentyne said."

The player stepped to the door and opened it. The Lord Chamberlain's Men waited outside, dressed in Green Man costumes. "Sam Gilbourne," Shakespeare called. The smallest Green Man stepped forward and lifted his mask. It was Sam.

"I have a role for you of great import."

"A role?" Sam squeaked, smiling. "Of great import?"

"Aye," Shakespeare said. He crooked a finger. "But first we must find you a wig and a frock."

Minutes later Shakespeare followed Valentyne down the hallway. He was wearing the giant's Herne costume, an enormous bearskin cloak that swamped him and dragged on the floor so that he stumbled on its hem. A rack of deer antlers rose from a crown of mistletoe on his head. His face was painted to look like the bark of a tree. In his left hand he carried a heavy lantern. On his right arm a live horned owl dug its claws into his gauntleted fist. "Tis murderous heavy," he complained. "I can scarce stand, let alone walk!"

Valentyne led him to a side door to the great hall. "Stand ready. Your entrance will be commanded by the blast of a hunting horn."

CHAPTER 65: DARK DOINGS IN THE CELLAR

I've already told you this bit, how I shamble through the Inn, the murder following me down to the cellar, and then me getting launched when they barge the cellar door open. I do a nice face-plant on the cold stone flags and lose the gun.

Bloody typical of my luck.

I roll over and sit up, the palms of both hands stinging from the fall. It's dark in the cellar, but there's enough filtered light to show me that *Double Falshood* surrounds me in a loose scattering of pages. I look up at the doorway. The silhouette framed there is curvy and svelte. My murderer is a woman.

"Where's the manuscript," she asks.

The voice is Gillian's, who else?

"It's yours," I say gathering up the nearest sheets and smearing even more blood on them. "Just let me live."

"What are you talking about?"

"An exchange. Toss your gun down and I'll give you the manuscript."

"Gun? I don't have a gun!"

This throws me. I am at a loss for words. I really expected her to have a gun.

"Hold on," she says, "let me turn the light on." Her hand gropes the wall until she finds the wall switch and flips it. The overhead fluorescents stutter into life and the cellar twitches beneath its pulsing light. "Ohmigod!" she says, when she sees me on the floor, bloody pages scrunched in my arms. "You've been shot!"

"Yes," I say in a sort of James Bond-cool I don't feel. "Thought I'd save you the trouble."

"What are you talking about?"

"I got your message." I do the voice: *"I'm going to kill you*! I heard you smash the window to get in. That's when the gun went off."

"Smash the window? I have no idea what you're talking about. I came in through the front door. It wasn't locked."

"It wasn't?" Oh yeah. I was so busy talking to the tree service I forgot to lock up.

"We have to get you to the hospi—"

As she goes to step forward, her words are cut off by a dark figure that jumps her from behind, throwing one hand around her throat. She struggles, flailing and her arm knocks the wall switch off, plunging us into darkness. Gillian shrieks as she is hurled forward into the cellar. She lands sprawling close to me.

Now a male silhouette chokes the cellar doorway.

"I warned you," the voice snarls. It takes a moment until I realise he's talking to me. "A tiger's heart wrapp'd in a woman's hide. She's a ball-breaking bitch."

It's Broody Brendan! Only I'm not sure whether this is a domestic dispute, or if he's here for the play. I don't have time to find out, either. A large shape looms behind him, blocking the light. A thick arm raises a tire iron and brings it down on the back of Brendan's head. WHUNK! He crumples untidily to the floor.

A tall and hairy Sasquatch shape steps over him. The overhead lights shiver on, painting Hedgehog frozen with his hand on the light switch. His eyes quickly take everything in: Brendan. Me. Gill. The manuscript in my hands. And the bloodstain widening across my chest.

"Bugger me!" he exclaims. "What happened to you?"

"That bloody gun you sold me, that's what!"

His laughter erases any hope he's to rescue us. "Dear oh, dear. I did warn you about that trigger ... very touchy."

A figure appears in the doorway behind him. Ohmigod, it's Sidney. He must have come back for something. I need to distract Hedgehog, keep him talking. I make eye contact with Sidney and nod to let him know that Hedgehog is standing next to the door. But as usual, Sidney is completely oblivious and blunders into the cellar as if we were having a birthday party.

"Hello, Hedgehog," Sidney says.

Hedgehog spins around, taken by surprise, the tire iron raised.

Sidney," I yell. "Don't just stand there. Clock him. He's here to steal the manuscript!"

I expect Sidney to spring and wrestle him to the floor, but the two just smile at one another. Instead Sidney reaches into the pocket of his corduroy jacket. Pulls out a pipe and slides it in his gob. On the floor, Broody Brendon moans and rolls over. He tries to sit up but passes out again. The back of his head hits the stone flags with a nauseating thud.

"Whash happened to him?" Sidney asks, nodding

"Vauxhall Astra jack handle," Hedgehog says, flourishing the shiny chrome club.

Sidney tisk-tisks. He nods at me. "You shoot him?"

Hedgehog shakes his werewolf head. "Nah. Silly bugger shot himself."

"Accident prone bunch!" Sidney chuckles, shoulders heaving as he wheezes laughter like a cartoon dog.

"I wouldn't laugh if I were you," I say, "I tripped the silent alarm. The Rozzers will be here any minute."

"Not likely," Hedgehog sneers. "I cut the phone lines, didn't I? How do you think the alarm sends out a signal, by magic?"

He chortles and Sidney joins in, like a pair of naughty schoolboys gadding about.

A hand squeezes my leg. It's Gillian. She nods to the open mouth of the tunnel. It's just inches away, but I shake my head. I'm in no condition. I'd never make it. Then I spot the dropped Beretta, lying close to Gillian's foot.

"The gun," I mumble to her. "By your foot."

"What?" she says and looks around.

It alerts Hedgehog, who wanders over and spots the pistol.

"Thanks, darlin'," he says. "Don't want any more accidents, now do we?"

Hedgehog flashes me a golden grin. "Told you ya shoulda bought the revolver. Much safer."

But as he scoops the Beretta up from the stone flags there a sharp *Crack!*—hardly louder than an electric typewriter—that makes Hedgehog flinch. He straightens up, but when he turns around, there's a trickle of blood running from a hole in his forehead.

"Bugger me!" he says. His one step forward turns into a wobbly-legged run and he crashes into Sidney's arms, staggering the pair of them backwards.

"Now!" Gillian shouts. She throws herself into the open tunnel shaft, dragging me with her. I fall backwards, cracking my head on every ladder rung—ouch-ouch-ouch-ouch-ouch—

until I lie sprawled at the bottom of the shaft.

"Come on," she says.

"Leave me," I whimper, lying there in a big puddle of self-pity. "I'm already dead."

"It's not a fatal wound," she insists,

"How the hell do *you* know?"

"Because if it was you'd be dead already."

I'm tempted to argue. I'm pretty sure that lying down is standard etiquette when you've just been shot. I just want to lie down and die peacefully like people do in films. After all, you never see people get shot and then jump up and run a four-minute mile. But Gill drags me to my feet and we lurch off down the tunnel. I hear a jangle of car keys close by and suddenly an eye-wateringly bright cone of light flares, illuminating the way ahead. She's got one of those little squeeze lights on her BMW key fob.

She must have been a girl scout.

"We've got to get to Wexcombe Hall," she says. "The place is wired with every kind of alarm system." She plays the beam across me, blindingly. "You still have the manuscript?"

The rolled scroll of papers is clenched in my right hand, but it hurts like hell when I raise my arm.

"Don't drop it." she says, "Oh . . . and try not to bleed on it."

Even now Gill is cold and calculating and I realise that if I didn't have the manuscript I'd probably be lying on the cellar floor next to Broody Brendan. We're both soon puffing and gasping. It's a good thing Gillian is jogged to perfection, because she's half-carrying/half-dragging my fat arse.

"I'm going to kill you!" the metallic robot voice sizzles in our ears. Sidney is in the tunnel and he's following close behind. His electro-taunt is followed by a deafening BOOM! I can almost feel the bullet whiz past, striking sparks as it skips off the stone wall.

"Gill!" I gasp. "Stop. He wants the play. I'll just drop it here."

"Don't you bloody dare!" she says and drags me faster.

"BOOM!" Another cacophonous blast leaves us with a tinny ringing sound in our ears.

She lets her light go out. Instead we navigate with one hand dragging along the wall. It's slower, but there's nothing for Sidney to shoot at. But after a few minutes my dizziness, coupled with the darkness-induced vertigo, really starts to kick in. I fall down once and then again. Each time Gill drags me back to my feet, but we can both hear Sidney's lumbering footsteps behind, closing in. As if being shot at wasn't bad enough, the noise, the darkness and the pursuit ratchets our terror to Hitchcockian levels.

Another fifty paces and Gill flashes the tiny torch for a brief moment, long enough to see the stairs up ahead. We've reached Wexcombe House. Sidney must see it, too, because he starts up with the voice changer like a psychotic parrot: "I'm going to kill you! I'm going to kill you! I'm going to kill you! I'm going to kill you!"

Then BOOM BOOM BOOM. He fires three shots in rapid succession. The din hurts like having a pointed stick rammed in each ear.

My ears haven't rung this much since I went to a Clash concert when I was nineteen.

Gill turns the light back on, just as we reach the stone stairs. Every step up the tall stone stairs is like a dagger plunging in my chest. BOOM! Sidney fires again and this time the bullet hits within inches, peppering my face with sharp-edged chips of stone. We labour to the top of the steps, Gill nearly carrying me at this point. "He must only have one shot left," I say. But the secret passage is slower going than the tunnel, as it is filled with rubble and debris. "We need to get to the library," she pants.

"I'm going to killllllll yoooooooooooooooooooooooo!" Sidney calls after us, really bloody close now and starting to sound like manic-depressive Dalek.

We collide with the wall as the passage turns left. Gill flips the light on long enough to locate a door catch and handle. I hear Sidney's size elevens pound around the corner as the latch snicks. The door is stiff, as it probably hasn't been opened in four hundred years, and makes a horrible grating squeal, but only opens part-way, too tight to squeeze through.

"Ha! Ha! Too late!" Sidney shouts as he sees us.

We both heave at the door and it scrunches open a reluctant inch. Gill squeezes through and then I do, wheezing, sweating, and really wishing I'd lost that weight. We crash through the library, throw open the door and hurl ourselves into the hallway. We must have tripped a dozen hidden sensors by now. I'm expecting sirens, flashing lights, klaxons, clanging bells.

Nothing.

The hallway is dim and silent.

"I thought you said there were alarms?"

"Probably silent," she says, hurrying me along. "I'm sure the police are on their way."

"I bloody hope so."

We limp to an outside door, but it's locked. We start to double back when Sidney appears in the hallway. "This way!" Gill shouts and drags me through an open door. But too late, he's seen us.

We're in the Great Hall, a huge, echoing space. The room is dimly lit by auxiliary safety lighting, enough faint illumination to make out rows of folding chairs and the huge Shakespeare banners hanging on either side of the stage. The Bard smiles down at us from the shadows, evidently enjoying a bit of 21st Century drama.

Doors rattle and clash as Sidney tries to open one of the sets of doors into the hall but they're locked. He tries the next set. They're locked too. Still, it's only a matter of time before he finds the same unlocked doors we came in through.

I grab Gill's arm and push *Double Falshood* into her hands. "Here," I say. "Take it."

"But—"

"Shush," I say. "For once do as I say."

She complies.

"Now step away."

I settle myself gingerly on the floor. It hurts to get down. I reach a hand inside my cardigan. The left side of my chest is warm and sticky with blood. I run my fingers through it then paint the corners of my mouth with its fresh redness. Then I flop and let my head sag to one side, eyes wide and glassy. The only acting I ever did was to play the corpse in a school Agatha Christie play. I think it was *The Mousetrap*. I can't remember. I volunteered not for my love of drama but for my love of skiving out of two hours of lessons. And I didn't even have to memorise a single line. All I had to do was lie still and look dead. We'll see how convincing I am in a moment. I reach one hand into my cardigan pocket and finger the pommel of the small dagger.

Sidney steps into the Great Hall. "I'm here, kiddies! Time to die!" he says in a sizzling electronic drone, and tosses the Voice Morpher 2000 aside." That . . . that . . . that was quite a chase," he says, panting. (The lazy bastard is more out of breath than me, and I've been shot!) "But I'm afraid it was all for nothing." He levels the gun at me for a moment, but I seem to be dead or close to it, so he points the business end at Gill. It doesn't even look like Sidney's face, the mask of slothful dimness has peeled away, revealing an expression of crafty alertness I didn't know his face muscles were capable of moulding.

"The manuscript, if you please," he says to Gill, holding out a hand. She just laughs at him.

"What can you possibly find funny about the situation you're in?"

"I just realised something," Gillian says. "I know who you are."

Surprise flashes across his face. "I very much doubt that—"

"A certain used bookstore in London? Manuscripts of a dodgy and questionable origin?"

He feigns a sceptical look, but then his poker face cracks and falls apart. "That was fifteen years ago. You have a good memory."

"Where have you been since then?"

"Here and there. A few years in prison ..."

"You must've picked up the same trail that I found; the one that lead me here."

"Yes, but neither of us is really that clever. I've been searching every inch of this inn for six months. He waves the gun at me. "It took a bumbling idiot falling through an old trap door to make the literary find of the century."

"Sometimes even bumbling idiots get lucky."

If I wasn't playing dead I would take exception to that description, but I am, so I don't.

"Pity you won't be so lucky." He raises his gun, pointing straight at her, ready to shoot. "I know the police are on the way, so please, don't try to play for time. Yes, as you've no doubt deduced, I have only one bullet left. But that is more than enough to make you very dead."

I have the dagger in my grip, but I can only draw my hand from my cardy pocket with time-lapse slowness, or he'll catch the movement. Plus, he's too far away. Sidney helps me out by taking two steps forward. He drops his gaze from Gill and kicks me in the face with the toe of his scuffed loafer to check I'm really dead. It hurts like hell and it's all I can do to keep my eyes from flickering. I let my head loll, trying to look like the deadest dead man ever to expire and die. Then a fly lands on my face. My skin crawls. Inside my clothes I'm sweating, screaming, crying, but I try to ignore as it crawls across my face, and even across my wide-open eye. My acting is Oscar-worthy.

Sidney's gaze returns to Gill who is defiant: "I'm not giving you the manuscript. You'll probably going to shoot me anyway."

He smiles. I had no idea Sidney's face could assume any expression approximating cunning but he's just managed it. Gotta hand it to the big bastard. If anyone's the actor, it's him. "You're quite right, of course, I am going to shoot you. But now you need to be a good girl and hand me the manuscript."

"Well, then," Gill breathes. "I guess there's nothing else to do."

I see him tense, anticipating her move. But all she does is throw the manuscript in the air. Pages flutter down, settling in cloud all around us. One lands on me. The distraction gives me just enough time to draw the dagger from my pocket and hold it ready, my fist clenched tight around it.

"Was that supposed to startle me? Sidney asks calmly. "Make me waste my last bullet?" He tut-tuts. "Childish and pointless." He gestures with the gun. "Now pick up the pages like a good girl ... and then I'll shoot you."

Gill shouts and runs for the doors. Sidney lifts the gun and aims at her fleeing back, his finger tightening on the trigger. I roll forward, shouting with pain and drive the dagger into his kneecap with everything I've got. Sidney howls in agony. The gun bangs and kicks in his hand.

When the smoke clears, he is lying on his back, screaming in agony, the dagger impaled to the hilt in his knee.

Gill suddenly appears, cautiously creeping closer. She reaches down a hand and pulls me to my feet.

"You fat little bastard!" Sidney growls.

"That's no way to refer to a lady," I say.

"I meant you!" he yells, and then goes back to moaning in agony.

For once I've surprised even the astute Gill. "Where did you get that from?" she asks.

"It's the dagger you found in the tunnel."

"Ohmigod," Gill says, putting her hands to her face. "That was a poison dagger! The handle is filled with a deadly neurotoxin!"

Sidney starts to blubber. His sweaty face purples. "Help me!" he shouts. "Call for an ambulance! Do something! " He sucks in a shuddering breath and adds in a whiny voice: "Pleeeeeeeze …"

He is still shouting as Gill limps me down the hall to the nearest emergency exit, which opens to our push, setting off a clanging fire alarm. We step from Wexcombe House into pulsing blue lights and the crackle of police radios.

It's a shame to die at this point. To come so close only to slip away. But I can hold on no longer, and fade away, dissolving a molecule at a time into the seething blue mist. The warmth of Gill's body pressed against my side is my last earthly memory.

CHAPTER 66: DANCE THE MADRIGAL

I nside the Great hall, a wood nymph with glittering wings scampered up to one of the giant oak trees and rapped upon it three times.

"Awaken, mighty Herne!" the nymph trilled in a silvery voice.

A hunting horn trumped.

Nothing happened.

The wood nymph looked a little unsure, and rapped again, harder.

"AWAKEN, MIGHTY HERNE!" the nymph bellowed. The hunting horn blared a mighty trump. A hidden door in the trunk sprung open, knocking the wood nymph backward as Shakespeare, clad in the Herne costume, stumbled out, blinking at the light.

In the interlude, the hall had been transformed once again. Hunting horns and bows and quivers of arrows hung from the trunks of the oak trees. The benches and chairs had been cleared, and now courtiers in costume danced a madrigal. Shakespeare gaped. Recog nising who was who would be nigh impossible. The men were bedecked in dazzling costumes that featured feather plumes, and sparkling gemstones, their faces hidden behind half-masks. The women were completely unrecognisable. Each floated across the floor in huge and spectacular dresses with enormous winged collars, their faces hidden behind silver hart masks topped with antlers. In all, nearly a thousand costumed figures moved about the hall in a slow, counter clockwise flow to the stately beat of a madrigal, amid the clapping of hands and the excited shouts of "Volpe" as gentleman hoisted their partners onto their hips.

Shakespeare took a step but found that the hidden door had swung shut behind, trapping the corner of his shaggy robe. He snatched it loose, tearing the fabric, and lumbered into the hall. A male performer in the rustic dress of a gamekeeper approached, singing in a high falsetto—a song imploring Herne to descend into the wood and bless the hunt.

Shakespeare gathered up the robe and stumbled after, the owl fluttering wildly on his arm. His eyes scanned the couples whirling past, but there was no way of telling friend from foe. He knew that Burbage and the Lord Chamberlain's Men should be about the hall, but they were lost in the masses. And then he noticed an empty throne on a dais raised above the dancers. The queen loved to dance and would be among the throngs, but the ageing monarch tired easily and would often watch the dances as she rested. Once she ascended the throne, Shakespeare could identify which costume she wore, but then so could the assassins and the murder was set to take place at the end of the Masque.

A pair of youths dressed as faeries skipped before him. The dancers stopped and cleared a path to where a hunting horn sat atop a plinth. It was clear they were waiting for him to blow it.

The high tenor sang, "Blow ye horn o Herne and bless our hunt."

Shakespeare put the horn to his lips and blew, but produced only a rude, wet blaaaaaaaattttt! The dancing courtiers guffawed. The tenor looked horror-struck. The music stopped, and then lurched forward again. Shakespeare sucked in a breath, pursed his lips and blew until his cheeks cracked. This time the horn blared a loud trump. The courtiers applauded and the dance recommenced. Shakespeare set down the horn and let himself be led by the huntsman tenor and the faeries. A side door into the hall opened and Valentyne slipped in. He gestured wildly to Shakespeare to keep moving. Apparently Herne was to circumnavigate the great hall while the dance proceeded.

Shakespeare shambled forward, his arms weighted down by the heavy lantern and the restless owl. And then, in an opening in the dancers, his eye was caught by the flash of gold—a lady in fabulous gown embroidered with golden thread coruscating with gems and pearls. Like the other dancers, a hind mask hid her face; but where all others wore silver masks, this mask alone was of shining gold.

The queen. He knew it instinctively. The golden mask would be reserved for her majesty. A lord and lady danced nearby. The lady was dressed in a silver gown with a silver hind mask, but a large gold crucifix swung from her neck—Sybilla, and within striking distance of the queen! Her partner wore a costume festooned with peacock feathers. While his upper face was hidden, the haughty pout beneath the half-mask left no doubt that it was Philip Mortlake. The Stratford poet needed to reach the queen and warn her. He let himself be led on by the faeries, capering clumsily to the music. As he passed one of the oaks he spied a bow and a quiver of arrows hanging from the trunk. He tried to linger close to it, but the dancers surged forward, blocking his way.

"Will!" He heard someone shout his name above the music. He scanned the crowd until he saw a large man dressed like a hedgerow. No, it was Richard Burbage in his green man disguise. Burbage pointed to the back of the hall, where the rest of the green men, players from the Lord Chamberlain's Men, lurked. Shakespeare raised the arm laden with the owl and tried to point where he had last seen the queen. Burbage, a head above the rest of the crowd, shook his masked head. Shakespeare pressed closer and suddenly two masked men appeared from the crowd, one tall, one unnaturally short. The men roughly grabbed the faeries and spun them away. They drew poison daggers from their sheaths, and kept them low, shielding them from sight of the courtiers dancing by.

"Base, interfering fool!" the dwarfish one spat and lunged at Shakespeare. With no other weapon, the player flung his arm forward, launching the owl, which ravaged Hyde's face, the great claws shredding the mask, the razor beak pecking and tearing at his skin. Flailing his arms and screaming, Hyde staggered back into the melee in a flurry of wings. Thinking it part of the spectacle, courtiers applauded. Finch hesitated a moment. Shakespeare swung the lantern at him. Finch dodged backwards, flashed his teeth in an angry snarl and looked ready to attack again, but then a thick arm flung around his neck, dragged him backward through the crowd and behind an oak tree. Oofs and grunts ensued and then Richard Burbage, clad in a Green Man costume, stepped from behind the tree. He cut an awkward caper and pranced over to join his friend.

"Will," Burbage muttered beneath his breath. "The Chamberlain's Men are scattered about the hall. Have you seen the queen?"

"I have," Shakespeare said. "She wears the mask of a golden hind. But beware—Sybilla is close by. You will know her by the great cross around her neck." For a moment, Rafe Foxe's words echoed in his mind: *Fools believe their eyes.* "It is a sham," he added. "The crucifix conceals a poison dagger. She means to kill the queen at masque's end!"

As he spoke, the dancer in the golden hind mask broke from her partner, plodded her weary feet up the steps of the raised dais and sank heavily onto the throne. The man she had been dancing with, undoubtedly Essex, found a new partner and danced away. Now the queen was completely isolated.

The assassins had their chance.

A dancer in a silver mask broke from her partner and began to mount the steps toward Elizabeth. Shakespeare saw the heavy gold cross swinging from her neck. He began to push through the swirl of dancers, earning himself curses and a cuff to the back of the head. A space opened in the crowd and he stumbled forward, colliding with a dancer.

"Base peasant!"

He looked up into the face of a man dressed like a giant peacock. Even beneath the layers of fancy dress, each man recognised the other at the same instant.

"You! Philip spat. "The fool player!" He drew a dagger from his cloak and flung himself at Shakespeare, stabbing wildly.

Shakespeare yelled with fear, reeling backward through the press of dancers as Philip stabbed again and again. Knowing that even a scratch could prove fatal, he warded off the thrusts, taking them on his arms. Thickly padded by the enormous bearskin, the point of the dagger could not penetrate. The courtiers applauded once more, thinking it was part of the pageant, a symbolic action. The acid poison sizzled and white smoke tendriled up from the suit. Philip backed Shakespeare into one of the oaks and hissed beneath the mask. "Interfering fool, here is your poison death."

But at that moment, Burbage stepped forward and clubbed Philip over the head with the large hunting horn, knocking him senseless to the floor.

"The queen!" Shakespeare said, pointing.

Sybilla had mounted the dais and stood over the sitting queen. She drew the golden dagger from its sheath in the crucifix and raised it high overhead. Shakespeare noticed a bow and arrow hanging from the nearby oak and snatched it down. He knocked the arrow to the string, drew back the bow, and sited along the shaft. Under his tremoring hands, the arrow dithered, its point circling upon Sybilla's back. By now even the courtiers had discerned that something was amiss. The madrigal stumbled and fell apart, instruments squealing into silence. All eyes in the great hall fixed upon the terrible spectacle.

"Will, loose your arrow!" Burbage urged.

"Should I miss . . ." Shakespeare muttered through gritted teeth. ". . . I will kill the queen!"

"You must shoot!"

"Thus dies a tyrant!" Sybilla shouted raising the crucifix dagger high. "And England returns to the true Catholic religion."

The bow shook in Shakespeare's hands. He willed himself to loose the arrow, but his trembling fingers would not obey. He closed his eyes and brought the most precious thing he knew to mind: the image of young Hamnet's smiling face. At the image, he breathed out, relaxed his grip, and the bowstring twanged through his fingertips.

The arrow whistled low over the heads of countless nobles, slicing through the feathers of a courtier's headdress ...

... and struck Sybilla in the shoulder blade.

She shrieked in shock and pain. The gold dagger slipped from her hand. She staggered a moment, doubled over, and fell, rolling down the steps of the dais.

Shakespeare and Burbage pushed toward the throne even as panicked courtiers surged back, opening a space around the fallen form. One of the dancing couples stepped forward. The gentleman undid the ribbons holding the lady's mask and the woman removed her silver hind mask.

It was the queen, Elizabeth.

The crowd gasped and fell to its knees. The queen stepped forward and stood looking down on the wounded Sybilla with contempt. "So, wicked girl, you thought to assassinate a queen?" She made a gesture and the doors of the Great Hall crashed open. Soldiers bearing halberds poured in and encircled the queen in a ring of iron. Richard Topcliffe entered, followed by his feral men, who each had an arm around the throat of John Thomas and Walt Gedding. Soon the remaining conspirators: Philip Mortlake, John Finch, and the dwarfish Thomas Hyde, his clawed face torn and bloodied, were dragged forward, railing and cursing, and forced to kneel before the queen.

When Elizabeth spoke, her voice shook with indignant thunder. "This most foul conspiracy has been revealed by the grace of God. You all, like any who seek to shed a prince's blood, shall die a traitor's death. One that will draw pity."

But Sybilla's venom was far from spent. As the queen spoke, she stirred from where she lay, her fingers stretching to fumble up the dropped dagger. She staggered to her feet with a cry, threatening with the blade any that dared approach. The crowd gasped and Elizabeth took a cautious step backward.

Sybilla words dripped with venom. "I would rather die by my own hand than live a day, an hour, a second, as your prisoner!" She threw a wild look around at the courtiers, flourishing the blade. "Thus I end my own life, as I have lived it … slave to no man … no woman … no false queen … no false God!"

With that she drove the dagger into her own stomach and crumpled around it.

Because the crucifix dagger held only a small amount of poison, Sybilla's death was slow and horrible to watch. Her eyes widened as the poison took effect. The beautiful face turned hideous, swept by tremors and convulsions. She fell to choking as if she could not draw breath. At last, her body twitched, her eyes rolled back and a final, saw tooth breath rasped from her lips.

The queen watched Sybilla's death rattle without pity. When it was finally done, she looked up at the figure seated on her throne and said, "Nobly done, pygmy. Though, I hope I dance more prettily than you."

With that, the figure removed the golden hind mask. Beneath it, clad, improbably, in one of the queen's most splendid gowns, was her spaniel-eyed Secretary of State, Sir Robert Cecil.

The queen turned her smile upon the figure drowning in his oversized Herne costume. "And you, master Herne, You have saved my best servant with your skills as archer. Remove your mask and show your queen whom she must reward."

Shakespeare nudged Burbage. Both men drew off their masks.

"Ah, Master Shakespeare and Master Burbage," Elizabeth said. "I see now how your play ends. You spoke true. Tis neither comedy nor tragedy."

She looked around at her courtiers. "The queen thinks that is enough entertainment for one night." She nodded and Essex came forward to take her hand. The soldiers of the queen's Life Guard opened an avenue in the crowd of courtiers and she strolled away on the arm of her young dandy. But before she left the hall she paused and turned to impart one last thought.

"Oh, and Master Shakespeare. Come see me tomorrow and I'll give you payment for your most entertaining play."

∾

Despite the trill of the harpsichord, William Shakespeare's stomach clenched with something worse than stage fright. The stony-faced soldiers guarding the doors jerked their cruel-bladed halberds aside. The doors parted and he was issued inside. His eyes swept the room. The short, crooked figure of Lord Cecil nodded in recognition and bade him enter further with a beckoning gesture.

Elizabeth was seated at the harpsichord, playing a madrigal, lit, like the vision of a saint, in a shaft of light slanting in through the window that made the gems and pearls sewn into her frock flash and scintillate. A beautiful young woman sat on a cushion close by, her combed and coiffed blonde hair shining silky in the light. Ladies-in-waited hovered discretely at the corners of the room, needles sparkling as they busied at their sewing. The final notes of the madrigal thrilled the air and subsided. After a moment's silence, Lord Cecil and the ladies-in-waiting applauded politely.

The queen, smiling with delight at her own skill, looked up and noticed the Stratford player for the first time. "Master Shakespeare, do you like my playing?"

Shakespeare threw her a low bow with a flourish. "Before I entered the room, majesty, I thought me an angel strummed a celestial harp."

The queen laughed with delight, "Sweet flattery as only a poet could speak." She stood and placed a motherly hand on the shoulder of the young woman.

Shakespeare had tried not to stare when first he entered the room, but now his gaze fell full upon the beauty and amazement flooded across his face. The young woman looked up for the first time and met Shakespeare's gaze. She was dressed in a rich green gown, her hair coiffed and pinned up with jewelled brooches. The doe-like eyes, a cerulean shade of blue, filled with recognition for a moment, but then the spark of intellect fizzled and her gaze fell back to the child's doll clutched in her hands.

"Lady Verity's mind still wanders in a wilderness," the queen said.

"But she is under our royal protection now and we shall see she is kept safe in her own house."

Emotions swept Shakespeare's face. He spoke in a voice crushed by sadness. "Majesty ... I, I ... have no words."

"There are times Master Shakespeare, when words—even your words—will fail you." The queen noticed that his gaze had fallen upon the sheath of papers sitting atop the harpsichord. She picked them up.

"In happier matters, I have read your play, sir. Though I must confess you have a rather mean and cramped hand ..."

The player cleared his throat. He struggled to find an apt response, but finally shrugged resignedly. "Aye madam."

She fingered the pages. "This play has no ending."

"Fortune prevented me from finishing it."

The queen gave the pages a cursory riffle. "I think it should end happily."

"'Tis not a comedy, majesty."

"True enough, it begins with tragedy, but we know it ends well."

"For some."

"When you have lived as long as I have, sir, you will find that every story ends happily for some and for others ..." her eyes strayed to the Lady Verity, who was listlessly stroking her doll's hair. "... less happily." The queen flipped the ink-blotted pages with her thumb. "You had a mind to publish this?"

"It is my how I have my living Majesty."

"And how much are you normally paid for such works?"

Shakespeare thought of a figure and then doubled it. "A hundred pounds."

Elizabeth arched a sceptical eyebrow, suppressing a smile. ""A goodly sum." She cleared her throat. "Very well," she said. "I wish to buy it."

"But madam, I had hoped to perform the play and thereby reap the benefit—"

"This play has had one performance," the Queen interrupted, her voice hardening. "It shall have no other." She set the play aside and returned to the Lady Verity, stroking a gentle hand on her head.

"Though the names be altered, and the setting changed, its subject touches too closely upon treason and the assassination of a prince. Thus it comes dangerous close to sedition. I believe a fellow playwright of yours found himself in Marshalsea Prison for writing such a seditious play." The ageing monarch turned and looked him full in the face. "I trust you have no desire to join him?"

Shakespeare's stomach tightened. For all he knew Ben Jonson still languished in jail. He shook his head.

"But to insure against your loss of labour I shall purchase the play." She threw a look at Robert Cecil. "Pay Master Shakespeare a hundred pounds, pygmy."

Irritation flashed across Cecil's face at being addressed in public that way, but he bit his lip and stepped to a walnut table where he opened a fine wooden money box and counted out a hundred pounds. The heavy crowns made a happy chink as they spilled from Cecil's hand into a leather purse. He nodded to Shakespeare and slapped the purse in his hand. The Secretary's sour expression betrayed his happiness at giving away the crown's money.

The Queen settled upon her seat at the harpsichord and asked, "Where are the Lord Chamberlain's Men bound for now?"

"To Marlborough, majesty. To play some of the large houses there."

"I recommend you return to London post-haste. When you reach the city you will find the play houses are all reopened." She returned her attention to the sheet music, placed her beringed fingers on the keys and began to play the madrigal again.

Shakespeare bowed deeply and backed to the door. His royal audience was over.

When Anthony Munday rode up to the White Hart Inn, the soldiers were busy fastening chains and manacles to the remaining plotters: Philip Mortlake, Father John Finch, Father Thomas Hyde, Walt Gedding, and John Thomas. Sybilla Mortlake was close by, nailed into a cheap deal coffin. She would be travelling to

London in the same cart as her co-conspirators, where her pretty face would look down from its spike atop London Bridge. Here, her beauty would soon fade into corruption, pecked at by greedy crows.

Maud, the innkeeper's zaftig wife, and Conny, his daughter, watched in tears. Maud wailed loudly for the fate of her husband. The conspirators shuffled forward one at a time as a blacksmith heated a new link to cherry red in a small brazier, and then pounded it closed over the next link, lengthening the chain binding them together.

Philip Mortlake, who now lacked the backbone he had previously borrowed from his sister Sybilla, sprawled on the dusty ground, unable to stand. All the conspirators were clothed in the mantle of despair worn by condemned men. Father Thomas Hyde alone seemed to exult in his doomed status. He was wearing a red shirt—the colour of Catholic martyrs—and shouted defiance when he saw Munday ride up.

"The time is coming, Master Double-Speak, when you shall kneel before God and all your masks and falsehoods will be purged away in flame. There you may scream for the rest of eternity, chained upon a lake of fire! The skin will be flayed from your bones each night and regenerated the next day so that your agonies shall never—"

"Silence, fool!" Father John Finch bellowed in Hyde's face. "Save your brave speeches for the scaffold!" The words seemed to cow Finch, who fell silent, and contented himself with hurling poisonous looks.

Munday paused before the burning brazier. He removed a sheaf of papers tucked in his doublet.

"The play?"

He looked up. Father Finch was watching him closely.

"Aye," he said nodding. "The queen told me it must never see the light of day, but …" he paused, the heat of the brazier hot on his cheeks. "… there has been too much burning of late." He slipped the play back inside his doublet and carried on inside.

In the cellar his Sergeant at Arms, Fen Crugg, was directing several stone masons hired to seal up the trap door to the secret passage.

"How goes it, Fen?" Munday asked.

"The door that opened into the attic cupboard has been filled in with wattle and daub and painted so that no trace remains. These fellows are drilling a hole through the slab so we may pin the massy stone in place with an iron rod."

The shrill squeal of a brace and bit drilling through stone set everyone's teeth on edge. Munday stepped to the edge of the tunnel and stared down as into a well pooled with liquid night. "Is anyone down there?" he asked.

"Nay, tis empty of men."

Munday nodded sagely. "Hold, you fellows," he said to the masons. "Stand back a moment, I would take one last look to be sure there are no infernal devices left behind."

The stonemasons stopped work and stepped aside. Anthony Munday eased a leg into the hole, searching blindly with his foot for the first rung and then climbed down. Seconds later he stood several yards inside the tunnel.

A cold, dry breeze blew in his face. It originated at the distant Wexcombe House, drawn down the tunnel like a chimney. In the tunnel, a solitary candle still burned in its niche, quivering on the edge of extinguishment.

This play must never see the light of day. Those were the words the Queen spoke to him as she handed him the manuscript of *Double Falshood*. Not *destroy this,* or *burn this,* or *tear this to tatters.*

This play must never see the light of day.

Munday pulled the sheaf of papers from his doublet. In the shifting light he could barely make out the jittery lines of Shakespeare's handwriting. He set the play on the shelf of the niche, a safe distance from the candle flame. Once the candle burned out, the play would likely never again see the light of day. Or maybe it would, in some unfathomable future, when someone broke into this tunnel and found it. But by then, nothing may remain of Shakespeare's great words than a fistful of dust.

"Master Munday!" It was Fen Crugg's voice calling from above.

"Aye?"

"Are you well, sir?"

"Aye," Munday shouted back. "Nothing remains behind. I am coming back."

But instead, Anthony Munday reached into his doublet, feeling for a leather scabbard fitted tight to his body. His fingers closed upon a leather pommel and he carefully drew the weapon he kept concealed there.

A poison dagger.

It was one of a set of twelve that had been made in Spain a year ago and distributed to those Catholic martyrs who had sworn to assassinate Elizabeth, the heretic bitch who sat on the throne of England.

Although Munday was a secret Catholic, he was foremost a pragmatist and his was a double loyalty shown equally to both sides. Had this assassination plot proved successful, he would have murdered Oswyn Scrope with the poison dagger he carried. As the plot had failed, he would retain his post as pursuivant, hunting down and executing Catholics who plotted treason against his queen. Munday knew that the only way to win the game was to play both sides against the other.

He set the poison dagger atop the sheaf of papers, so that its weight held the papers down. Then he licked his fingers and pinched out the flame.

Unrestrained, four hundred years of darkness—yet to come—tumbled in upon him.

~

The Lord Chamberlain's Men traipsed the Great West Road behind a rickety horse cart laden with props and costumes, heading east this time, toward London. Sam Guilbourne drove as before, but could scarce keep his eyes on the road, for the wild-eyed glances he threw about, expecting ghosts and horrible demons to leap out from the oaks that towered around them.

"Peace, Young Sam," Burbage shouted. "Nothing lurks in the trees hereabout.

But as he said it, a dark figure stepped from the trees ahead and waited in the shadows.

The players stumbled to a halt.

"Tis a ghost!" Sam quavered.

"Or a coney-catching beggar," Thom Pope spat.

"Nay, Burbage said, settling a hand on his dagger. "More likely a highwayman. Look for his fellows hiding in the greensward."

Shakespeare squinted at the distant figure and a smile of recognition flashed across his face. "Neither, tis Anthony Munday." And he was right. When the Chamberlain's Men drew closer they saw it was their rival player, clad in his pursuivant's black clothes, his horse tied to a tree. "Master Munday!" Shakespeare said, and shook his hand. "Why do you tarry here?"

Munday tugged the black hat from his head and fanned himself with it. "I travel to London and wonder if I could share the journey."

"A fellow player is always welcome!" Shakespeare said, although Burbage, who never liked Munday, gave him a sour look.

"Have you taken your Master Scrope's position?"

Munday shook his head. "No. In truth, I go to resign my post as Queen's Messenger. I have lost my stomach for hunting Jesuits."

Shakespeare asked, "How will you have your living?"

"I have thought on it, and will take up my pen again. Though being a writer pays little, it is perhaps all I am good for. And I may once again tread the boards." He laughed at their doubting expressions. "Be not afeared, I shall contain my extemporising."

"A player again?" Shakespeare said. "I am right glad to hear it!"

"The Lord Chamberlain's Men have all the players we need," Burbage quickly interjected. "Unless you could unbreak your voice and wear a lady's dress."

It was clear Munday knew Burbage didn't like him, still he laughed at the jibe. He threw a glance at the Stratford player walking beside him. "And what does the future hold for Will Shakespeare? I hear you received a handsome sum from the queen."

Shakespeare smiled. "The Lord Chamberlain's Men are to build a new theatre, and I shall be a sharer. Then, come the autumn, I shall go back to Stratford to see my darling girls."

"And your good wife?" Munday added.

Shakespeare's smile faltered. "Aye, like as not I will see her, too. Tis unavoidable. And then I shall buy me the biggest house in Stratford, such as befits a gentleman."

They continued onward and soon, as always, Shakespeare and Munday trailed far behind the rest of the players. Without prompting, Munday suddenly confessed in a low voice that only Shakespeare could hear: "I am a Catholic."

Shakespeare nodded. "Aye ... I guessed as much."

Munday looked surprised. "How is it you knew when none suspected?

"We are both men of letters, you and I. The words we leave out often speak louder than those we write." Shakespeare grinned mischievously to break the tension. "Plus I have heard of your exploits as pursuivant. You chase Catholics the way my cat chases squirrels—just so fast he rarely catches one."

It was obvious that Munday burned to find out Shakespeare's true allegiance. "And you . . . are you also a Catholic?" he cautiously ventured. The former pursuivant did not expect the pain that flashed across Shakespeare's face.

"I confess I am neither Catholic nor Protestant, atheist nor believer."

"You must be something. Every man must be something."

The bard shook his head, his expression grew miserable. "Last year my darling boy, Hamnet died, taken by the plague. He was scarce eleven years old."

"You blame God?"

"Who else?" His eyes grew dark. "If there be one."

Munday said nothing for several moments. "No doubt, it is your grief that speaks. Then where do you find mirth in your heart to write comedies?"

"Comedy is the only safe ground my mind may tread. For there are regions of my soul so dark and blasted I dare not step foot there."

"So *Double Falshood* was your last tragedy?"

He was answered by Shakespeare's sardonic laugh. "A man with no son, no heir, has no legacy but Tragedy. However, there is a work I catch a glimpse of now and then. It is a dark storm gathering in my soul. A Tempest of fire to set the skies afire. When it breaks it will burn me to dust and ash stirred by the wind. To mere atomies. After that, I think I may never write again, having said all a man was born to say."

Far ahead, Thom Pope flung a chestnut at Will Kempe. It pinged off his head and he dropped the three apples he was juggling. Kempe stood rubbing the back of noggin. Although his words did not carry, it was clear he was giving Pope a curse-filled tongue-lashing.

"It will be a dark work," Shakespeare continued. "But not in the fashion of a revenger's tragedy—a tale of dull minds and sharp knives. At its heart I will pit the struggle of quick life versus cold, inanimate clay, and ask the question that vexes my dreams: why, if God gave us free will, should Man choose the pain of existence over the balm of death?" Shakespeare's face reflected the earnestness of his words. "All my powers, all my skill, all I am, I will pour into this one work. It will be the best play, the best anything, I have ever writ."

"Do you have an inkling of what it shall be called?"

"I shall name it in remembrance of my son, and the title shall be ... Hamlet."

CHAPTER 67: THIS PLAY HAS NO ENDING

Did you actually think that I really died? What are you, stupid? How the bloody hell could I have written what you've just been reading if I'd actually died? Honestly, I blame television. It rots people's brains.

No, of course I didn't die. That would've been ridiculous. Yes, I spent a few weeks in hospital. They patched my lung, but no permanent damage. Right now I'm standing behind the bar at the White Hart Inn. The doctors wanted me to stay off my feet for a few more weeks, but they obviously no idea of how little work I do.

Oh, and Sidney? No, he didn't die either. After four hundred years the poison in the dagger was all dried up. I saw him on yesterday's news. Well, I didn't actually see his face. I saw them bundle him into court, a coat over his head as uniform officers whisked him past rows of photographers machine-gunning him with flashes. I saw Gill a while back. She popped into the pub with guess who: Broody Brandon. It appears they're back together. I gather their relationship is a little unconventional and centres on whips, masks, and leather restraints. You know what I mean: *A tyger's heart wrapped in a woman's hide.* Too bloody true. I'm well out of that.

My new barmaid's name is Brenda. She's not much in the looks department, and is frankly a bit of a carthorse, but she's got nice legs and a huge pair of knockers, which she dusts me off with every time she squeezes by.

"You look posh," Brenda says as she pulls a pint. The pub is busy these days, what with all the publicity. We've even got an official blue plaque on the wall outside, saying Will Shakespeare & Co. slept here. Bloody brill for business! Oh, the priceless manuscript? I donated it to the British Library. Yeah, I didn't ask for a penny. Weeeelll, what the hell else could I do? Anyway, now I earn a fair amount of dosh appearing on telly and at Shakespeare events. I made the queen's New Year's Honour list. There's even rumours of a possible O.B.E. in the works. I'm a bit of a national hero—the man who saved literature. Yeah, I know, what a larf! Cue the irony.

"Why are you so dressed up?" Brenda asks, giving me a triple-X massage with her love pillows as she squeezes past to grab a punter a bag of pork cracklings.

"Got a date," I explain. And as I say it, she appears. Her name is Eveline. She's lovely and she's divorced, too. We met through one of those Internet dating sites. (No snarky comments, please.) As we are already in full irony mode, I need to add that Eveline works at Wexcombe house, just up the road. She's a tour guide. Eveline kisses me hello. I grab my tux jacket and as we head for the door she asks if I have the tickets.

"Right here!" I say flourishing them.

We're going to see a Shakespeare play. Yeah, that's right, me at a Shakespeare play. I already know I'm going to hate it—probably need to prop my eyes open with matchsticks—but the tickets were free (Gillian sent them). One thing that is a bit weird, though, the play has no ending. Bizarre, eh? I'll be interested to see how they pull that off. The play? Oh, yeah, that's the best part. You might have heard of it by now, it's called *Double Falshood*.

The End

END NOTES

2. CHAPTER 2: A BLOODY MURDER

1. The main road running from London to the West country
2. The main road running from London to the West country
3. Buckram: a course cotton fabric
4. Poison daggers were popular in Elizabethan days—at least in the popular imagination, although there are reputed to have been some real examples especially fashioned for assassination.
5. Vizard: a mask
6. Face; appearance
7. A dagger
8. A short dagger
9. An infamous figure in the Elizabethan world, Richard Topcliffe was the queen's principal interrogator and torturer. He may have been mentally unbalanced, as he often bragged of having sexual relations with the queen, although that boast seems highly improbable. His reputation as a sadistic torturer earned him the moniker "the most feared man in England."
10. Garments

3. CHAPTER 3: THE PLAYERS' QUARREL

1. A conceited dandy; a fop
2. An acting troupe Shakespeare wrote for. Its patron was Henry Carey, 1st Baron Hunsdon, the Lord Chamberlain in charge of court entertainments.
3. Buboe: swollen and inflamed lymph glands caused by bubonic plague.
4. A body of senior advisors to the queen
5. The department head responsible from the coordination of theatrical entertainment at court.
6. Thieves; robbers; highwaymen
7. An old and tired horse
8. Shareholders in the theatre entitled to a percentage of ticket sales
9. Smeared; fouled

4. CHAPTER 4: THE QUEEN'S PURSUIVANTS

1. A steel helmet similar to those worn by Spanish conquistadors
2. In Elizabeth's time, an officer especially tasked with tracking down and arresting Roman Catholic priests

3. Priest hole: a secret space specially constructed in the fabric of a building to hide a Jesuit Priest
4. A Roman Catholic who refused to attend Church of England services and was obliged to pay a fine

5. CHAPTER 5: EXEUNT, PURSUED BY A GHOST

1. A body of advisors to the monarch; in this case, Elizabeth I
2. A former castle that earned infamy as a prison for traitors
3. Titus Andronicus; Shakespeare's bloodiest and most popular play
4. A type of entertainment performed by masked players, often incorporating music, dance and poetry
5. Ghosts or spectres

8. CHAPTER 8: THE WHITE HART INN

1. A cockerel castrated to improve the flesh for food
2. Money in coins, so-called because of the noise it makes when shaken
3. A fortified wine imported from Spain
4. An ancient board game, similar to Chinese Checkers
5. An old English coin, worth 4 pennies

9. CHAPTER 9: FOUR DAYS EARLIER—HOW THIS WHOLE BLOODY MESS BEGAN

1. A classic British touring car

13. CHAPTER 13: THE DEVIL'S LUCK

1. In the parlance of the times, a Coney-Catcher was a confidence trickster, a rascal who wandered the country, living off his wits by swindling and cozening innocent folk

23. CHAPTER 23: A PURITAN INQUISITION

1. A wooden framework on a post with holes for the head and hands of a prisoner so he may be exposed to public shame and ridicule

31. CHAPTER 31: PURSUIVANTS AND PRETENDERS

1. A loaf of bread made from the best flour

36. CHAPTER 36: AFTER THE TEMPEST

1. Quarrel: a short crossbow arrow

64. CHAPTER 64: FROM BAD TO VERSE

1. Dressing rooms

PLEASE LEAVE ME A REVIEW

Did you enjoy this book? If so, please leave a review on Amazon or GoodReads. Reviews really help build readership and ensure more novels like this in the future. Here's how to leave a review on Amazon:

- Go to Amazon
- Type in Double Falshood: A Shakespearean Thriller
- Scroll down to Customer Reviews. Nearby you'll see a box labeled Write A Review. Click on it
- If you've never left a review before they might ask you to create a name
- Reviews can be as simple as "Love the Book!" (Please don't include spoilers.)

And that's it. Please feel free to bask in the knowledge that you have done a kind and noble deed!

Thank you in advance and warmest wishes.

Vaughn Entwistle, Cheltenham, England 2020

ABOUT THE AUTHOR

Vaughn Entwistle grew up in Northern England, but spent many years living in the United States, first in Michigan, (where he earned a Master's Degree in English at Oakland University), and then in Seattle (where he worked as an editor/writer and also ran a successful gargoyle sculpting business for ten years. (Yes, really!) He currently lives in the English spa town of Cheltenham.

Find out more about the author and his books and sign up for his newsletter at his website: www.vaughnentwistle.com

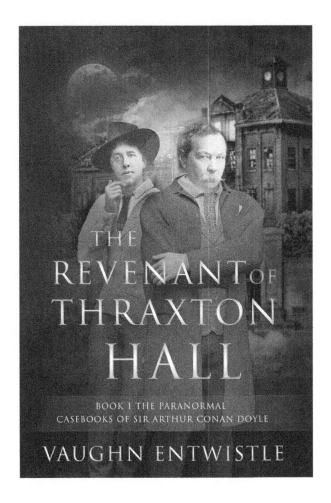

The Revenant of Thraxton Hall

"My murder will take place in a darkened séance room—shot twice in the chest." The words are a premonition related to Arthur Conan Doyle when he answers a summons for help from a mysterious woman who identifies herself only as "a Spiritualist Medium of some renown." The house is a fashionable address in London. The woman's voice is young, cultured and ethereal. But even with his Holmesian powers of observation, Conan Doyle can only guess at her true identity, for the interview takes place in total darkness. Suspicious of being drawn into a web of charlatanism, the author is initially reluctant. However, the mystery deepens when he returns the next day and finds the residence abandoned.

1893 is a tumultuous year in the life of the 34-year old Conan Doyle: his alcoholic father dies in an insane asylum, his wife is diagnosed with galloping consumption, and his most famous literary creation, Sherlock Holmes, is killed off in *The Adventure of the Final Problem*. It is a move that backfires, making the author the most hated man in England. But despite the fact that his personal life is in turmoil, the lure of an intrigue proves irresistible. Conan Doyle assumes the mantle of his fictional consulting detective and recruits a redoubtable Watson in the Irish playwright, Oscar Wilde, who brings to the sleuthing duo a razor-keen mind, an effervescent wit, and an outrageous sense of fashion.

"The game is a afoot" as the two friends board a steam train for Northern England to attend the first meeting of the *Society for Psychical Research*, held at the mysterious medium's ancestral home of Thraxton Hall—a brooding Gothic pile swarmed by ghosts. Here, they encounter an eccentric mélange of seers, scientists, psychics and skeptics—each with an inflated ego and a motive for murder. As the night of the fateful séance draws near, the two writers find themselves entangled in a Gordian Knot that would confound even the powers of a Sherlock Holmes to unravel—how to solve a murder *before* it is committed."

"Marvellous fun . . . delightfully swift reading, and when all is said and done, rather spiffy too."—**British Fantasy Society**

"Grand Guignol fun. Entwistle is an original who has assembled a delicious, extravagantly eccentric cast of characters."—**Open Letters, An Arts and Literature Review**

"London's gaslights sputter and the game's afoot in The Revenant of Thraxton Hall, a witty, atmospheric tale featuring the unique detecting duo of Arthur Conan Doyle and Oscar Wilde." – **Cara Black**

"The Revenant of Thraxton Hall is a delight. It's a treat to meet the great detective's creator (Arthur Conan Doyle) as a sleuth in his own right. And partnered with Oscar Wilde—what a bold and wonderful conceit!"—**John Lescroart**

The Angel of Highgate

People die . . . but love endures immortal.

Lord Geoffrey Thraxton is notorious in Victorian society—a Byronesque rake-hell with a reputation as the "wickedest man in London."

After surviving a pistol duel, Thraxton boasts his contempt for death and insults the attending physician. It is a mistake he will regret, for Silas Garrette is a deranged sociopath and chloroform-addict whose mind was broken on the battlefields of Crimea.

Oblivious to the danger, Thraxton's pursuit of idle pleasure leads him through the fog shrouded streets of London—from champagne soirees in the mummy room of the British Museum, to its high-class brothels and low-class opium dens. But when Thraxton falls in love with a mysterious woman who haunts Highgate Cemetery by night, he unwittingly provides the murderous doctor with the perfect means to punish a man with no fear of death.

A magnificently written, provocative novel."—**Kirkus Reviews**

"Chock-full of thrills, action, suspense and derring-do."—**British Fantasy Society**

"A heady mix of Victorian melodrama and murder mystery."—***Books Monthly***

Daringly original . . . Entwistle's cheerfully confident prose sparkles and unsettles by turns"—**Historical Novel Society**

Gothic Novel of the Year (Shortlisted) **The Dracula Society**

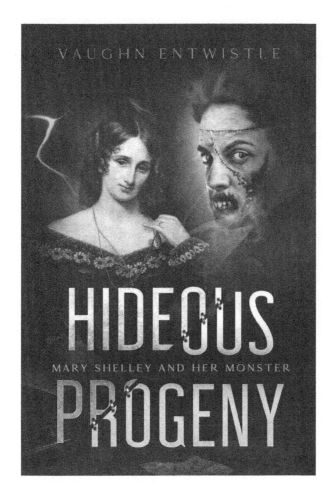

Hideous Progeny: Mary Shelley and Her Monster

It never had life . . . but now it must die . . .

During a night of apocalyptic thunderstorms, 18-year old Mary Shelley's imagination birthed a nameless monster that would make her name famous and haunt the world for generations. But since the dark nativity of her "hideous progeny", Mary's life has been cursed by tragedy, loss and grief: a dead sister, a dead husband, and three dead children. Now aged 48, and suffering debilitating headaches from the brain tumour that will finally claim her life, Mary sees her monster as a malevolence that has cursed her life and which now threatens her only living child. Seeking release, Mary travels from London to the Somerset estate of Andrew Crosse, the gentlemen scientist who first inspired her Dr. Frankenstein. Crosse is an electrical experimenter known to the terrified locals as "The Thunder and Lightning Man". Mary has sought him out in hopes that the same *Dread Engine* that conjured her monster can finally lay that ghost to rest.

Made in the USA
Coppell, TX
15 September 2021